image COMICS PRESENTS

INVINCIBLE

A DIFFERENT WORLD

CREATED BY
ROBERT KIRKMAN
& CORY WALKER

image®

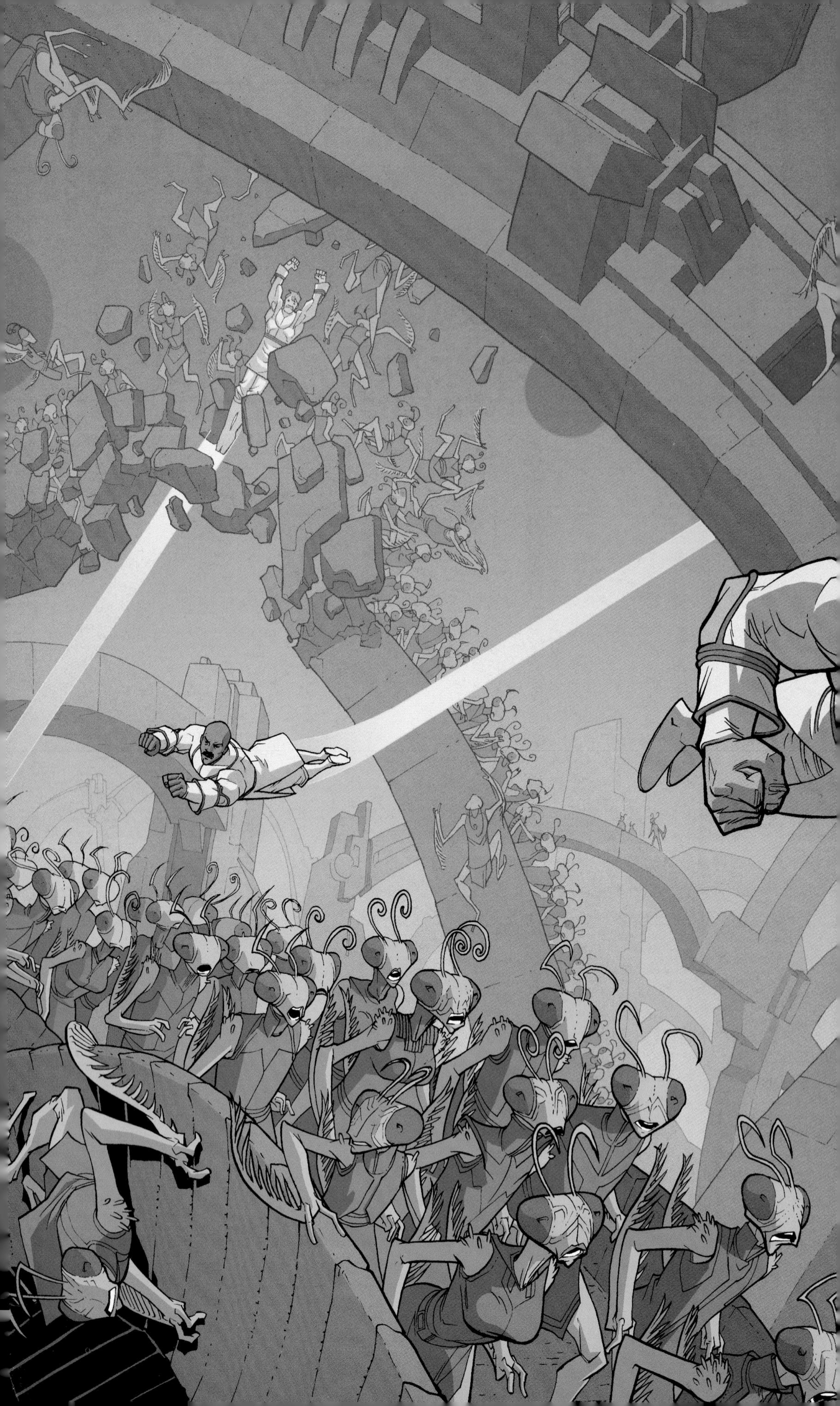

writer

ROBERT KIRKMAN

penciler, inker

RYAN OTTLEY

inker
(chapters 4-6)

CLIFF RATHBURN

colorist

BILL CRABTREE

letterer

RUS WOOTON

cover

RYAN OTTLEY & BILL CRABTREE

www.imagecomics.com

IMAGE COMICS, INC.

Erik Larsen - *Publisher*
Todd McFarlane - *President*
Marc Silvestri - *CEO*
Jim Valentino - *Vice-President*

Eric Stephenson - *Executive Director*
Jim Demonakos - *PR & Marketing*
Mia MacHatton - *Accounts Manager*
Traci Hui - *Administrative Assistant*
Joe Keatinge - *Traffic Manager*
Laurenn McCubbin - *Designer*
Allen Hui - *Production Manager*
Jonathan Chan - *Production Artist*
Drew Gill - *Production Artist*

INTRODUCTION

A year ago, I wasn't even reading Invincible. Sure, I'd heard about how good it was, but frankly, I felt there were more than enough superhero books on the market from Marvel and DC, and I didn't feel the need to check out any others. But I was reading Walking Dead, because, well... Zombies. Anyway, I'm talking to Robert Kirkman at the Emerald City Comicon in Seattle, and he asks if I've ever read Invincible, and proceeds to give me the first three trades. A few days and one marathon comics reading session later, I no longer care about Walking Dead. I just want to read more Invincible. What the hell is up with that?

Okay, I do still read Walking Dead, but Invincible is my favorite Kirkman book, by far. And I'm a grim guy a lot of the time. My favorite books and movies tend to be things like "The Killer Inside Me" or "Get Carter." But Invincible really taps into the other side of my psyche, the part that loves old John Romita Spider-Man comics, the movies of Miyazaki, Toy Story, Harriet the Spy... the part of every creative person that is always a bit of a kid. That's what Invincible is about, to me. Kirkman found a way to do superhero comics that remind me why I liked them in the first place, without seeming like an actual comic from the 70s or early 80s, most of which are better in memory than in actuality. I really dig reading about Mark Grayson and his friends and fellow superheroes. I dig all the names that Kirkman comes up with for the side heroes of his world (Dupli-Kate? Come on, and her little brother is Multi-Paul. That's gold, solid gold). I dig all the costumes that Cory Walker and then Ryan Ottley put them all in (especially Atom Eve). And I know that eventually Robot will be revealed to be bad... I just know it.

And let's not even talk about how lucky this Kirkman bastard is with artists. I don't know a single writer who wouldn't kill to work with Ryan Ottley. Ryan draws how many panels a page, all of them great, he draws amazing action in every issue, and most importantly, you care about his characters when you watch them talk. People who don't work in comics may not realize that simple part, the facial expressions and body language of the characters when they aren't fighting, is the key ingredient in making a good script great. Ryan is one of the best, and Kirkman is more than lucky to have him. (In fact, Ryan, if you're reading this, call me, buddy, I've got ideas).

You know how big a fan I am of Invincible? I made Robert send me the PDFs of the last three issues of the story collected here even though I never planned on mentioning them in this intro. I just wanted to read them early. But, of course, now I just have longer to wait until the next issue...

ED
BRUBAKER
Seattle 2006

Brubaker's credits include -- SLEEPER, GOTHAM CENTRAL, SCENE OF THE CRIME, CAPTAIN AMERICA, DAREDEVIL and UNCANNY X-MEN

CHAPTER ONE

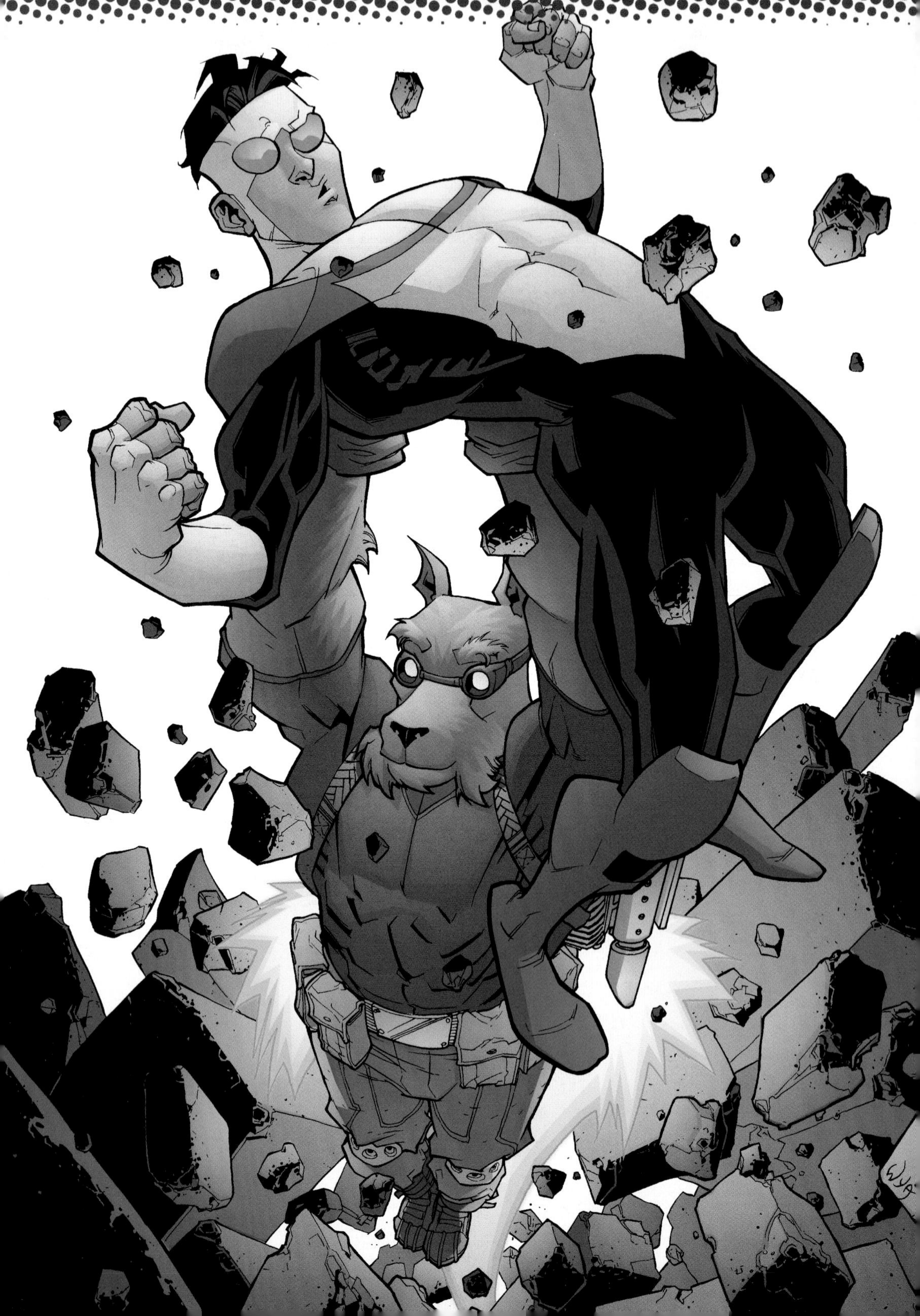

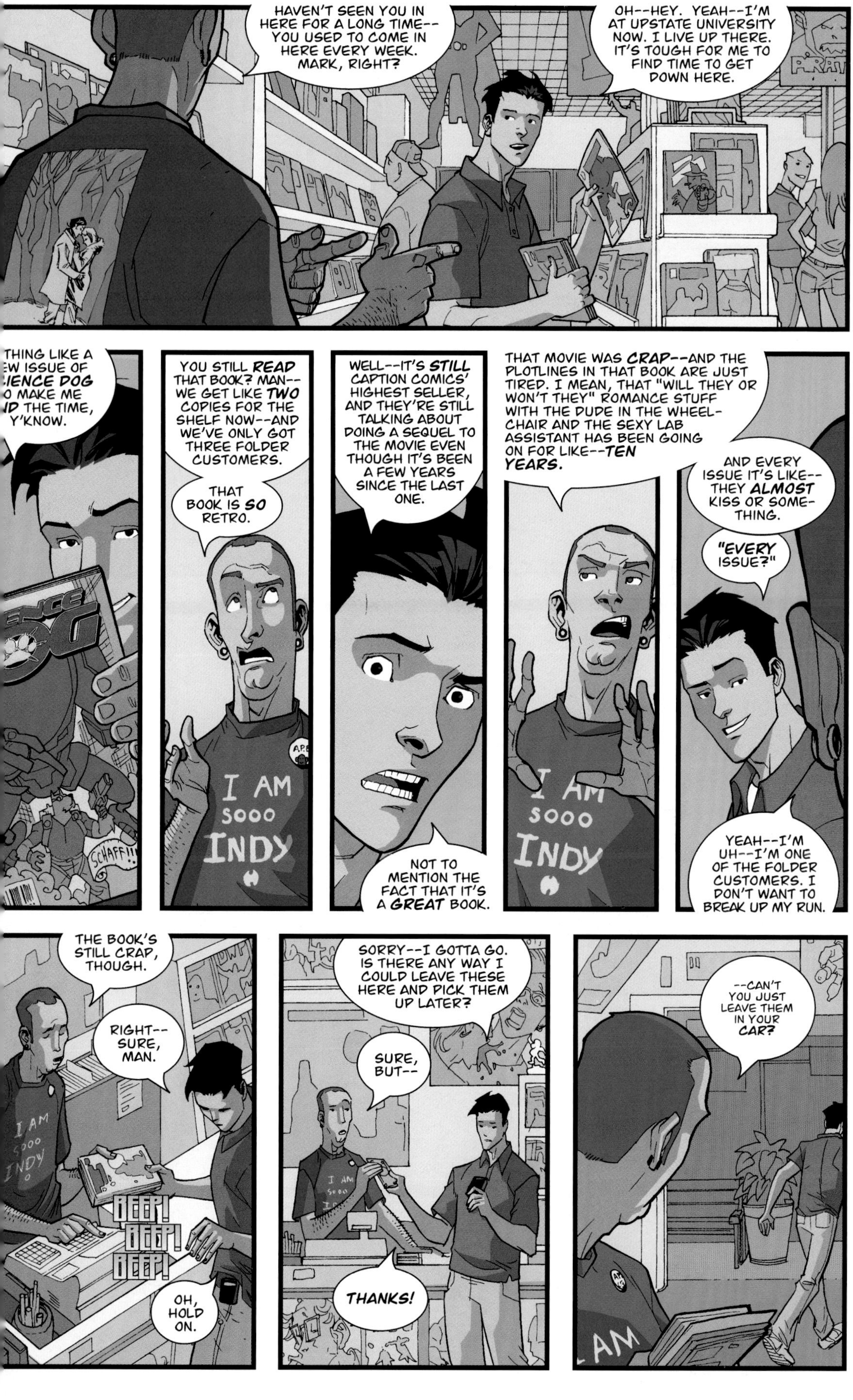

HAVEN'T SEEN YOU IN HERE FOR A LONG TIME--YOU USED TO COME IN HERE EVERY WEEK. MARK, RIGHT?
OH--HEY. YEAH--I'M AT UPSTATE UNIVERSITY NOW. I LIVE UP THERE. IT'S TOUGH FOR ME TO FIND TIME TO GET DOWN HERE.
THING LIKE A EW ISSUE OF IENCE DOG O MAKE ME D THE TIME, Y'KNOW.
YOU STILL READ THAT BOOK? MAN--WE GET LIKE TWO COPIES FOR THE SHELF NOW--AND WE'VE ONLY GOT THREE FOLDER CUSTOMERS.
THAT BOOK IS SO RETRO.
WELL--IT'S STILL CAPTION COMICS' HIGHEST SELLER, AND THEY'RE STILL TALKING ABOUT DOING A SEQUEL TO THE MOVIE EVEN THOUGH IT'S BEEN A FEW YEARS SINCE THE LAST ONE.
NOT TO MENTION THE FACT THAT IT'S A GREAT BOOK.
THAT MOVIE WAS CRAP--AND THE PLOTLINES IN THAT BOOK ARE JUST TIRED. I MEAN, THAT "WILL THEY OR WON'T THEY" ROMANCE STUFF WITH THE DUDE IN THE WHEEL-CHAIR AND THE SEXY LAB ASSISTANT HAS BEEN GOING ON FOR LIKE--TEN YEARS.
I AM SOOO INDY
AND EVERY ISSUE IT'S LIKE--THEY ALMOST KISS OR SOME-THING.
"EVERY ISSUE?"
YEAH--I'M UH--I'M ONE OF THE FOLDER CUSTOMERS. I DON'T WANT TO BREAK UP MY RUN.
THE BOOK'S STILL CRAP, THOUGH.
RIGHT--SURE, MAN.
BEEP! BEEP! BEEP!
OH, HOLD ON.
SORRY--I GOTTA GO. IS THERE ANY WAY I COULD LEAVE THESE HERE AND PICK THEM UP LATER?
SURE, BUT--
THANKS!
--CAN'T YOU JUST LEAVE THEM IN YOUR CAR?

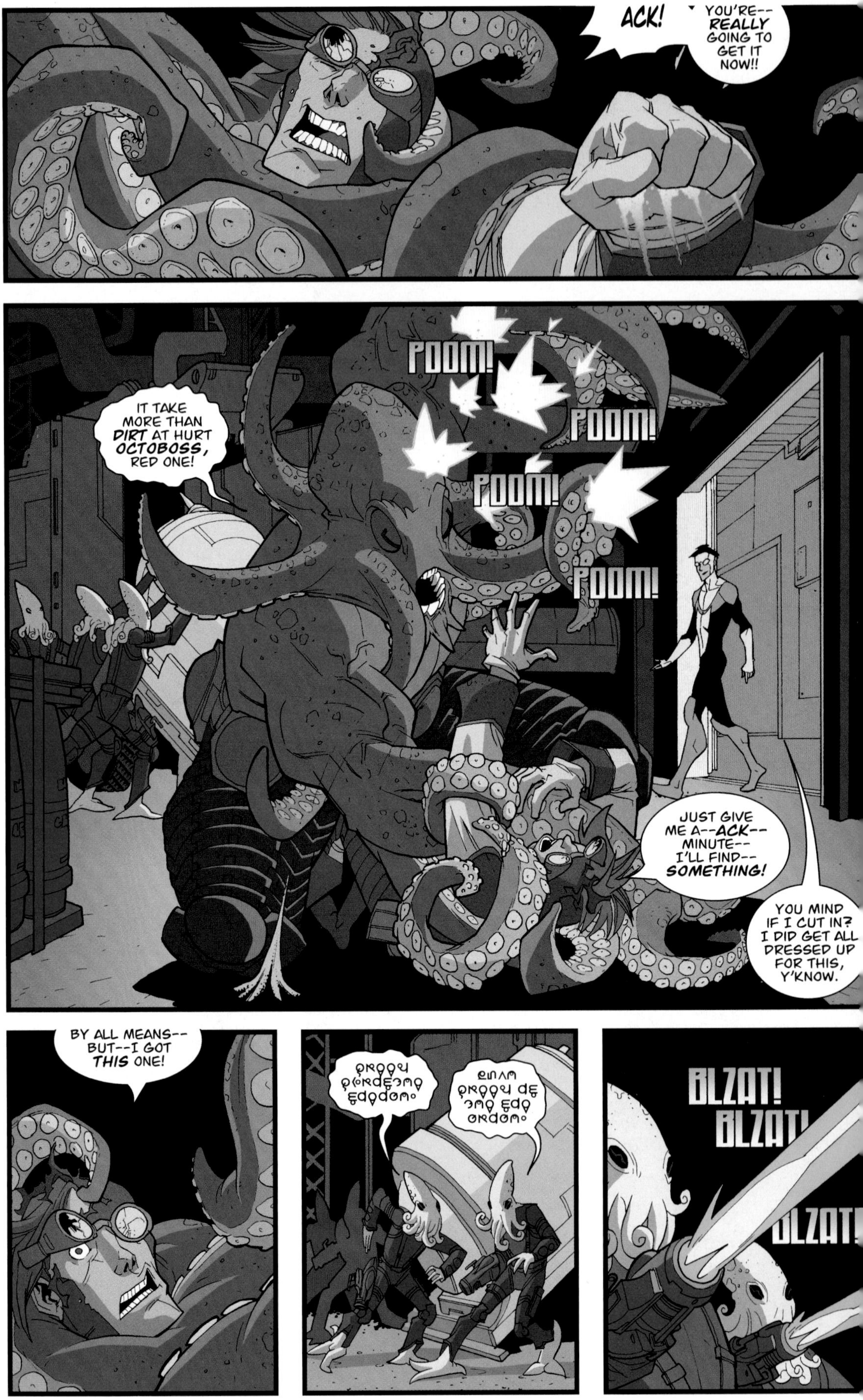
ACK!
YOU'RE--REALLY GOING TO GET IT NOW!!
POOM!
POOM!
POOM!
POOM!
IT TAKE MORE THAN DIRT AT HURT OCTOBOSS, RED ONE!
JUST GIVE ME A--ACK--MINUTE--I'LL FIND--SOMETHING!
YOU MIND IF I CUT IN? I DID GET ALL DRESSED UP FOR THIS, Y'KNOW.
BY ALL MEANS--BUT--I GOT THIS ONE!
BLZAT!
BLZAT!
BLZAT!

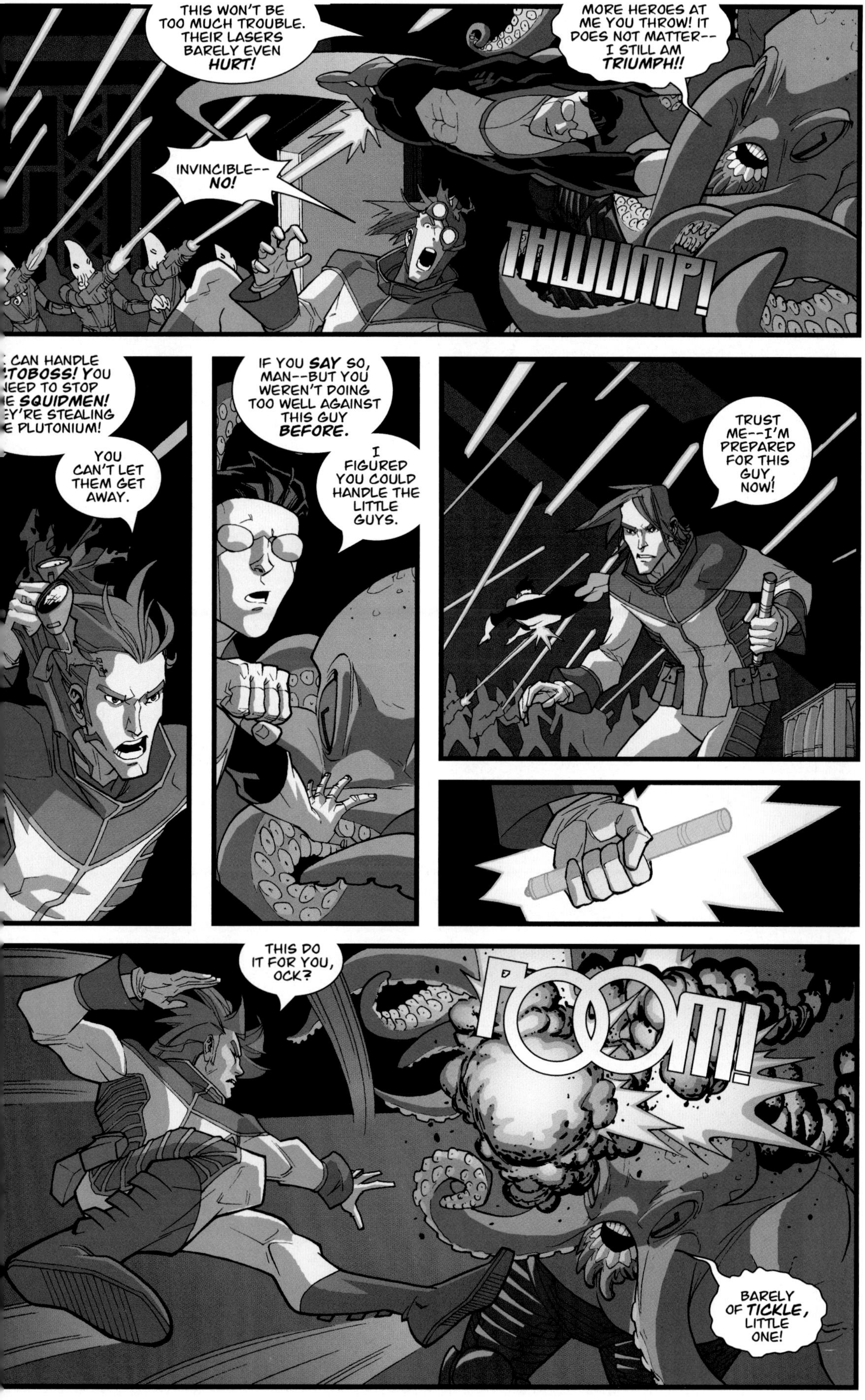
THIS WON'T BE TOO MUCH TROUBLE. THEIR LASERS BARELY EVEN HURT!
MORE HEROES AT ME YOU THROW! IT DOES NOT MATTER-- I STILL AM TRIUMPH!!
INVINCIBLE-- NO!
THWUMP!
CAN HANDLE CTOBOSS! YOU NEED TO STOP E SQUIDMEN! EY'RE STEALING E PLUTONIUM!
YOU CAN'T LET THEM GET AWAY.
IF YOU SAY SO, MAN--BUT YOU WEREN'T DOING TOO WELL AGAINST THIS GUY BEFORE.
I FIGURED YOU COULD HANDLE THE LITTLE GUYS.
TRUST ME--I'M PREPARED FOR THIS GUY, NOW!
THIS DO IT FOR YOU, OCK?
POOOM!
BARELY OF TICKLE, LITTLE ONE!

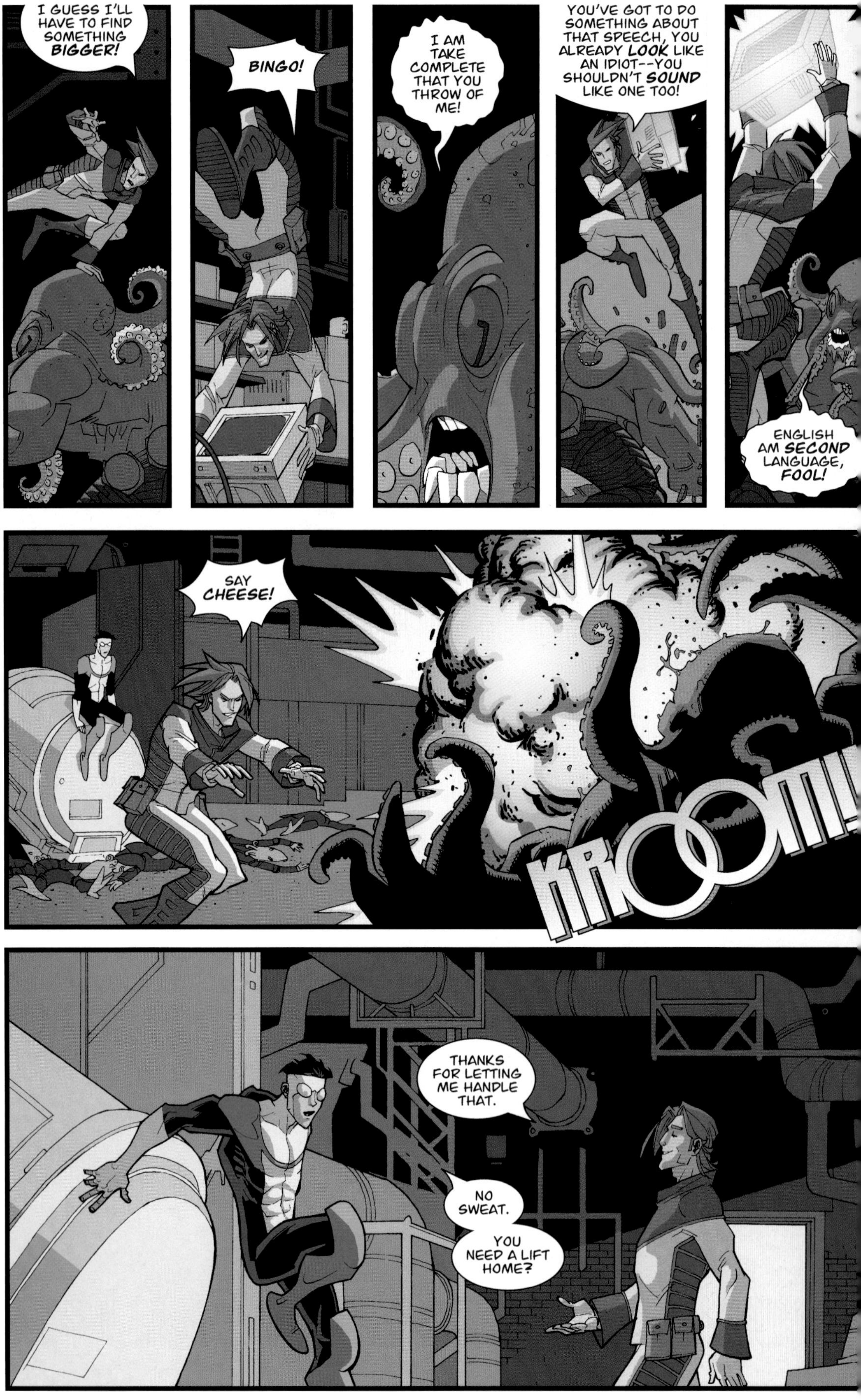
I GUESS I'LL HAVE TO FIND SOMETHING **BIGGER!**
BINGO!
I AM TAKE COMPLETE THAT YOU THROW OF ME!
YOU'VE GOT TO DO SOMETHING ABOUT THAT SPEECH, YOU ALREADY **LOOK** LIKE AN IDIOT--YOU SHOULDN'T **SOUND** LIKE ONE TOO!
ENGLISH AM **SECOND** LANGUAGE, **FOOL!**
SAY **CHEESE!**
KROOOM!!
THANKS FOR LETTING ME HANDLE THAT.
NO SWEAT.
YOU NEED A LIFT HOME?

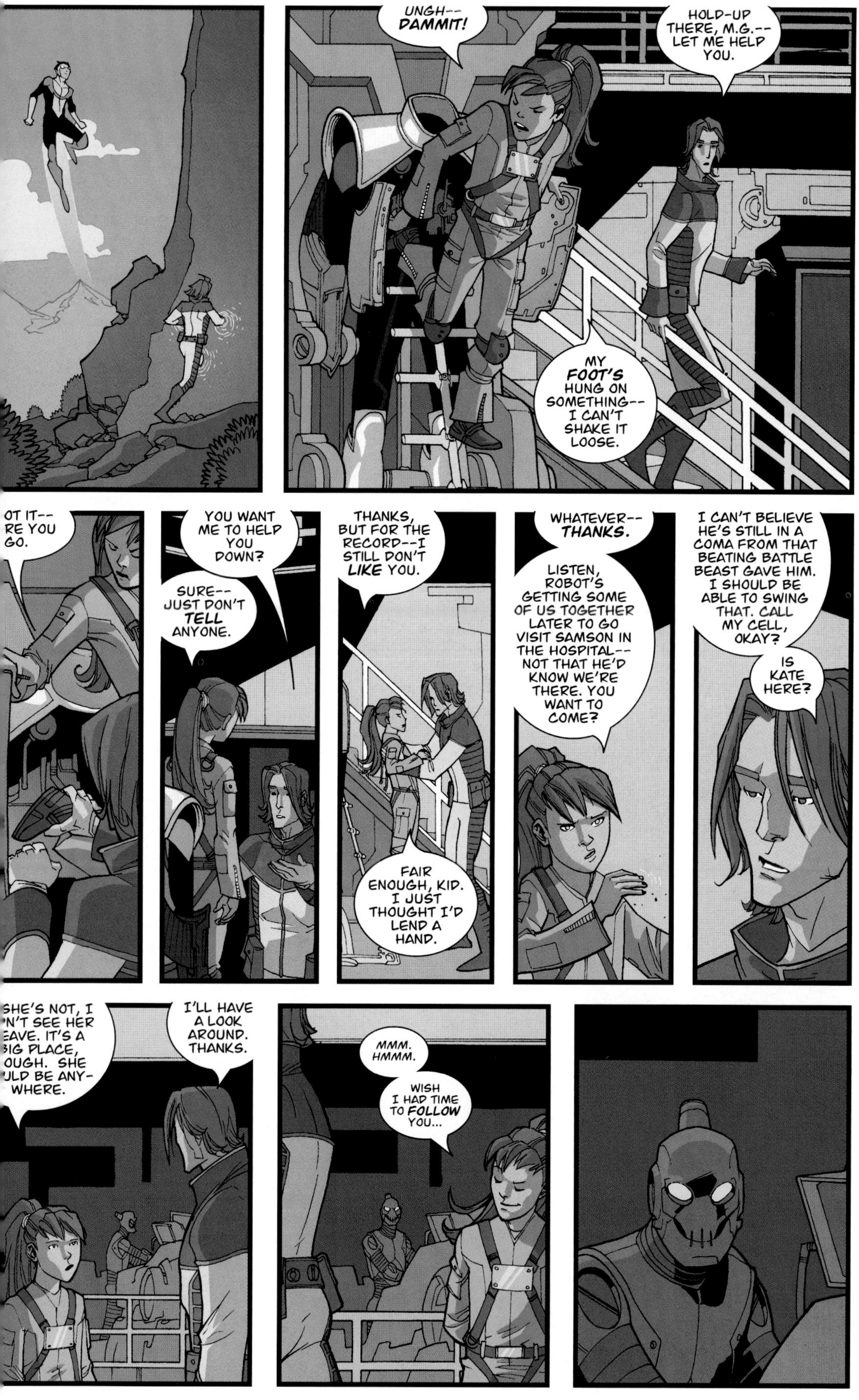
UNGH--
DAMMIT!
HOLD-UP THERE, M.G.-- LET ME HELP YOU.
MY FOOT'S HUNG ON SOMETHING-- I CAN'T SHAKE IT LOOSE.
OT IT-- RE YOU GO.
YOU WANT ME TO HELP YOU DOWN?
SURE-- JUST DON'T TELL ANYONE.
THANKS, BUT FOR THE RECORD--I STILL DON'T LIKE YOU.
FAIR ENOUGH, KID. I JUST THOUGHT I'D LEND A HAND.
WHATEVER-- THANKS.
LISTEN, ROBOT'S GETTING SOME OF US TOGETHER LATER TO GO VISIT SAMSON IN THE HOSPITAL-- NOT THAT HE'D KNOW WE'RE THERE. YOU WANT TO COME?
I CAN'T BELIEVE HE'S STILL IN A COMA FROM THAT BEATING BATTLE BEAST GAVE HIM. I SHOULD BE ABLE TO SWING THAT. CALL MY CELL, OKAY?
IS KATE HERE?
SHE'S NOT, I N'T SEE HER EAVE. IT'S A BIG PLACE, OUGH. SHE ULD BE ANY-WHERE.
I'LL HAVE A LOOK AROUND. THANKS.
MMM. HMMM.
WISH I HAD TIME TO FOLLOW YOU...

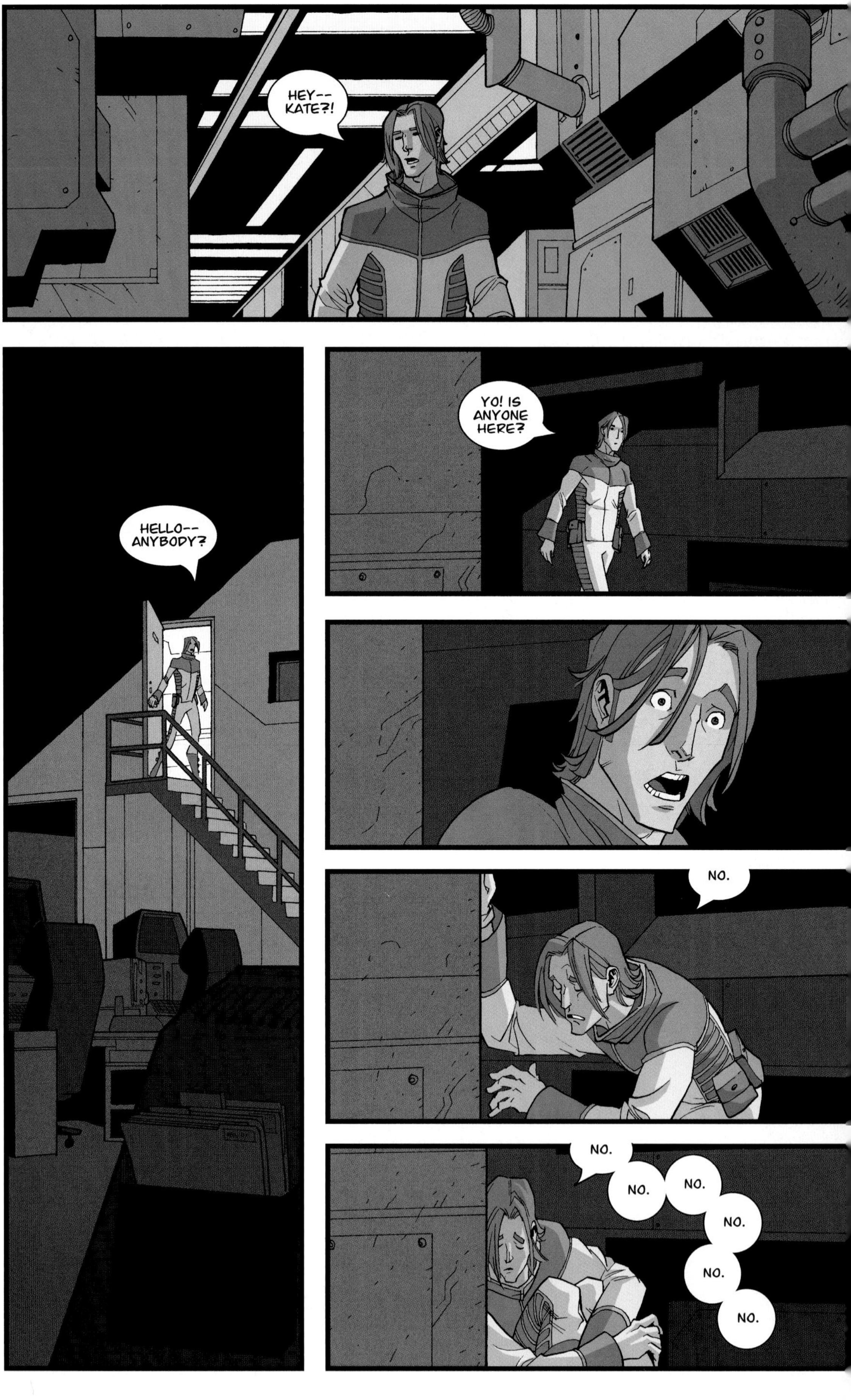
HEY--
KATE?!
HELLO--
ANYBODY?
YO! IS
ANYONE
HERE?
NO.
NO.
NO.
NO.
NO.
NO.
NO.

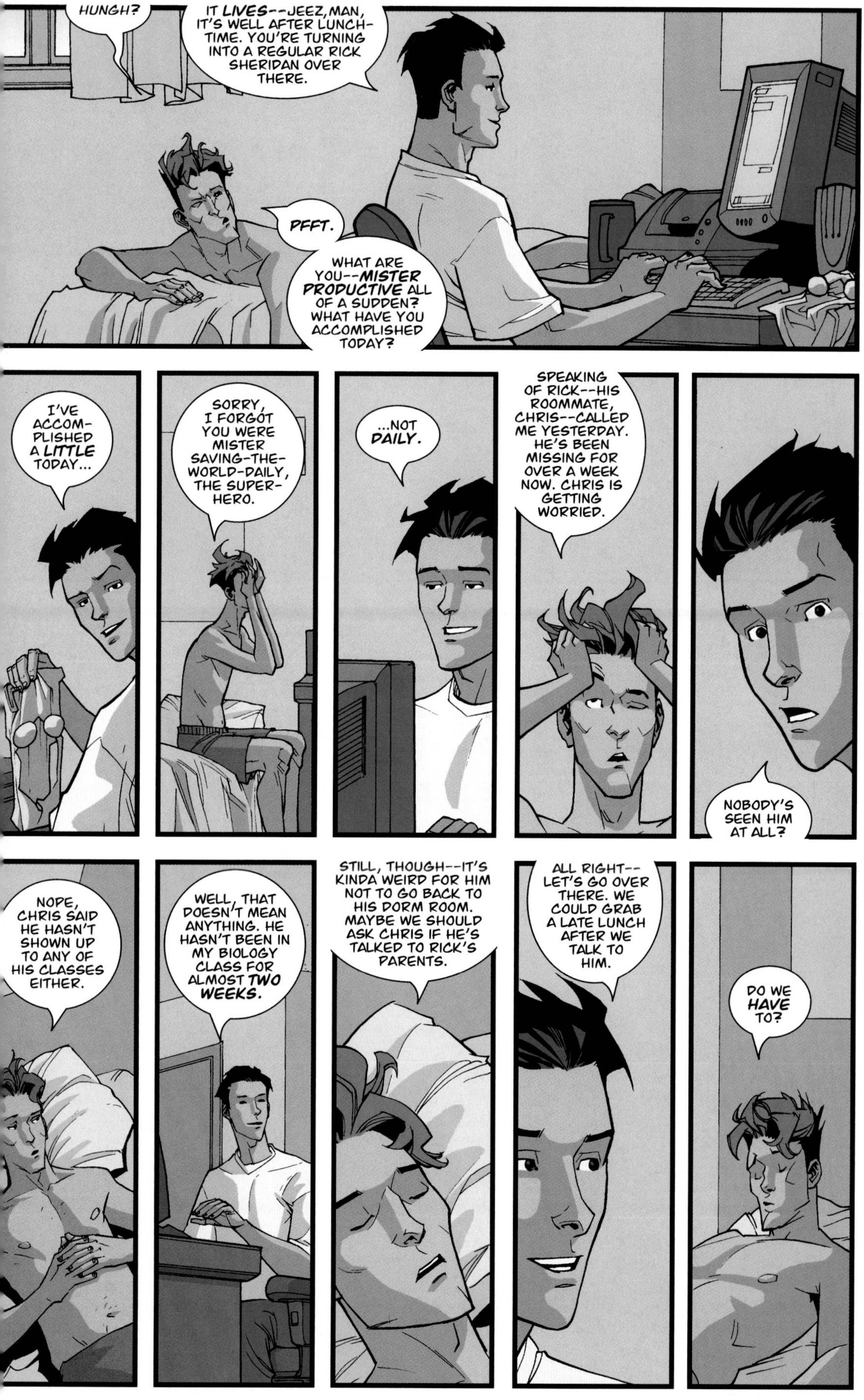
HUNGH?
IT LIVES--JEEZ, MAN, IT'S WELL AFTER LUNCH-TIME. YOU'RE TURNING INTO A REGULAR RICK SHERIDAN OVER THERE.
PFFT.
WHAT ARE YOU--MISTER PRODUCTIVE ALL OF A SUDDEN? WHAT HAVE YOU ACCOMPLISHED TODAY?
I'VE ACCOM-PLISHED A LITTLE TODAY...
SORRY, I FORGOT YOU WERE MISTER SAVING-THE-WORLD-DAILY, THE SUPER-HERO.
...NOT DAILY.
SPEAKING OF RICK--HIS ROOMMATE, CHRIS--CALLED ME YESTERDAY. HE'S BEEN MISSING FOR OVER A WEEK NOW. CHRIS IS GETTING WORRIED.
NOBODY'S SEEN HIM AT ALL?
NOPE, CHRIS SAID HE HASN'T SHOWN UP TO ANY OF HIS CLASSES EITHER.
WELL, THAT DOESN'T MEAN ANYTHING. HE HASN'T BEEN IN MY BIOLOGY CLASS FOR ALMOST TWO WEEKS.
STILL, THOUGH--IT'S KINDA WEIRD FOR HIM NOT TO GO BACK TO HIS DORM ROOM. MAYBE WE SHOULD ASK CHRIS IF HE'S TALKED TO RICK'S PARENTS.
ALL RIGHT--LET'S GO OVER THERE. WE COULD GRAB A LATE LUNCH AFTER WE TALK TO HIM.
DO WE HAVE TO?

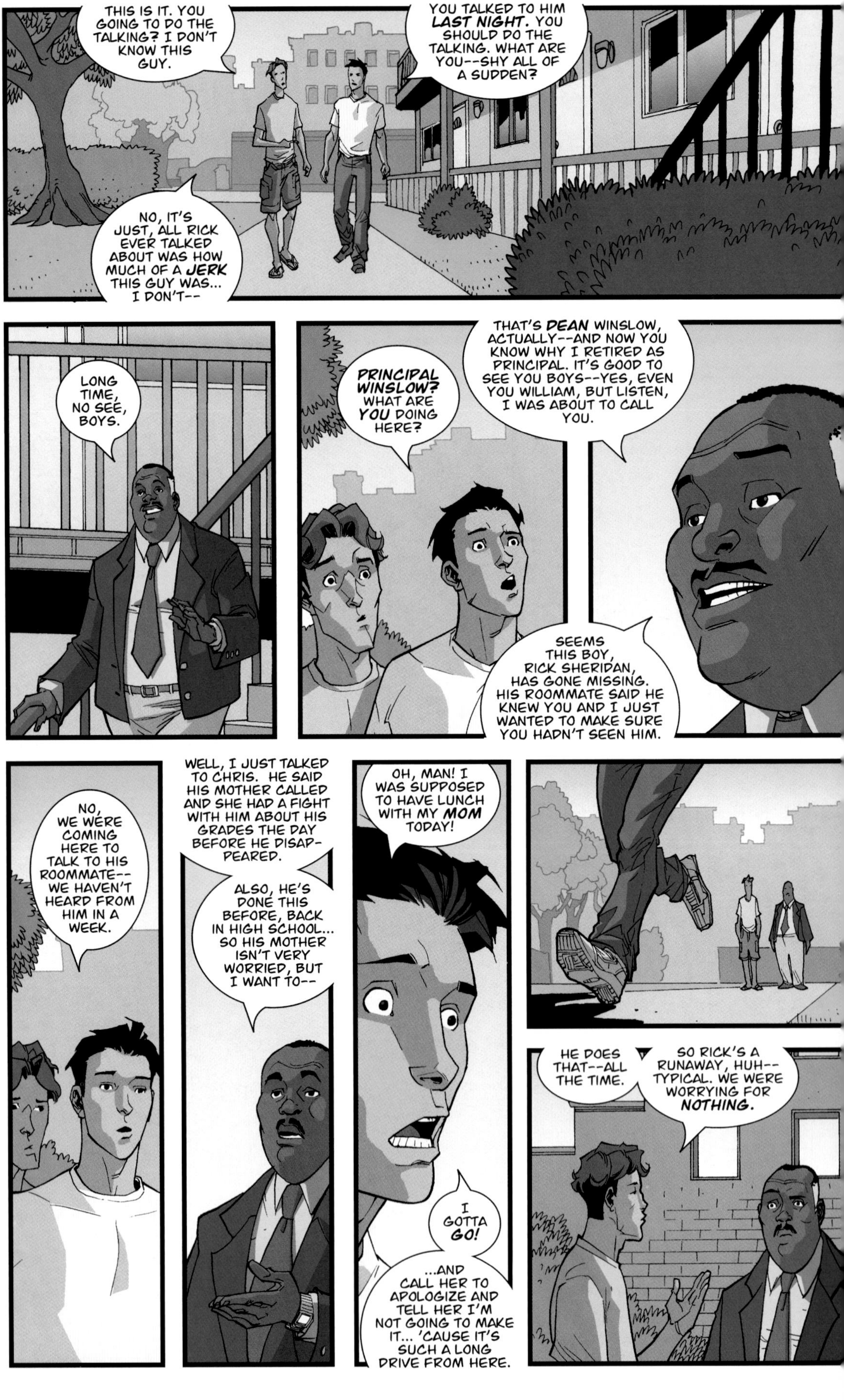
THIS IS IT. YOU GOING TO DO THE TALKING? I DON'T KNOW THIS GUY.
YOU TALKED TO HIM LAST NIGHT. YOU SHOULD DO THE TALKING. WHAT ARE YOU--SHY ALL OF A SUDDEN?
NO, IT'S JUST, ALL RICK EVER TALKED ABOUT WAS HOW MUCH OF A JERK THIS GUY WAS... I DON'T--
LONG TIME, NO SEE, BOYS.
PRINCIPAL WINSLOW? WHAT ARE YOU DOING HERE?
THAT'S DEAN WINSLOW, ACTUALLY--AND NOW YOU KNOW WHY I RETIRED AS PRINCIPAL. IT'S GOOD TO SEE YOU BOYS--YES, EVEN YOU WILLIAM, BUT LISTEN, I WAS ABOUT TO CALL YOU.
SEEMS THIS BOY, RICK SHERIDAN, HAS GONE MISSING. HIS ROOMMATE SAID HE KNEW YOU AND I JUST WANTED TO MAKE SURE YOU HADN'T SEEN HIM.
NO, WE WERE COMING HERE TO TALK TO HIS ROOMMATE--WE HAVEN'T HEARD FROM HIM IN A WEEK.
WELL, I JUST TALKED TO CHRIS. HE SAID HIS MOTHER CALLED AND SHE HAD A FIGHT WITH HIM ABOUT HIS GRADES THE DAY BEFORE HE DISAP-PEARED.
ALSO, HE'S DONE THIS BEFORE, BACK IN HIGH SCHOOL... SO HIS MOTHER ISN'T VERY WORRIED, BUT I WANT TO--
OH, MAN! I WAS SUPPOSED TO HAVE LUNCH WITH MY MOM TODAY!
I GOTTA GO!
...AND CALL HER TO APOLOGIZE AND TELL HER I'M NOT GOING TO MAKE IT... 'CAUSE IT'S SUCH A LONG DRIVE FROM HERE.
HE DOES THAT--ALL THE TIME.
SO RICK'S A RUNAWAY, HUH--TYPICAL. WE WERE WORRYING FOR NOTHING.

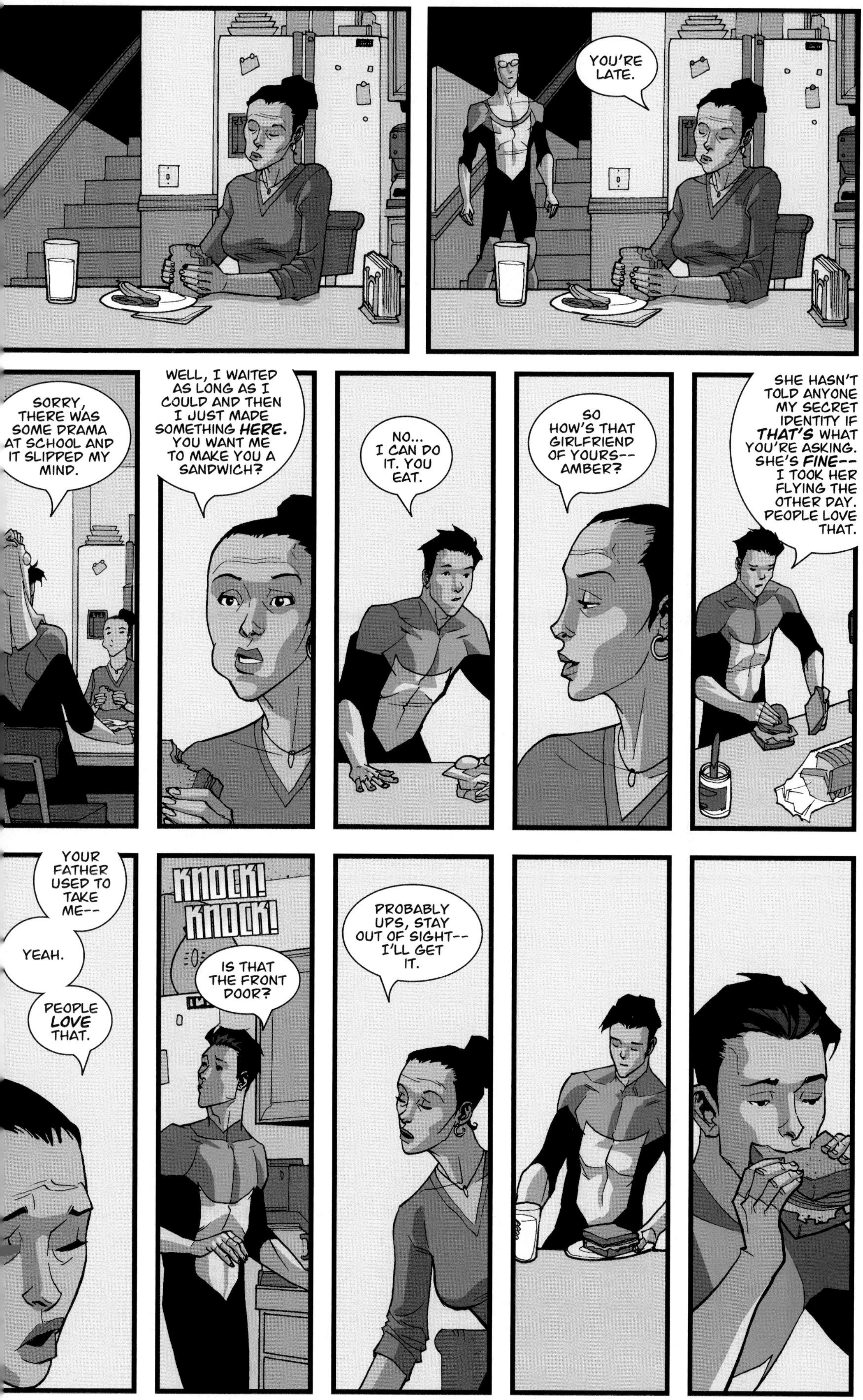

YOU'RE LATE.
SORRY, THERE WAS SOME DRAMA AT SCHOOL AND IT SLIPPED MY MIND.
WELL, I WAITED AS LONG AS I COULD AND THEN I JUST MADE SOMETHING HERE. YOU WANT ME TO MAKE YOU A SANDWICH?
NO... I CAN DO IT. YOU EAT.
SO HOW'S THAT GIRLFRIEND OF YOURS-- AMBER?
SHE HASN'T TOLD ANYONE MY SECRET IDENTITY IF THAT'S WHAT YOU'RE ASKING. SHE'S FINE-- I TOOK HER FLYING THE OTHER DAY. PEOPLE LOVE THAT.
YOUR FATHER USED TO TAKE ME--
YEAH.
PEOPLE LOVE THAT.
KNOCK! KNOCK!
IS THAT THE FRONT DOOR?
PROBABLY UPS, STAY OUT OF SIGHT-- I'LL GET IT.

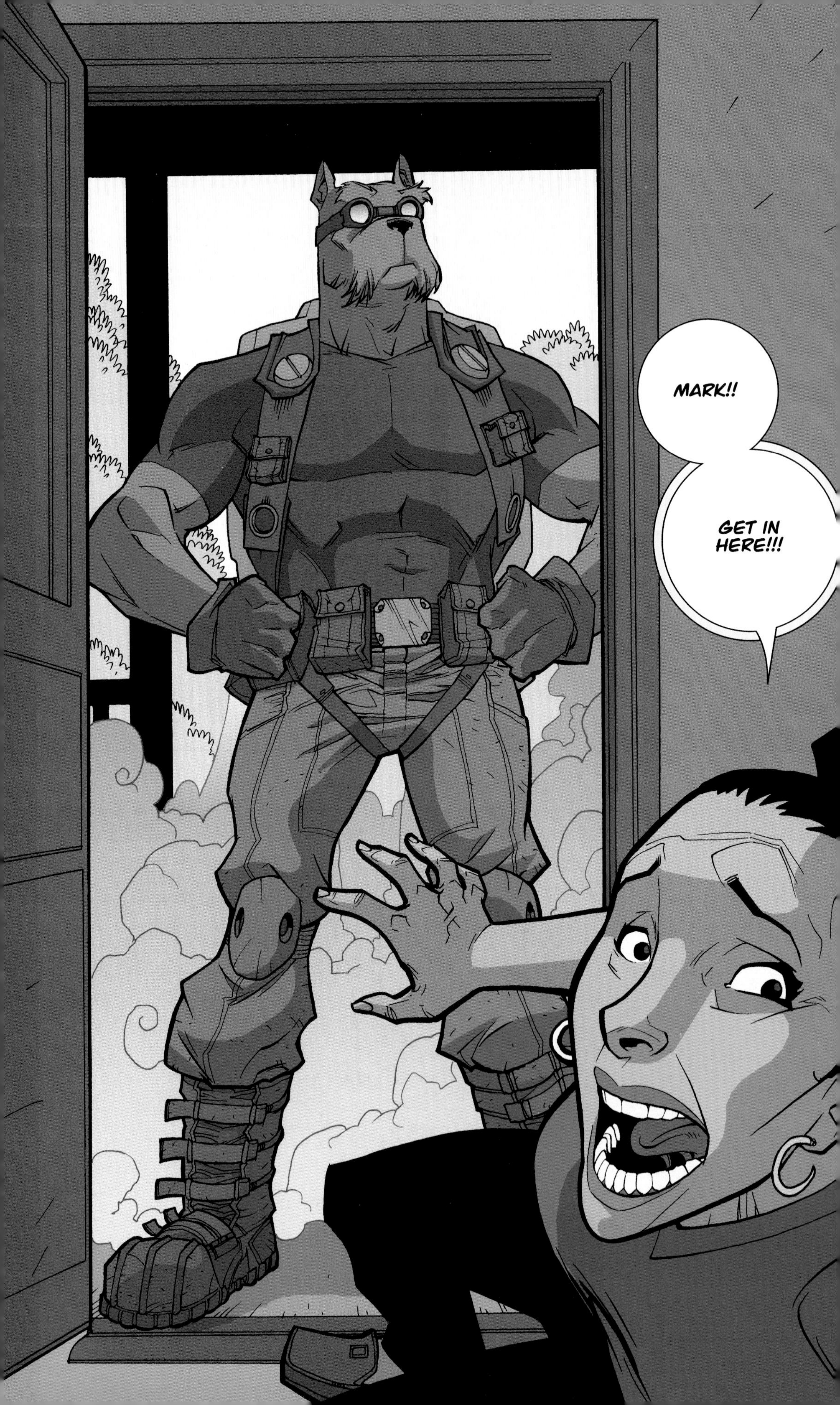
MARK!!
GET IN HERE!!!

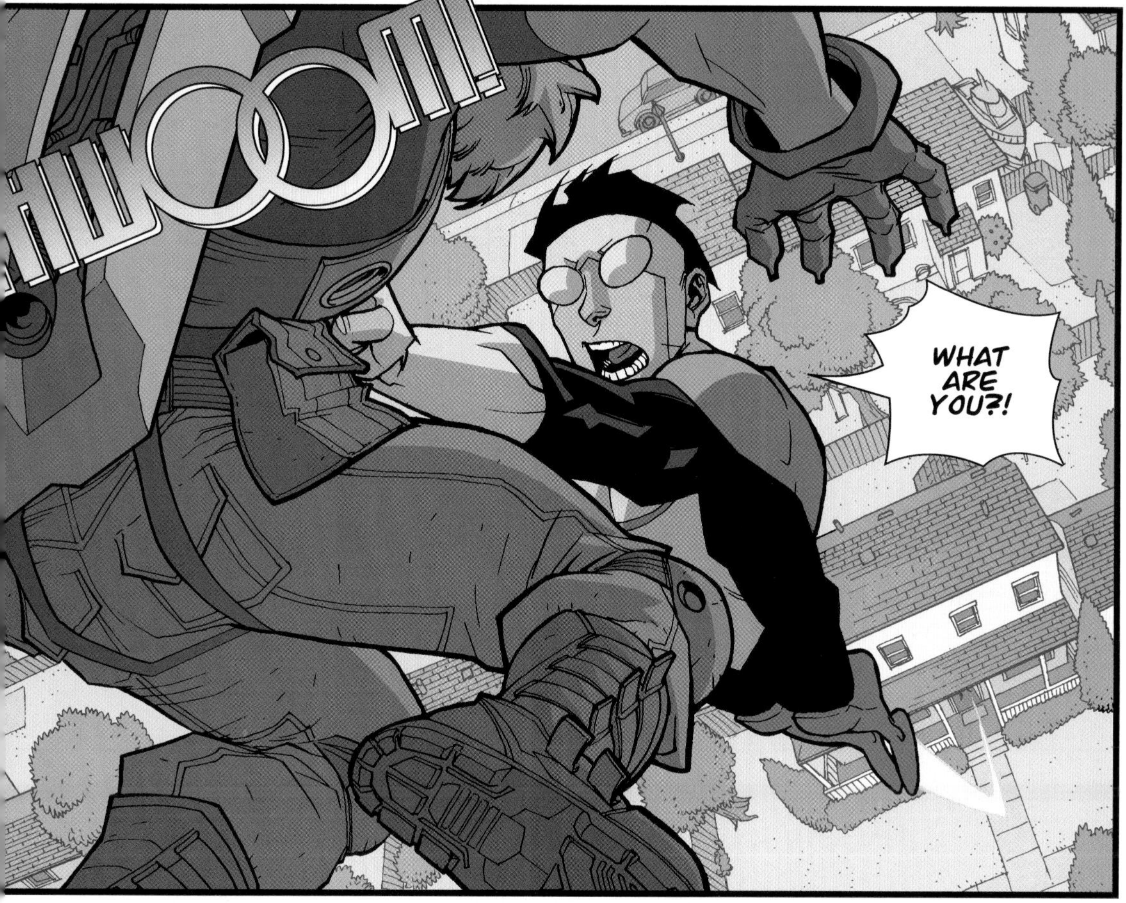

HWOOM!
WHAT ARE YOU?!

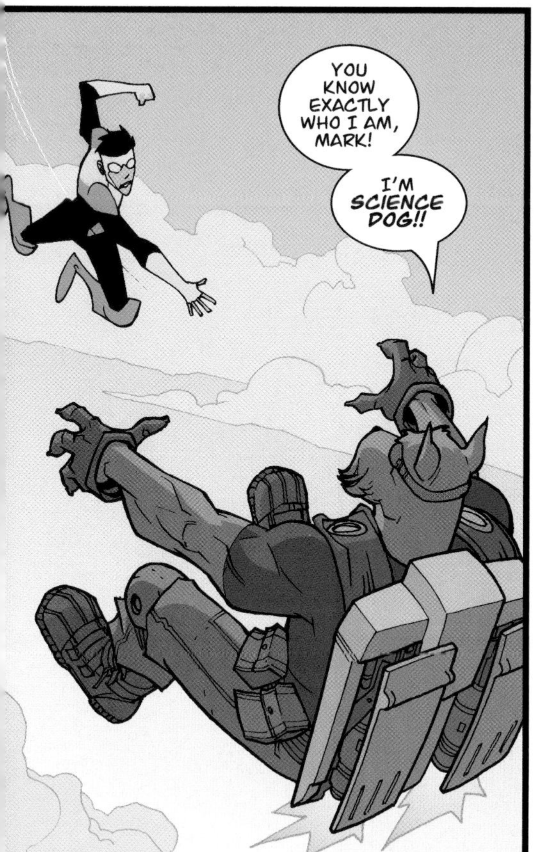

YOU KNOW EXACTLY WHO I AM, MARK!
I'M SCIENCE DOG!!

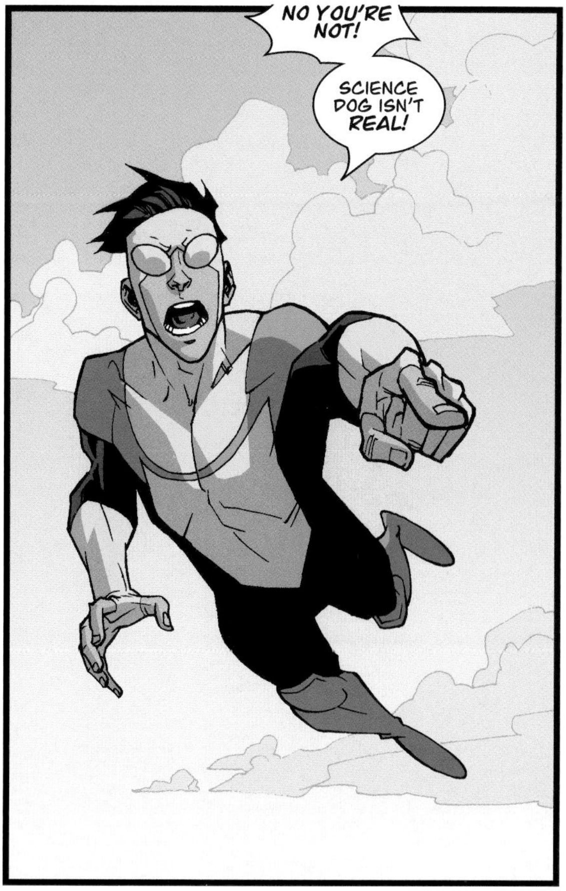

NO YOU'RE NOT!
SCIENCE DOG ISN'T REAL!

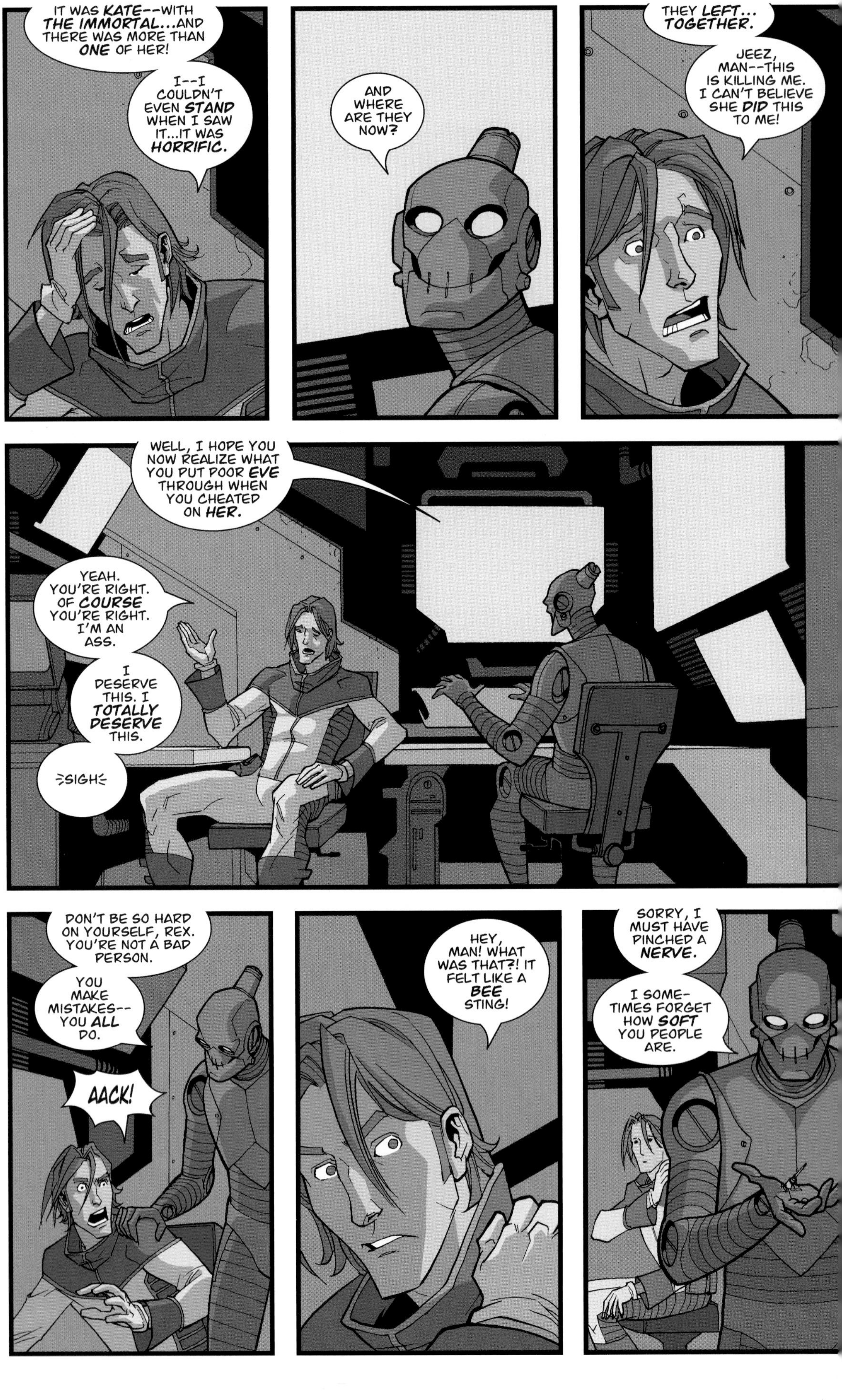
IT WAS KATE--WITH THE IMMORTAL...AND THERE WAS MORE THAN ONE OF HER!
I--I COULDN'T EVEN STAND WHEN I SAW IT...IT WAS HORRIFIC.
AND WHERE ARE THEY NOW?
THEY LEFT... TOGETHER.
JEEZ, MAN--THIS IS KILLING ME. I CAN'T BELIEVE SHE DID THIS TO ME!
WELL, I HOPE YOU NOW REALIZE WHAT YOU PUT POOR EVE THROUGH WHEN YOU CHEATED ON HER.
YEAH. YOU'RE RIGHT. OF COURSE YOU'RE RIGHT. I'M AN ASS.
I DESERVE THIS. I TOTALLY DESERVE THIS.
SIGH
DON'T BE SO HARD ON YOURSELF, REX. YOU'RE NOT A BAD PERSON.
YOU MAKE MISTAKES--YOU ALL DO.
AACK!
HEY, MAN! WHAT WAS THAT?! IT FELT LIKE A BEE STING!
SORRY, I MUST HAVE PINCHED A NERVE.
I SOMETIMES FORGET HOW SOFT YOU PEOPLE ARE.

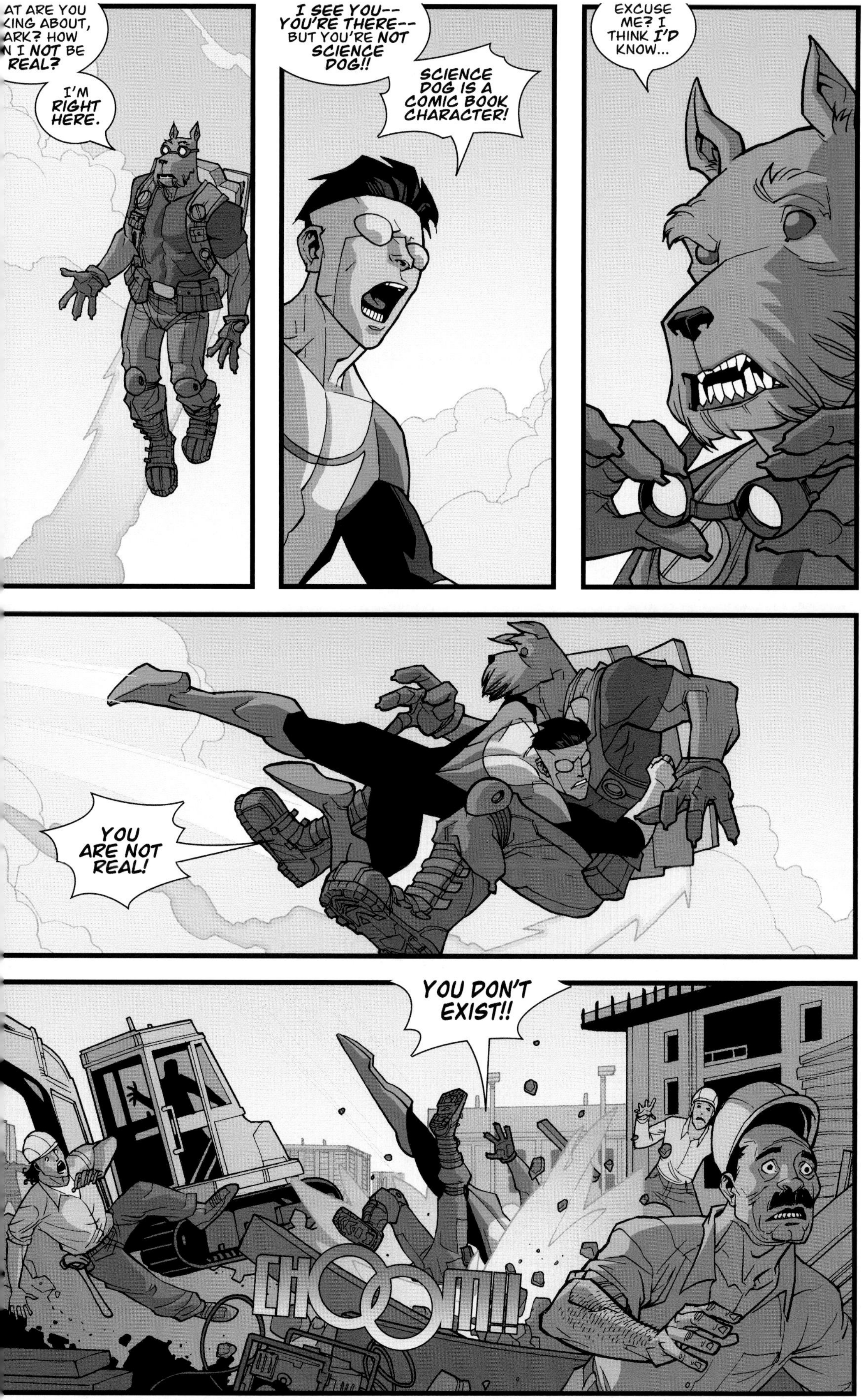
AT ARE YOU
KING ABOUT,
ARK? HOW
N I NOT BE
REAL?
I'M RIGHT HERE.
I SEE YOU-- YOU'RE THERE-- BUT YOU'RE NOT SCIENCE DOG!!
SCIENCE DOG IS A COMIC BOOK CHARACTER!
EXCUSE ME? I THINK I'D KNOW...
YOU ARE NOT REAL!
YOU DON'T EXIST!!
CHOOOM!!

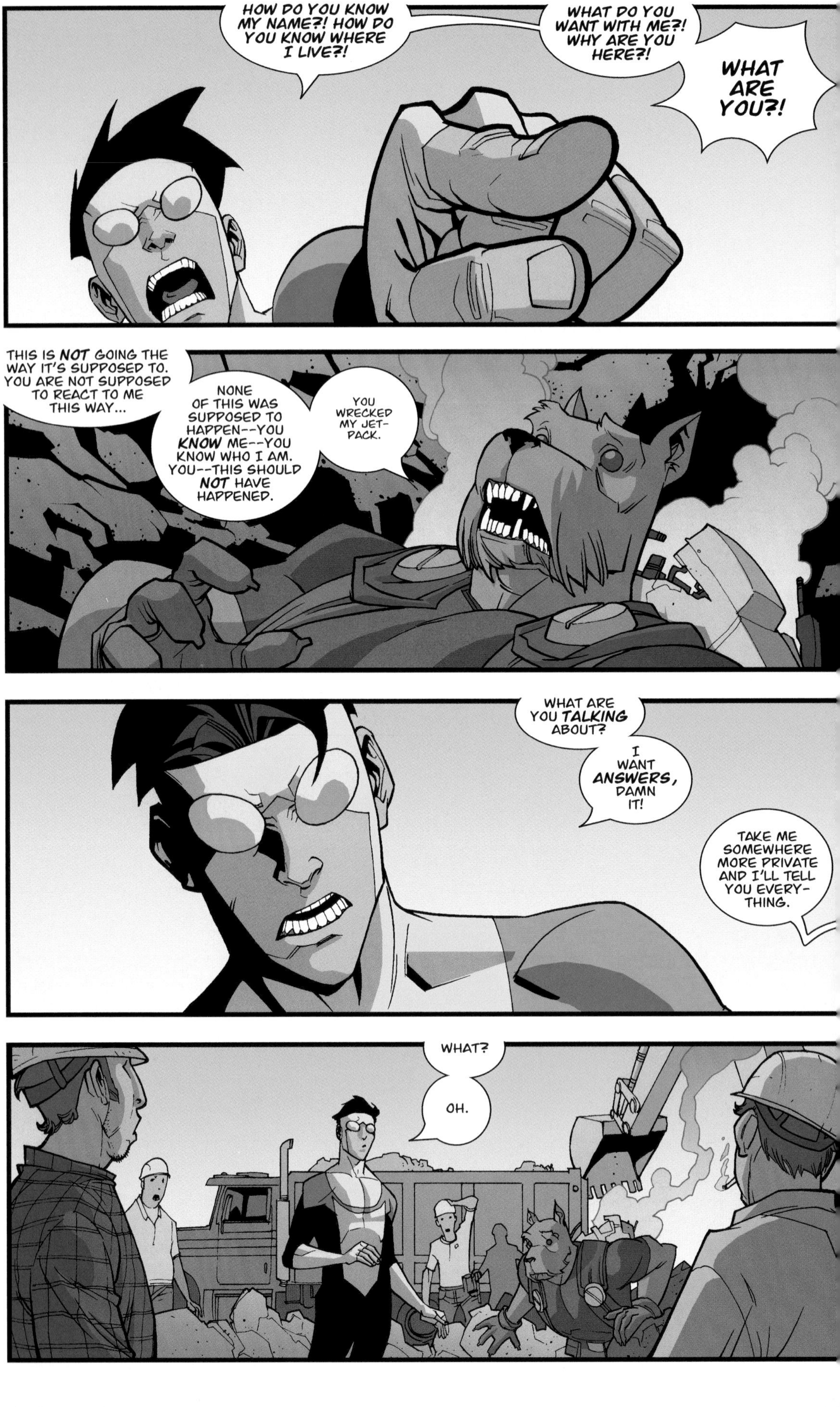
HOW DO YOU KNOW MY NAME?! HOW DO YOU KNOW WHERE I LIVE?!
WHAT DO YOU WANT WITH ME?! WHY ARE YOU HERE?!
WHAT ARE YOU?!
THIS IS NOT GOING THE WAY IT'S SUPPOSED TO. YOU ARE NOT SUPPOSED TO REACT TO ME THIS WAY...
NONE OF THIS WAS SUPPOSED TO HAPPEN--YOU KNOW ME--YOU KNOW WHO I AM. YOU--THIS SHOULD NOT HAVE HAPPENED.
YOU WRECKED MY JET-PACK.
WHAT ARE YOU TALKING ABOUT?
I WANT ANSWERS, DAMN IT!
TAKE ME SOMEWHERE MORE PRIVATE AND I'LL TELL YOU EVERY-THING.
WHAT?
OH.

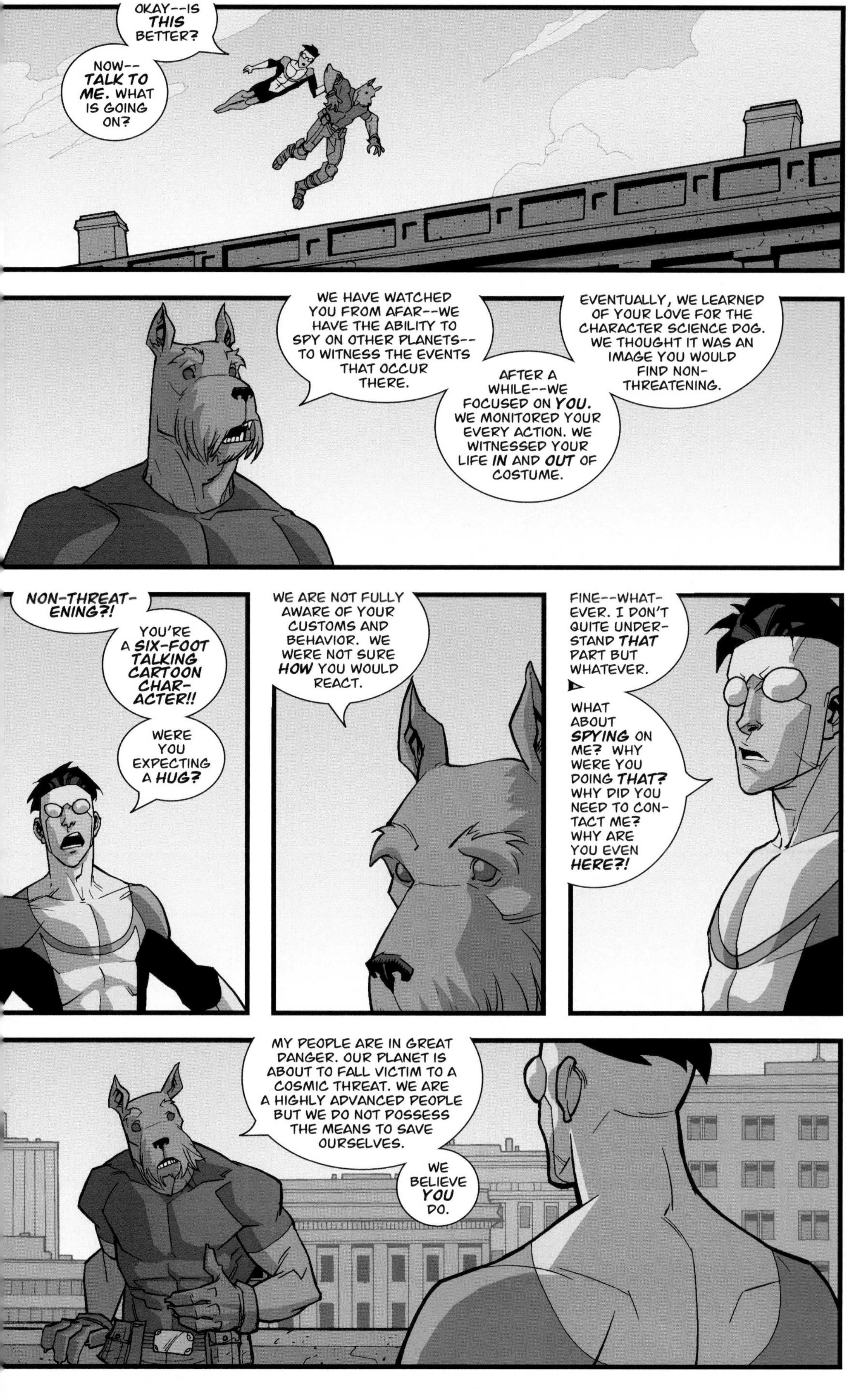
OKAY--IS THIS BETTER?
NOW--TALK TO ME. WHAT IS GOING ON?
WE HAVE WATCHED YOU FROM AFAR--WE HAVE THE ABILITY TO SPY ON OTHER PLANETS--TO WITNESS THE EVENTS THAT OCCUR THERE.
AFTER A WHILE--WE FOCUSED ON YOU. WE MONITORED YOUR EVERY ACTION. WE WITNESSED YOUR LIFE IN AND OUT OF COSTUME.
EVENTUALLY, WE LEARNED OF YOUR LOVE FOR THE CHARACTER SCIENCE DOG. WE THOUGHT IT WAS AN IMAGE YOU WOULD FIND NON-THREATENING.
NON-THREAT-ENING?!
YOU'RE A SIX-FOOT TALKING CARTOON CHAR-ACTER!!
WERE YOU EXPECTING A HUG?
WE ARE NOT FULLY AWARE OF YOUR CUSTOMS AND BEHAVIOR. WE WERE NOT SURE HOW YOU WOULD REACT.
FINE--WHAT-EVER. I DON'T QUITE UNDER-STAND THAT PART BUT WHATEVER.
WHAT ABOUT SPYING ON ME? WHY WERE YOU DOING THAT? WHY DID YOU NEED TO CON-TACT ME? WHY ARE YOU EVEN HERE?!
MY PEOPLE ARE IN GREAT DANGER. OUR PLANET IS ABOUT TO FALL VICTIM TO A COSMIC THREAT. WE ARE A HIGHLY ADVANCED PEOPLE BUT WE DO NOT POSSESS THE MEANS TO SAVE OURSELVES.
WE BELIEVE YOU DO.

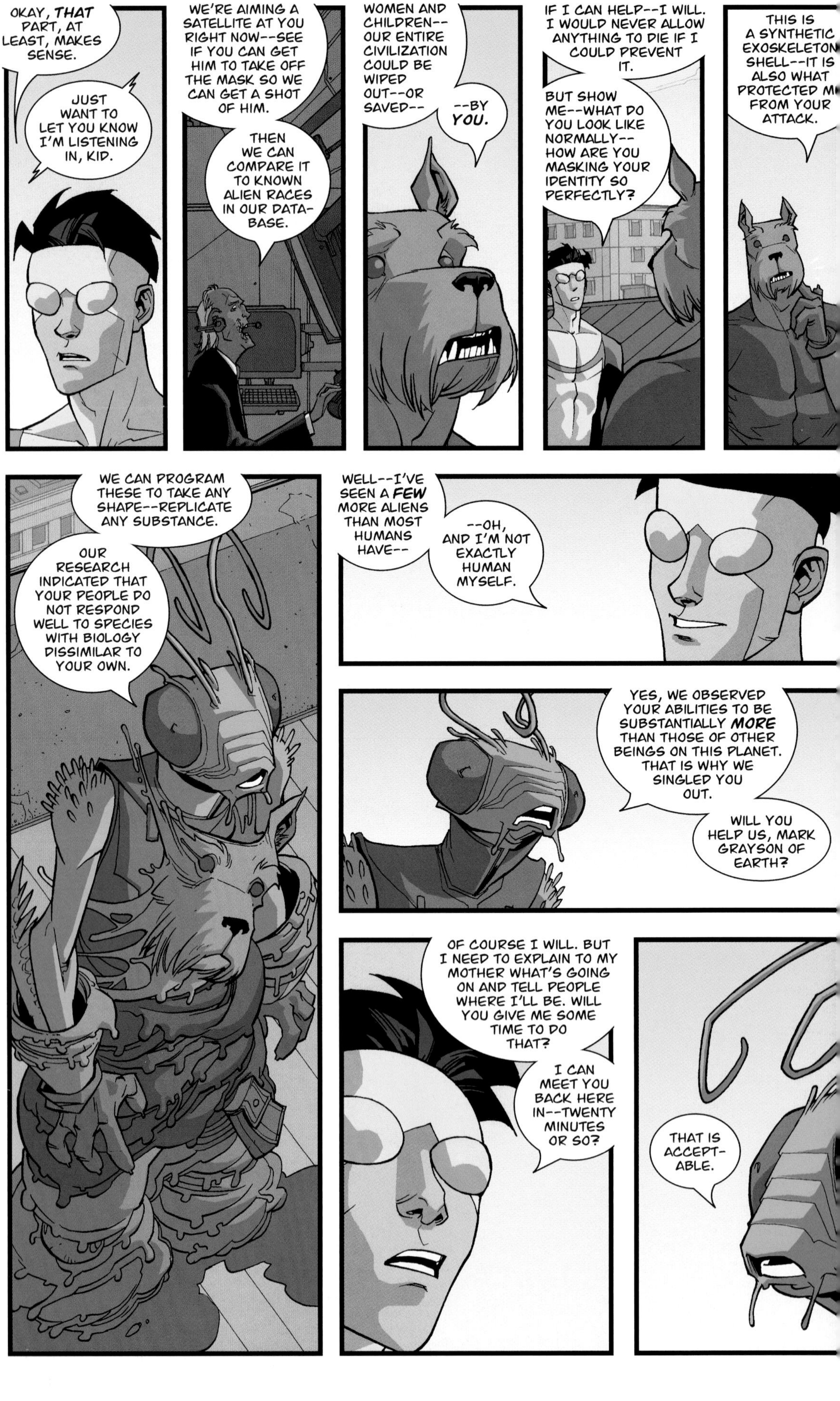
OKAY, THAT PART, AT LEAST, MAKES SENSE.
JUST WANT TO LET YOU KNOW I'M LISTENING IN, KID.
WE'RE AIMING A SATELLITE AT YOU RIGHT NOW--SEE IF YOU CAN GET HIM TO TAKE OFF THE MASK SO WE CAN GET A SHOT OF HIM.
THEN WE CAN COMPARE IT TO KNOWN ALIEN RACES IN OUR DATA-BASE.
WOMEN AND CHILDREN--OUR ENTIRE CIVILIZATION COULD BE WIPED OUT--OR SAVED--
--BY YOU.
IF I CAN HELP--I WILL. I WOULD NEVER ALLOW ANYTHING TO DIE IF I COULD PREVENT IT.
BUT SHOW ME--WHAT DO YOU LOOK LIKE NORMALLY--HOW ARE YOU MASKING YOUR IDENTITY SO PERFECTLY?
THIS IS A SYNTHETIC EXOSKELETON SHELL--IT IS ALSO WHAT PROTECTED M FROM YOUR ATTACK.
WE CAN PROGRAM THESE TO TAKE ANY SHAPE--REPLICATE ANY SUBSTANCE.
OUR RESEARCH INDICATED THAT YOUR PEOPLE DO NOT RESPOND WELL TO SPECIES WITH BIOLOGY DISSIMILAR TO YOUR OWN.
WELL--I'VE SEEN A FEW MORE ALIENS THAN MOST HUMANS HAVE--
--OH, AND I'M NOT EXACTLY HUMAN MYSELF.
YES, WE OBSERVED YOUR ABILITIES TO BE SUBSTANTIALLY MORE THAN THOSE OF OTHER BEINGS ON THIS PLANET. THAT IS WHY WE SINGLED YOU OUT.
WILL YOU HELP US, MARK GRAYSON OF EARTH?
OF COURSE I WILL. BUT I NEED TO EXPLAIN TO MY MOTHER WHAT'S GOING ON AND TELL PEOPLE WHERE I'LL BE. WILL YOU GIVE ME SOME TIME TO DO THAT?
I CAN MEET YOU BACK HERE IN--TWENTY MINUTES OR SO?
THAT IS ACCEPT-ABLE.

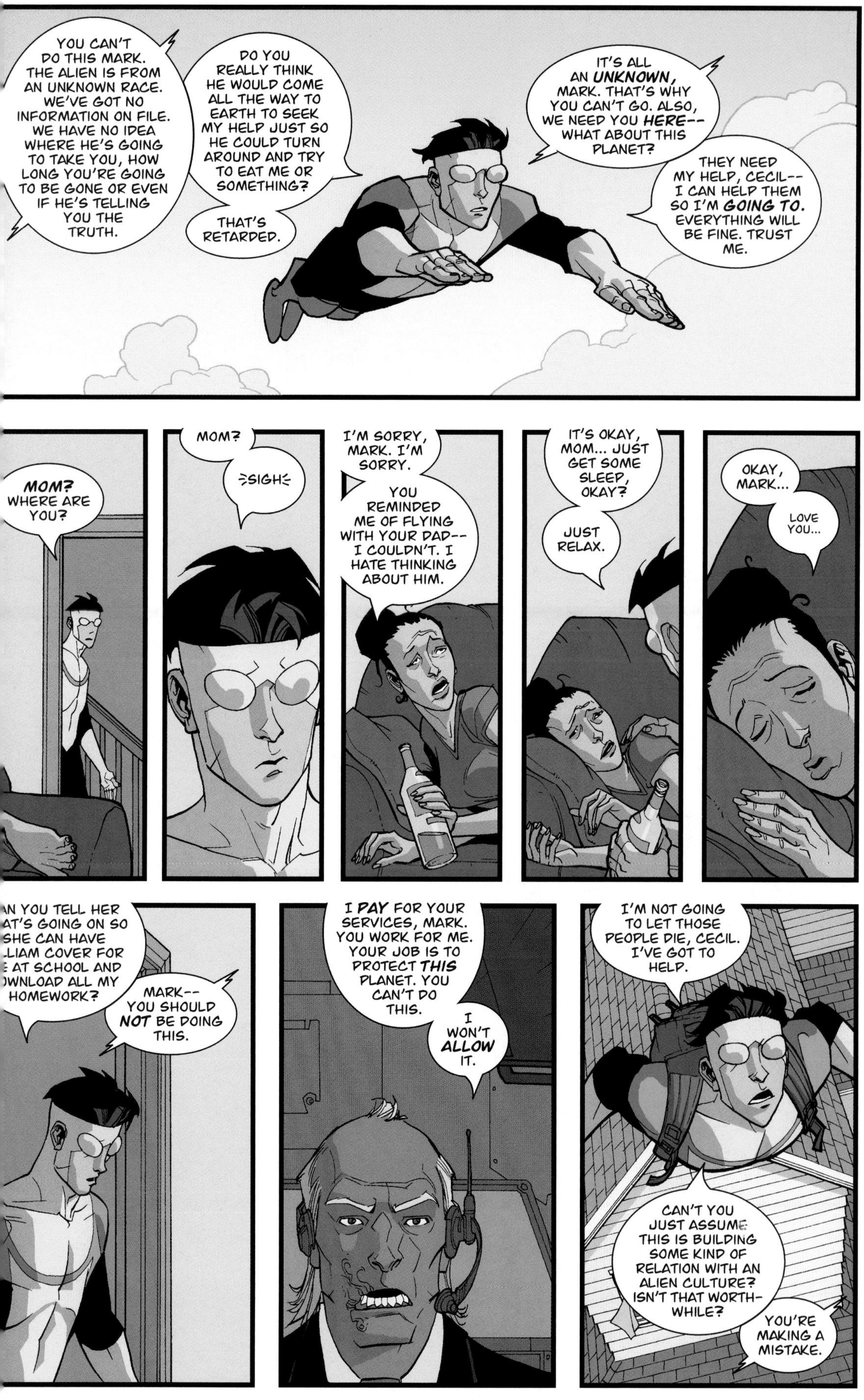
YOU CAN'T DO THIS MARK. THE ALIEN IS FROM AN UNKNOWN RACE. WE'VE GOT NO INFORMATION ON FILE. WE HAVE NO IDEA WHERE HE'S GOING TO TAKE YOU, HOW LONG YOU'RE GOING TO BE GONE OR EVEN IF HE'S TELLING YOU THE TRUTH.
DO YOU REALLY THINK HE WOULD COME ALL THE WAY TO EARTH TO SEEK MY HELP JUST SO HE COULD TURN AROUND AND TRY TO EAT ME OR SOMETHING?
THAT'S RETARDED.
IT'S ALL AN UNKNOWN, MARK. THAT'S WHY YOU CAN'T GO. ALSO, WE NEED YOU HERE-- WHAT ABOUT THIS PLANET?
THEY NEED MY HELP, CECIL-- I CAN HELP THEM SO I'M GOING TO. EVERYTHING WILL BE FINE. TRUST ME.
MOM? WHERE ARE YOU?
MOM?
SIGH
I'M SORRY, MARK. I'M SORRY.
YOU REMINDED ME OF FLYING WITH YOUR DAD-- I COULDN'T. I HATE THINKING ABOUT HIM.
IT'S OKAY, MOM... JUST GET SOME SLEEP, OKAY?
JUST RELAX.
OKAY, MARK...
LOVE YOU...
AN YOU TELL HER AT'S GOING ON SO SHE CAN HAVE LLIAM COVER FOR E AT SCHOOL AND WNLOAD ALL MY HOMEWORK?
MARK-- YOU SHOULD NOT BE DOING THIS.
I PAY FOR YOUR SERVICES, MARK. YOU WORK FOR ME. YOUR JOB IS TO PROTECT THIS PLANET. YOU CAN'T DO THIS.
I WON'T ALLOW IT.
I'M NOT GOING TO LET THOSE PEOPLE DIE, CECIL. I'VE GOT TO HELP.
CAN'T YOU JUST ASSUME THIS IS BUILDING SOME KIND OF RELATION WITH AN ALIEN CULTURE? ISN'T THAT WORTH-WHILE?
YOU'RE MAKING A MISTAKE.

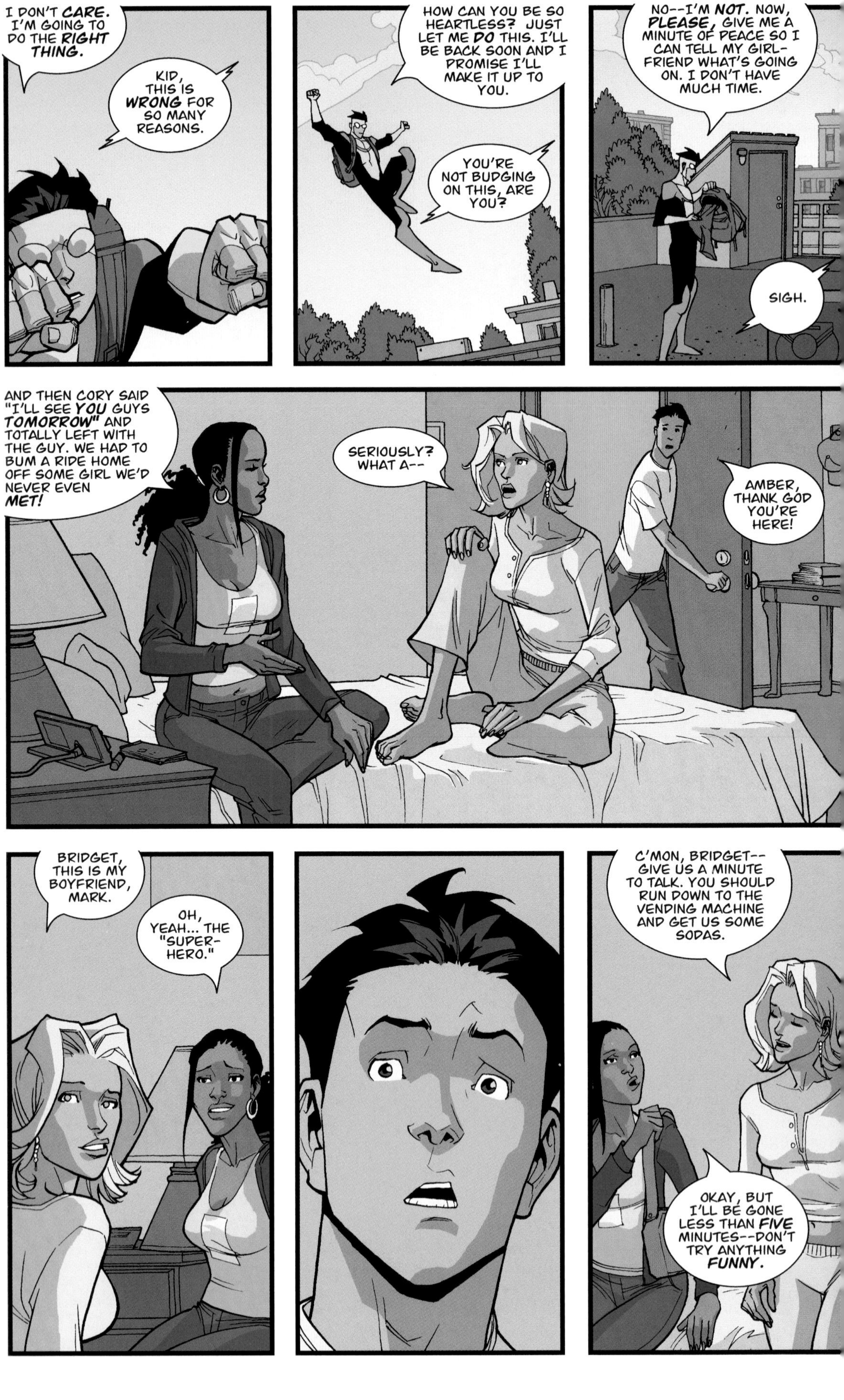

I DON'T CARE. I'M GOING TO DO THE RIGHT THING.
KID, THIS IS WRONG FOR SO MANY REASONS.
HOW CAN YOU BE SO HEARTLESS? JUST LET ME DO THIS. I'LL BE BACK SOON AND I PROMISE I'LL MAKE IT UP TO YOU.
YOU'RE NOT BUDGING ON THIS, ARE YOU?
NO--I'M NOT. NOW, PLEASE, GIVE ME A MINUTE OF PEACE SO I CAN TELL MY GIRL-FRIEND WHAT'S GOING ON. I DON'T HAVE MUCH TIME.
SIGH.
AND THEN CORY SAID "I'LL SEE YOU GUYS TOMORROW" AND TOTALLY LEFT WITH THE GUY. WE HAD TO BUM A RIDE HOME OFF SOME GIRL WE'D NEVER EVEN MET!
SERIOUSLY? WHAT A--
AMBER, THANK GOD YOU'RE HERE!
BRIDGET, THIS IS MY BOYFRIEND, MARK.
OH, YEAH... THE "SUPER-HERO."
C'MON, BRIDGET--GIVE US A MINUTE TO TALK. YOU SHOULD RUN DOWN TO THE VENDING MACHINE AND GET US SOME SODAS.
OKAY, BUT I'LL BE GONE LESS THAN FIVE MINUTES--DON'T TRY ANYTHING FUNNY.

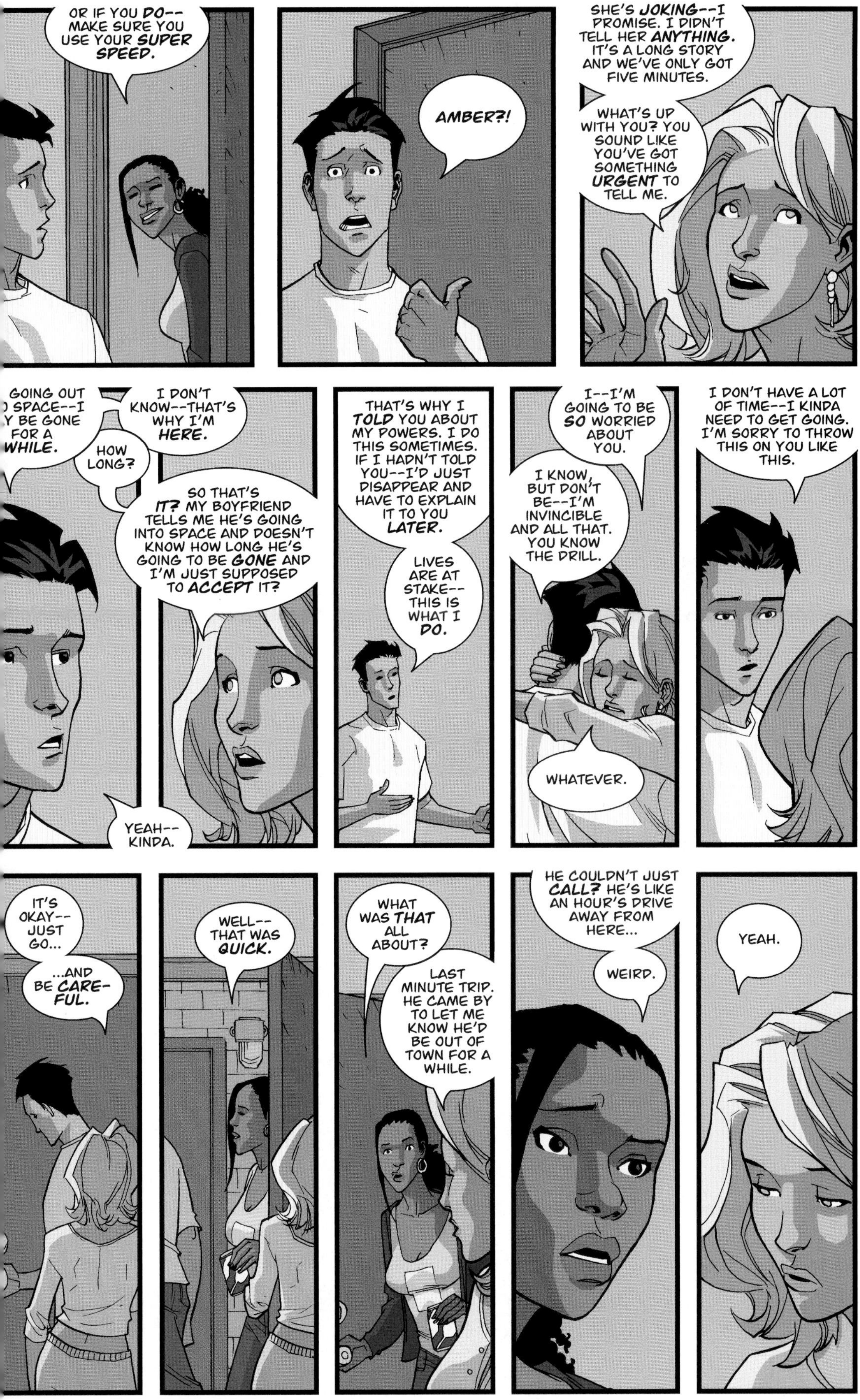
OR IF YOU DO--
MAKE SURE YOU
USE YOUR SUPER
SPEED.
AMBER?!
SHE'S JOKING--I PROMISE. I DIDN'T TELL HER ANYTHING. IT'S A LONG STORY AND WE'VE ONLY GOT FIVE MINUTES.
WHAT'S UP WITH YOU? YOU SOUND LIKE YOU'VE GOT SOMETHING URGENT TO TELL ME.
GOING OUT SPACE--I BE GONE FOR A WHILE.
HOW LONG?
I DON'T KNOW--THAT'S WHY I'M HERE.
SO THAT'S IT? MY BOYFRIEND TELLS ME HE'S GOING INTO SPACE AND DOESN'T KNOW HOW LONG HE'S GOING TO BE GONE AND I'M JUST SUPPOSED TO ACCEPT IT?
YEAH--KINDA.
THAT'S WHY I TOLD YOU ABOUT MY POWERS. I DO THIS SOMETIMES. IF I HADN'T TOLD YOU--I'D JUST DISAPPEAR AND HAVE TO EXPLAIN IT TO YOU LATER.
LIVES ARE AT STAKE--THIS IS WHAT I DO.
I--I'M GOING TO BE SO WORRIED ABOUT YOU.
I KNOW, BUT DON'T BE--I'M INVINCIBLE AND ALL THAT. YOU KNOW THE DRILL.
WHATEVER.
I DON'T HAVE A LOT OF TIME--I KINDA NEED TO GET GOING. I'M SORRY TO THROW THIS ON YOU LIKE THIS.
IT'S OKAY--JUST GO...
...AND BE CARE-FUL.
WELL--THAT WAS QUICK.
WHAT WAS THAT ALL ABOUT?
LAST MINUTE TRIP. HE CAME BY TO LET ME KNOW HE'D BE OUT OF TOWN FOR A WHILE.
HE COULDN'T JUST CALL? HE'S LIKE AN HOUR'S DRIVE AWAY FROM HERE...
WEIRD.
YEAH.

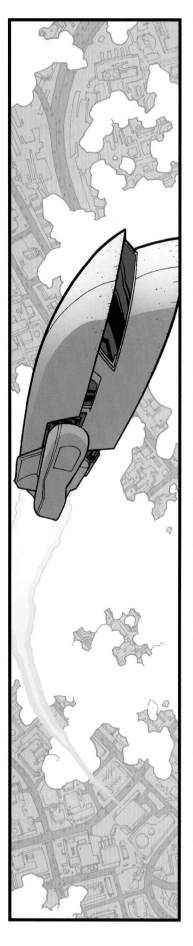

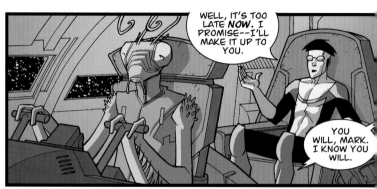
WELL, IT'S TOO LATE *NOW*. I PROMISE--I'LL MAKE IT UP TO YOU.

YOU WILL, MARK. I KNOW YOU WILL.

WHATEVER, *FINE*. JUST DON'T FORGET TO TELL MY *MOM* WHAT'S GOING ON.

I'LL MAKE SURE ⇒SQUIT⇐ ⇒SQUEEE⇐ ⇒SKRIK⇐

BLAST!!

MUST BE OUT OF RANGE...

ARE YOU COMFORTABLE?

YES. THANKS.

GOOD. THE TRIP WILL TAKE SIX OF YOUR EARTH DAYS.

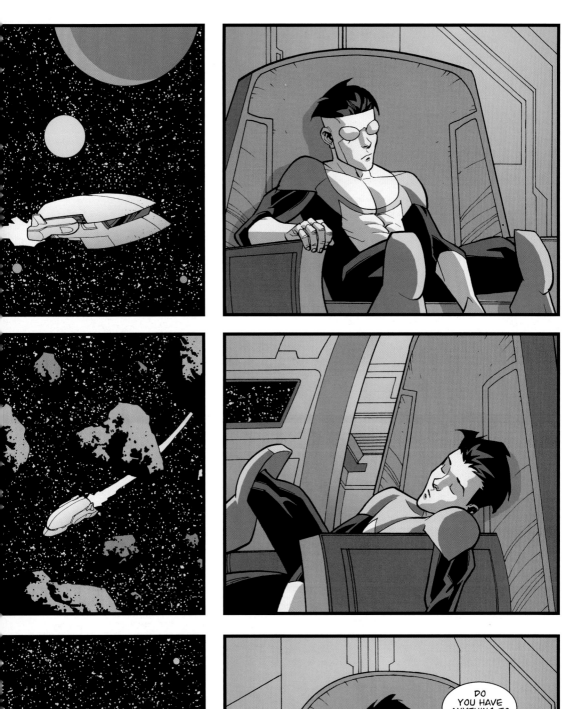

DO YOU HAVE ANYTHING TO **READ?**

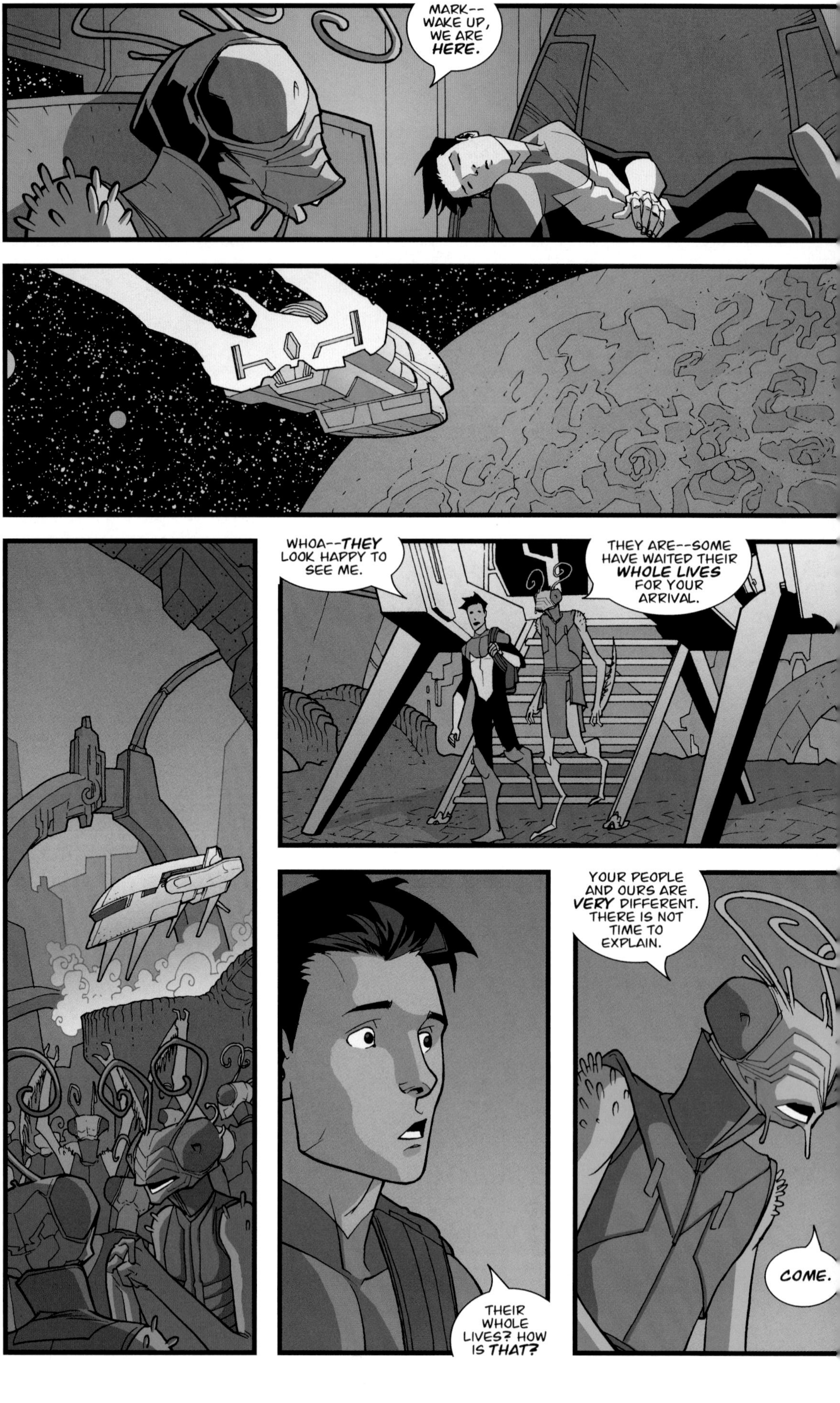
MARK--
WAKE UP,
WE ARE
HERE.
WHOA--THEY
LOOK HAPPY TO
SEE ME.
THEY ARE--SOME
HAVE WAITED THEIR
WHOLE LIVES
FOR YOUR
ARRIVAL.
THEIR
WHOLE
LIVES? HOW
IS THAT?
YOUR PEOPLE
AND OURS ARE
VERY DIFFERENT.
THERE IS NOT
TIME TO
EXPLAIN.
COME.

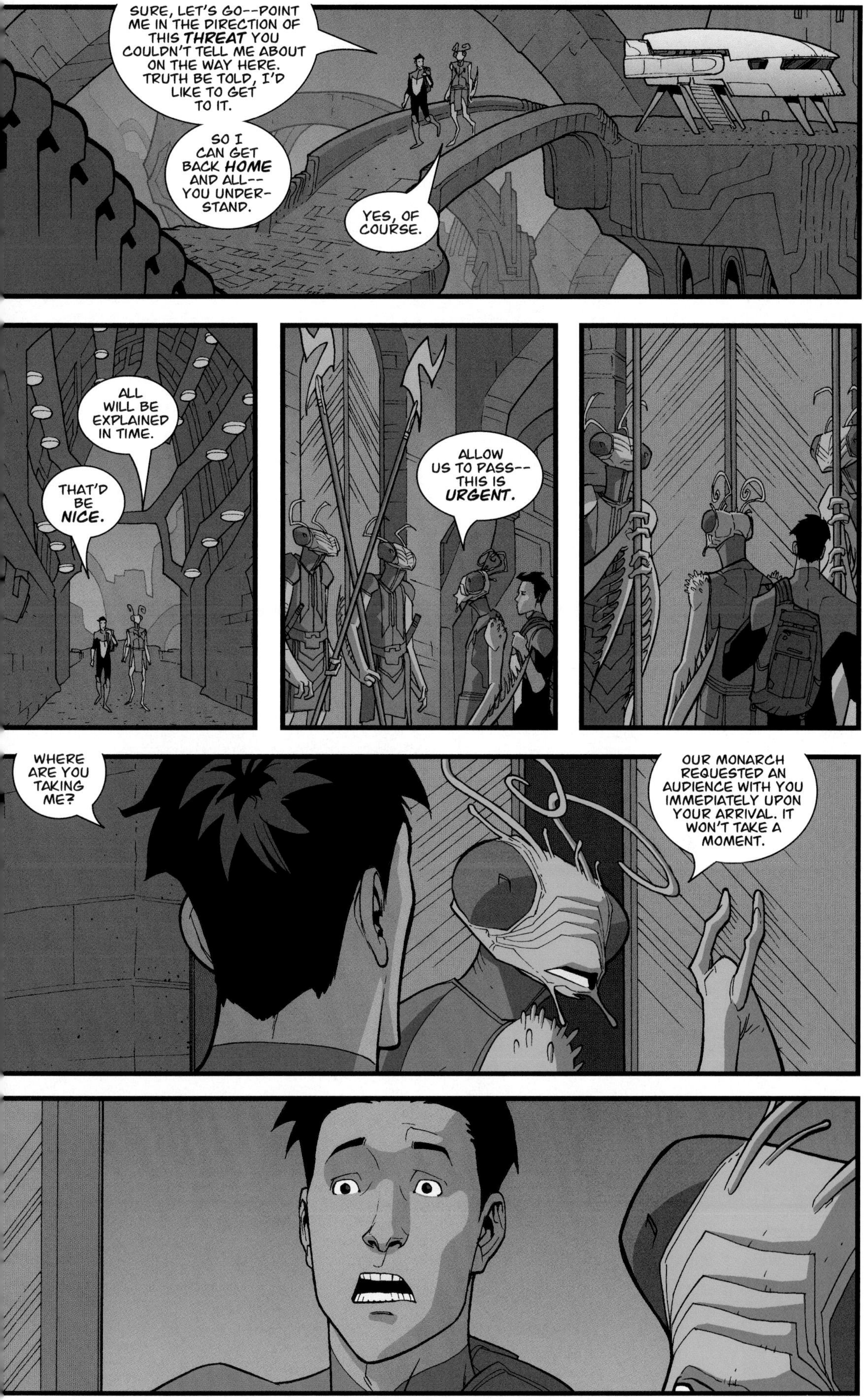
SURE, LET'S GO--POINT ME IN THE DIRECTION OF THIS THREAT YOU COULDN'T TELL ME ABOUT ON THE WAY HERE. TRUTH BE TOLD, I'D LIKE TO GET TO IT.
SO I CAN GET BACK HOME AND ALL--YOU UNDERSTAND.
YES, OF COURSE.
ALL WILL BE EXPLAINED IN TIME.
THAT'D BE NICE.
ALLOW US TO PASS--THIS IS URGENT.
WHERE ARE YOU TAKING ME?
OUR MONARCH REQUESTED AN AUDIENCE WITH YOU IMMEDIATELY UPON YOUR ARRIVAL. IT WON'T TAKE A MOMENT.

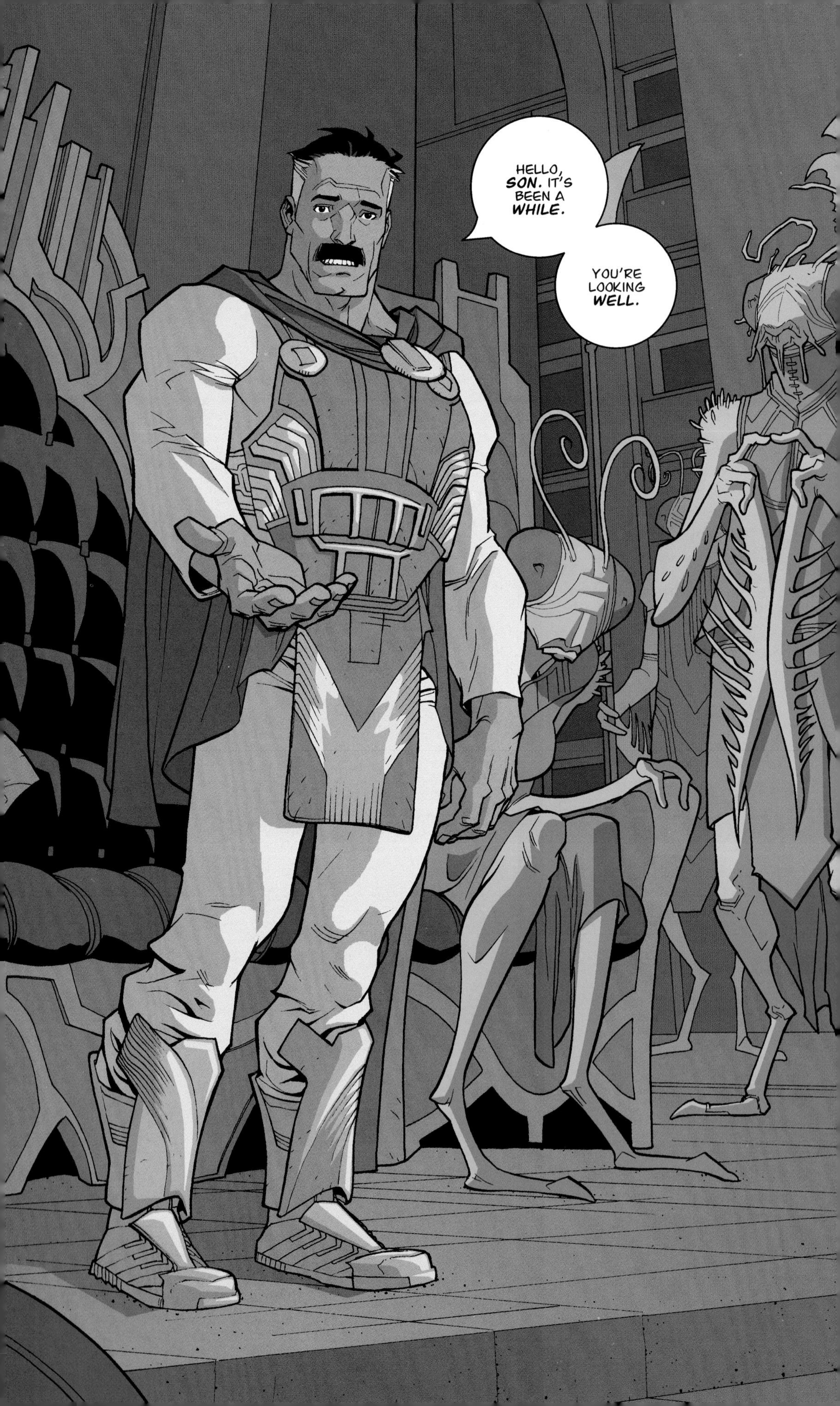
HELLO, SON. IT'S BEEN A WHILE.
YOU'RE LOOKING WELL.

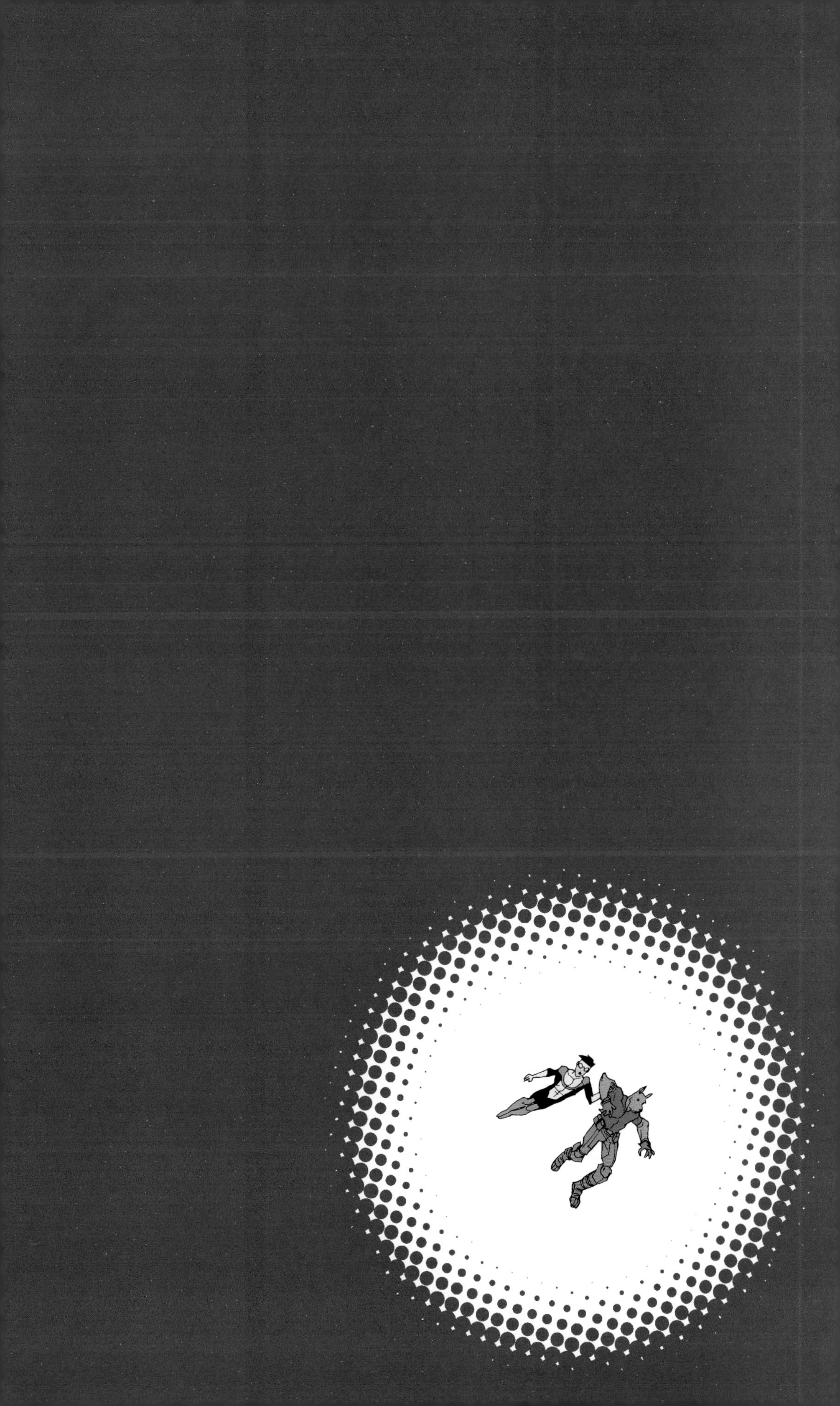

CHAPTER TWO

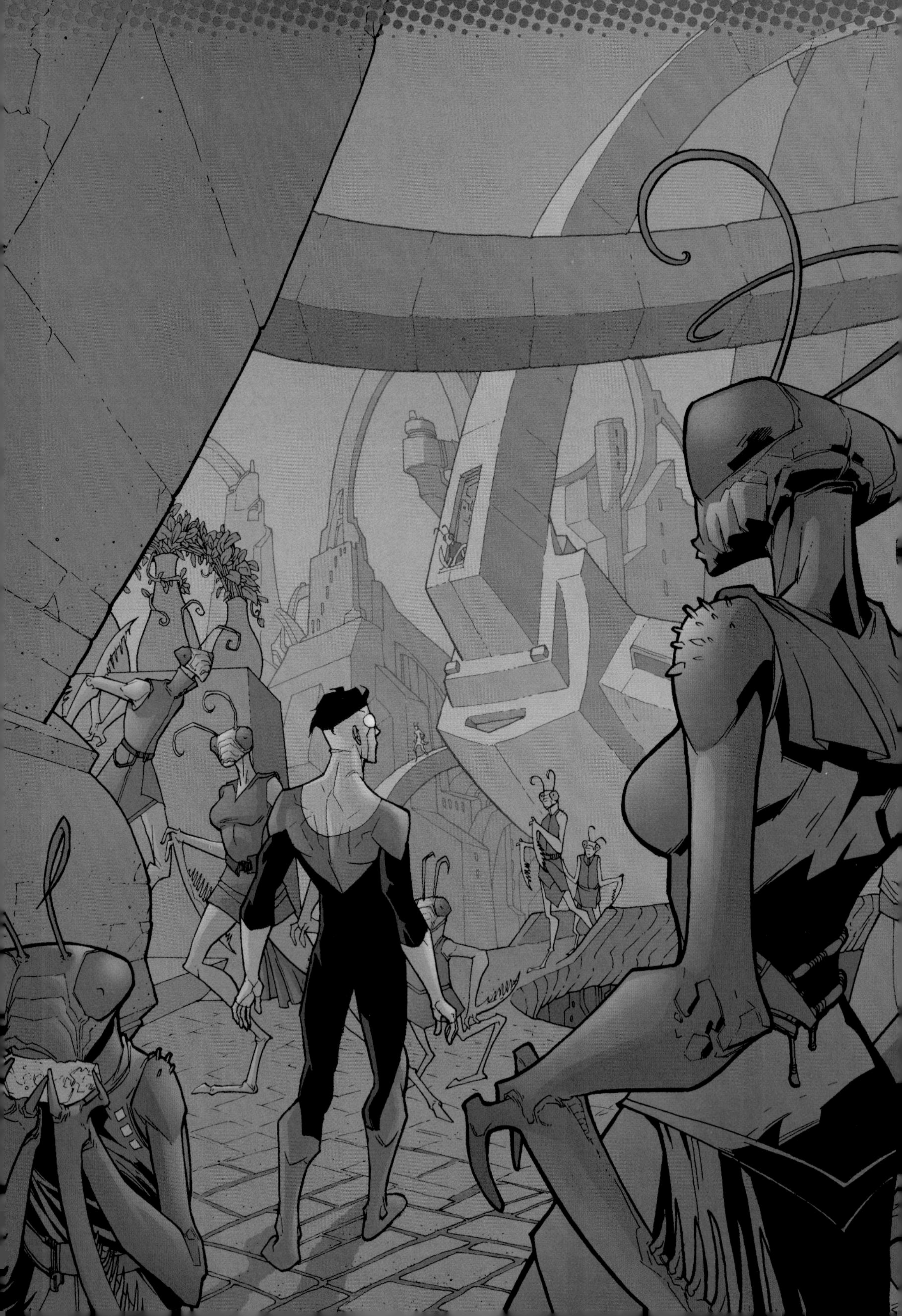

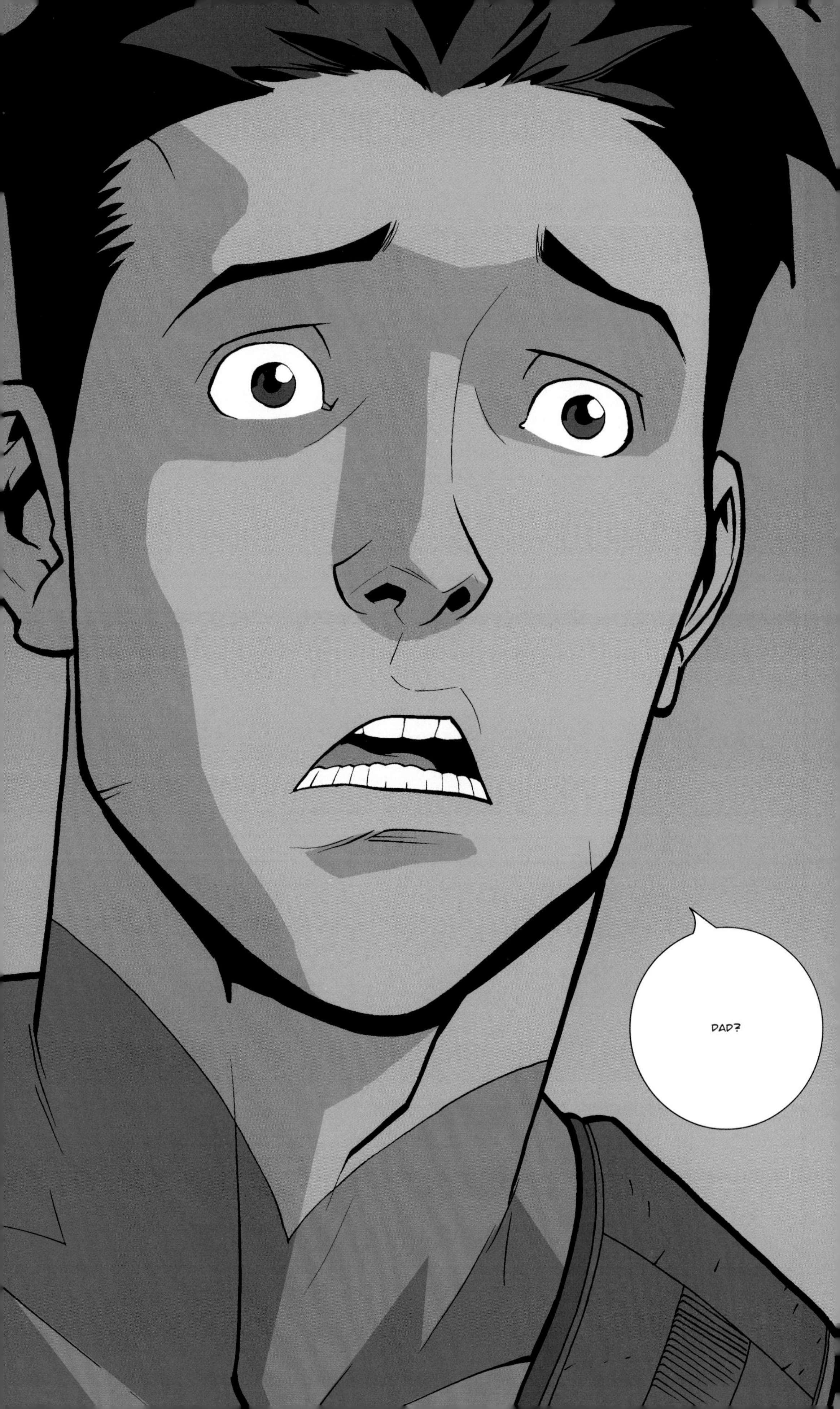
DAD?

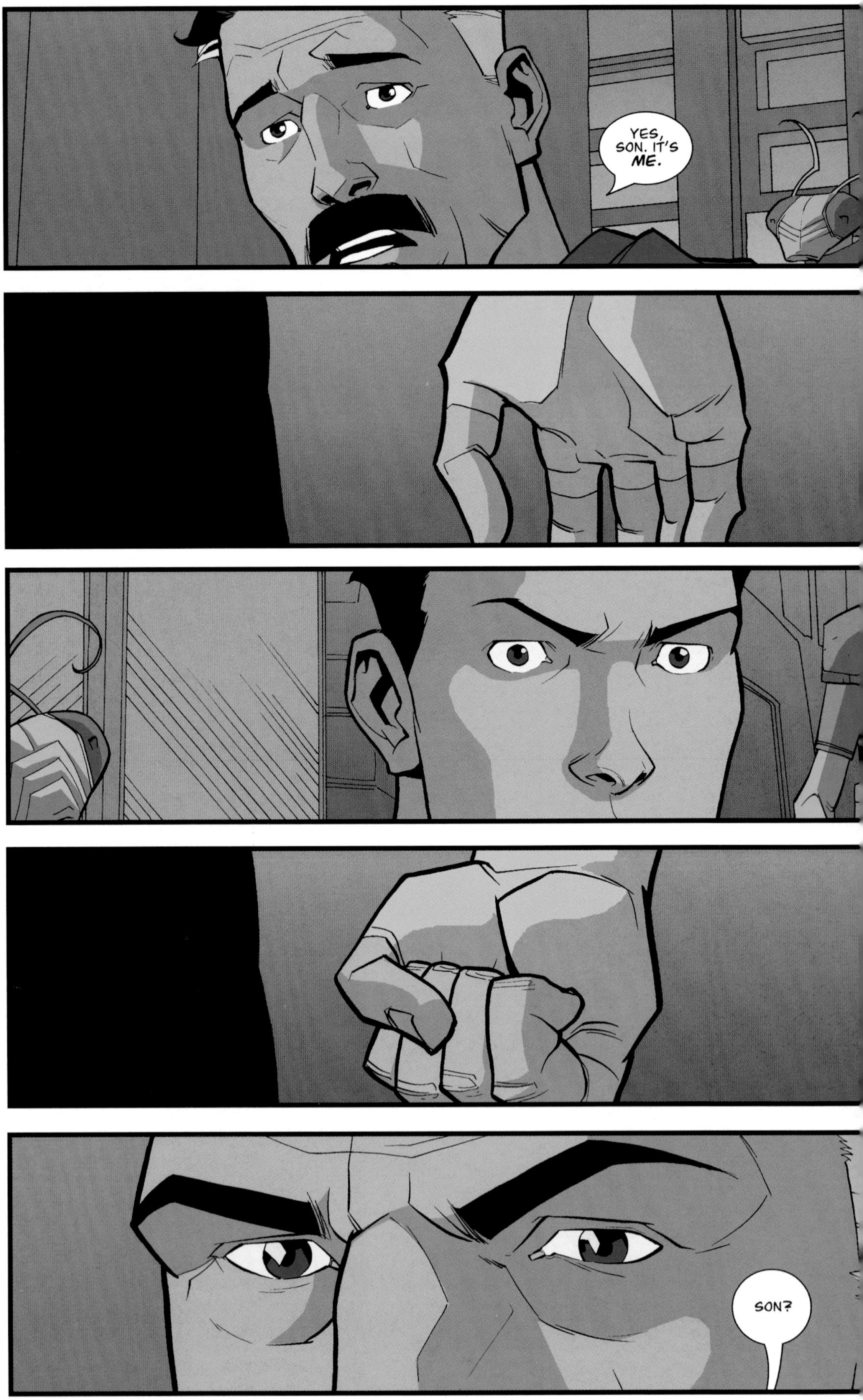
YES, SON. IT'S ME.
SON?

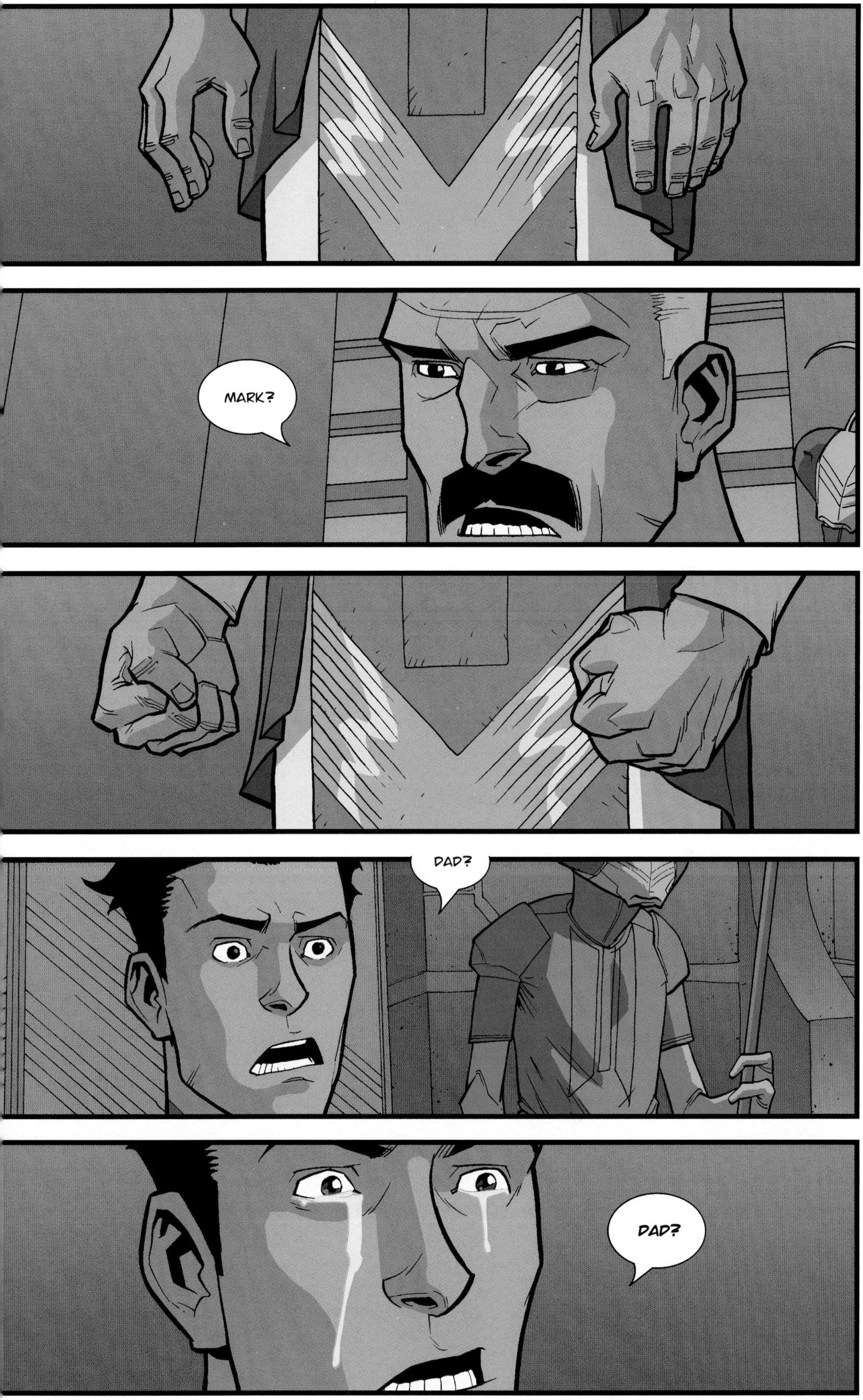
MARK?
DAD?
DAD?

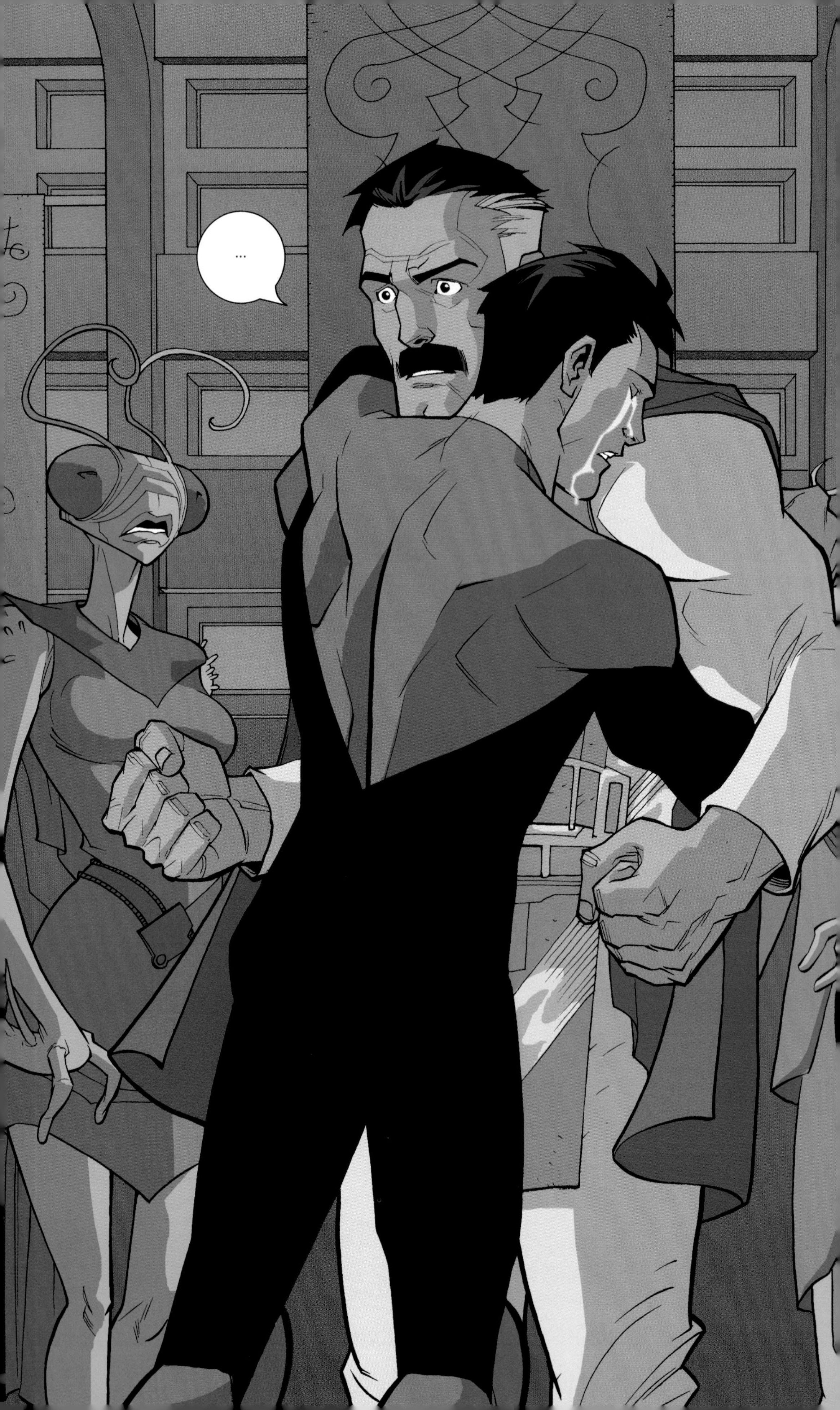
...

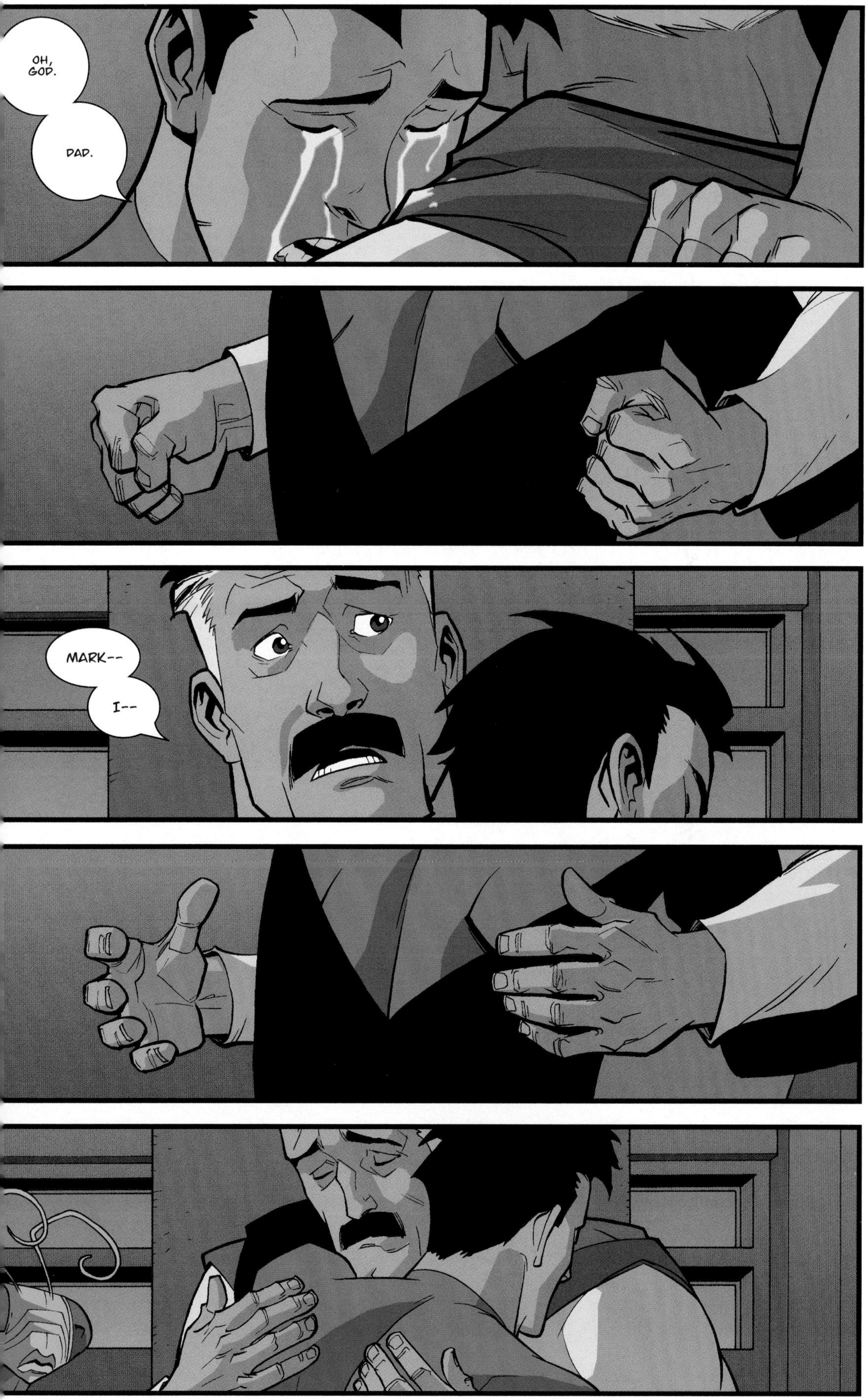
OH, GOD.
DAD.
MARK--
I--

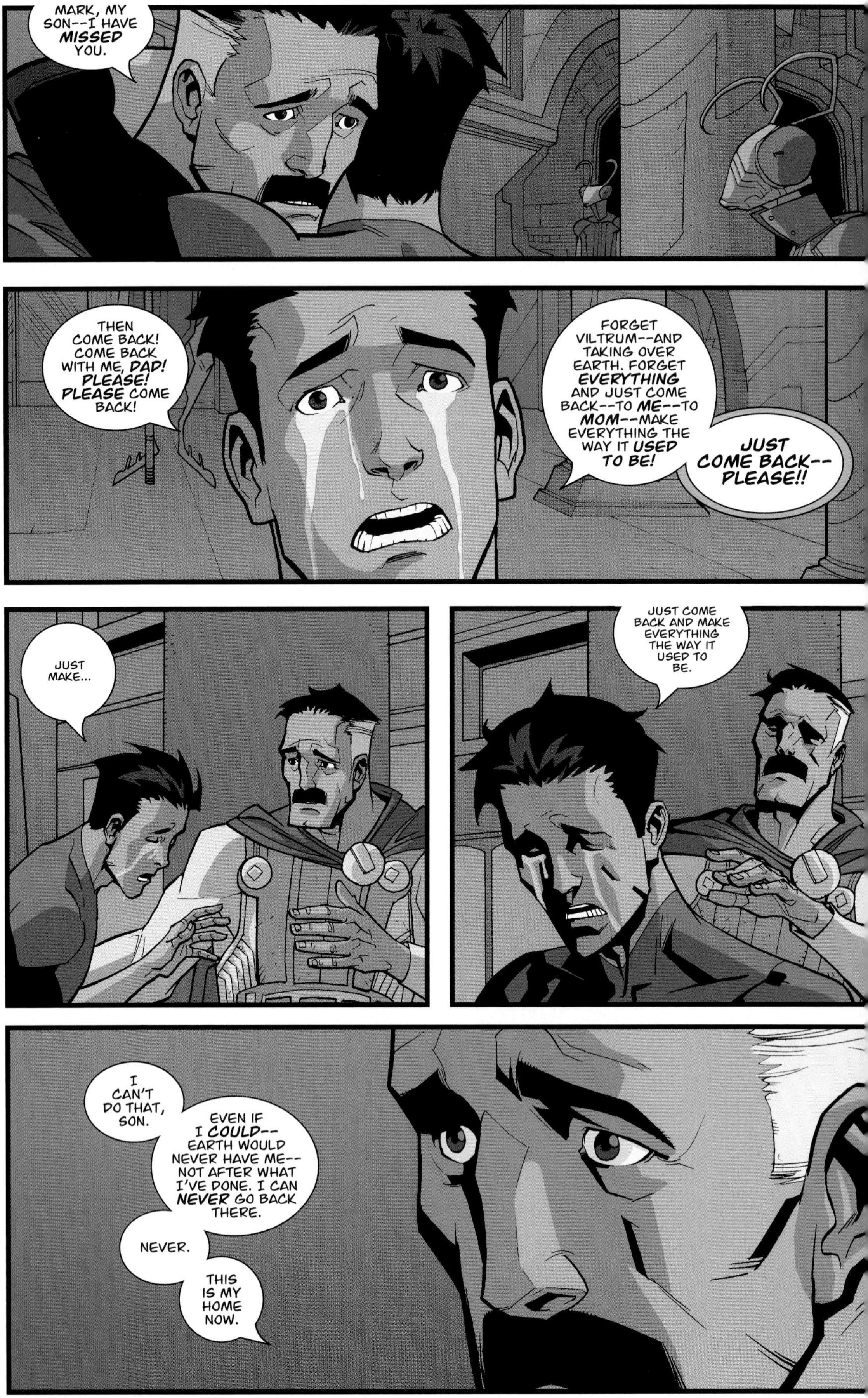
MARK, MY SON--I HAVE MISSED YOU.
THEN COME BACK! COME BACK WITH ME, DAD! PLEASE! PLEASE COME BACK!
FORGET VILTRUM--AND TAKING OVER EARTH. FORGET EVERYTHING AND JUST COME BACK--TO ME--TO MOM--MAKE EVERYTHING THE WAY IT USED TO BE!
JUST COME BACK-- PLEASE!!
JUST MAKE...
JUST COME BACK AND MAKE EVERYTHING THE WAY IT USED TO BE.
I CAN'T DO THAT, SON.
EVEN IF I COULD--EARTH WOULD NEVER HAVE ME--NOT AFTER WHAT I'VE DONE. I CAN NEVER GO BACK THERE.
NEVER.
THIS IS MY HOME NOW.

OKAY--I THINK THAT'S EVERYTHING. I CAN DO A LITTLE STUDYING AT RED LIGHTS ON THE WAY--AND I'LL HAVE TWENTY MINUTES ONCE I GET THERE TO LOOK OVER THINGS ONE LAST TIME BEFORE THE EXAM STARTS.

YOU'RE GOING TO PASS, DEBBIE. DON'T WORRY--YOU'RE GOING TO PASS.

GREETINGS FROM THE US GOVERNMENT.

MISTER STEDMAN! HOW MANY TIMES HAVE I TOLD YOU NOT TO TELEPORT DIRECTLY INTO THE HOUSE?

YOU'RE GOING TO GIVE SOMEONE A HEART ATTACK.

MISS GRAYSON. HOW MANY TIMES HAVE I TOLD YOU TO CALL ME CECIL? BESIDES, IF I START TELEPORTING INTO THE FRONT LAWN, HOW LONG DO YOU THINK YOUR SON'S SECRET IDENTITY WILL LAST?

I WOULD STILL PREFER YOU USED THE BACK YARD OR GARAGE OR SOME-THING.

WHAT IS IT YOU'RE HERE FOR? MARK IS STILL IN SPACE, ISN'T HE?

SO YOU DID GET MY MESSAGE. I'VE BEEN VERY BUSY THIS PAST WEEK AND I JUST WANTED TO APOLOGIZE FOR NOT CONTACTING YOU IN PERSON BEFORE.

AND TO APOLOGIZE FOR ALLOWING MARK TO VENTURE OUT INTO THE UNKNOWN LIKE HE HAS. I TRIED TO STOP HIM, I ASSURE YOU.

THE MAN WHO DELIVERED THE MESSAGE, DONALD--I THINK, WAS VERY KIND.

AND AS FAR AS MARK GOING OUT INTO SPACE, HE THINKS IT'S THE RIGHT THING AND SO HE'S DOING THE RIGHT THING. I'M PROUD OF HIM. WORRIED, BUT PROUD.

NOW IF YOU'LL EXCUSE ME.

WHERE ARE YOU OFF TO IN SUCH A HURRY?

I'VE GOT THE FINAL EXAM FOR MY REAL ESTATE CLASS TODAY. I THOUGHT YOU GOVERNMENT TYPES KNEW EVERYTHING.

REAL ESTATE-- AREN'T WE PAYING YOU ENOUGH?

THAT'S NOT IT AT ALL. I JUST NEED SOME-THING TO DO WITH MY TIME. SOMETHING TO KEEP ME BUSY.

WHY, MISS GRAYSON-- IF YOU WANTED TO DO SOMETHING TO EARN THAT MONEY--ALL YOU HAD TO DO WAS SAY SO.

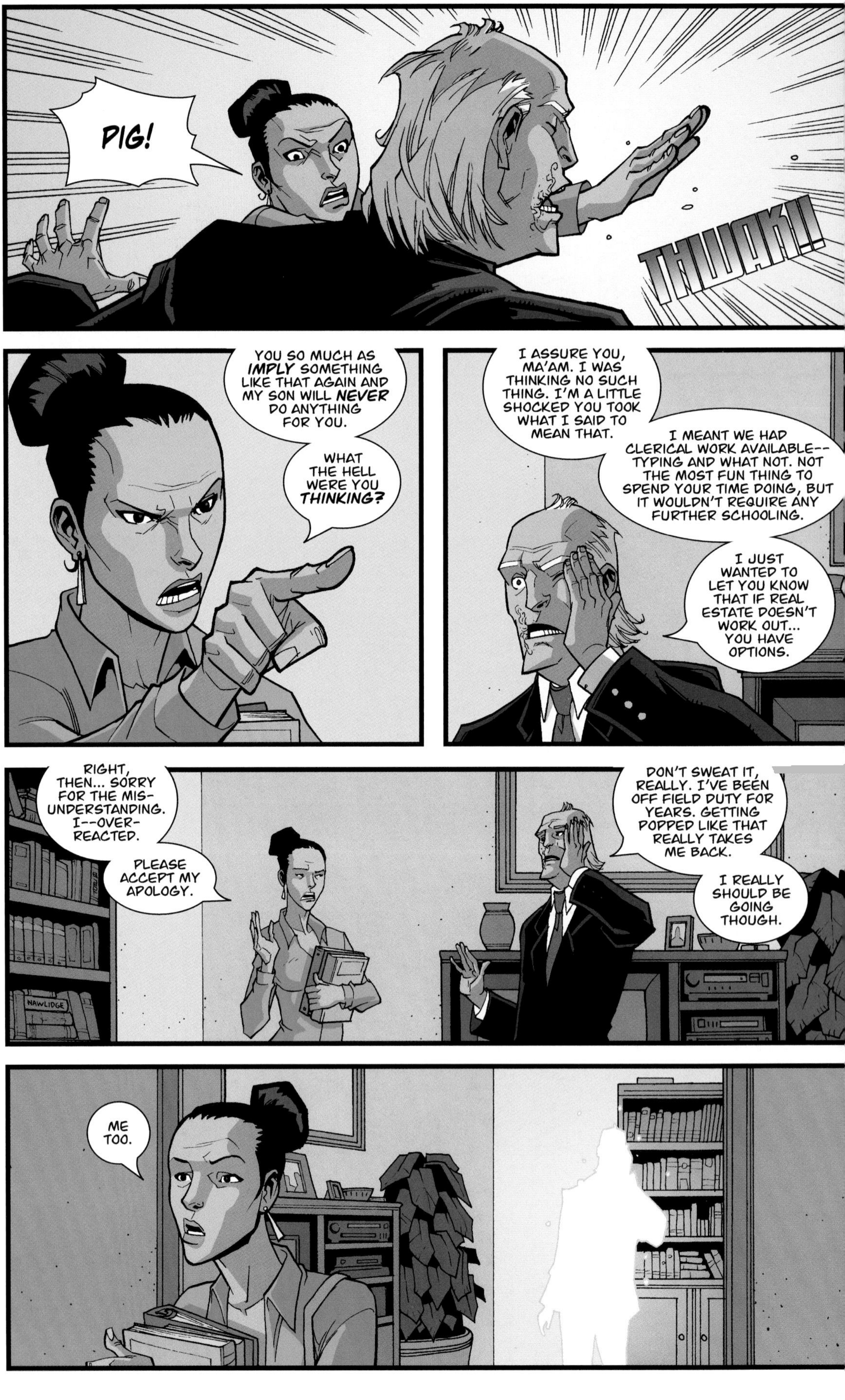
PIG!
THWAK!!
YOU SO MUCH AS IMPLY SOMETHING LIKE THAT AGAIN AND MY SON WILL NEVER DO ANYTHING FOR YOU.
WHAT THE HELL WERE YOU THINKING?
I ASSURE YOU, MA'AM. I WAS THINKING NO SUCH THING. I'M A LITTLE SHOCKED YOU TOOK WHAT I SAID TO MEAN THAT.
I MEANT WE HAD CLERICAL WORK AVAILABLE-- TYPING AND WHAT NOT. NOT THE MOST FUN THING TO SPEND YOUR TIME DOING, BUT IT WOULDN'T REQUIRE ANY FURTHER SCHOOLING.
I JUST WANTED TO LET YOU KNOW THAT IF REAL ESTATE DOESN'T WORK OUT... YOU HAVE OPTIONS.
RIGHT, THEN... SORRY FOR THE MIS-UNDERSTANDING. I--OVER-REACTED.
PLEASE ACCEPT MY APOLOGY.
DON'T SWEAT IT, REALLY. I'VE BEEN OFF FIELD DUTY FOR YEARS. GETTING POPPED LIKE THAT REALLY TAKES ME BACK.
I REALLY SHOULD BE GOING THOUGH.
NAWLIDGE
ME TOO.

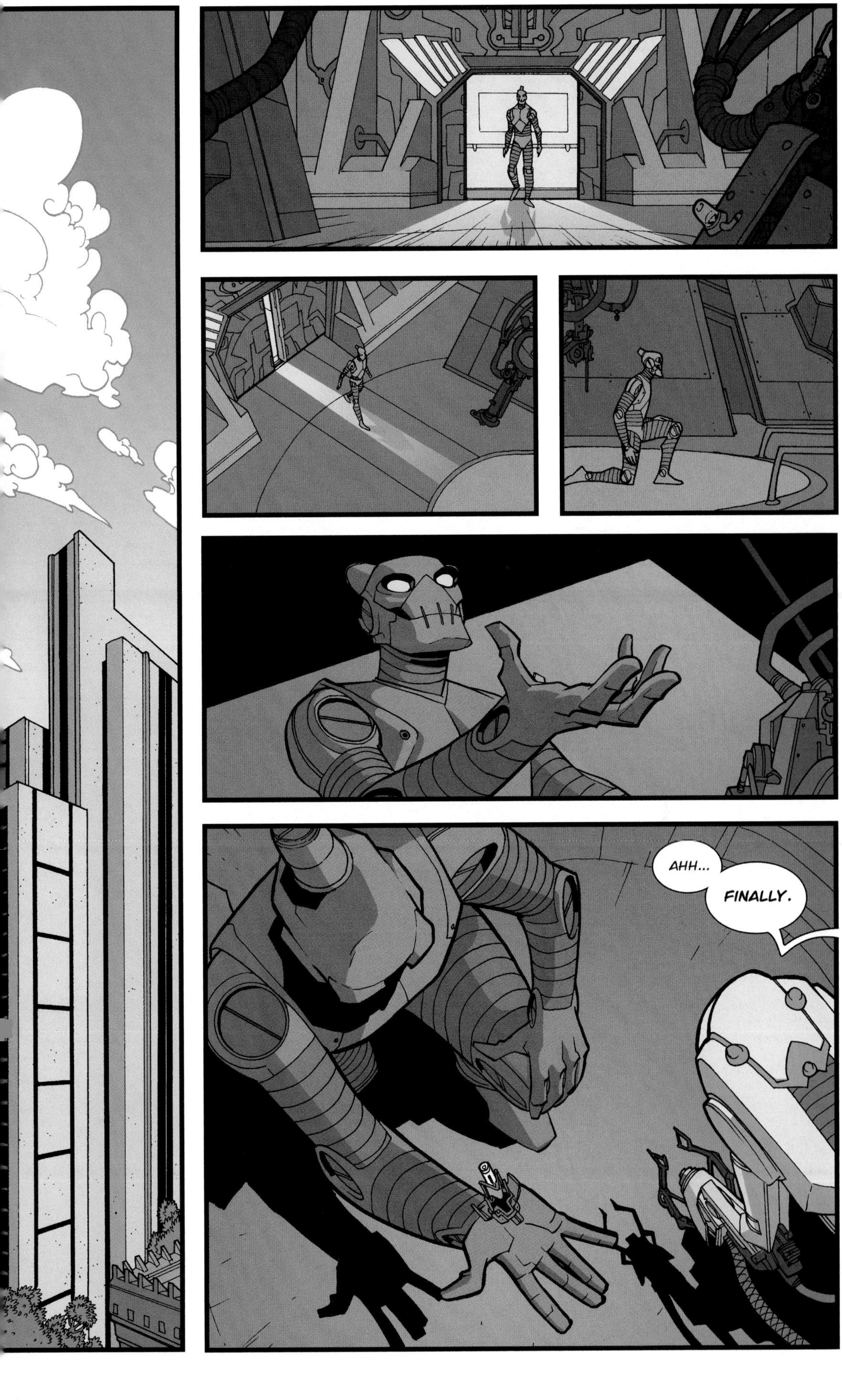

AHH...
FINALLY.

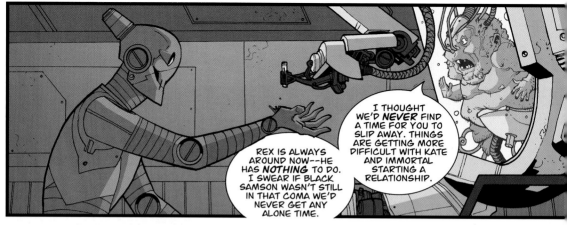

REX IS ALWAYS AROUND NOW--HE HAS **NOTHING** TO DO. I SWEAR IF BLACK SAMSON WASN'T STILL IN THAT COMA WE'D NEVER GET ANY ALONE TIME.

I THOUGHT WE'D **NEVER** FIND A TIME FOR YOU TO SLIP AWAY. THINGS ARE GETTING MORE DIFFICULT WITH KATE AND IMMORTAL STARTING A RELATIONSHIP.

DO YOU REALIZE WHAT I HOLD IN MY HANDS? DO YOU REALIZE THE POWER I NOW HAVE?

OF **COURSE** YOU DON'T.

THIS DNA SAMPLE FROM REX SPLODE COULD WELL MAKE YOU OBSOLETE. I WOULD NO LONGER **NEED** YOU.

IF ALL GOES ACCORDING TO PLAN I'LL BE ABLE TO MOVE FREELY AMONG THEM, WITHOUT CAUSING ANY PAUSE. THEY'LL ACCEPT ME AS ONE OF THEIR OWN.

I'LL BE ONE OF THEM.

AND FROM THERE I CAN MOVE ON TO **PHASE TWO!**

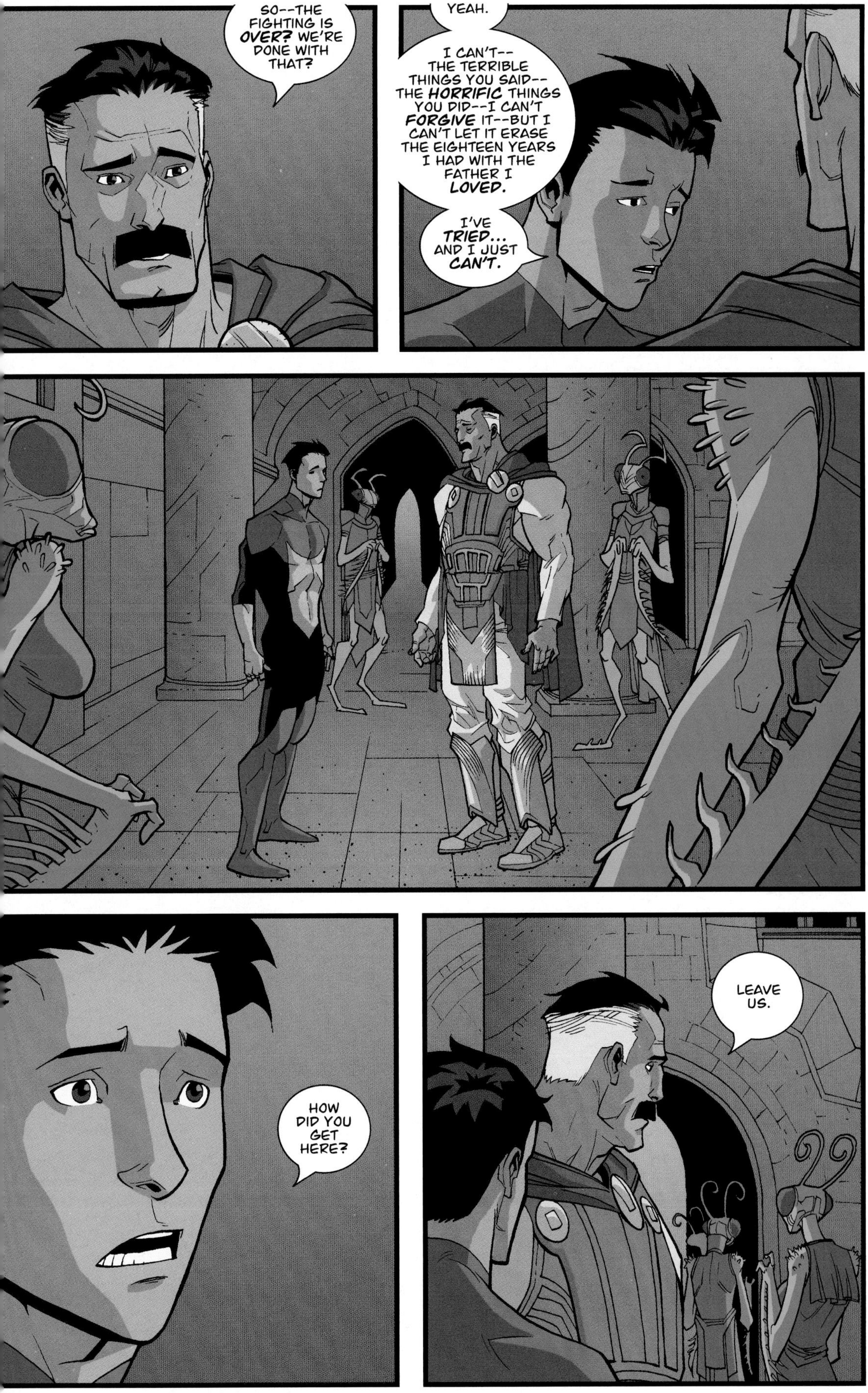
SO--THE FIGHTING IS OVER? WE'RE DONE WITH THAT?
YEAH.
I CAN'T-- THE TERRIBLE THINGS YOU SAID-- THE HORRIFIC THINGS YOU DID--I CAN'T FORGIVE IT--BUT I CAN'T LET IT ERASE THE EIGHTEEN YEARS I HAD WITH THE FATHER I LOVED.
I'VE TRIED... AND I JUST CAN'T.
HOW DID YOU GET HERE?
LEAVE US.

I LIVED AS A VILTRUMITE FOR THOUSANDS OF YEARS BEFORE I CAME TO EARTH--BUT WHAT LITTLE TIME I SPENT THERE-- CHANGED ME.
I WAS READY TO KILL YOU WHEN YOU DEFIED ME. I WOULD HAVE. THOSE ARE THE WAYS OF THE VILTRUMITE.
YOU WERE WEAK. YOU DESERVED TO DIE.
BUT WHEN IT BECAME CLEAR THAT I WOULD HAVE TO KILL YOU--THAT YOU WOULD NOT JOIN ME--WHEN IT BECAME CLEAR THAT I WOULD HAVE NO OTHER OPTION...
...I COULDN'T DO IT.
I HAD TWO CHOICES. I COULD KILL YOU AND ENSLAVE EARTH AS I WAS MEANT TO. OR I COULD LEAVE EARTH--AND LEAVE YOU.
I CHOSE TO LEAVE.

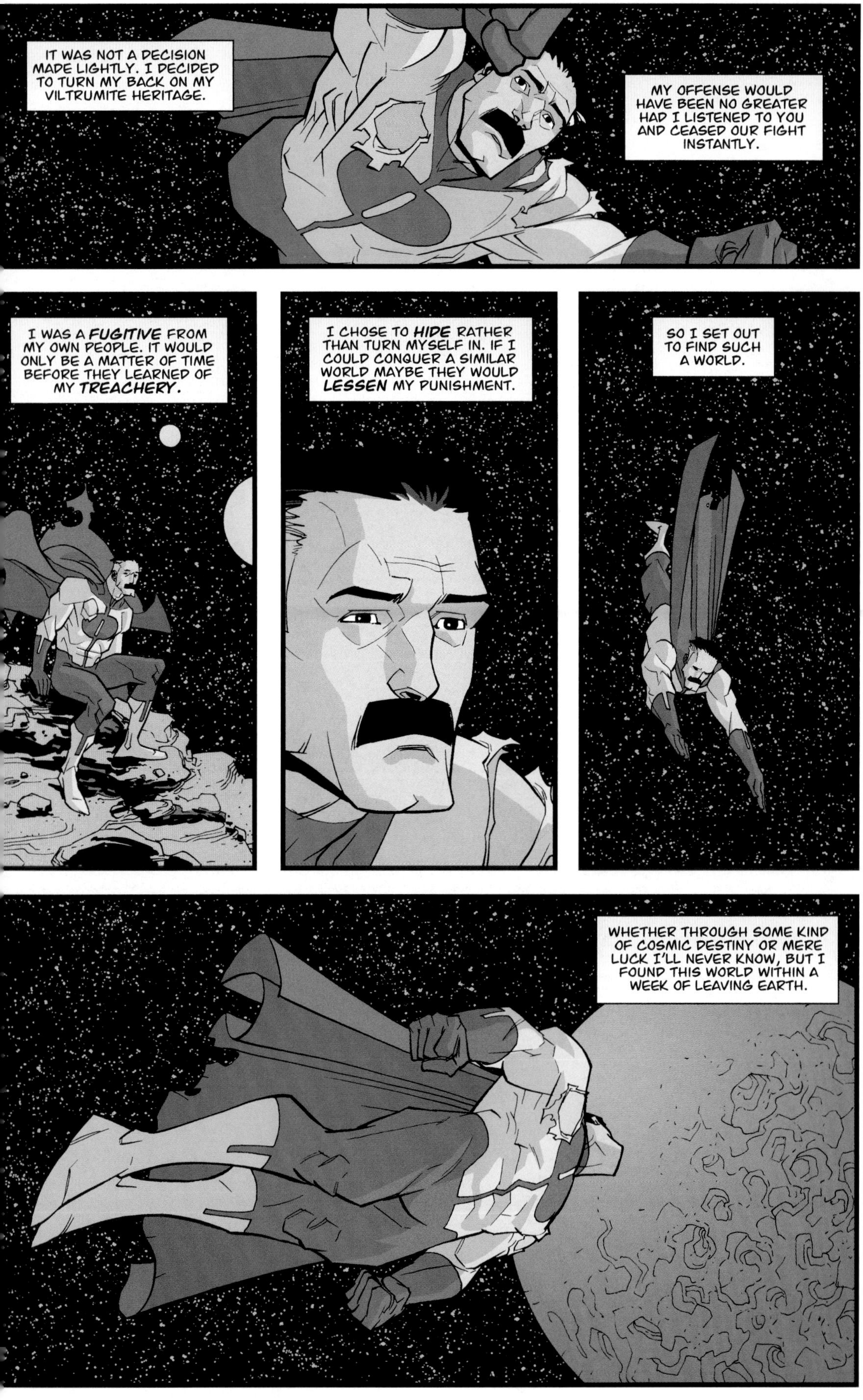
IT WAS NOT A DECISION MADE LIGHTLY. I DECIDED TO TURN MY BACK ON MY VILTRUMITE HERITAGE.
MY OFFENSE WOULD HAVE BEEN NO GREATER HAD I LISTENED TO YOU AND CEASED OUR FIGHT INSTANTLY.
I WAS A *FUGITIVE* FROM MY OWN PEOPLE. IT WOULD ONLY BE A MATTER OF TIME BEFORE THEY LEARNED OF MY *TREACHERY.*
I CHOSE TO *HIDE* RATHER THAN TURN MYSELF IN. IF I COULD CONQUER A SIMILAR WORLD MAYBE THEY WOULD *LESSEN* MY PUNISHMENT.
SO I SET OUT TO FIND SUCH A WORLD.
WHETHER THROUGH SOME KIND OF COSMIC DESTINY OR MERE LUCK I'LL NEVER KNOW, BUT I FOUND THIS WORLD WITHIN A WEEK OF LEAVING EARTH.

THEY ARE A PEOPLE **VASTLY** DIFFERENT THAN THOSE OF EARTH. THOUGH THEIR TECHNOLOGY AND ADVANCEMENT AS A SPECIES ARE VERY SIMILAR.

IN SOME WAYS THEY ARE **LESS** ADVANCED, IN OTHER WAYS, THEY ARE **MORE** ADVANCED.

I DECIDED ON THIS WORLD ALMOST **INSTANTLY**.

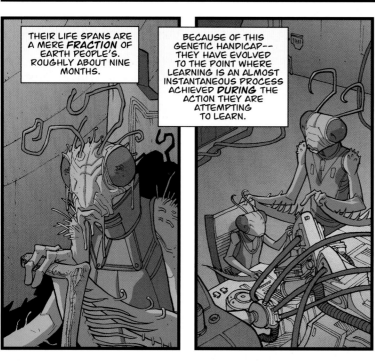

THEIR LIFE SPANS ARE A MERE **FRACTION** OF EARTH PEOPLE'S. ROUGHLY ABOUT NINE MONTHS.

BECAUSE OF THIS GENETIC HANDICAP-- THEY HAVE EVOLVED TO THE POINT WHERE LEARNING IS AN ALMOST INSTANTANEOUS PROCESS ACHIEVED **DURING** THE ACTION THEY ARE ATTEMPTING TO LEARN.

THEIR ELDERS ARE THE RULING CLASS. THE ELDEST KNOWN MEMBER OF THE SPECIES IS CROWNED RULER OF THE ENTIRE PLANET.

THEY CYCLED THROUGH LEADERS AT A VERY RAPID PACE.

NEEDLESS TO SAY IT WAS INCREDIBLY **EASY** TO ASSUME CONTROL OF THIS PLANET. ONCE THEY LEARNED HOW OLD I WAS--I WAS ELECTED RULER ALMOST IMMEDIATELY.

THINGS MOVE VERY **FAST** HERE.

THEY JUST HANDED THE WHOLE PLANET OVER TO YOU? NO QUESTIONS ASKED?

YES, SON-- THEY *DID*.

THINGS ARE VERY DIFFERENT HERE, MARK. THEIR LIFE SPAN ACCOUNTS FOR A GREAT MANY DIFFERENCES.

AFTER NINE MONTHS HERE, NO ONE WILL BE ALIVE TO REMEMBER HOW THEIR PLANET WAS BEFORE MY RULE. THINK ABOUT THAT.

YOU OUT LIVE AN ENTIRE GENERATION IN *HALF A YEAR*.

UPPOSE YOU'RE GHT. I CAN SEE W THAT WOULD KE A TAKEOVER EASIER TO ACCEPT.

COME. THERE IS STILL *MUCH* TO DISCUSS.

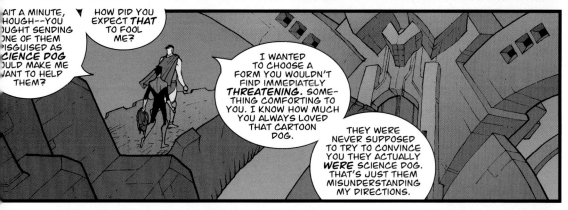

AIT A MINUTE, HOUGH--YOU OUGHT SENDING NE OF THEM ISGUISED AS CIENCE DOG OULD MAKE ME ANT TO HELP THEM?

HOW DID YOU EXPECT *THAT* TO FOOL ME?

I WANTED TO CHOOSE A FORM YOU WOULDN'T FIND IMMEDIATELY *THREATENING*. SOME- THING COMFORTING TO YOU. I KNOW HOW MUCH YOU ALWAYS LOVED THAT CARTOON DOG.

THEY WERE NEVER SUPPOSED TO TRY TO CONVINCE YOU THEY ACTUALLY *WERE* SCIENCE DOG. THAT'S JUST THEM MISUNDERSTANDING MY DIRECTIONS.

I SEE.

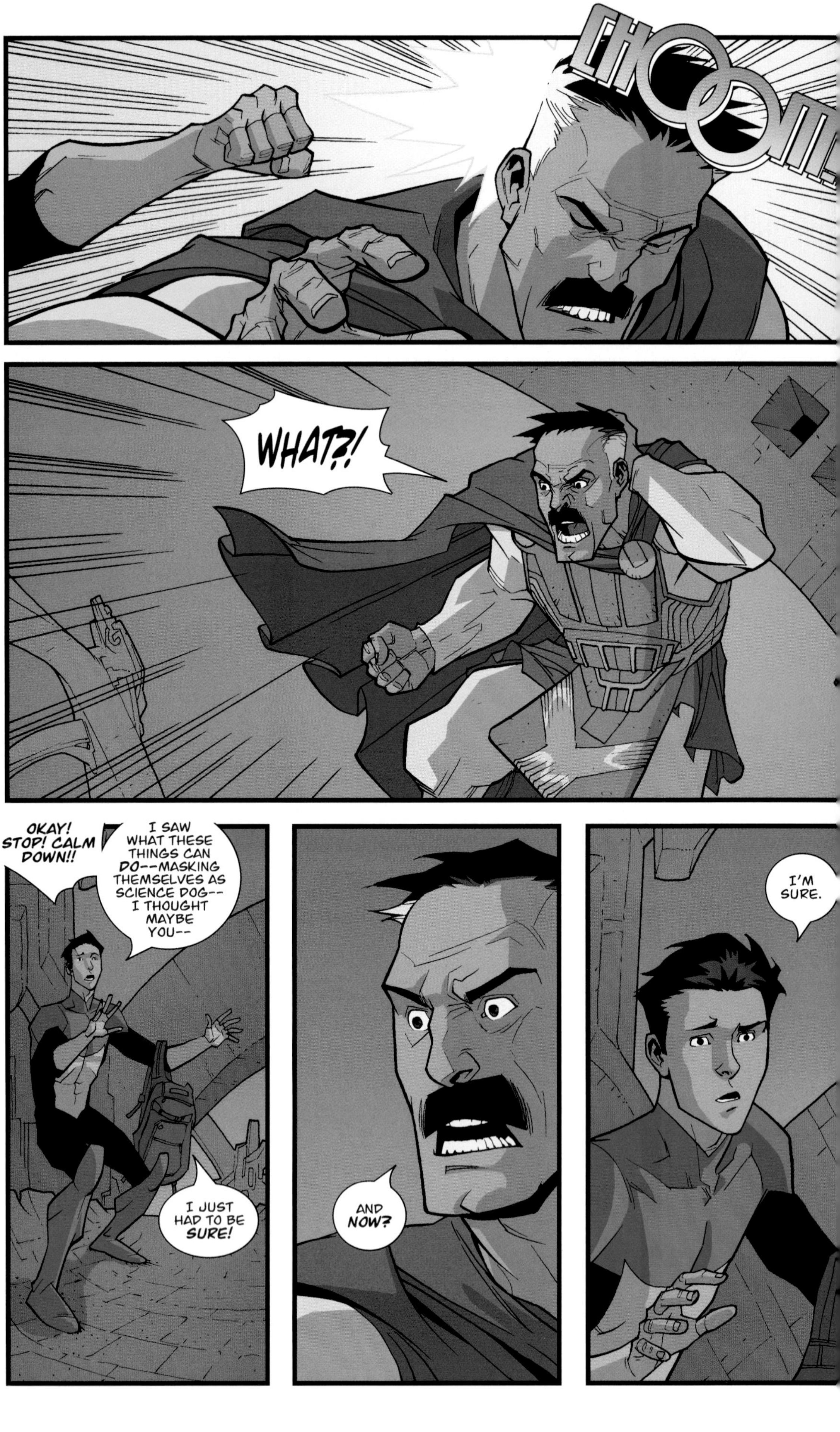
CHOOM
WHAT?!
OKAY! STOP! CALM DOWN!!
I SAW WHAT THESE THINGS CAN DO--MASKING THEMSELVES AS SCIENCE DOG--I THOUGHT MAYBE YOU--
I JUST HAD TO BE SURE!
AND NOW?
I'M SURE.

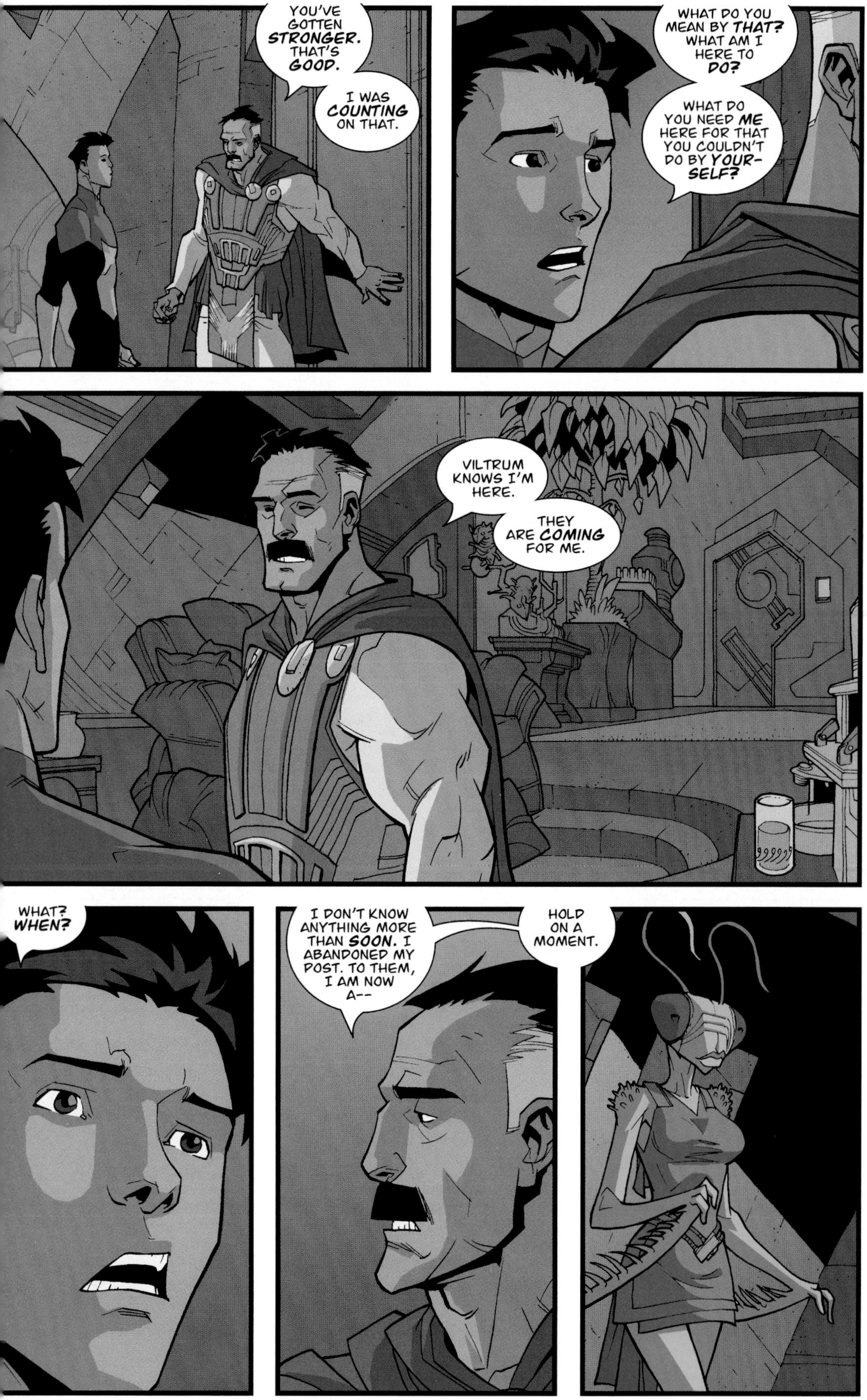
YOU'VE GOTTEN STRONGER. THAT'S GOOD.
I WAS COUNTING ON THAT.
WHAT DO YOU MEAN BY THAT? WHAT AM I HERE TO DO?
WHAT DO YOU NEED ME HERE FOR THAT YOU COULDN'T DO BY YOURSELF?
VILTRUM KNOWS I'M HERE.
THEY ARE COMING FOR ME.
WHAT? WHEN?
I DON'T KNOW ANYTHING MORE THAN SOON. I ABANDONED MY POST. TO THEM, I AM NOW A--
HOLD ON A MOMENT.

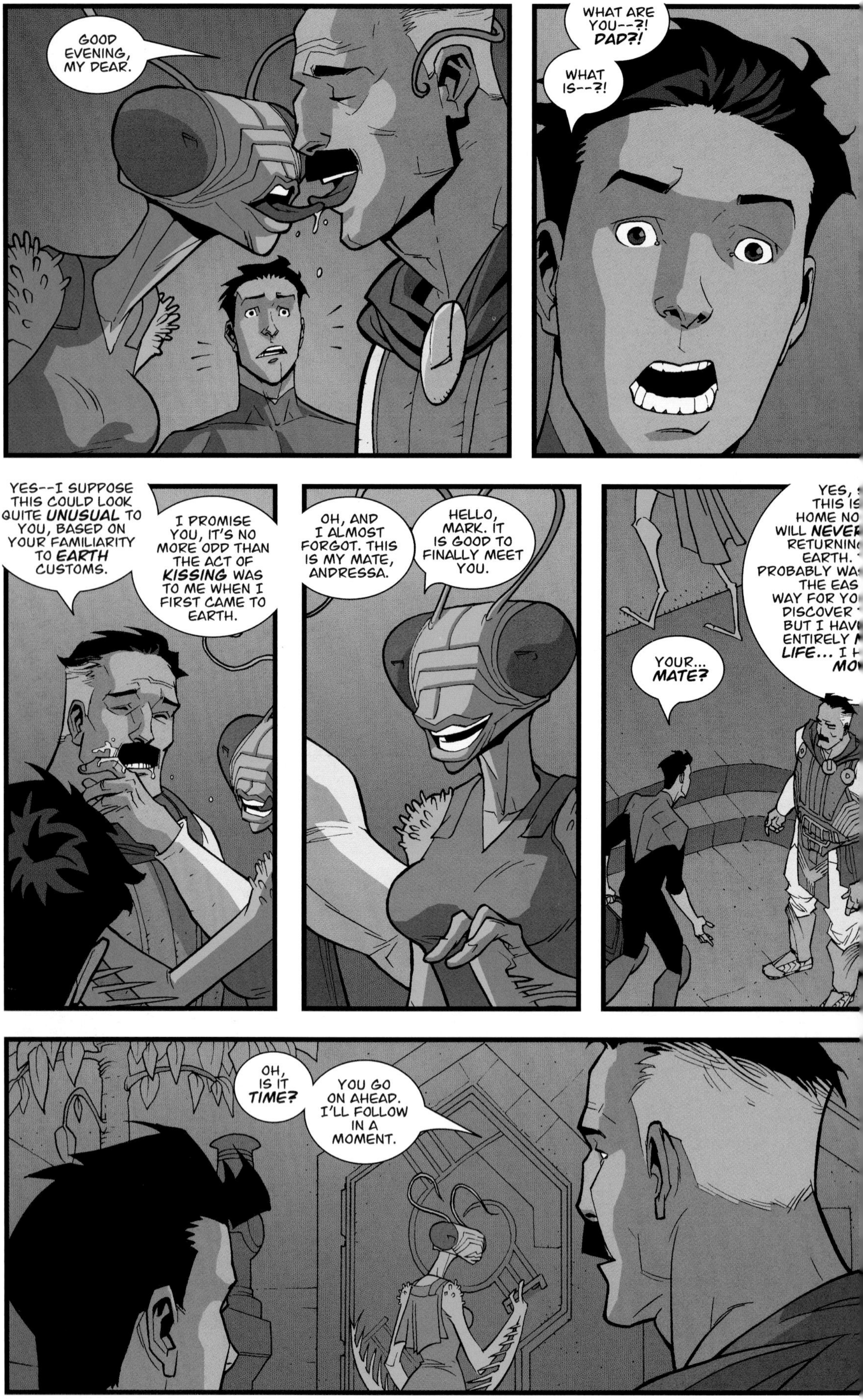
GOOD EVENING, MY DEAR.
WHAT ARE YOU--?! DAD?!
WHAT IS--?!
YES--I SUPPOSE THIS COULD LOOK QUITE UNUSUAL TO YOU, BASED ON YOUR FAMILIARITY TO EARTH CUSTOMS.
I PROMISE YOU, IT'S NO MORE ODD THAN THE ACT OF KISSING WAS TO ME WHEN I FIRST CAME TO EARTH.
OH, AND I ALMOST FORGOT. THIS IS MY MATE, ANDRESSA.
HELLO, MARK. IT IS GOOD TO FINALLY MEET YOU.
YOUR... MATE?
YES, THIS IS HOME NO WILL NEVER RETURNING EARTH. PROBABLY WAS THE EAS WAY FOR YO DISCOVER BUT I HAV ENTIRELY LIFE... I H MO
OH, IS IT TIME?
YOU GO ON AHEAD. I'LL FOLLOW IN A MOMENT.

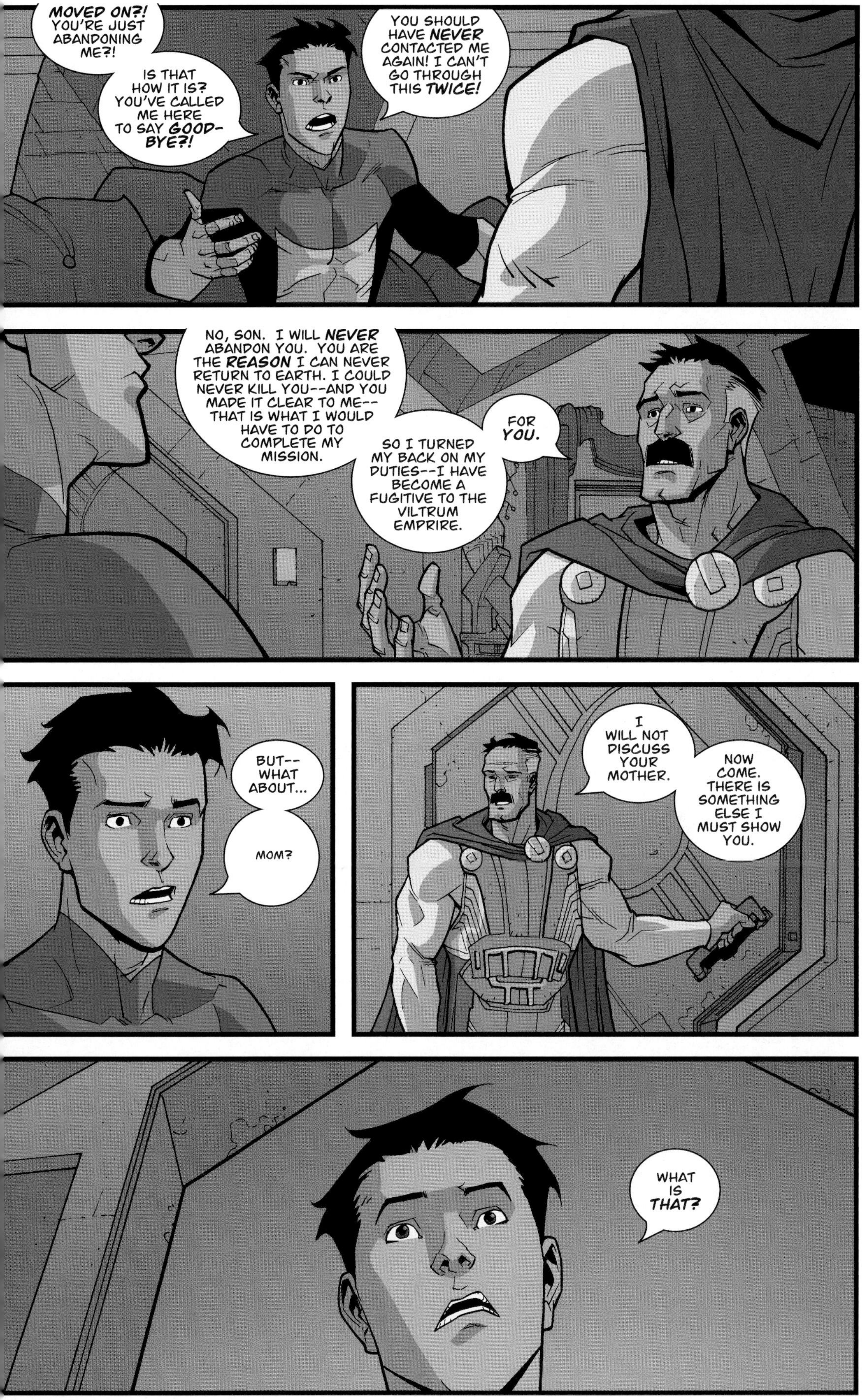
MOVED ON?! YOU'RE JUST ABANDONING ME?!
IS THAT HOW IT IS? YOU'VE CALLED ME HERE TO SAY GOOD-BYE?!
YOU SHOULD HAVE NEVER CONTACTED ME AGAIN! I CAN'T GO THROUGH THIS TWICE!
NO, SON. I WILL NEVER ABANDON YOU. YOU ARE THE REASON I CAN NEVER RETURN TO EARTH. I COULD NEVER KILL YOU--AND YOU MADE IT CLEAR TO ME--THAT IS WHAT I WOULD HAVE TO DO TO COMPLETE MY MISSION.
SO I TURNED MY BACK ON MY DUTIES--I HAVE BECOME A FUGITIVE TO THE VILTRUM EMPRIRE.
FOR YOU.
BUT-- WHAT ABOUT...
MOM?
I WILL NOT DISCUSS YOUR MOTHER.
NOW COME. THERE IS SOMETHING ELSE I MUST SHOW YOU.
WHAT IS THAT?

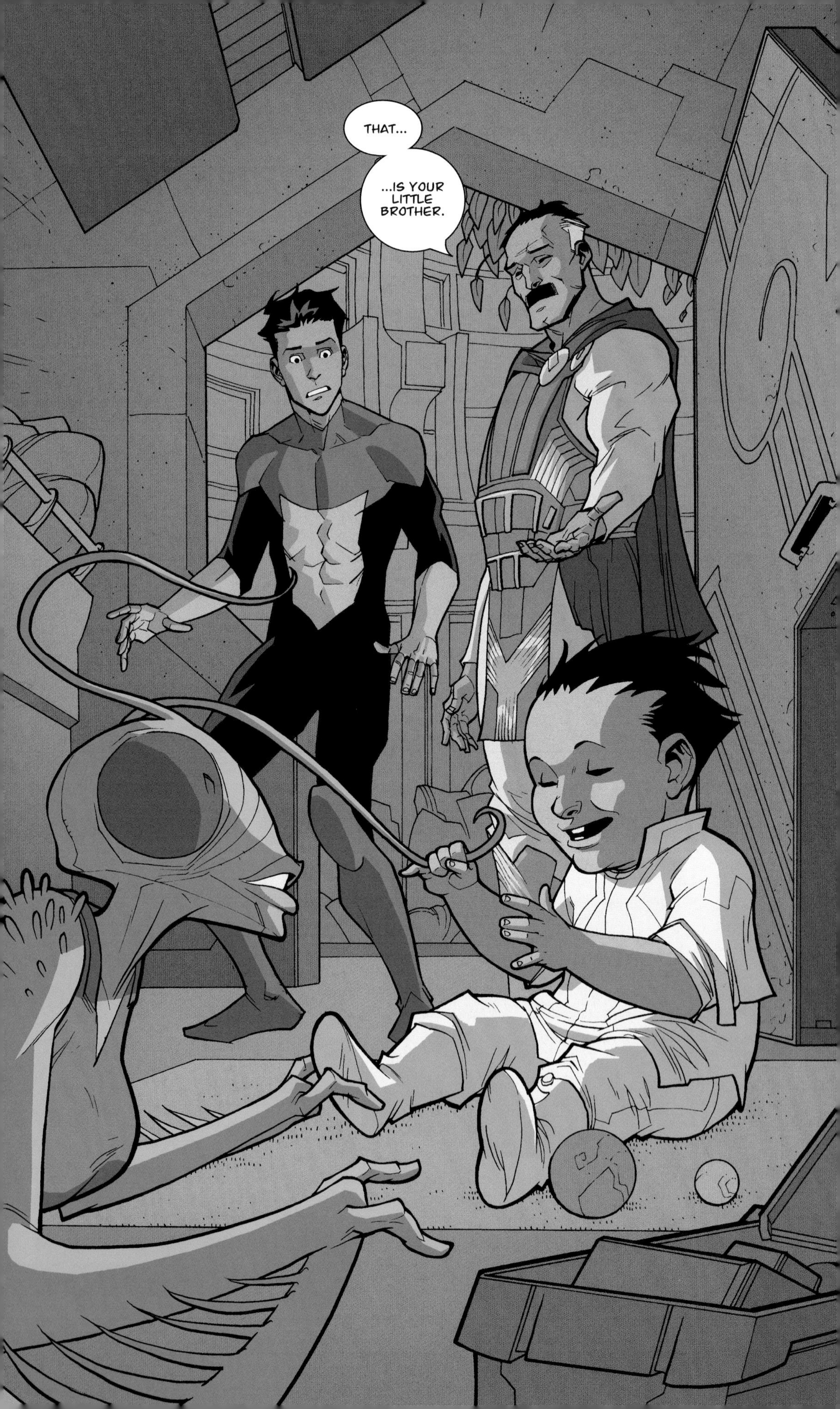
THAT...
...IS YOUR LITTLE BROTHER.

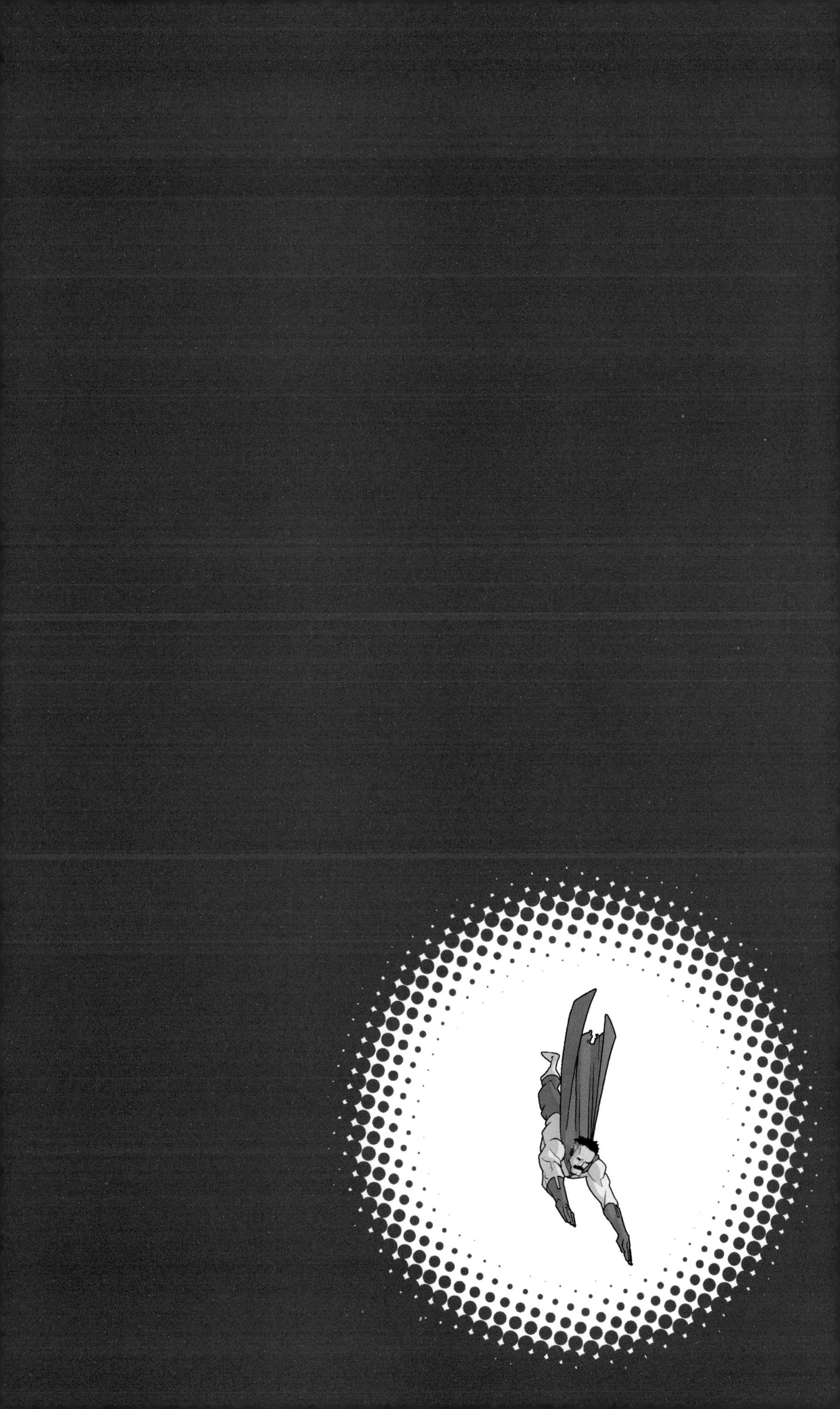

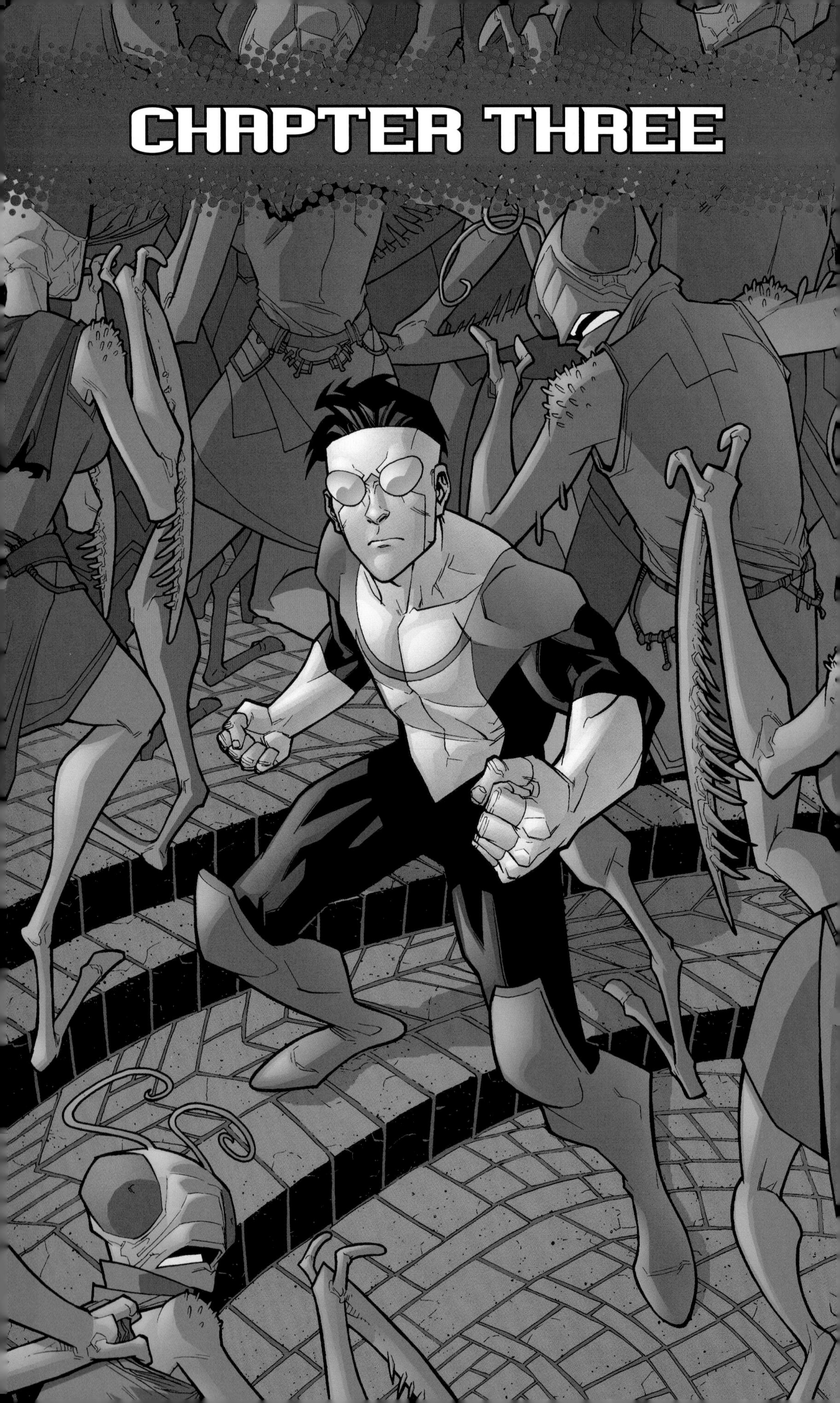
CHAPTER THREE

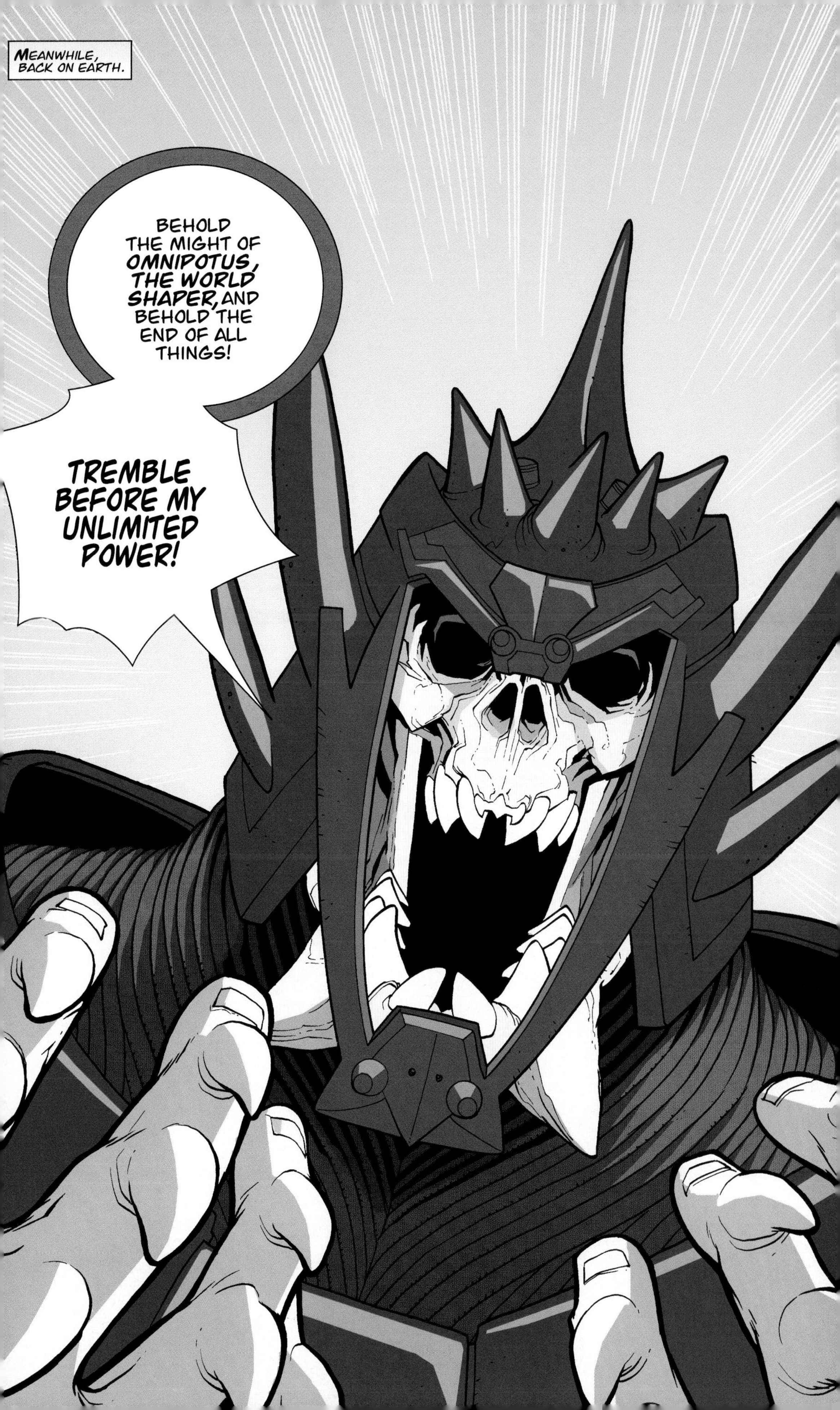
MEANWHILE, BACK ON EARTH.
BEHOLD THE MIGHT OF OMNIPOTUS, THE WORLD SHAPER, AND BEHOLD THE END OF ALL THINGS!
TREMBLE BEFORE MY UNLIMITED POWER!

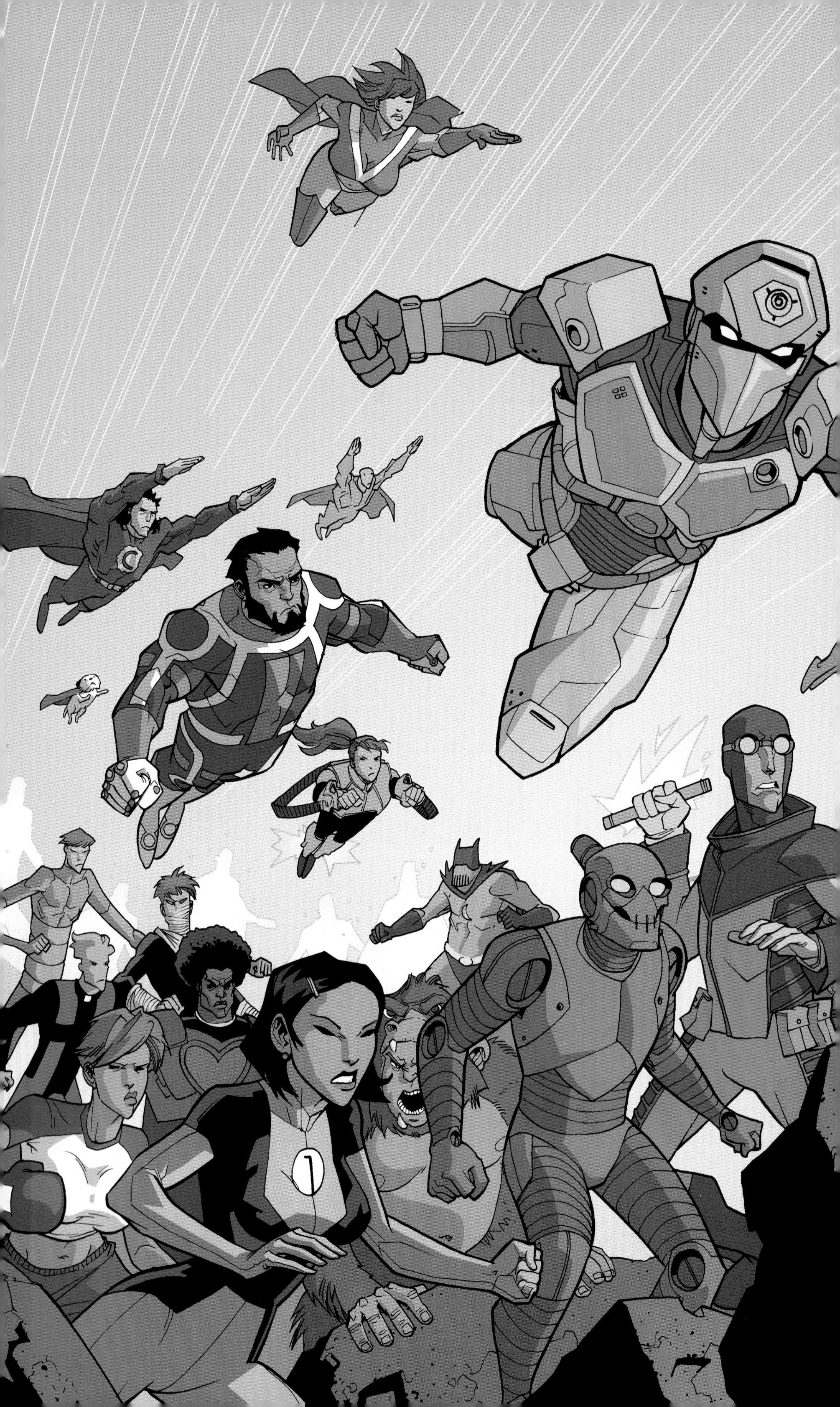

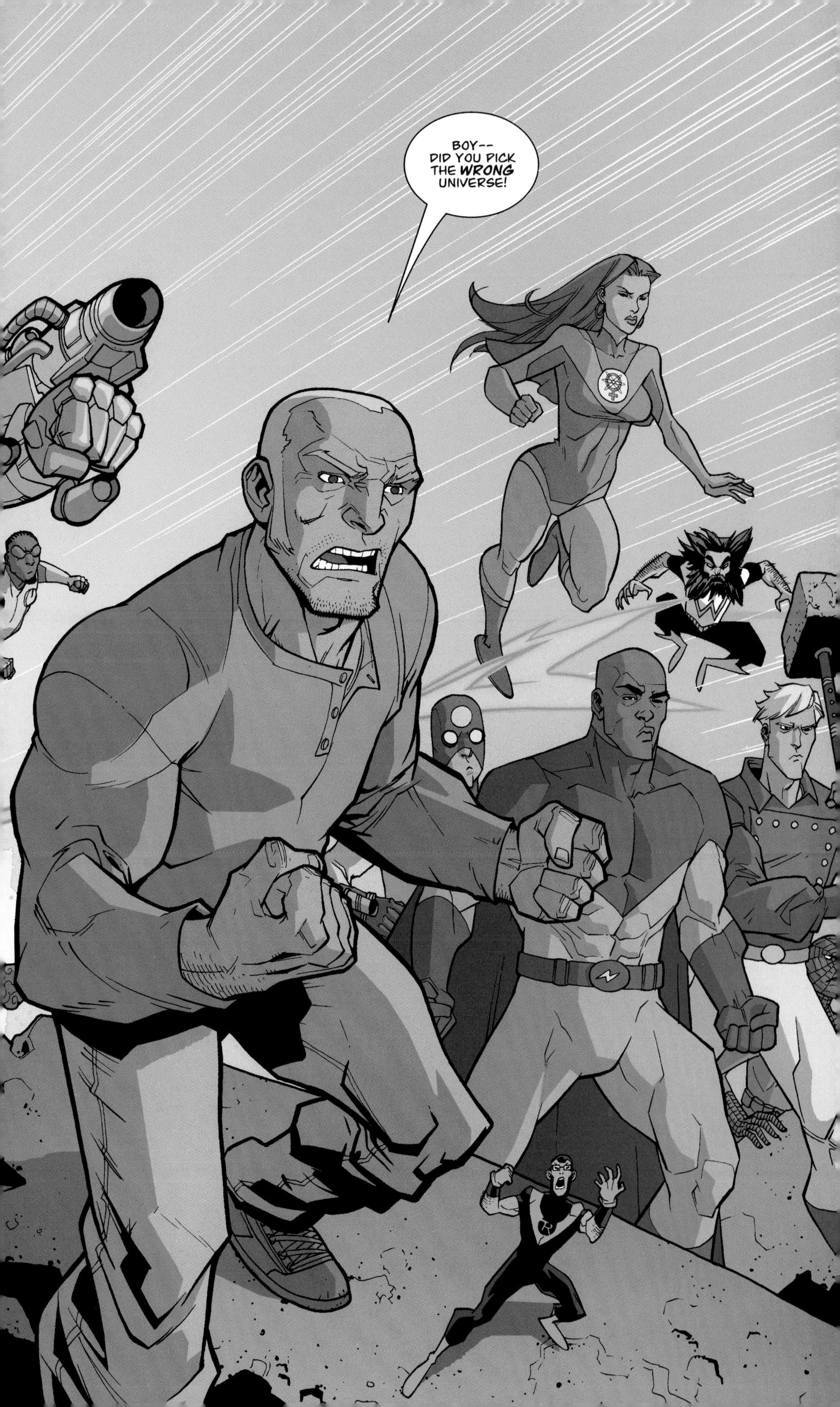
BOY-- DID YOU PICK THE WRONG UNIVERSE!

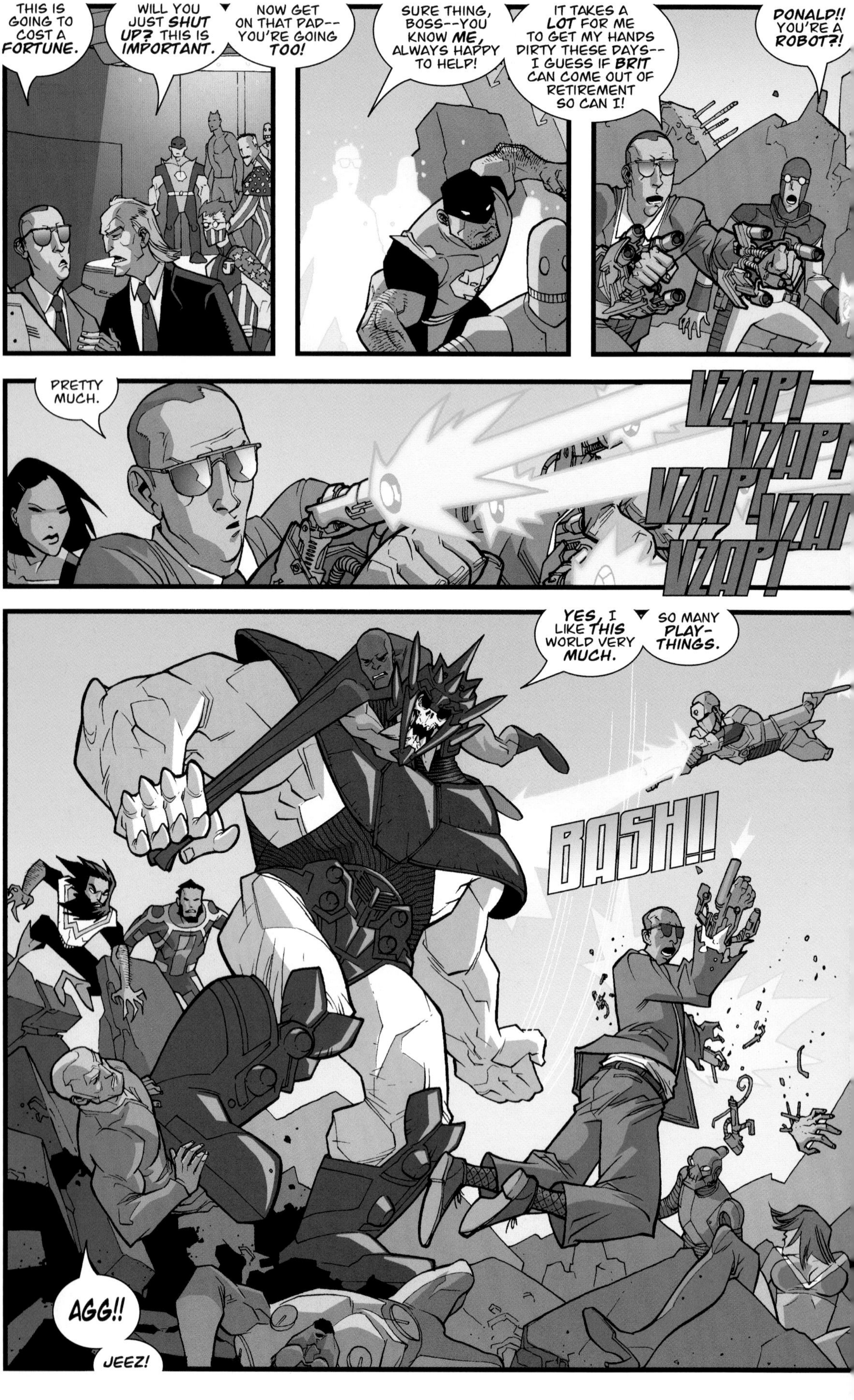
THIS IS GOING TO COST A FORTUNE.
WILL YOU JUST SHUT UP? THIS IS IMPORTANT.
NOW GET ON THAT PAD-- YOU'RE GOING TOO!
SURE THING, BOSS--YOU KNOW ME, ALWAYS HAPPY TO HELP!
IT TAKES A LOT FOR ME TO GET MY HANDS DIRTY THESE DAYS-- I GUESS IF BRIT CAN COME OUT OF RETIREMENT SO CAN I!
DONALD!! YOU'RE A ROBOT?!
PRETTY MUCH.
VZAP! VZAP! VZAP! VZAP! VZAP!
YES, I LIKE THIS WORLD VERY MUCH.
SO MANY PLAY-THINGS.
BASH!!
AGG!!
JEEZ!

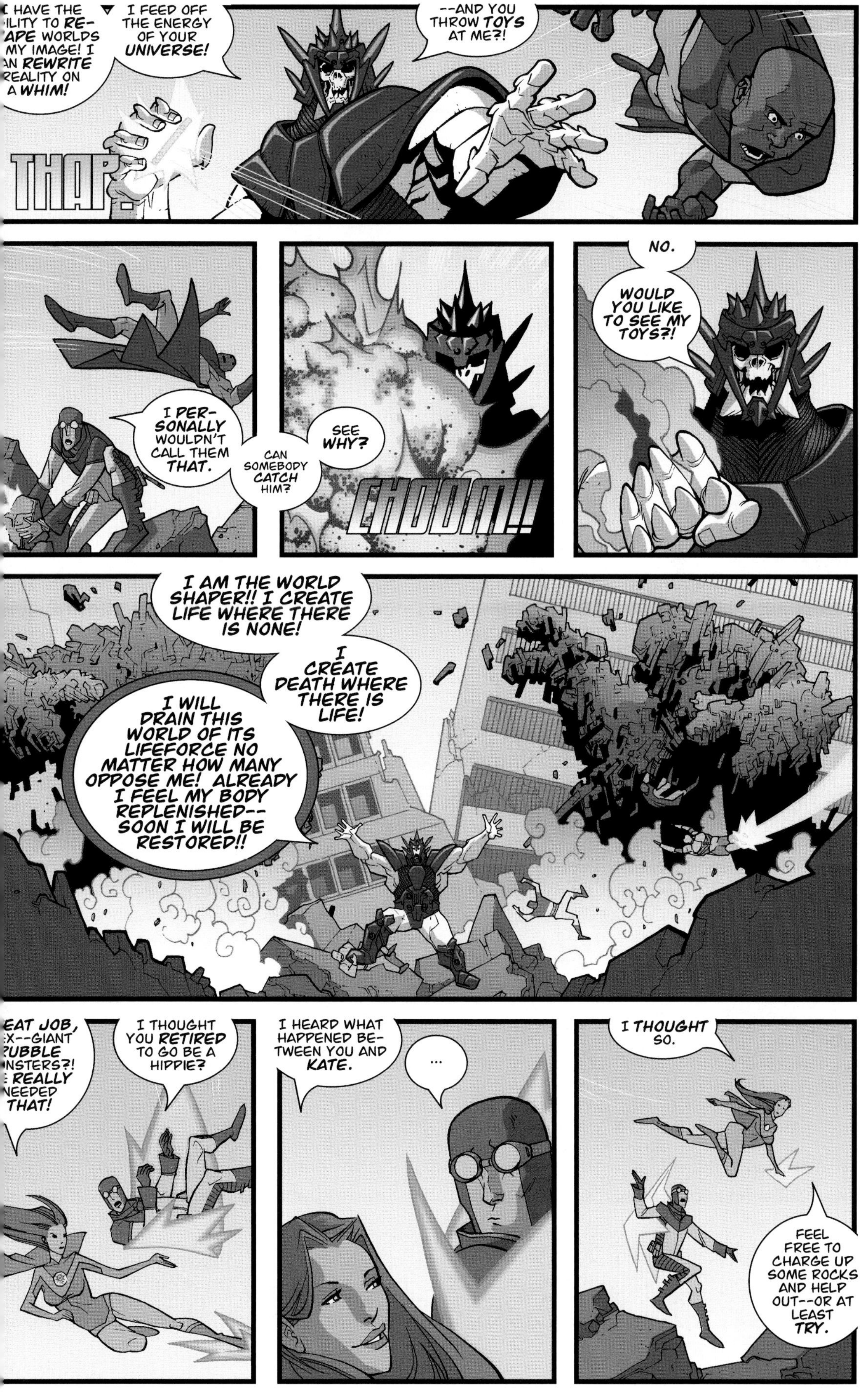

I HAVE THE ABILITY TO RE-SHAPE WORLDS IN MY IMAGE! I CAN REWRITE REALITY ON A WHIM!
I FEED OFF THE ENERGY OF YOUR UNIVERSE!
--AND YOU THROW TOYS AT ME?!
THAP!
I PER-SONALLY WOULDN'T CALL THEM THAT.
CAN SOMEBODY CATCH HIM?
SEE WHY?
CHOOM!!
NO.
WOULD YOU LIKE TO SEE MY TOYS?!
I AM THE WORLD SHAPER!! I CREATE LIFE WHERE THERE IS NONE!
I CREATE DEATH WHERE THERE IS LIFE!
I WILL DRAIN THIS WORLD OF ITS LIFEFORCE NO MATTER HOW MANY OPPOSE ME! ALREADY I FEEL MY BODY REPLENISHED-- SOON I WILL BE RESTORED!!
EAT JOB, EX--GIANT RUBBLE NSTERS?! E REALLY NEEDED THAT!
I THOUGHT YOU RETIRED TO GO BE A HIPPIE?
I HEARD WHAT HAPPENED BE-TWEEN YOU AND KATE.
...
I THOUGHT SO.
FEEL FREE TO CHARGE UP SOME ROCKS AND HELP OUT--OR AT LEAST TRY.

I'M TAKING THESE THINGS OUT!

WHOA!

I'M TURNING ITS LEG INTO FLOWERS. NOW, QUICK-- PUSH HIM OVER!

SURE THING, ROBOT.

ROAARRR!!

WHEW!

MY RESTORATION IS NEARLY COMPLETE-- YOU'D BE WISE TO SURRENDER.

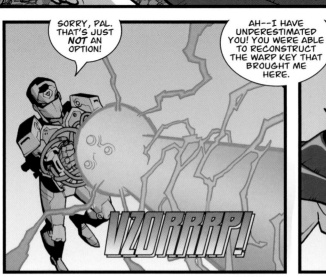

SORRY, PAL. THAT'S JUST NOT AN OPTION!

AH--I HAVE UNDERESTIMATED YOU! YOU WERE ABLE TO RECONSTRUCT THE WARP KEY THAT BROUGHT ME HERE.

YOU HAVE OPENED A PORTAL TO MY UNIVERSE--THE ONE I DRAINED AND DESTROYED!

VZORRRP!

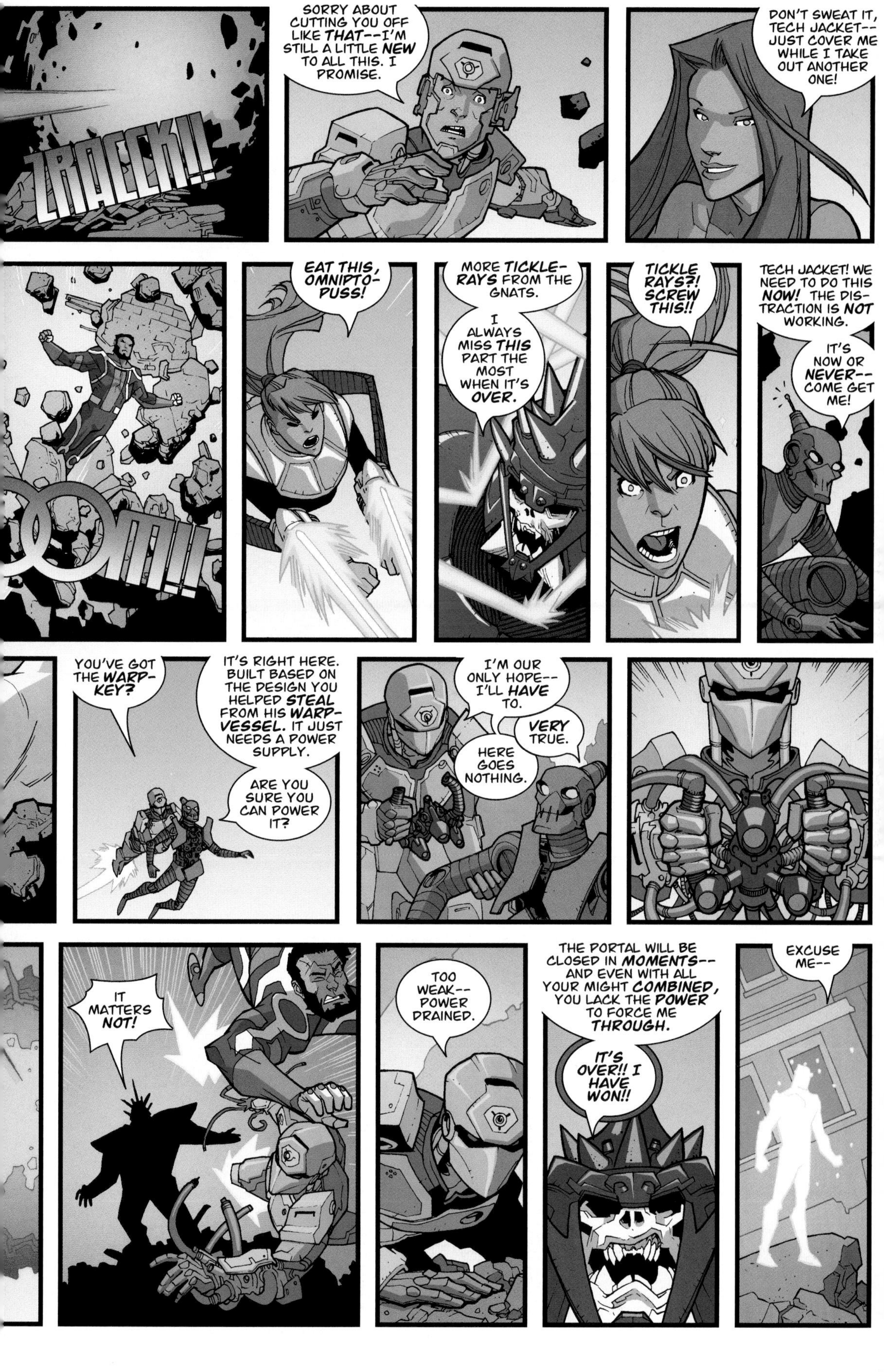
ZRACCK!!
SORRY ABOUT CUTTING YOU OFF LIKE THAT--I'M STILL A LITTLE NEW TO ALL THIS. I PROMISE.
DON'T SWEAT IT, TECH JACKET--JUST COVER ME WHILE I TAKE OUT ANOTHER ONE!
OOM!!!
EAT THIS, OMNIPTO-PUSS!
MORE TICKLE-RAYS FROM THE GNATS.
I ALWAYS MISS THIS PART THE MOST WHEN IT'S OVER.
TICKLE RAYS?! SCREW THIS!!
TECH JACKET! WE NEED TO DO THIS NOW! THE DIS-TRACTION IS NOT WORKING.
IT'S NOW OR NEVER--COME GET ME!
YOU'VE GOT THE WARP-KEY?
IT'S RIGHT HERE. BUILT BASED ON THE DESIGN YOU HELPED STEAL FROM HIS WARP-VESSEL. IT JUST NEEDS A POWER SUPPLY.
ARE YOU SURE YOU CAN POWER IT?
I'M OUR ONLY HOPE--I'LL HAVE TO.
VERY TRUE.
HERE GOES NOTHING.
IT MATTERS NOT!
TOO WEAK--POWER DRAINED.
THE PORTAL WILL BE CLOSED IN MOMENTS--AND EVEN WITH ALL YOUR MIGHT COMBINED, YOU LACK THE POWER TO FORCE ME THROUGH.
IT'S OVER!! I HAVE WON!!
EXCUSE ME--

--I WOKE UP TO COVERAGE OF THIS ORDEAL ON THE *NEWS.* YOU MIND IF I BUTT IN?

IT SEEMS I'VE BEEN OUT OF COMMISSION FOR A WHILE. I'D LIKE TO GET BACK INTO THE SWING OF THINGS.

CECIL TELEPORTED ME RIGHT OVER--I'D HATE TO *WASTE* ALL THAT TECHNOLOGY THAT BROUGHT ME HERE.

BLACK SAMSON--!

HOW CAN THIS BE--HE WAS--!

BUT HE'S BEEN IN A COMA FOR *MONTHS!*

THANK--GOD--

COULD IT REALLY BE--?!

KICK ASS!

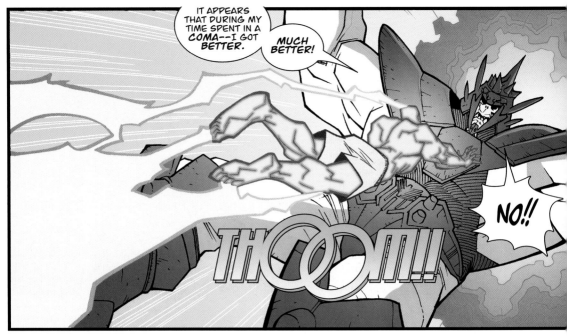

IT APPEARS THAT DURING MY TIME SPENT IN A *COMA*--I GOT *BETTER.*

MUCH BETTER!

THOOM!!

NO!!

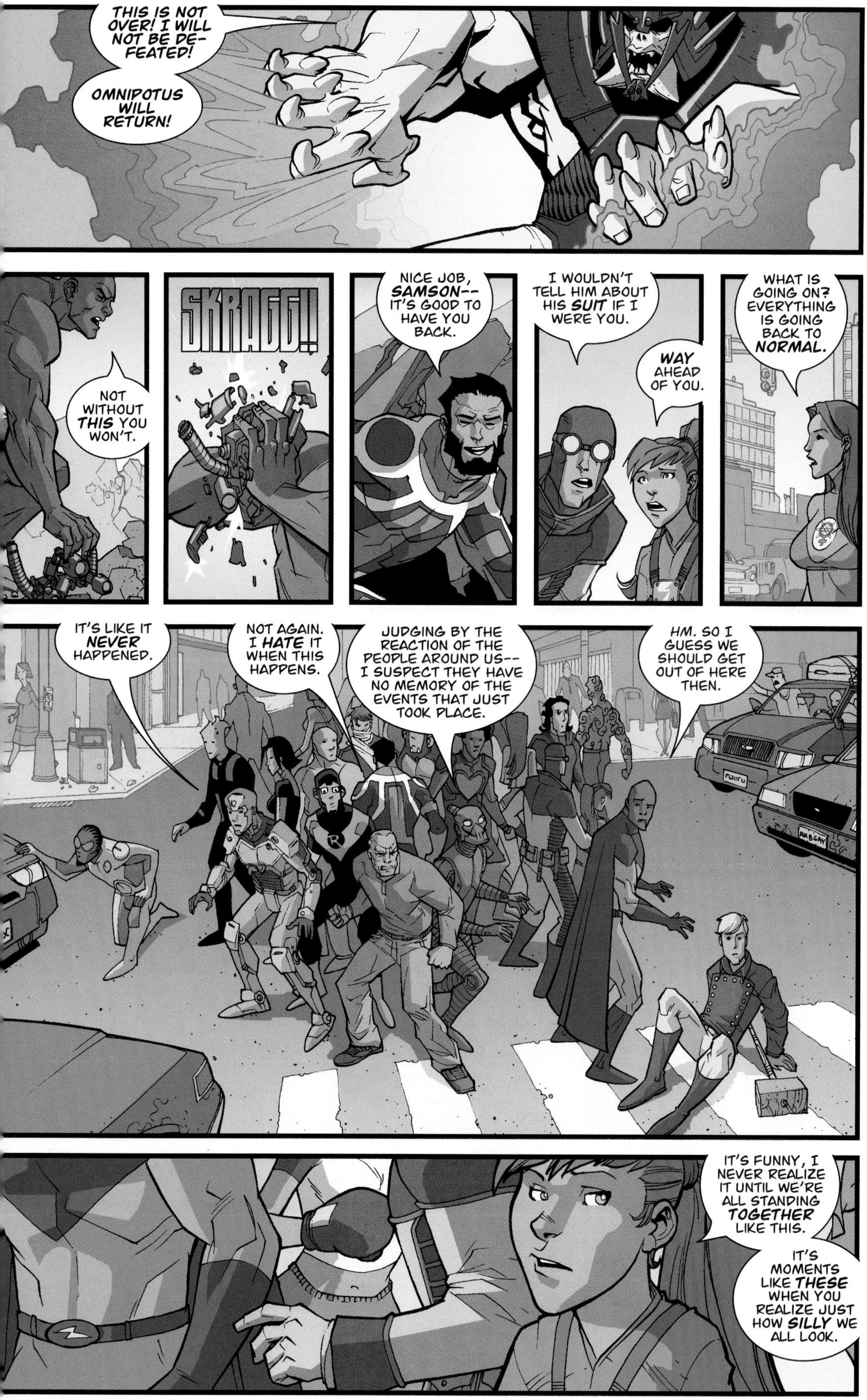
THIS IS NOT OVER! I WILL NOT BE DE-FEATED!
OMNIPOTUS WILL RETURN!
NOT WITHOUT THIS YOU WON'T.
SKRAGG!!
NICE JOB, SAMSON-- IT'S GOOD TO HAVE YOU BACK.
I WOULDN'T TELL HIM ABOUT HIS SUIT IF I WERE YOU.
WAY AHEAD OF YOU.
WHAT IS GOING ON? EVERYTHING IS GOING BACK TO NORMAL.
IT'S LIKE IT NEVER HAPPENED.
NOT AGAIN. I HATE IT WHEN THIS HAPPENS.
JUDGING BY THE REACTION OF THE PEOPLE AROUND US-- I SUSPECT THEY HAVE NO MEMORY OF THE EVENTS THAT JUST TOOK PLACE.
HM. SO I GUESS WE SHOULD GET OUT OF HERE THEN.
IT'S FUNNY, I NEVER REALIZE IT UNTIL WE'RE ALL STANDING TOGETHER LIKE THIS.
IT'S MOMENTS LIKE THESE WHEN YOU REALIZE JUST HOW SILLY WE ALL LOOK.

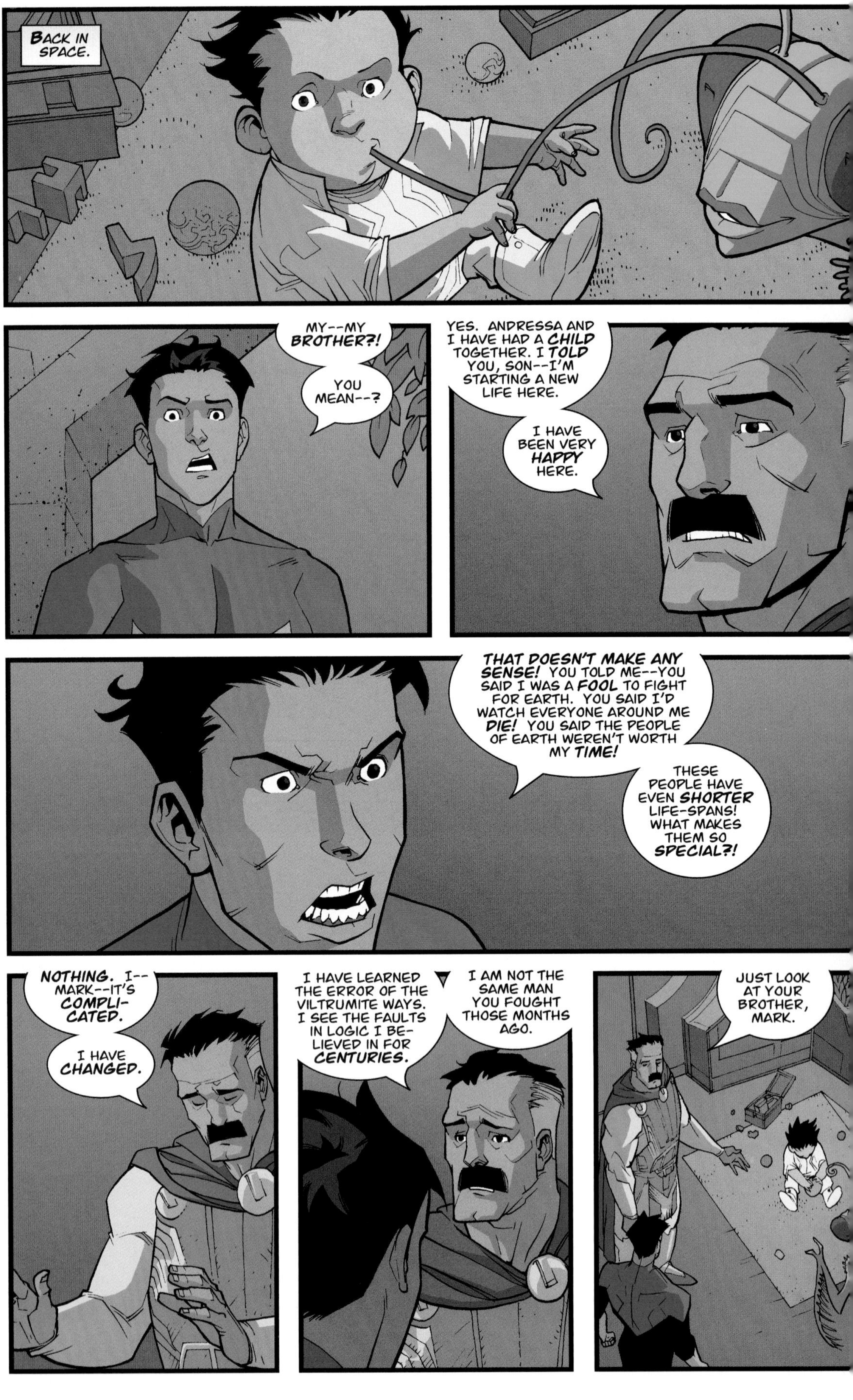
BACK IN SPACE.
MY--MY BROTHER?!
YOU MEAN--?
YES. ANDRESSA AND I HAVE HAD A CHILD TOGETHER. I TOLD YOU, SON--I'M STARTING A NEW LIFE HERE.
I HAVE BEEN VERY HAPPY HERE.
THAT DOESN'T MAKE ANY SENSE! YOU TOLD ME--YOU SAID I WAS A FOOL TO FIGHT FOR EARTH. YOU SAID I'D WATCH EVERYONE AROUND ME DIE! YOU SAID THE PEOPLE OF EARTH WEREN'T WORTH MY TIME!
THESE PEOPLE HAVE EVEN SHORTER LIFE-SPANS! WHAT MAKES THEM SO SPECIAL?!
NOTHING. I--MARK--IT'S COMPLICATED.
I HAVE CHANGED.
I HAVE LEARNED THE ERROR OF THE VILTRUMITE WAYS. I SEE THE FAULTS IN LOGIC I BELIEVED IN FOR CENTURIES.
I AM NOT THE SAME MAN YOU FOUGHT THOSE MONTHS AGO.
JUST LOOK AT YOUR BROTHER, MARK.

WHAT ABOUT HIM?

YOU SEE THE COLOR OF HIS SKIN, HOW IT'S *DIFFERENT* FROM OURS? THAT'S BECAUSE ANDRESSA'S PEOPLE ARE NOT AS COMPATIBLE WITH VILTRUMITE DNA AS HUMANS WERE.

YOU *THINK?!*

I WOULD APPRECIATE YOU GETTING RID OF THE *TONE,* SON. I'M STILL YOUR *FATHER.*

UNDER-STAND?

OKAY, *GOT IT.* PLEASE--GO ON. JUST MAKE THIS ALL MAKE SENSE TO ME, DAD. *PLEASE.*

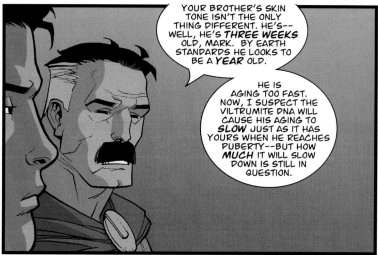

YOUR BROTHER'S SKIN TONE ISN'T THE ONLY THING DIFFERENT. HE'S--WELL, HE'S *THREE WEEKS* OLD, MARK. BY EARTH STANDARDS HE LOOKS TO BE A *YEAR* OLD.

HE IS AGING TOO FAST. NOW, I SUSPECT THE VILTRUMITE DNA WILL CAUSE HIS AGING TO *SLOW* JUST AS IT HAS YOURS WHEN HE REACHES PUBERTY--BUT HOW *MUCH* IT WILL SLOW DOWN IS STILL IN QUESTION.

IS HE GOING TO--? I MEAN, HOW LONG DO YOU THINK HE HAS?

HUNDREDS, IF NOT *THOUSANDS* OF YEARS. HE'LL BE *FINE.* HE'LL STILL LIVE A LONG AND HEALTHY LIFE, ESPECIALLY BY *HUMAN* STANDARDS AND AMONG THESE PEOPLE.

BUT ON VILTRUM... THAT WOULD BE A WHOLE OTHER STORY.

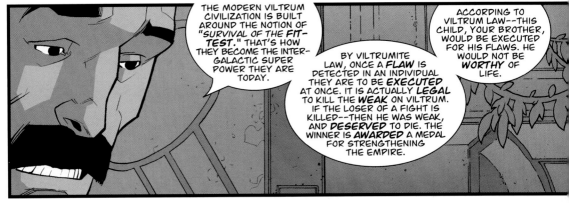

THE MODERN VILTRUM CIVILIZATION IS BUILT AROUND THE NOTION OF "SURVIVAL OF THE **FIT-TEST.**" THAT'S HOW THEY BECOME THE INTER-GALACTIC SUPER POWER THEY ARE TODAY.

BY VILTRUMITE LAW, ONCE A **FLAW** IS DETECTED IN AN INDIVIDUAL THEY ARE TO BE **EXECUTED** AT ONCE. IT IS ACTUALLY **LEGAL** TO KILL THE **WEAK** ON VILTRUM. IF THE LOSER OF A FIGHT IS KILLED--THEN HE WAS WEAK, AND **DESERVED** TO DIE. THE WINNER IS **AWARDED** A MEDAL FOR STRENGTHENING THE EMPIRE.

ACCORDING TO VILTRUM LAW--THIS CHILD, YOUR BROTHER, WOULD BE EXECUTED FOR HIS FLAWS. HE WOULD NOT BE **WORTHY** OF LIFE.

WHAT'S HIS **NAME?** YOU HAVEN'T CALLED HIM BY NAME YET, YOU KEEP SAYING "**SON**" OR "**YOUR BROTHER.**"

THE CUSTOM HERE IS FOR AN INDIVIDUAL TO **CHOOSE** THEIR OWN NAME ONCE THEY REACH ADULT-HOOD.

WHICH WOULD BE **TWO WEEKS** FROM NOW, WERE IT NOT FOR HIS VILTRUMITE BLOOD.

WHAT IS **YOUR** NAME?

I MEAN-- NOLAN IS AN **EARTH** NAME, RIGHT? YOU HAD TO HAVE A DIFFERENT NAME ON VILTRUM.

NO, NOLAN IS AND HAS ALWAYS BEEN MY NAME. THE VILTRUMITES HAVE NO NEED FOR LAST NAMES, SO GRAYSON WAS ADDED WHILE I WAS ON EARTH.

THE PRONUNCIATIO WAS JUST A BIT DIFFERENT, AS I RECALL. CLOSER T "NOWL-AHN" BUT MORE OR LESS THE SAME.

SOMEHOW THAT MAKES ME FEEL **BETTER.** ONE OF THE THINGS THAT GOT TO ME THE **MOST** WAS THAT I MORE THAN LIKELY DIDN'T EVEN KNOW YOUR **NAME** ANYMORE.

I HOPE THIS TALK WE'VE HAD IS SHOWING YOU THAT YOU KNEW ME BETTER THAN EVEN I WOULD LIKE TO HAVE ADMITTED.

I'M SORRY, SON-- FOR **EVERY-THING.**

THAT, THOUGH, DOESN'T HELP AT **ALL.**

AN APOLO JUST IS GOING CUT

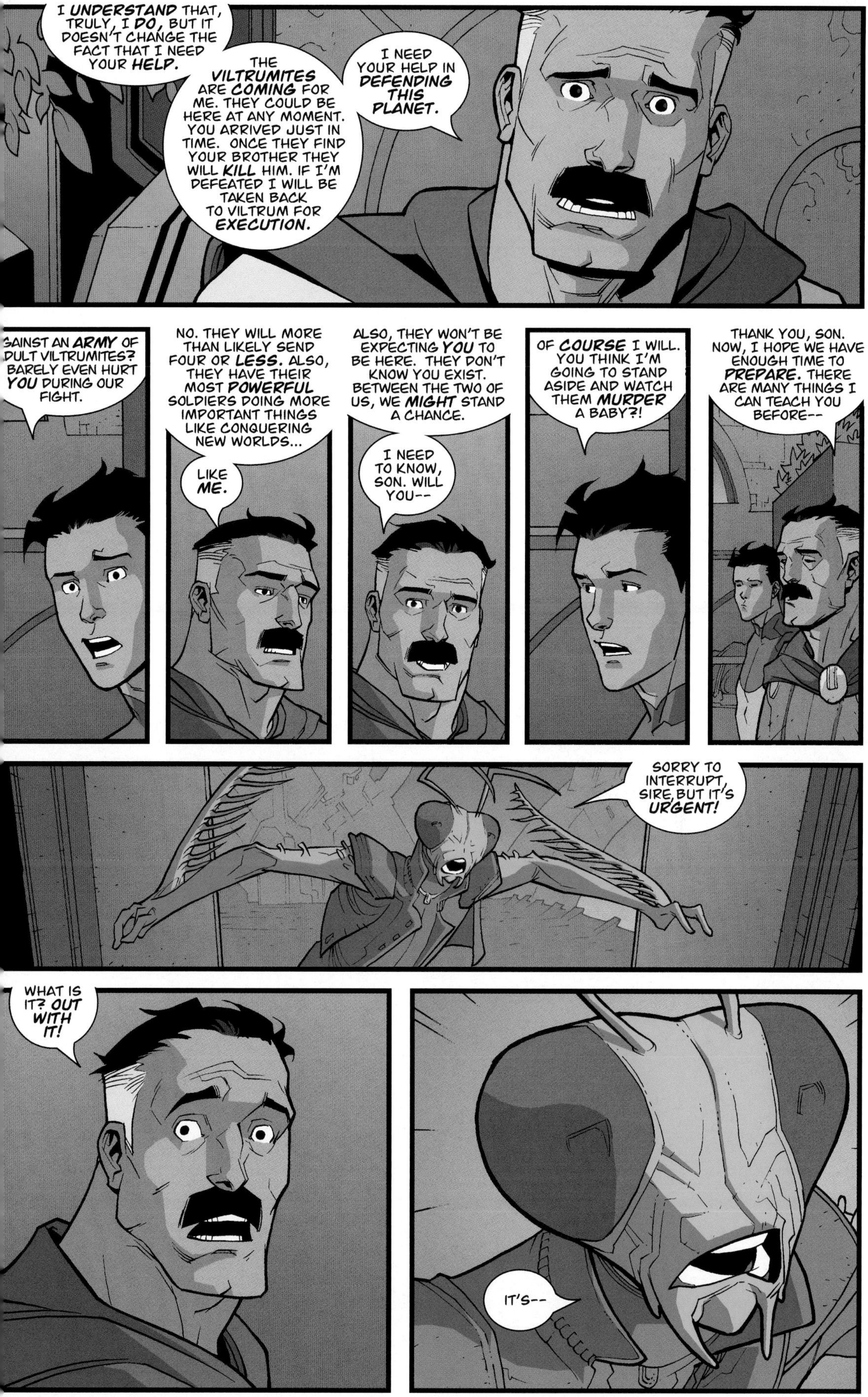

I UNDERSTAND THAT, TRULY, I DO, BUT IT DOESN'T CHANGE THE FACT THAT I NEED YOUR HELP.
THE VILTRUMITES ARE COMING FOR ME. THEY COULD BE HERE AT ANY MOMENT. YOU ARRIVED JUST IN TIME. ONCE THEY FIND YOUR BROTHER THEY WILL KILL HIM. IF I'M DEFEATED I WILL BE TAKEN BACK TO VILTRUM FOR EXECUTION.
I NEED YOUR HELP IN DEFENDING THIS PLANET.
GAINST AN ARMY OF DULT VILTRUMITES? BARELY EVEN HURT YOU DURING OUR FIGHT.
NO. THEY WILL MORE THAN LIKELY SEND FOUR OR LESS. ALSO, THEY HAVE THEIR MOST POWERFUL SOLDIERS DOING MORE IMPORTANT THINGS LIKE CONQUERING NEW WORLDS...
LIKE ME.
ALSO, THEY WON'T BE EXPECTING YOU TO BE HERE. THEY DON'T KNOW YOU EXIST. BETWEEN THE TWO OF US, WE MIGHT STAND A CHANCE.
I NEED TO KNOW, SON. WILL YOU--
OF COURSE I WILL. YOU THINK I'M GOING TO STAND ASIDE AND WATCH THEM MURDER A BABY?!
THANK YOU, SON. NOW, I HOPE WE HAVE ENOUGH TIME TO PREPARE. THERE ARE MANY THINGS I CAN TEACH YOU BEFORE--
SORRY TO INTERRUPT, SIRE, BUT IT'S URGENT!
WHAT IS IT? OUT WITH IT!
IT'S--

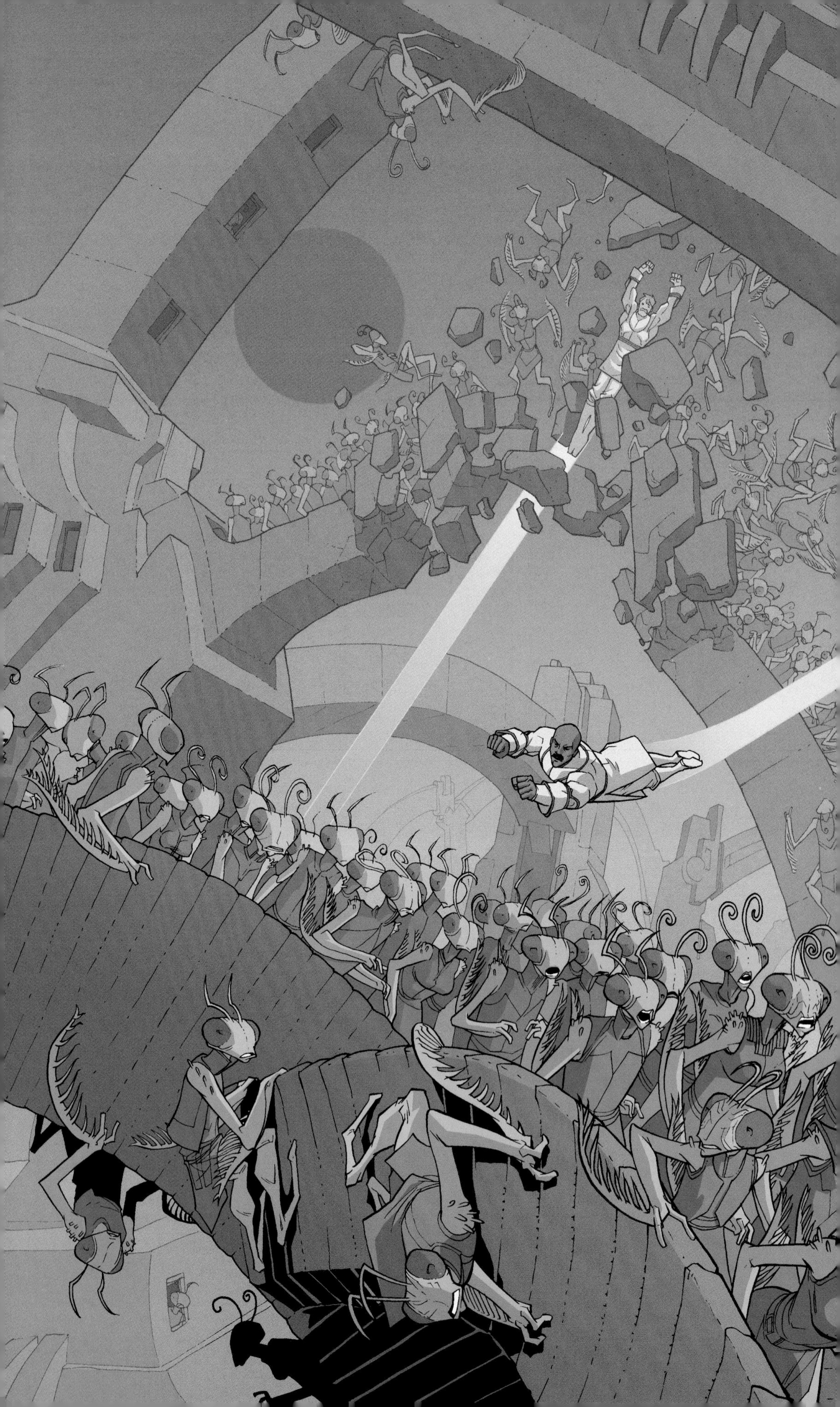

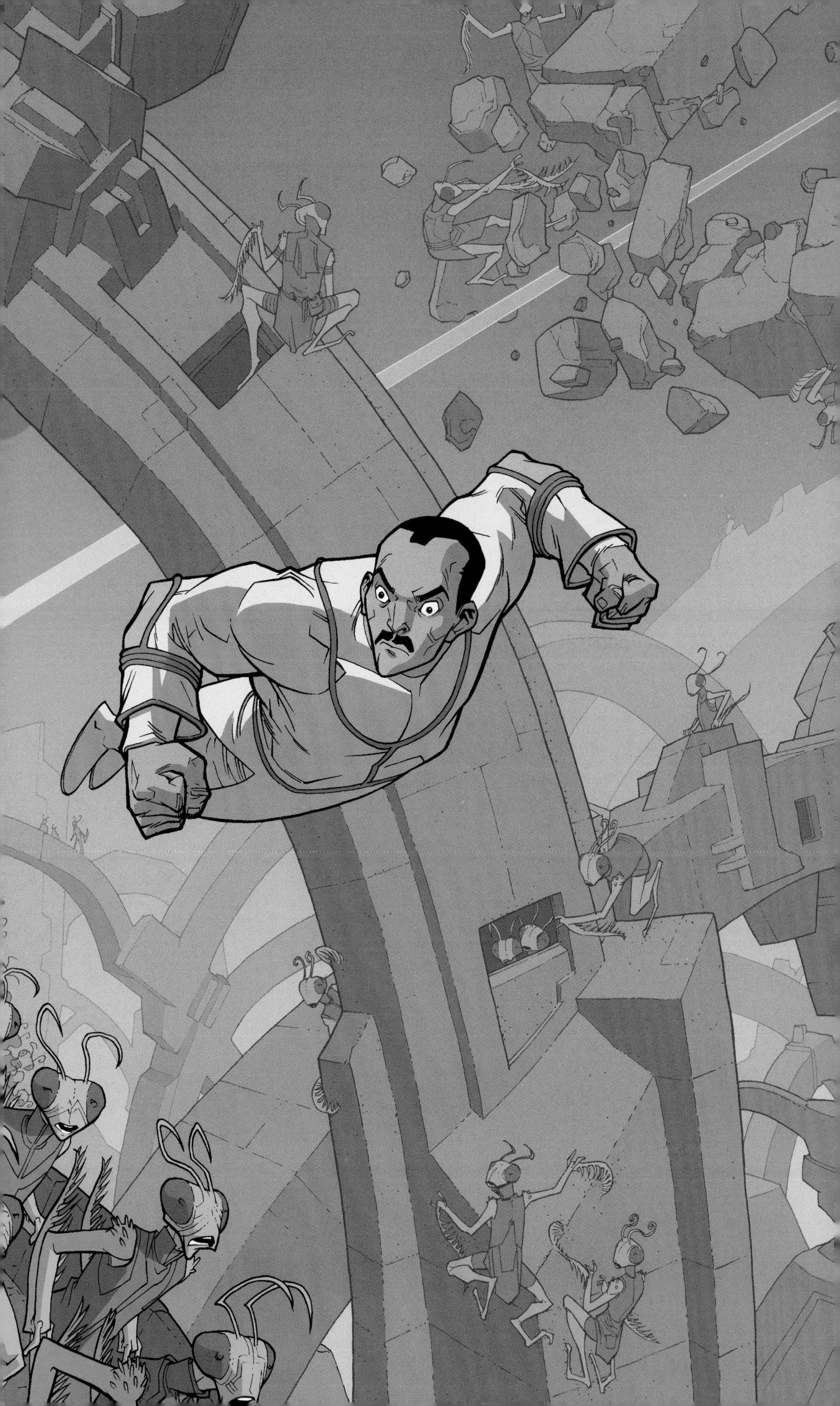

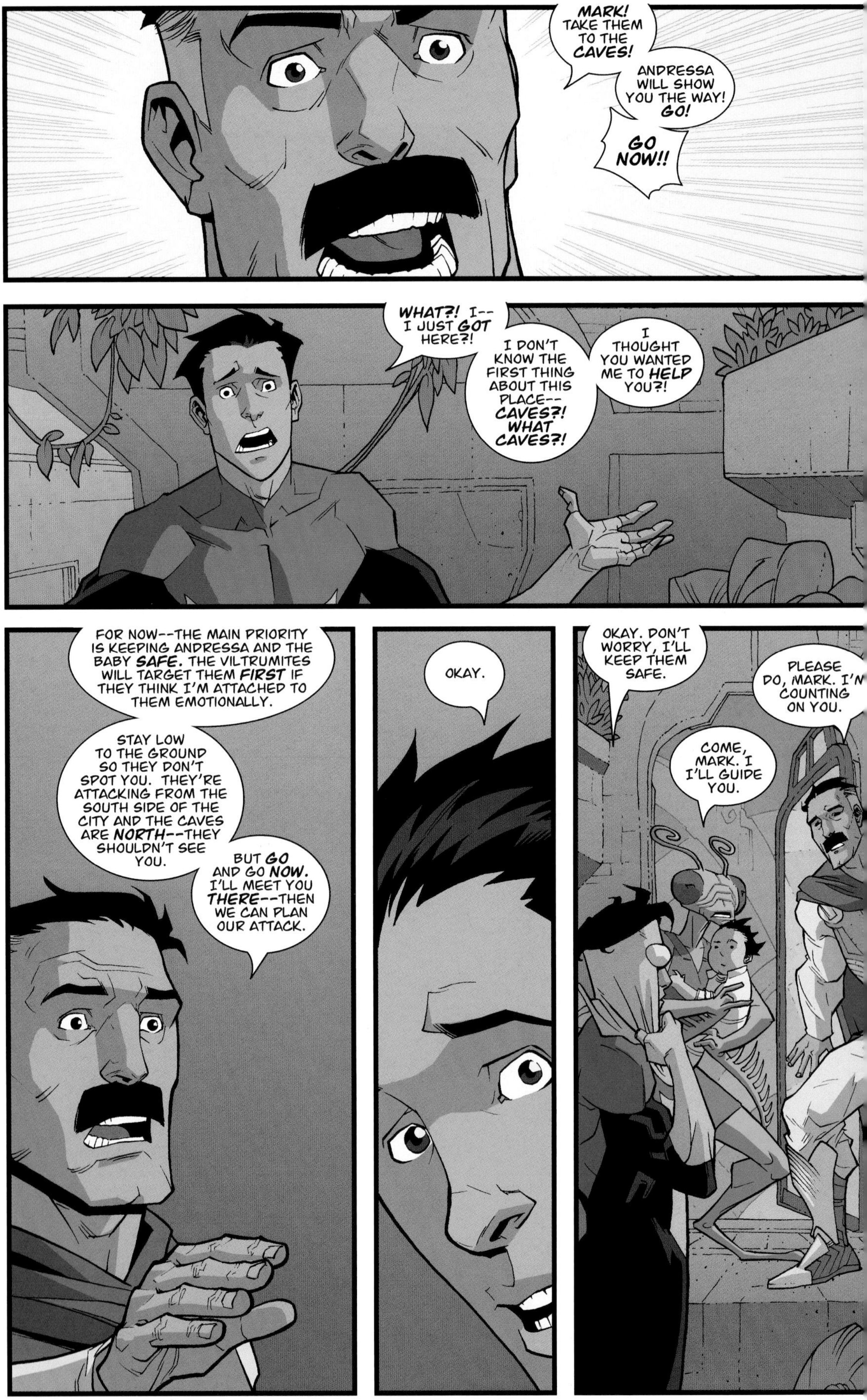
MARK! TAKE THEM TO THE CAVES!
ANDRESSA WILL SHOW YOU THE WAY! GO!
GO NOW!!
WHAT?! I-- I JUST GOT HERE?!
I DON'T KNOW THE FIRST THING ABOUT THIS PLACE-- CAVES?! WHAT CAVES?!
I THOUGHT YOU WANTED ME TO HELP YOU?!
FOR NOW--THE MAIN PRIORITY IS KEEPING ANDRESSA AND THE BABY SAFE. THE VILTRUMITES WILL TARGET THEM FIRST IF THEY THINK I'M ATTACHED TO THEM EMOTIONALLY.
STAY LOW TO THE GROUND SO THEY DON'T SPOT YOU. THEY'RE ATTACKING FROM THE SOUTH SIDE OF THE CITY AND THE CAVES ARE NORTH--THEY SHOULDN'T SEE YOU.
BUT GO AND GO NOW. I'LL MEET YOU THERE--THEN WE CAN PLAN OUR ATTACK.
OKAY.
OKAY. DON'T WORRY, I'LL KEEP THEM SAFE.
PLEASE DO, MARK. I'M COUNTING ON YOU.
COME, MARK. I I'LL GUIDE YOU.

HANG
ON!

VOOSH!!

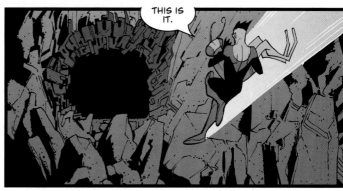

THIS IS
IT.

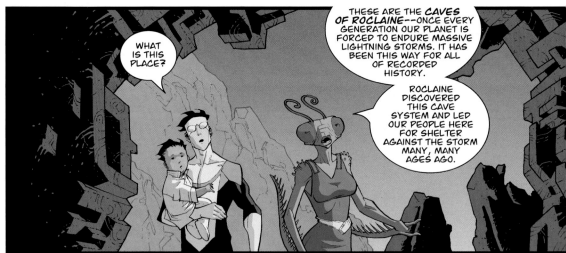

THESE ARE THE **CAVES OF ROCLAINE**--ONCE EVERY GENERATION OUR PLANET IS FORCED TO ENDURE MASSIVE LIGHTNING STORMS. IT HAS BEEN THIS WAY FOR ALL OF RECORDED HISTORY.

ROCLAINE DISCOVERED THIS CAVE SYSTEM AND LED OUR PEOPLE HERE FOR SHELTER AGAINST THE STORM MANY, MANY AGES AGO.

WHAT IS THIS PLACE?

IT WAS ALSO USED AS A **HAVEN** FOR OUR PEOPLE DURING THE WARS OF TIMES PAST BEFORE MY PEOPLE UNITED UNDER ONE WORLD RULER.

THAT'S INTERESTING.

WHAT ARE YOU DOING THERE?

THIS.

THE CAVES ARE NO LONGER USED FOR **PROTECTION.** OUR TECHNOLOGY HAS BUILT STRUCTURES THAT CAN WITHSTAND THE LIGHTNING STORMS.

NOW WE USE THE CAVES AS A PLACE FOR GATHERING, FOR STUDY, FOR MANY THINGS.

THE ENGRAVINGS WILL LIGHT THE WAY. THERE ARE **MANY** CAVERNS AHEAD, MANY LAVISHLY FURNISHED-- WE WILL BE QUITE COMFORTABLE HERE.

FOLLOW ME.

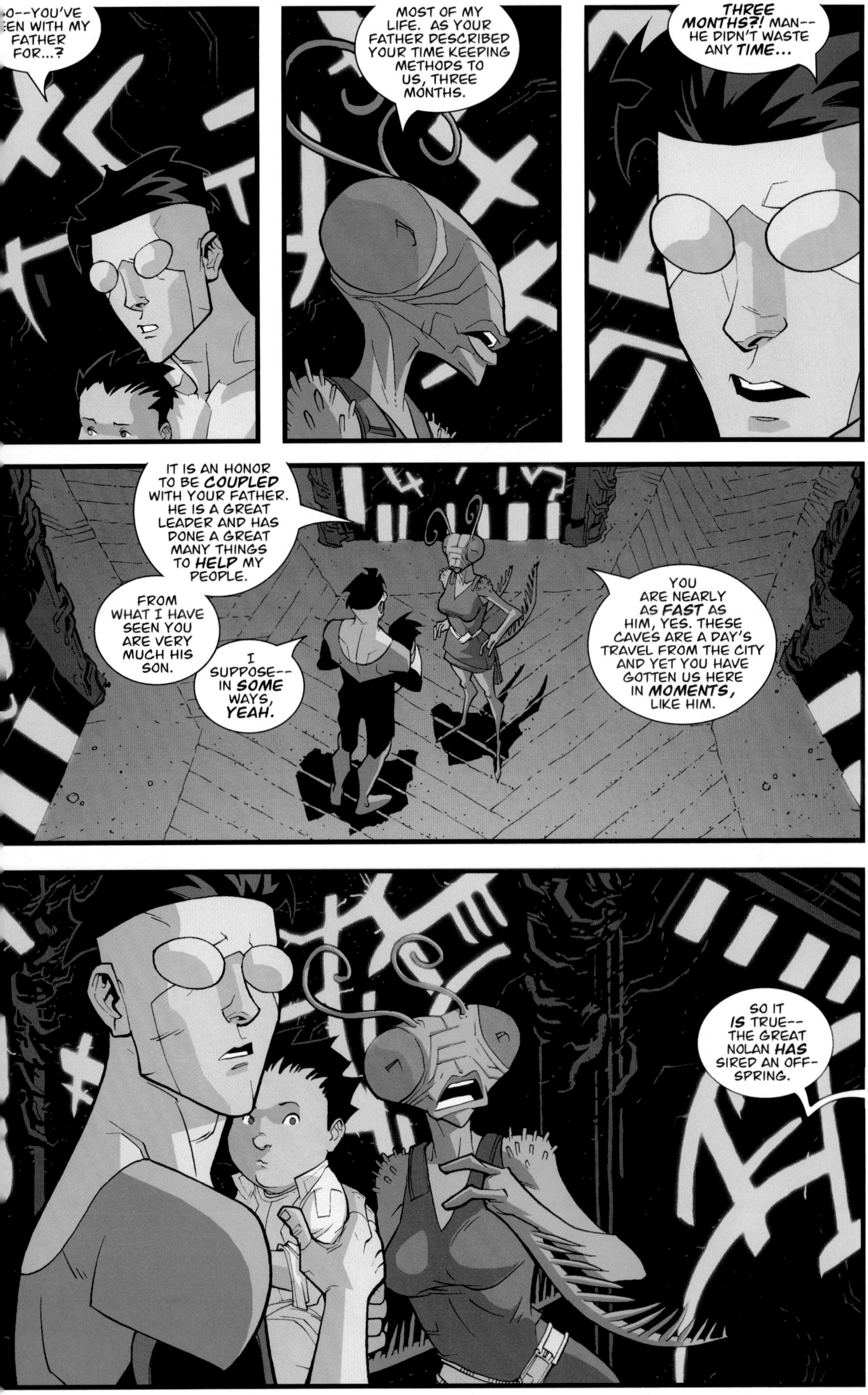

SO--YOU'VE BEEN WITH MY FATHER FOR...?
MOST OF MY LIFE. AS YOUR FATHER DESCRIBED YOUR TIME KEEPING METHODS TO US, THREE MONTHS.
THREE MONTHS?! MAN--HE DIDN'T WASTE ANY TIME...
IT IS AN HONOR TO BE COUPLED WITH YOUR FATHER. HE IS A GREAT LEADER AND HAS DONE A GREAT MANY THINGS TO HELP MY PEOPLE.
FROM WHAT I HAVE SEEN YOU ARE VERY MUCH HIS SON.
I SUPPOSE--IN SOME WAYS, YEAH.
YOU ARE NEARLY AS FAST AS HIM, YES. THESE CAVES ARE A DAY'S TRAVEL FROM THE CITY AND YET YOU HAVE GOTTEN US HERE IN MOMENTS, LIKE HIM.
SO IT IS TRUE--THE GREAT NOLAN HAS SIRED AN OFF-SPRING.

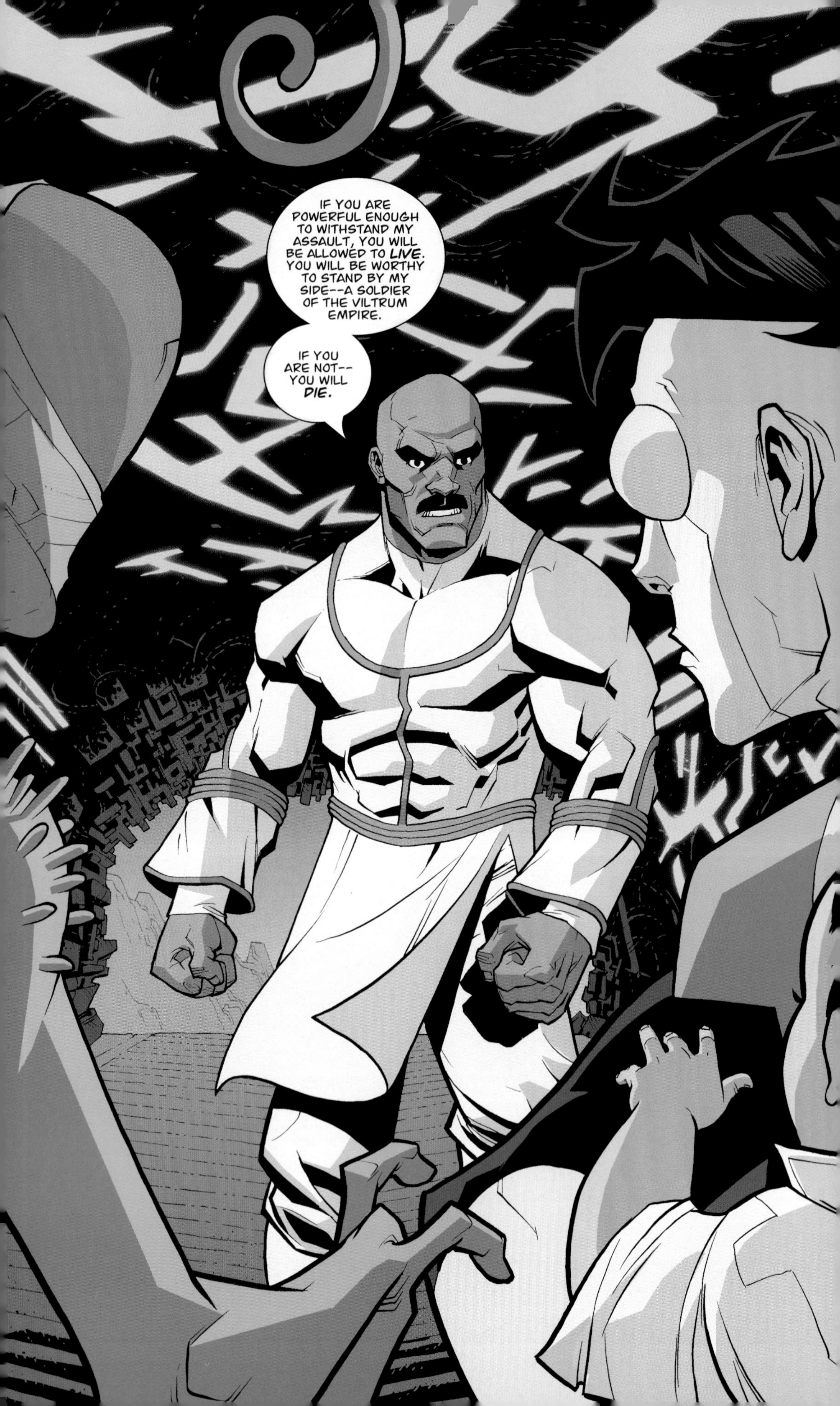
IF YOU ARE POWERFUL ENOUGH TO WITHSTAND MY ASSAULT, YOU WILL BE ALLOWED TO LIVE. YOU WILL BE WORTHY TO STAND BY MY SIDE--A SOLDIER OF THE VILTRUM EMPIRE.
IF YOU ARE NOT--YOU WILL DIE.

CHAPTER FOUR

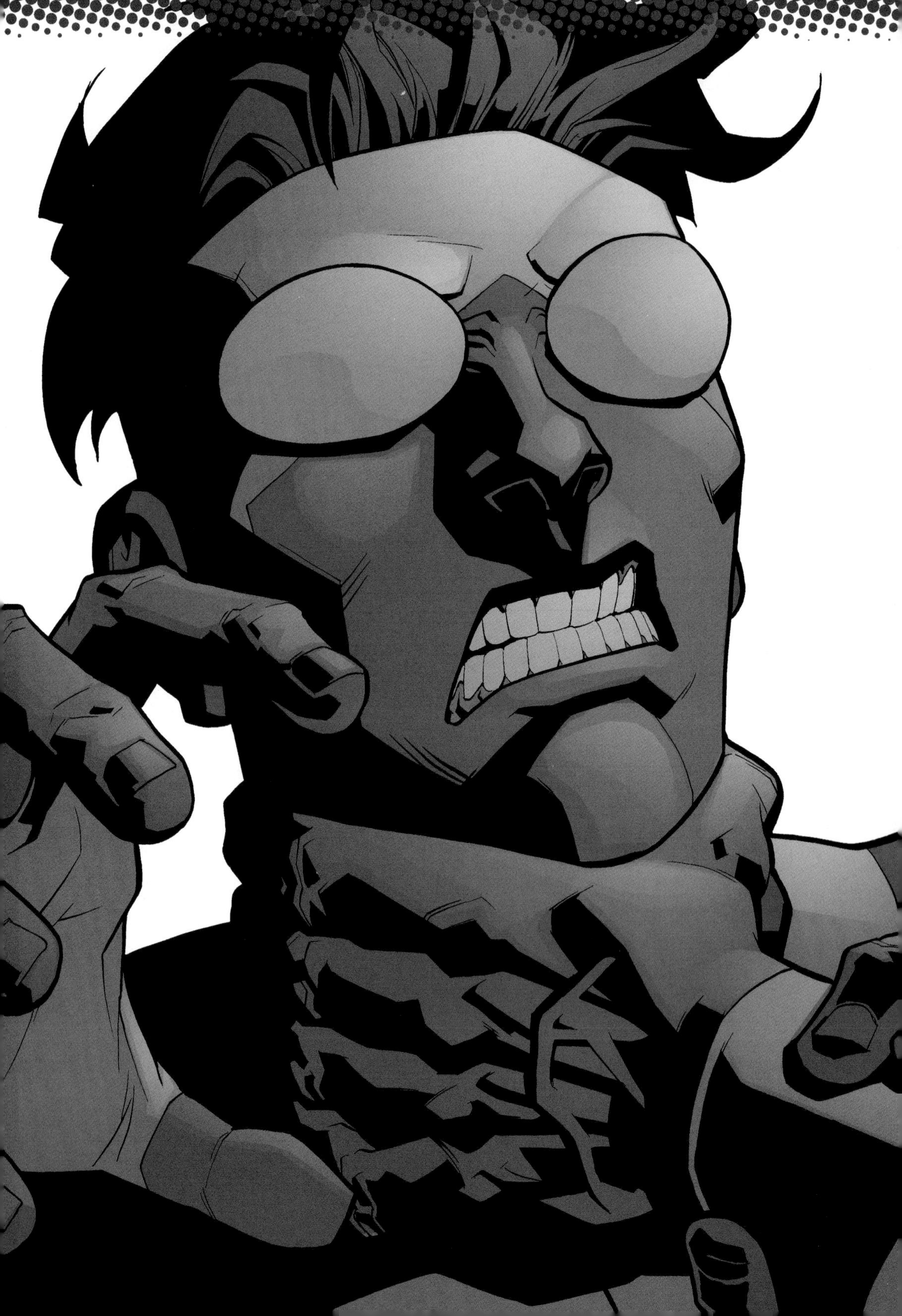

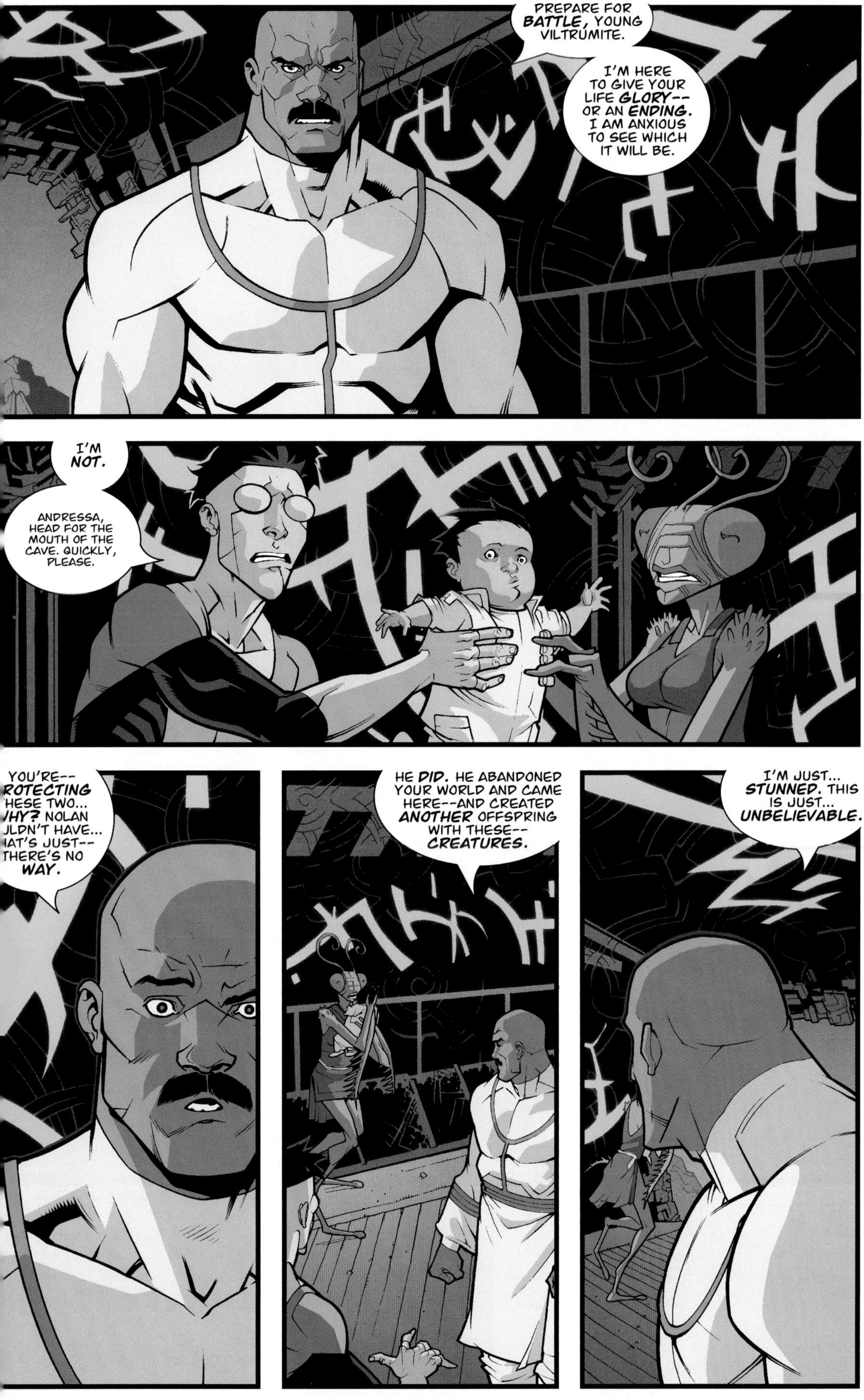
PREPARE FOR BATTLE, YOUNG VILTRUMITE.
I'M HERE TO GIVE YOUR LIFE GLORY-- OR AN ENDING. I AM ANXIOUS TO SEE WHICH IT WILL BE.
I'M NOT.
ANDRESSA, HEAD FOR THE MOUTH OF THE CAVE. QUICKLY, PLEASE.
YOU'RE-- ROTECTING HESE TWO... VHY? NOLAN ULDN'T HAVE... IAT'S JUST-- THERE'S NO WAY.
HE DID. HE ABANDONED YOUR WORLD AND CAME HERE--AND CREATED ANOTHER OFFSPRING WITH THESE-- CREATURES.
I'M JUST... STUNNED. THIS IS JUST... UNBELIEVABLE.

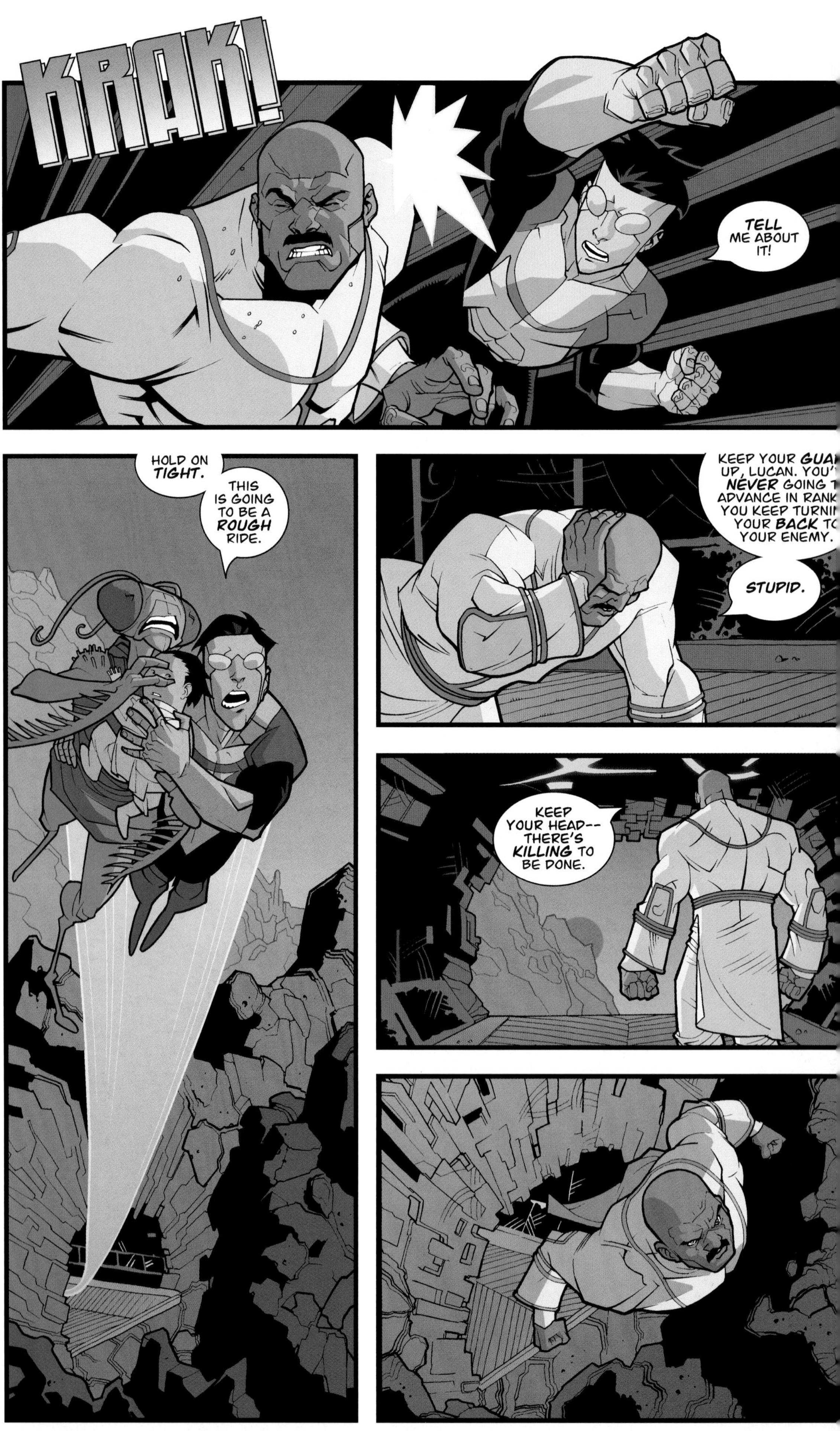
KRAK!
TELL ME ABOUT IT!
HOLD ON TIGHT.
THIS IS GOING TO BE A ROUGH RIDE.
KEEP YOUR GUA UP, LUCAN. YOU' NEVER GOING T ADVANCE IN RANK YOU KEEP TURNI YOUR BACK T YOUR ENEMY.
STUPID.
KEEP YOUR HEAD-- THERE'S KILLING TO BE DONE.

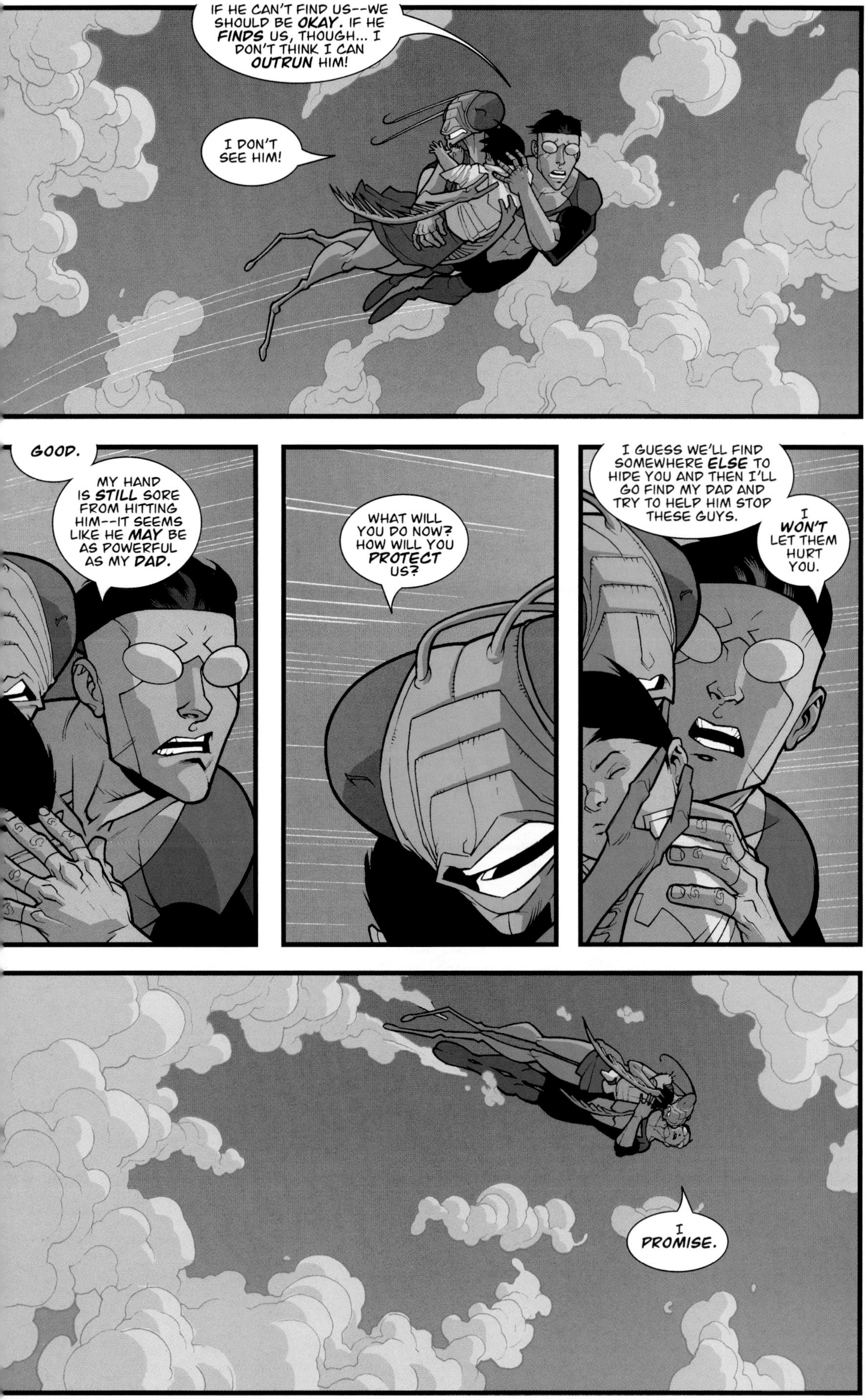

IF HE CAN'T FIND US--WE SHOULD BE OKAY. IF HE FINDS US, THOUGH... I DON'T THINK I CAN OUTRUN HIM!
I DON'T SEE HIM!
GOOD.
MY HAND IS STILL SORE FROM HITTING HIM--IT SEEMS LIKE HE MAY BE AS POWERFUL AS MY DAD.
WHAT WILL YOU DO NOW? HOW WILL YOU PROTECT US?
I GUESS WE'LL FIND SOMEWHERE ELSE TO HIDE YOU AND THEN I'LL GO FIND MY DAD AND TRY TO HELP HIM STOP THESE GUYS.
I WON'T LET THEM HURT YOU.
I PROMISE.

MARK?

WHAT IS IT--?

CRAP!

JUST TRY TO KEEP AN *EYE* ON HIM. WE CAN'T HIDE YOU *NOW* BUT I CAN TRY TO OUTRUN HIM... MAYBE HE'S *NOT* AS FAST AS *ME!*

I THINK HE'S GETTING *CLOSER.*

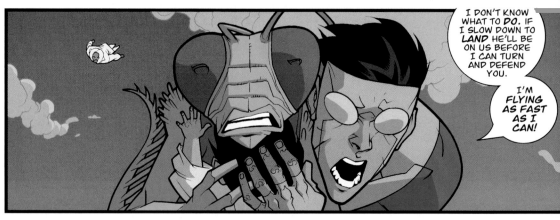

I DON'T KNOW WHAT TO *DO.* IF I SLOW DOWN TO *LAND* HE'LL BE ON US BEFORE I CAN TURN AND DEFEND YOU.

I'M *FLYING* AS FAST AS I CAN!

HOW BAD IS IT?

HOW *FAST* IS HE GAINING ON US?

FAST. HE WILL BE *ON* US IN MOMENTS.

I DON'T KNOW WHAT TO SAY-- I'M *SORRY.*

I DON'T KNOW IF WE'RE GOING TO SURVIVE *THIS.*

YOU CANNOT *HOPE* TO MATCH MY SPEED, *CHILD.*

WE *WILL* HAVE OUR CONTEST. BUT *FIRST* I'LL KILL THE *CREATURE* AND HER *HALF-BREED* OFF-SPRING!

YOU *ARE* FAST-- NO DOUBT-- JUST *NOT* FAST *ENOUGH.*

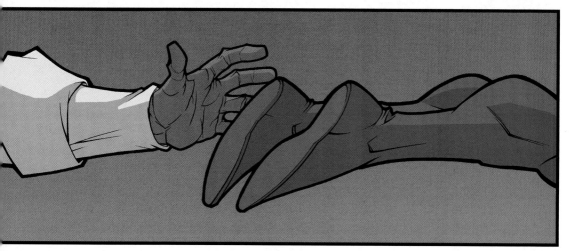

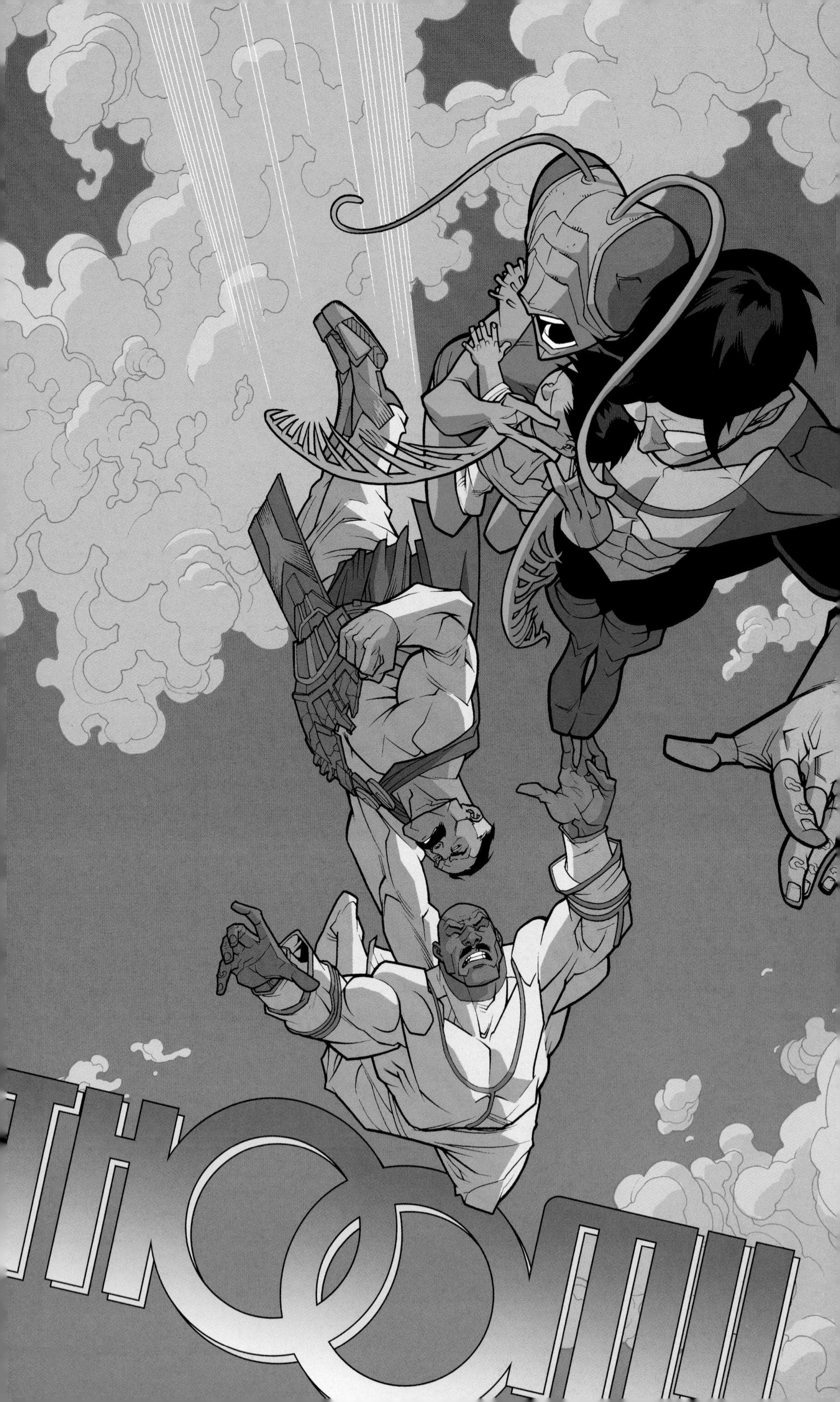
THOOM

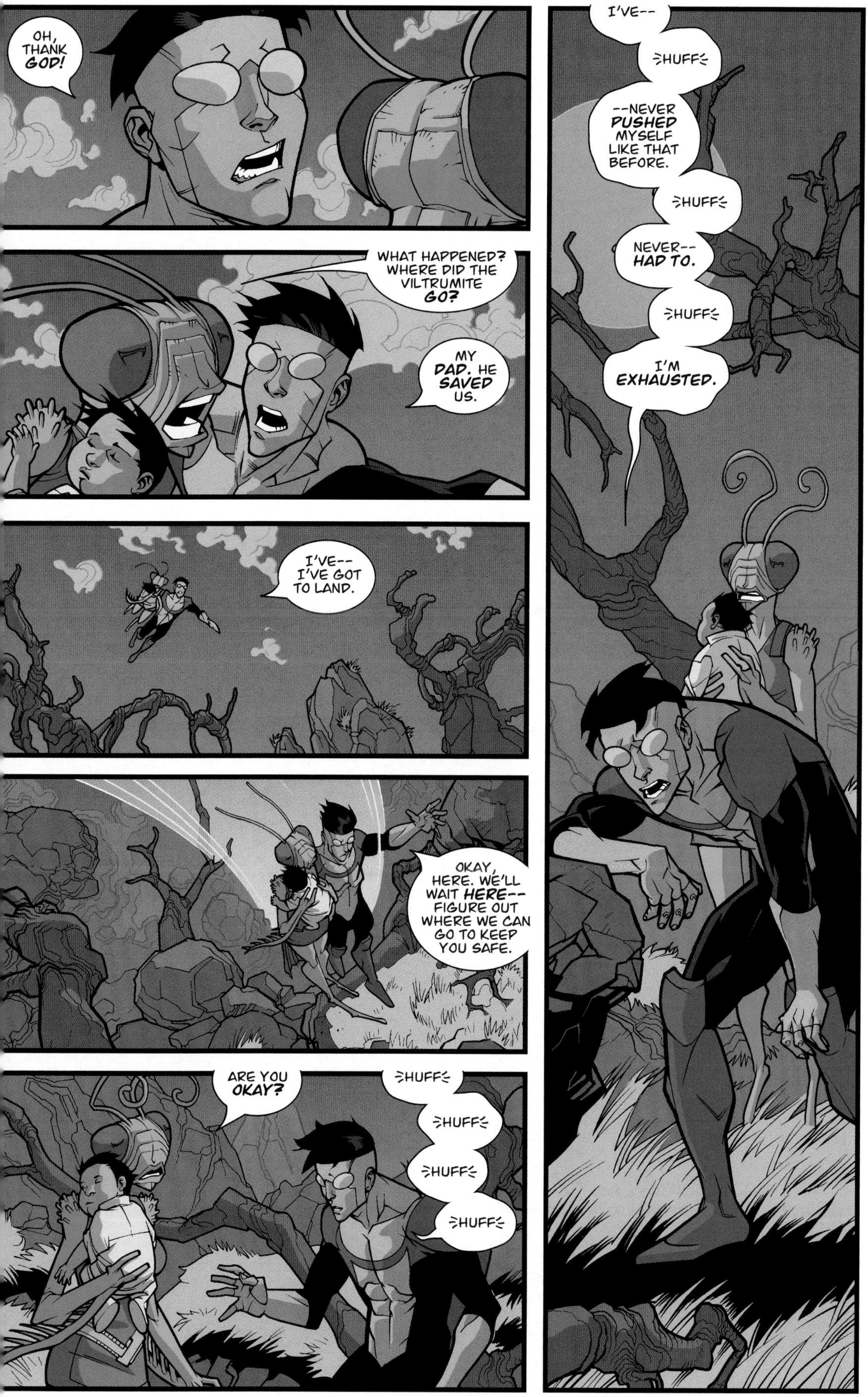

OH, THANK GOD!
WHAT HAPPENED? WHERE DID THE VILTRUMITE GO?
MY DAD. HE SAVED US.
I'VE-- I'VE GOT TO LAND.
OKAY, HERE. WE'LL WAIT HERE-- FIGURE OUT WHERE WE CAN GO TO KEEP YOU SAFE.
ARE YOU OKAY?
HUFF
HUFF
HUFF
HUFF
I'VE--
HUFF
--NEVER PUSHED MYSELF LIKE THAT BEFORE.
HUFF
NEVER-- HAD TO.
HUFF
I'M EXHAUSTED.

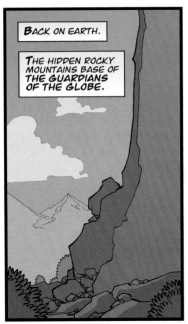

BACK ON EARTH.

THE HIDDEN ROCKY MOUNTAINS BASE OF **THE GUARDIANS OF THE GLOBE.**

SAMSON, I WAS WANTING TO--

--TALK TO YOU.

I KNOW. DATED. **VERY** DATED.

I'M PLANNING ON GETTING A **NEW** ONE. I PROMISE. I JUST WANTED TO TRY IT ON JUST IN CASE.

IT'S BEEN A **WHILE.**

MY POWER SUIT WAS **DESTROYED** BY MONSTER GIRL IN THE FIGHT WITH OMNIPOTUS, AND I'VE GOT MY POWERS BACK NOW, SO I DON'T REALLY **NEED** IT. SO I FIGURED I'D SEE IF THIS COSTUME WOULD STILL WORK.

IT **DOESN'T.**

HOW ARE YOU FEELING?

GOOD. I'VE GOT MY POWERS BACK. I'VE BEEN WORSE. MY POWER LEVELS ARE BACK DOWN TO **NORMAL.** OR WHAT THEY WERE BEFORE I LOST THEM.

BEING IN THE COMA, IT GAVE MY BODY A CHANCE TO **HEAL**-RESET ITSELF OR SOMETHING. ALL THAT TIME WITHOUT POWER SORT OF BUILD UP IN ME, GAVE THAT SUDDEN BURST OF **EXTRA** POWER NEEDED TO PUSH OMNIPOTUS BACK INTO HIS UNIVERSE.

BUT IT'S GONE NOW. I'M BACK TO BEING REGULAR OLD BLACK SAMSON.

JUST WANTED TO SAY... IT'S GOOD TO HAVE YOU BACK.

YEAH. SURE, MAN. LIKE YOU CARE.

EXCUSE ME?

I WAS IN A **COMA** FOR A FEW **MONTHS.** YOU **NEVER** VISITED ME. I ASKED AROUND. I KNOW YOU DON'T GIVE A **DAMN** ABOUT **ANY** OF US ON THIS TEAM. NEVER **DID.**

I'LL ADMIT IT. YOU'RE **RIGHT.** I DIDN'T.

BEFORE.

BUT THINGS ARE CHANGING. **I'M** CHANGING.

DO YOU KNOW **WHY** I NEVER VISITED YOU? WHY I NEVER **REALLY** ·OT TO KNOW ANY OF THE ORIGINAL GUARDIANS? ·HY I WAS SO DISTANT-- DISCONNECTED?

YOU KNOW MY **HISTORY**, THE THINGS I'VE BEEN THROUGH, HOW **LONG** I'VE BEEN AROUND. YOU KNOW **EVERYTHING.** YOU **ALL DID.** STILL, YOU NEVER QUITE **UNDERSTOOD.**

I'VE SEEN **THOUSANDS** DIE. MANY OF THEM **VERY** CLOSE TO ME. I'VE LOST HUNDREDS OF WIVES, FRIENDS--EVEN THE **ENEMIES** STARTED GETTING TO ME AFTER A WHILE, AND I **WANTED** SOME OF THEM DEAD.

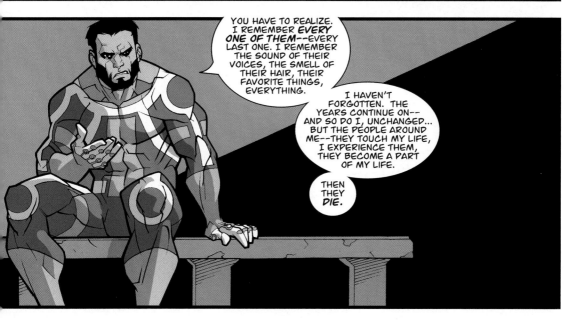

YOU HAVE TO REALIZE. I REMEMBER **EVERY ONE OF THEM**--EVERY LAST ONE. I REMEMBER THE SOUND OF THEIR VOICES, THE SMELL OF THEIR HAIR, THEIR FAVORITE THINGS, EVERYTHING.

I HAVEN'T FORGOTTEN. THE YEARS CONTINUE ON-- AND SO DO I, UNCHANGED... BUT THE PEOPLE AROUND ME--THEY TOUCH MY LIFE, I EXPERIENCE THEM, THEY BECOME A PART OF MY LIFE.

THEN THEY **DIE.**

SO I SHUT MYSELF OFF.

FOR THE LAST **FEW** DECADES I'VE LET VERY FEW PEOPLE INTO MY LIFE.

AND AFTER MY WIFE **GRACE** DIED...

NO ONE.

GRACE WAS A WONDERFUL WOMAN. WE WERE **ALL** UPSET OVER HER PASSING.

AFTER **HER**--I DECIDED TO FOCUS COMPLETELY ON THE **WORK**, PROTECTING OTHERS BUT NEVER GETTING TOO **CLOSE.**

I'VE COME TO REGRET PUSHING YOU ALL AWAY. ESPECIALLY NOW THAT EVERYONE BUT US IS **GONE.**

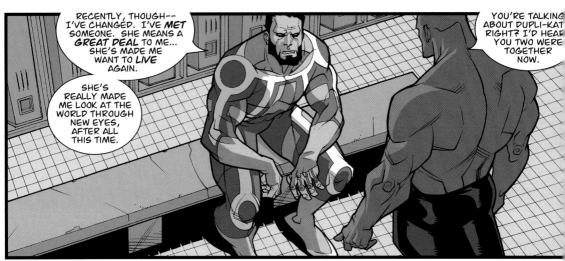

RECENTLY, THOUGH-- I'VE CHANGED. I'VE **MET** SOMEONE. SHE MEANS A **GREAT DEAL** TO ME... SHE'S MADE ME WANT TO **LIVE** AGAIN.

SHE'S REALLY MADE ME LOOK AT THE WORLD THROUGH NEW EYES, AFTER ALL THIS TIME.

YOU'RE TALKING ABOUT DUPLI-KAT RIGHT? I'D HEAR YOU TWO WERE TOGETHER NOW.

YEAH. IT'S KATE.

I KNOW THIS GOES FOR JUST ABOUT **ANYONE** AT THIS POINT-- BUT ISN'T SHE A LITTLE **YOUNG** FOR YOU?

SHE'S--

SHE CERTAINLY MAKES LIFE **INTERESTING.**

MEANWHILE...

SOMEWHERE ELSE ENTIRELY (THOUGH STILL ON EARTH).

AARRGGH!!

AAARRGGHGH!!

ELCOME TO HE LAND OF HE LIVING, CLONE.

I'M NOT THE CLONE, MY NEW FRIEND. YOU ARE.

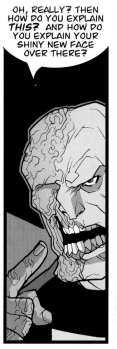

OH, REALLY? THEN HOW DO YOU EXPLAIN *THIS*? AND HOW DO YOU EXPLAIN YOUR SHINY NEW FACE OVER THERE?

BUT--MY MEMORIES-- I--I REMEMBER *MAKING* THIS BODY, I REMEMBER WORKING WITH ANGSTROM LEVY. BUT MY FACE--IT'S NOT--I *AM* THE CLONE.

I DIDN'T EVEN EXIST UNTIL A MOMENT AGO--UNTIL *YOU* GAVE ME LIFE.

FOR THE FIRST TIME, WE'RE GOING TO KNOW EXACTLY WHO IS THE COPY-- AND WHO IS *INFERIOR*.

IT'S *ME*...

THIS IS GOING TO WORK OUT *SO MUCH* BETTER.

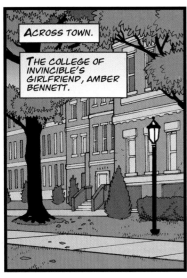

ACROSS TOWN.

THE COLLEGE OF INVINCIBLE'S GIRLFRIEND, AMBER BENNETT.

KNOCK.
KNOCK.

COME IN.

IT'S OPEN.

OH, JEEZ. I KNEW I SHOULDA **CALLED** FIRST. HE'S NOT BACK YET IS HE? YOU'RE GOING TO BE COMPLETELY **USELESS** TO ME UNTIL HE COMES BACK.

HAS HE EVEN **CALLED?**

NO, I TOLD YOU... HE'S OUT IN THE WOODS OR SOMETHING. THEY CAN'T GET A CELL PHONE SIGNAL.

SO YOUR BOYFRIEND RUNS UP HERE TO SAY GOODBYE TO YOU AND LETS YOU KNOW HE'S GOING ON A LAST MINUTE CAMPING TRIP--CAN'T TELL YOU **WHEN** HE'LL BE BACK AND CAN'T CALL YOU?

HE CAN EVEN M IT TO A F PHONE

HIS GRANDFATHER'S **SICK**, THEY'RE NOT **CAMPING**. HE COULD **DIE**. THEY'RE IN A SMALL TOWN.

A SMALL TOWN WITHOUT **PHONES?!**

SOMETHING LIKE THAT-- YEAH. WHAT'S THE BIG DEAL, BRIDGET?

AMBER, IT'S JUST--ARE YOU **SURE** HE'S NOT JUST CHEATING ON YOU?

PRETTY SURE.

I THI

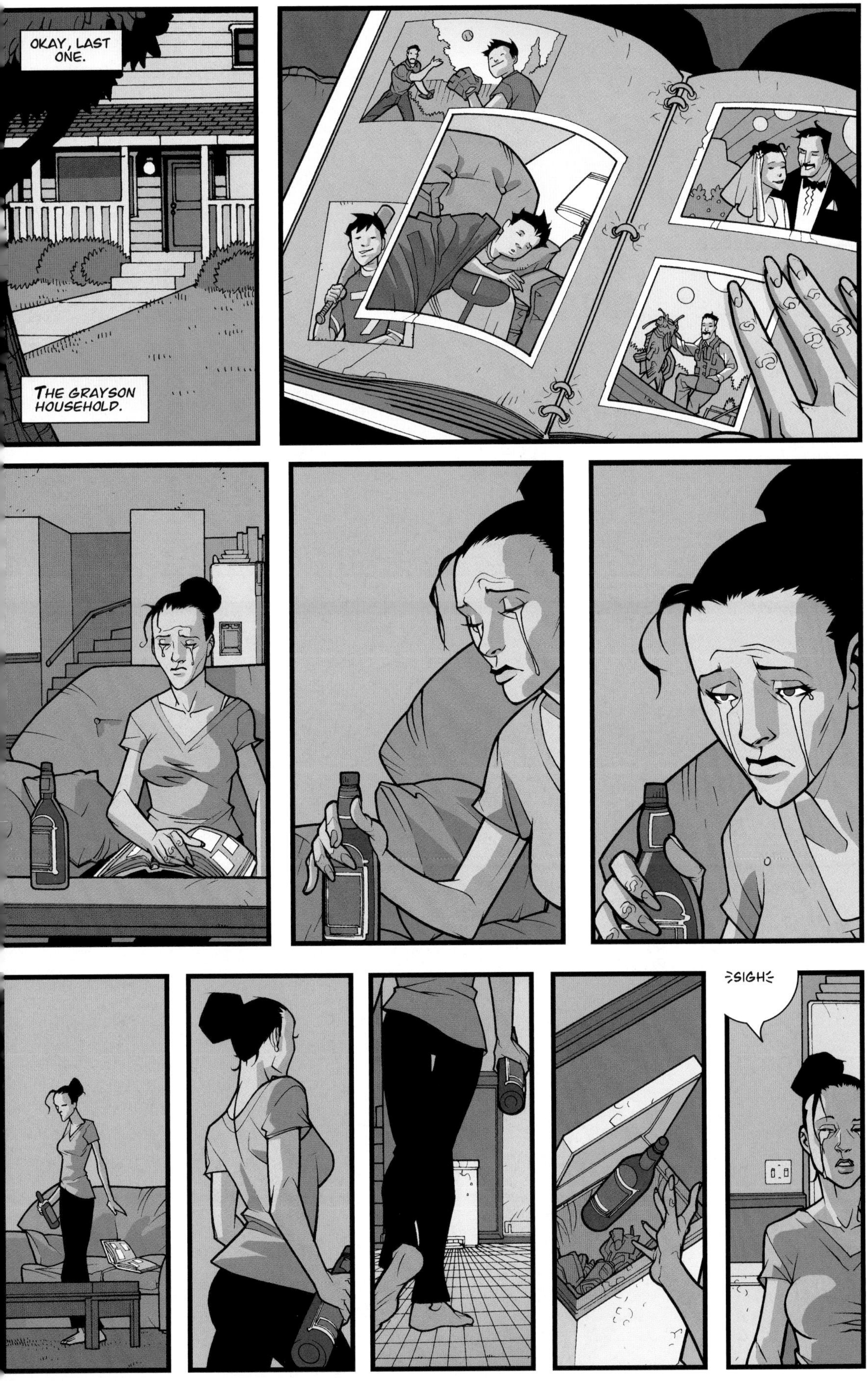
OKAY, LAST ONE.
THE GRAYSON HOUSEHOLD.
≋SIGH≋

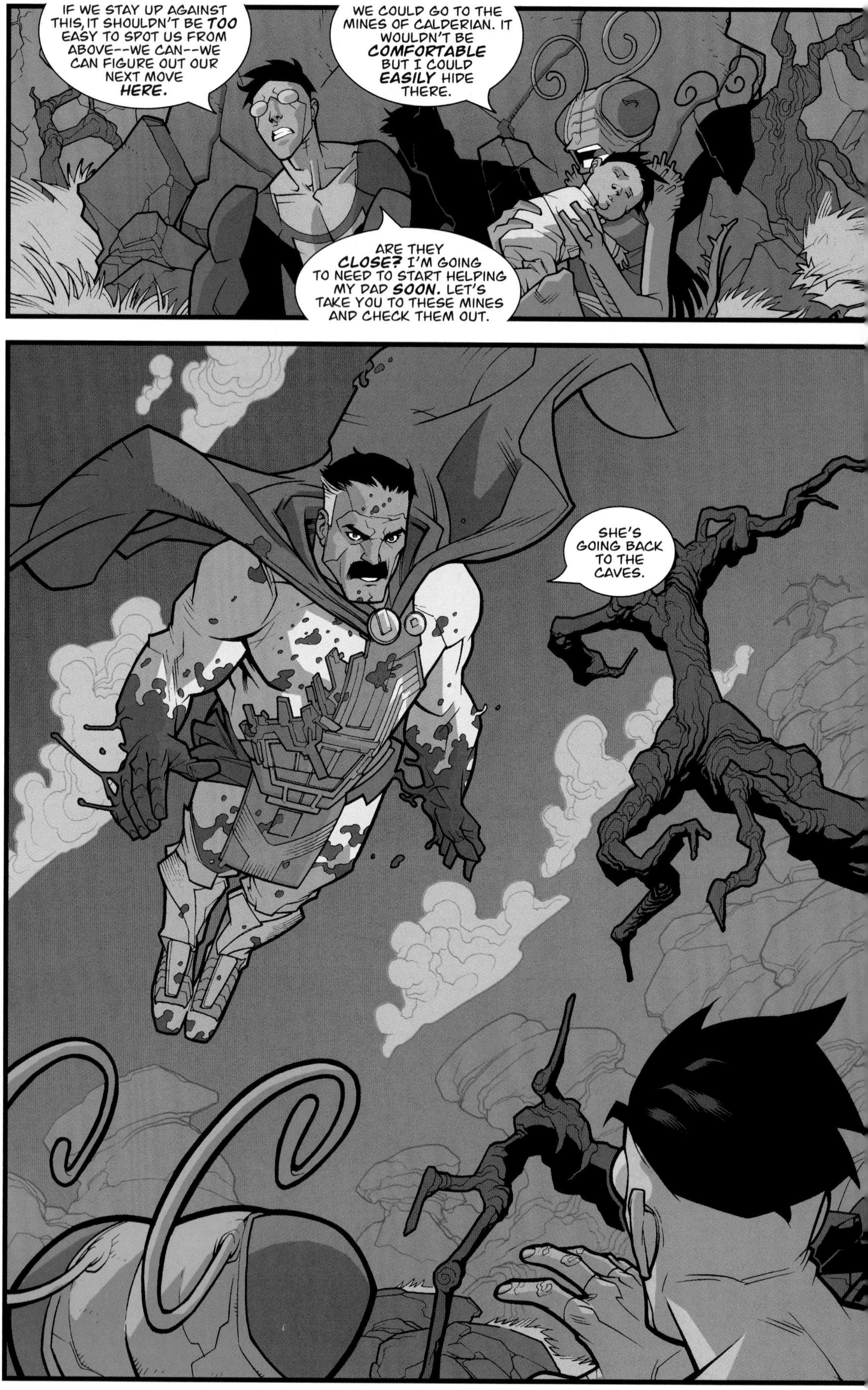
IF WE STAY UP AGAINST THIS, IT SHOULDN'T BE TOO EASY TO SPOT US FROM ABOVE--WE CAN--WE CAN FIGURE OUT OUR NEXT MOVE HERE.
WE COULD GO TO THE MINES OF CALDERIAN. IT WOULDN'T BE COMFORTABLE BUT I COULD EASILY HIDE THERE.
ARE THEY CLOSE? I'M GOING TO NEED TO START HELPING MY DAD SOON. LET'S TAKE YOU TO THESE MINES AND CHECK THEM OUT.
SHE'S GOING BACK TO THE CAVES.

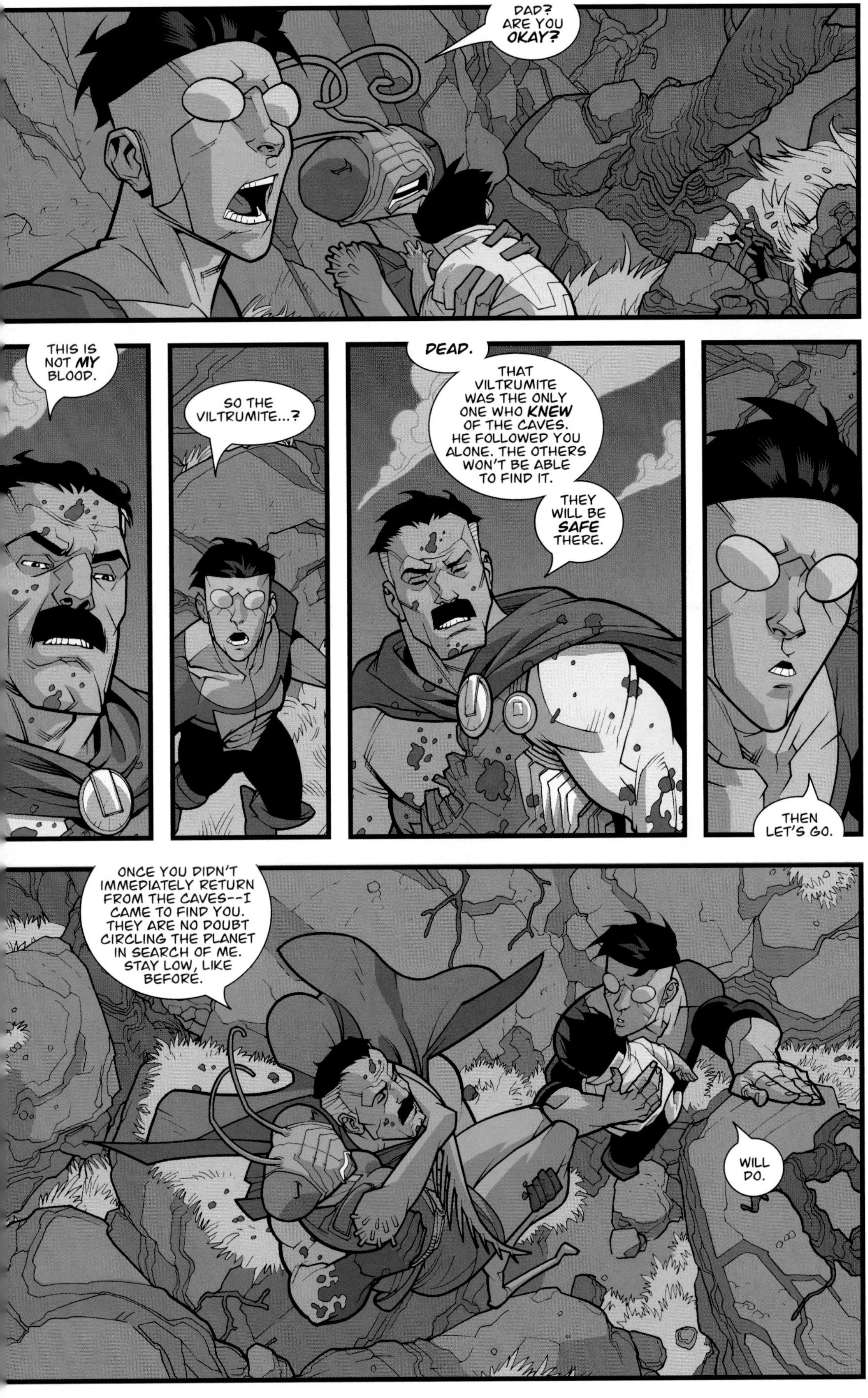
DAD? ARE YOU OKAY?
THIS IS NOT MY BLOOD.
SO THE VILTRUMITE...?
DEAD.
THAT VILTRUMITE WAS THE ONLY ONE WHO KNEW OF THE CAVES. HE FOLLOWED YOU ALONE. THE OTHERS WON'T BE ABLE TO FIND IT.
THEY WILL BE SAFE THERE.
THEN LET'S GO.
ONCE YOU DIDN'T IMMEDIATELY RETURN FROM THE CAVES--I CAME TO FIND YOU. THEY ARE NO DOUBT CIRCLING THE PLANET IN SEARCH OF ME. STAY LOW, LIKE BEFORE.
WILL DO.

BE READY TO CATCH ANDRESSA, MARK. IF THEY FIND US, I WILL THROW HER TO YOU AND YOU WILL TAKE BOTH OF THEM TO THE CAVES.

OKAY. SURE.

MARK. ARE YOU OKAY?

MARK. ARE YOU OKAY?

I GOT *TIRED*, DAD. I NEVER GOT TIRED BEFORE. I DIDN'T KNOW I *COULD* GET TIRED ANY MORE.

I GOT *TIRED*, DAD. I NEVER GOT TIRED BEFORE. I DIDN'T KNOW I *COULD* GET TIRED ANY MORE.

YOU HAVEN'T BEEN *PUSHING* YOURSEL YOU'RE NOT USED T USING YOUR POWER AS MUCH AS YOU'V HAD TO HERE.

YOU MEAN *EXERCISE?*

YES. PRETTY MUCH. YOU'VE GOT TO PUSH YOURSELF FROM TIME TO TIME--JUST IN CASE THINGS LIKE *THIS* HAPPEN.

I HADN'T EVER REALLY THOUGHT ABOUT IT.

WEIRD.

YOU TAKE TOO MUCH FOR GRANTED, SON. YOU'VE GOT TO RESPECT YOUR POWERS MORE.

UH... OKAY.

THER ARE TH CAVE

I'M HEADING BACK TO THE CITY. MEET ME THERE.

MAKE SURE THEY'RE *SAFE*.

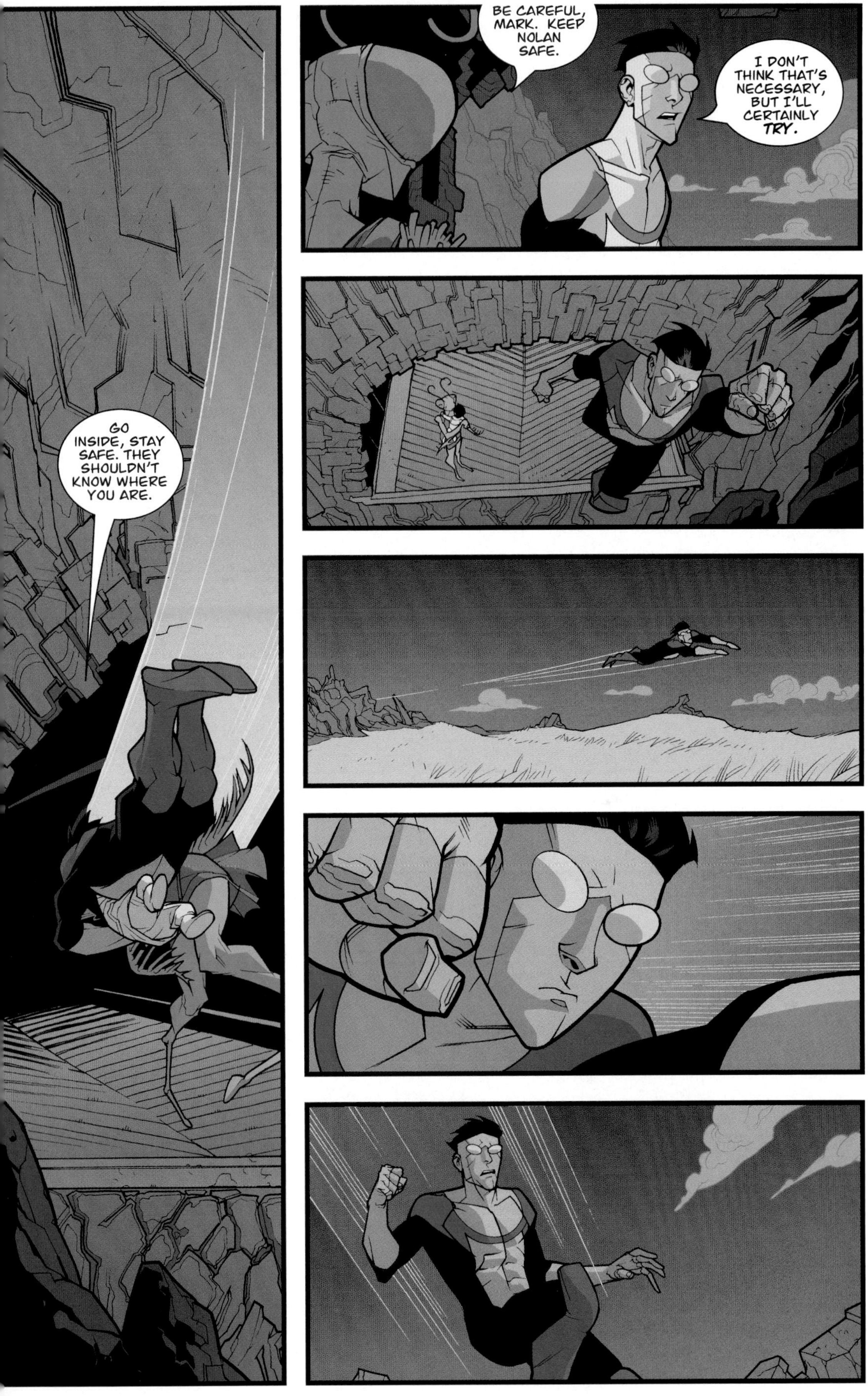
GO INSIDE, STAY SAFE. THEY SHOULDN'T KNOW WHERE YOU ARE.
BE CAREFUL, MARK. KEEP NOLAN SAFE.
I DON'T THINK THAT'S NECESSARY, BUT I'LL CERTAINLY TRY.

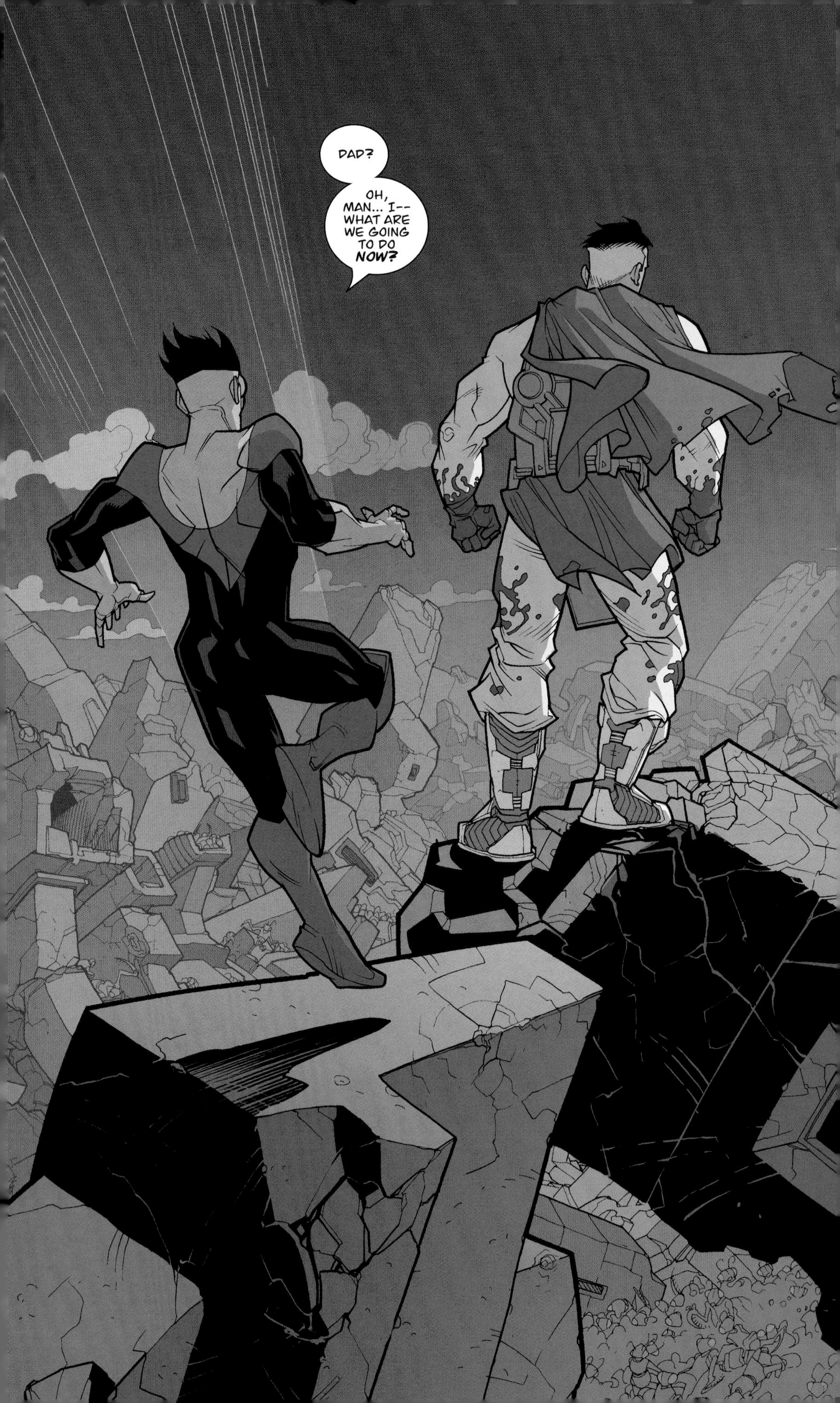
DAD?
OH, MAN... I-- WHAT ARE WE GOING TO DO NOW?

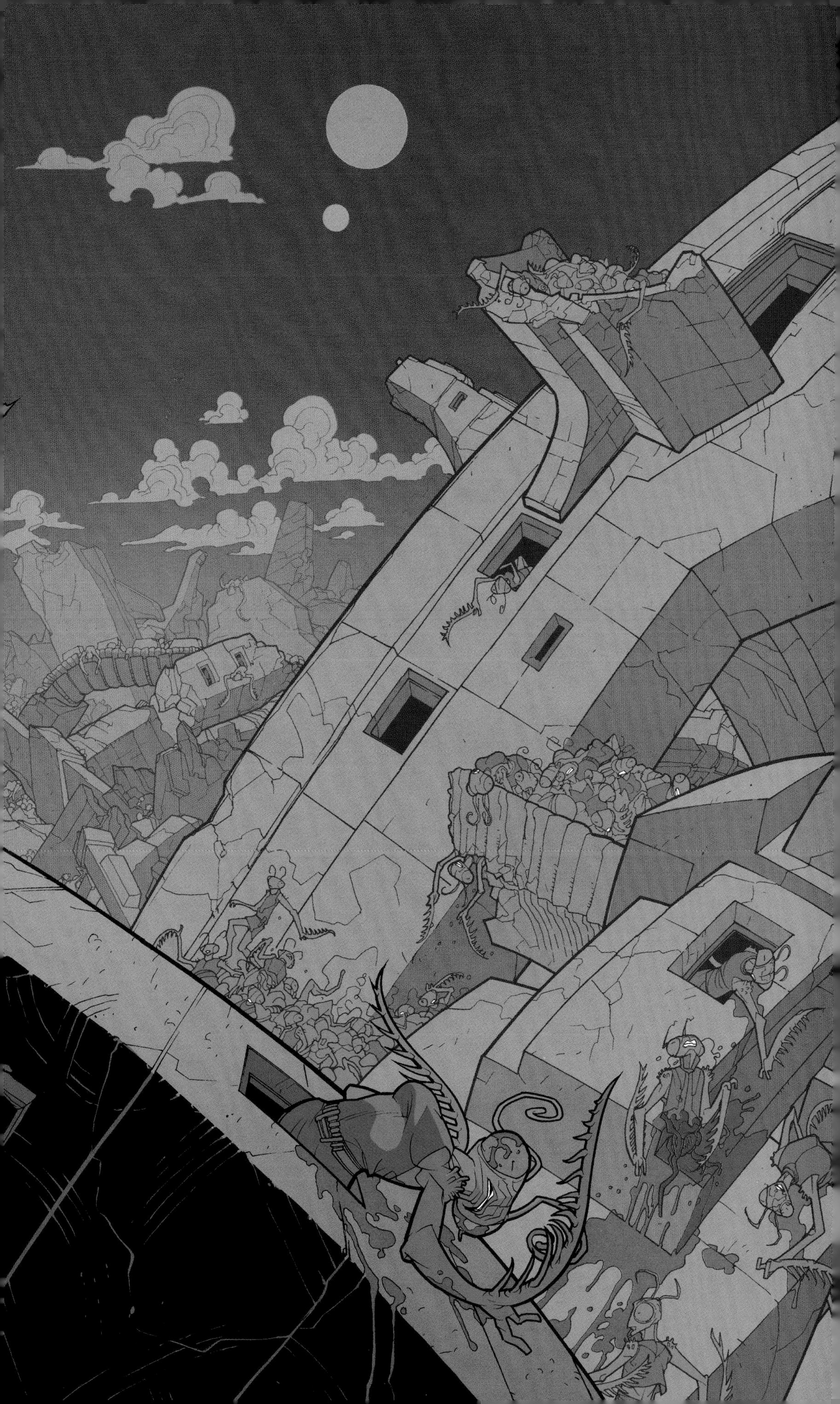

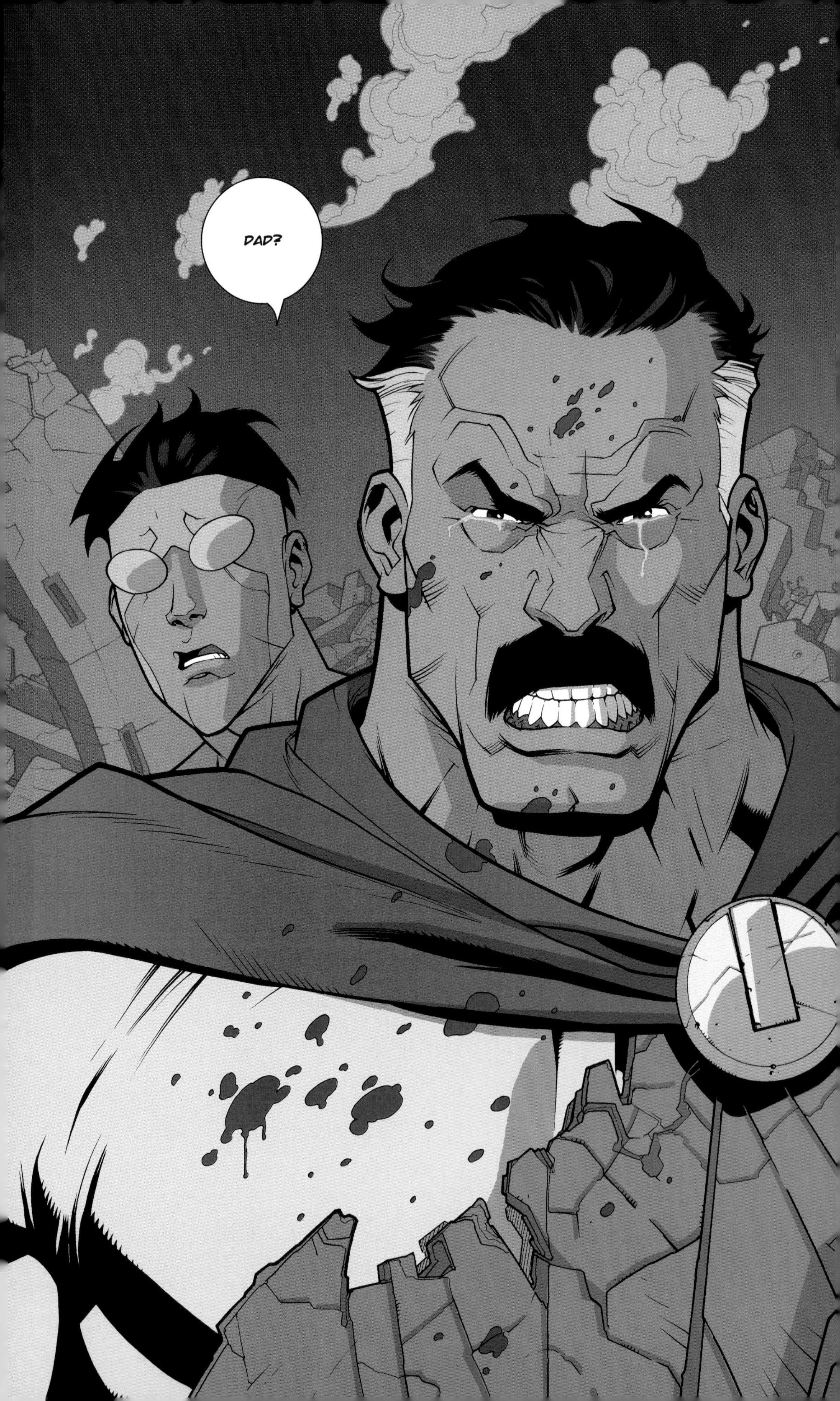
DAD?

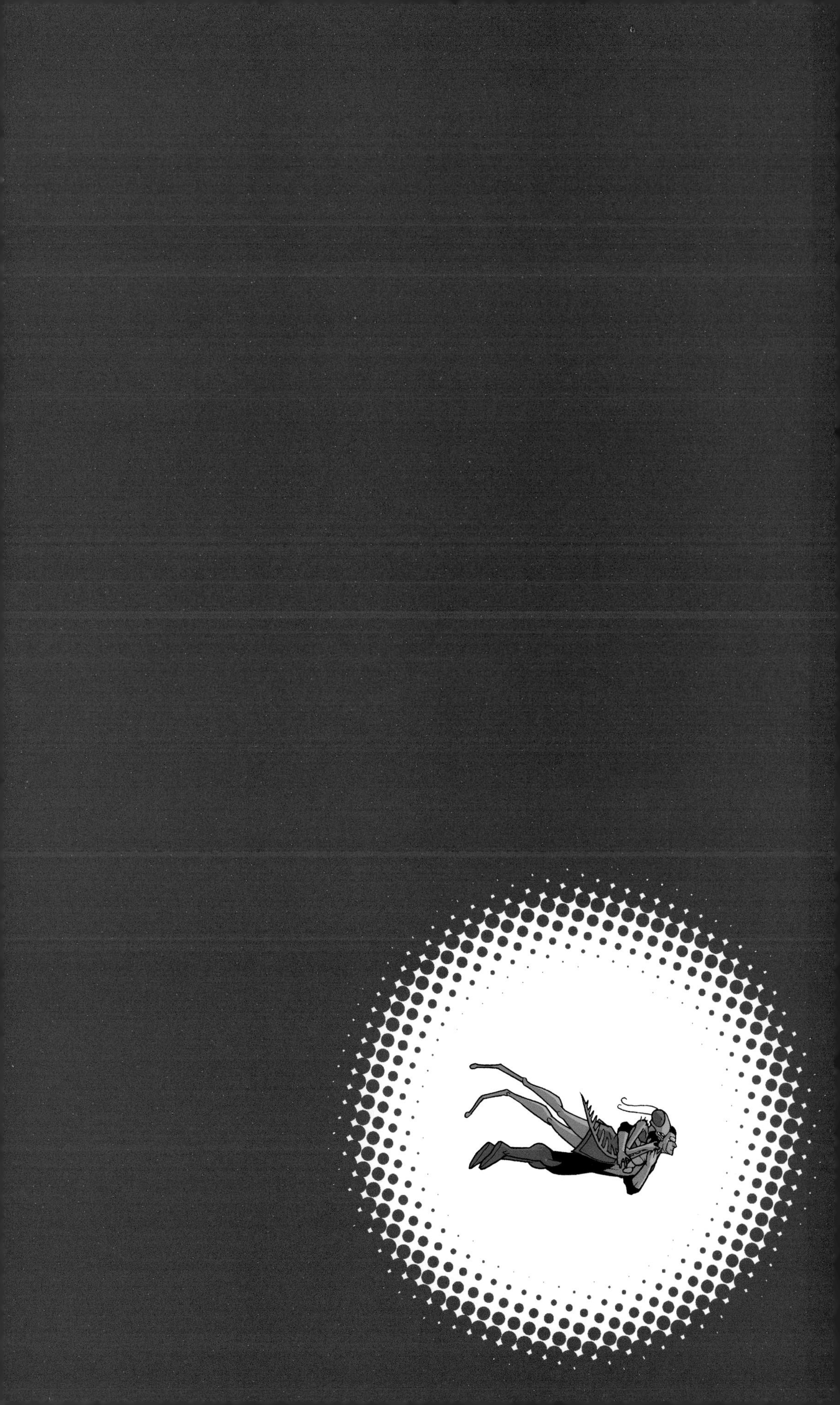

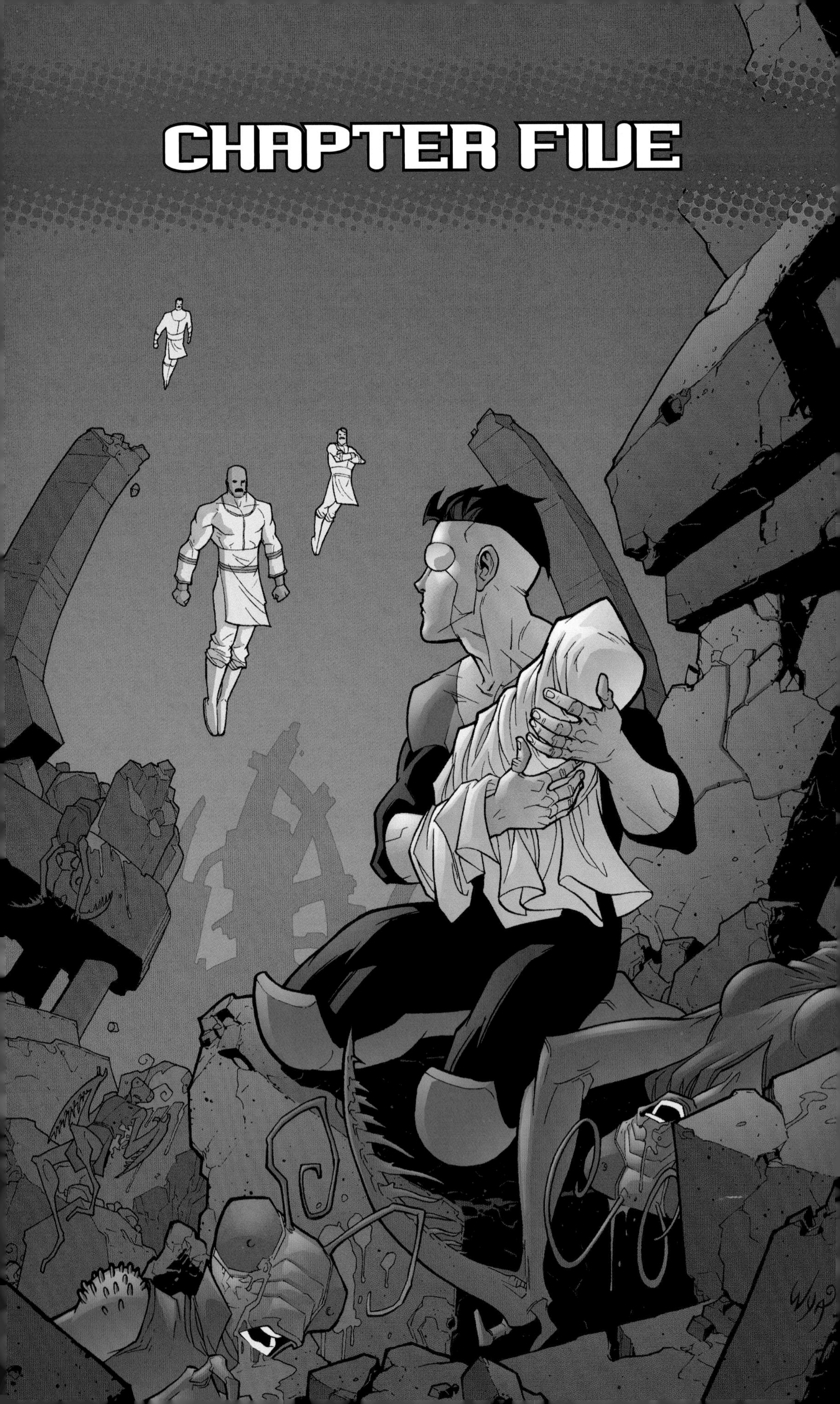
CHAPTER FIVE

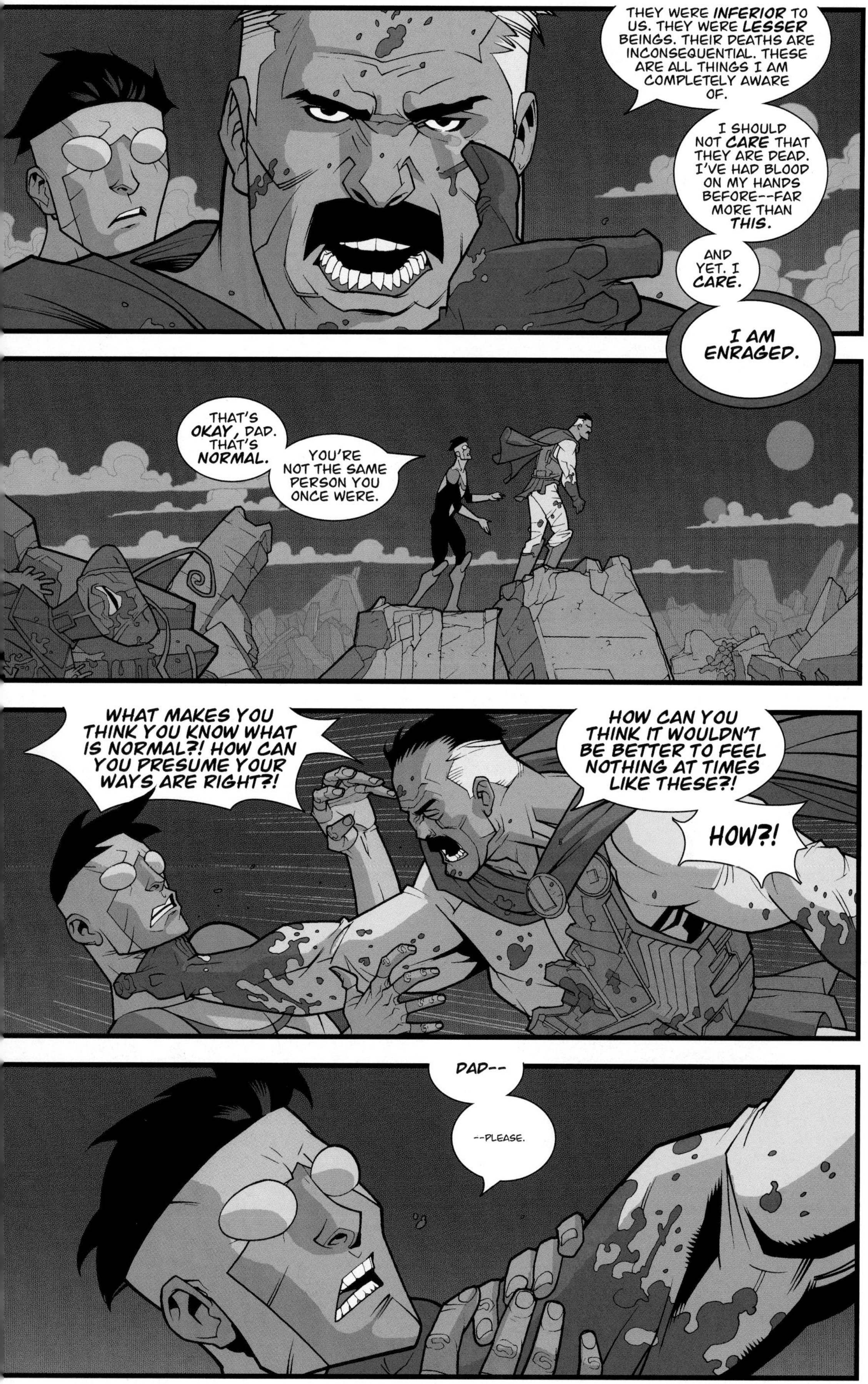
THEY WERE INFERIOR TO US. THEY WERE LESSER BEINGS. THEIR DEATHS ARE INCONSEQUENTIAL. THESE ARE ALL THINGS I AM COMPLETELY AWARE OF.
I SHOULD NOT CARE THAT THEY ARE DEAD. I'VE HAD BLOOD ON MY HANDS BEFORE--FAR MORE THAN THIS.
AND YET. I CARE.
I AM ENRAGED.
THAT'S OKAY, DAD. THAT'S NORMAL.
YOU'RE NOT THE SAME PERSON YOU ONCE WERE.
WHAT MAKES YOU THINK YOU KNOW WHAT IS NORMAL?! HOW CAN YOU PRESUME YOUR WAYS ARE RIGHT?!
HOW CAN YOU THINK IT WOULDN'T BE BETTER TO FEEL NOTHING AT TIMES LIKE THESE?!
HOW?!
DAD--
--PLEASE.

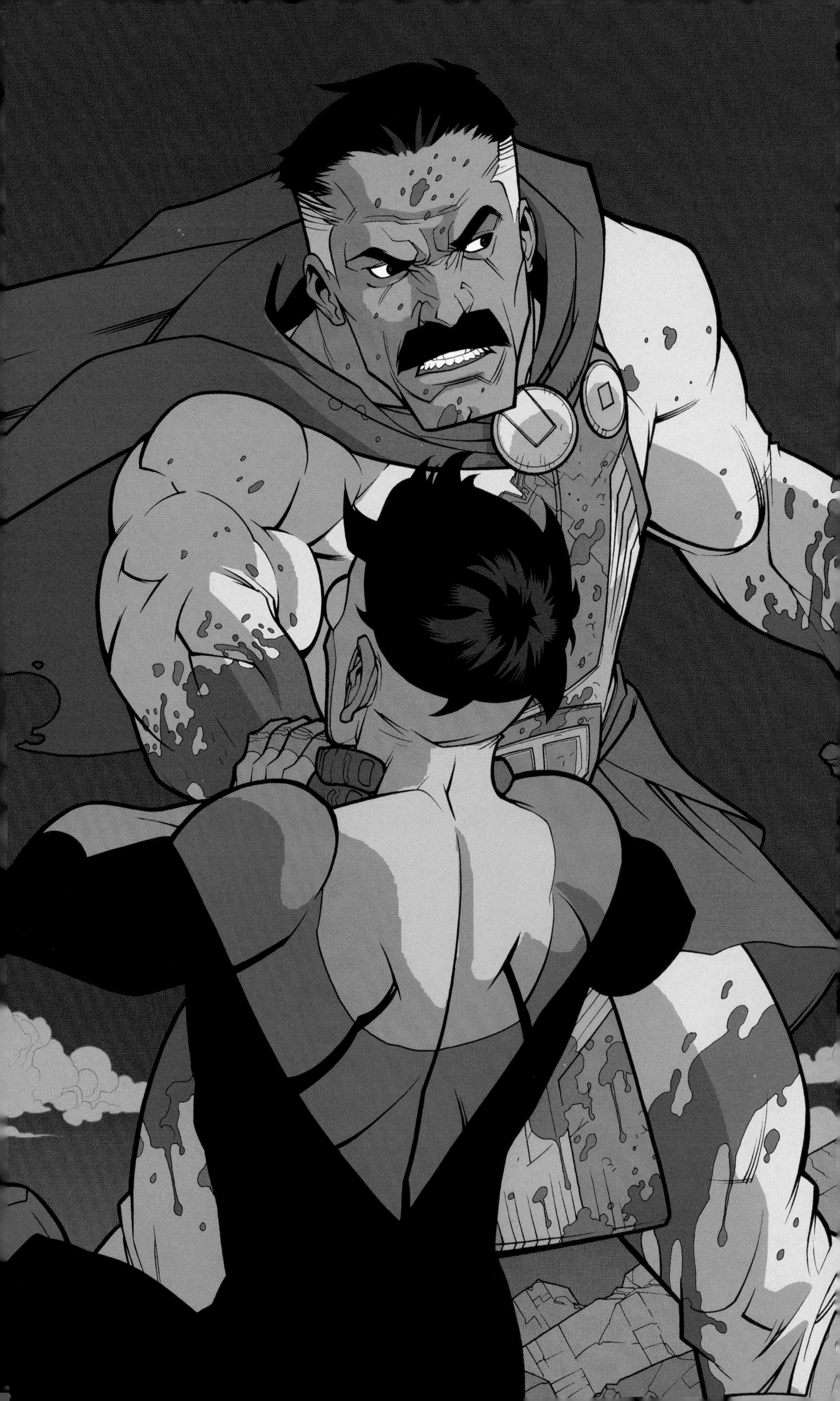

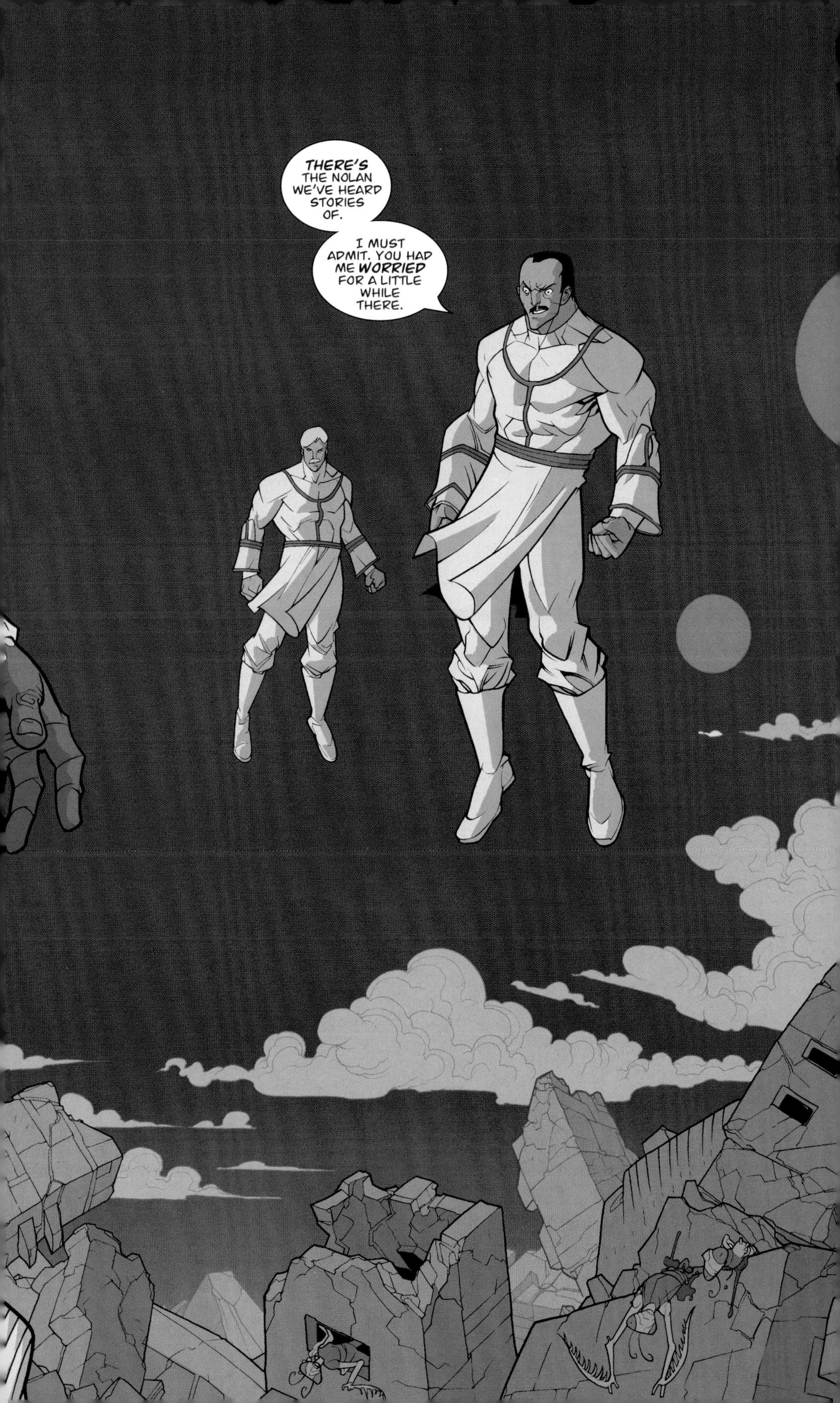
THERE'S THE NOLAN WE'VE HEARD STORIES OF.
I MUST ADMIT. YOU HAD ME WORRIED FOR A LITTLE WHILE THERE.

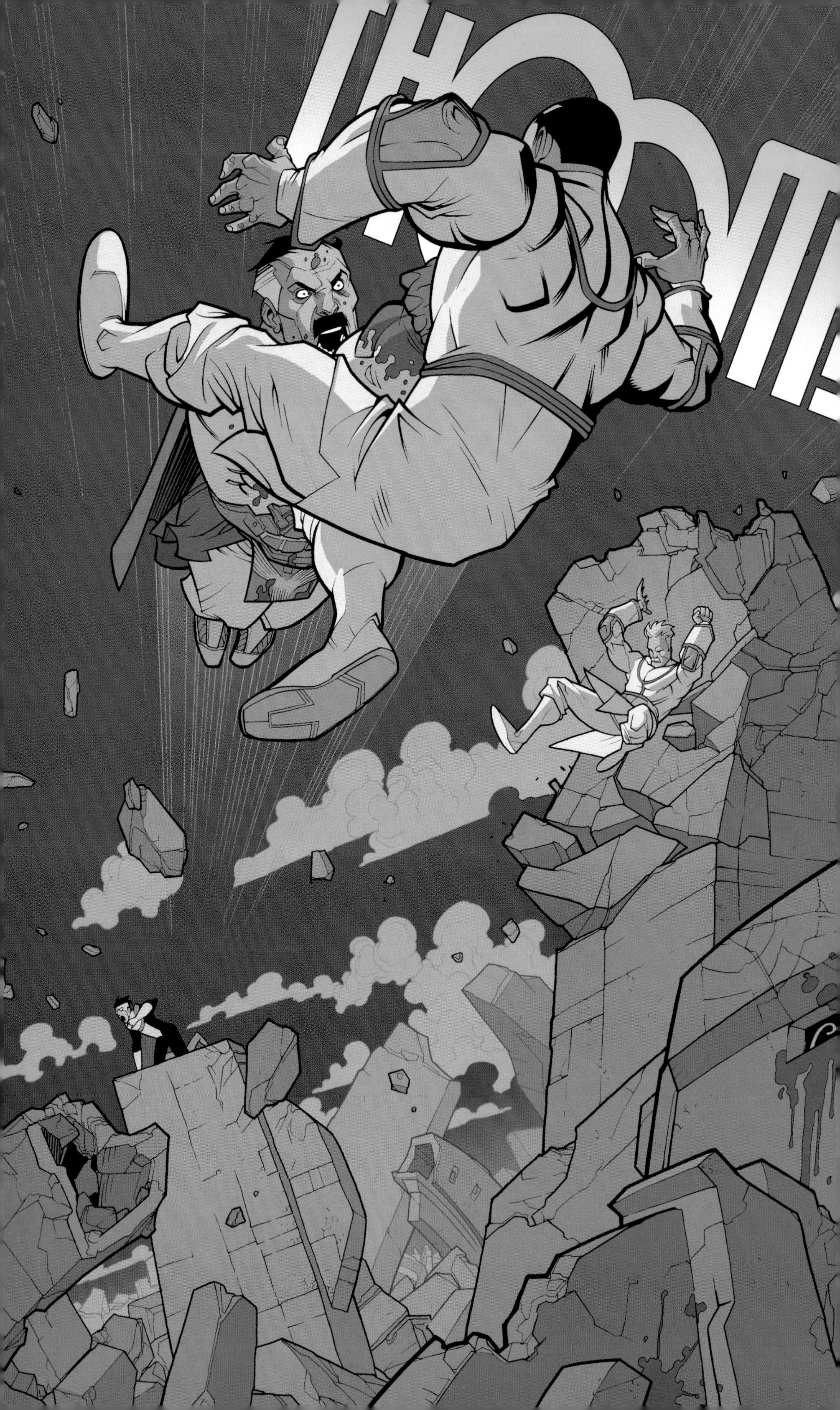
THOOM!

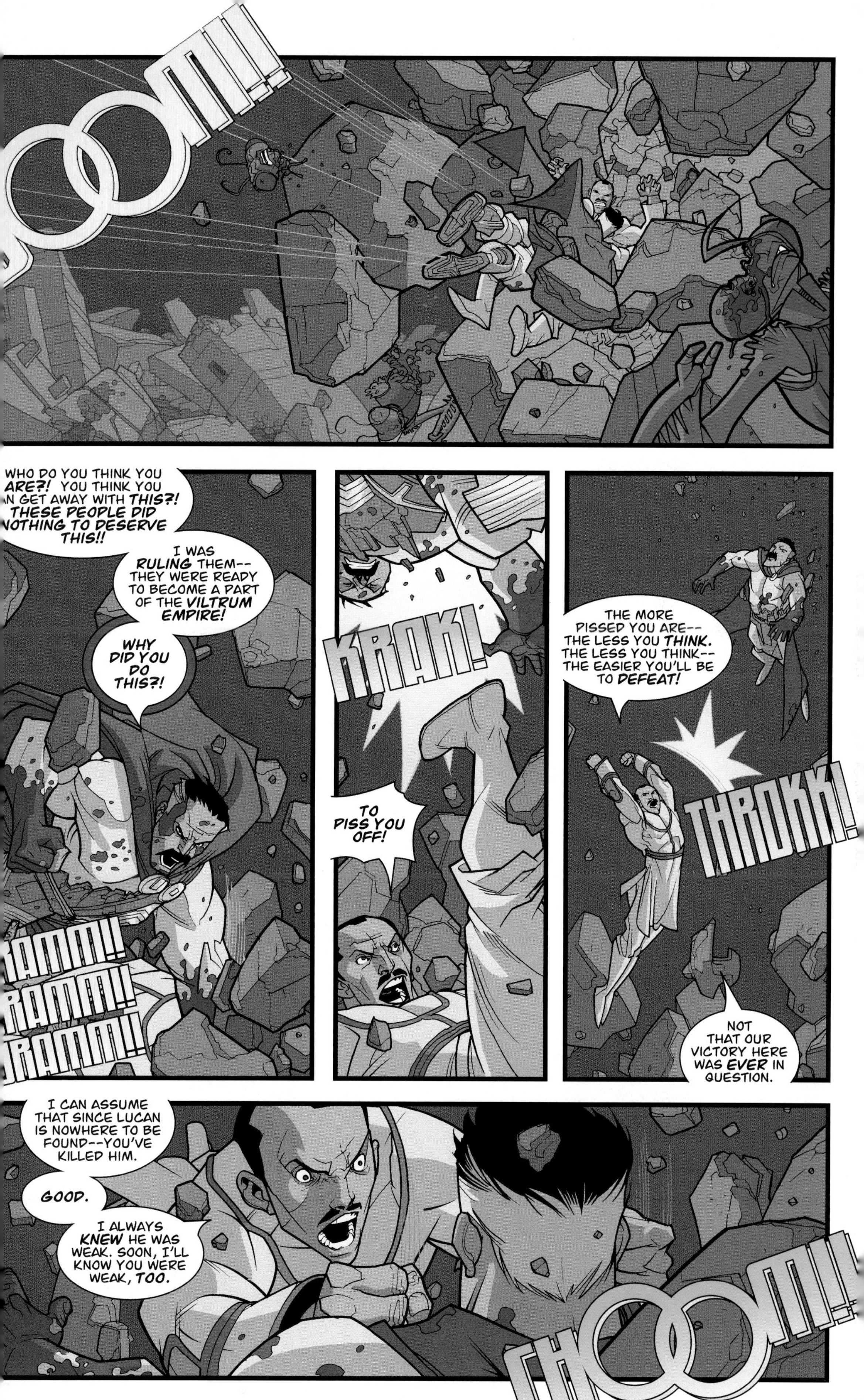
OOOM!!
WHO DO YOU THINK YOU ARE?! YOU THINK YOU N GET AWAY WITH THIS?! THESE PEOPLE DID NOTHING TO DESERVE THIS!!
I WAS RULING THEM-- THEY WERE READY TO BECOME A PART OF THE VILTRUM EMPIRE!
WHY DID YOU DO THIS?!
RAMM!! RAMM!! RAMM!!
KRAK!
TO PISS YOU OFF!
THE MORE PISSED YOU ARE-- THE LESS YOU THINK. THE LESS YOU THINK-- THE EASIER YOU'LL BE TO DEFEAT!
THROKK!
NOT THAT OUR VICTORY HERE WAS EVER IN QUESTION.
I CAN ASSUME THAT SINCE LUCAN IS NOWHERE TO BE FOUND--YOU'VE KILLED HIM.
GOOD.
I ALWAYS KNEW HE WAS WEAK. SOON, I'LL KNOW YOU WERE WEAK, TOO.
CHOOOM!!

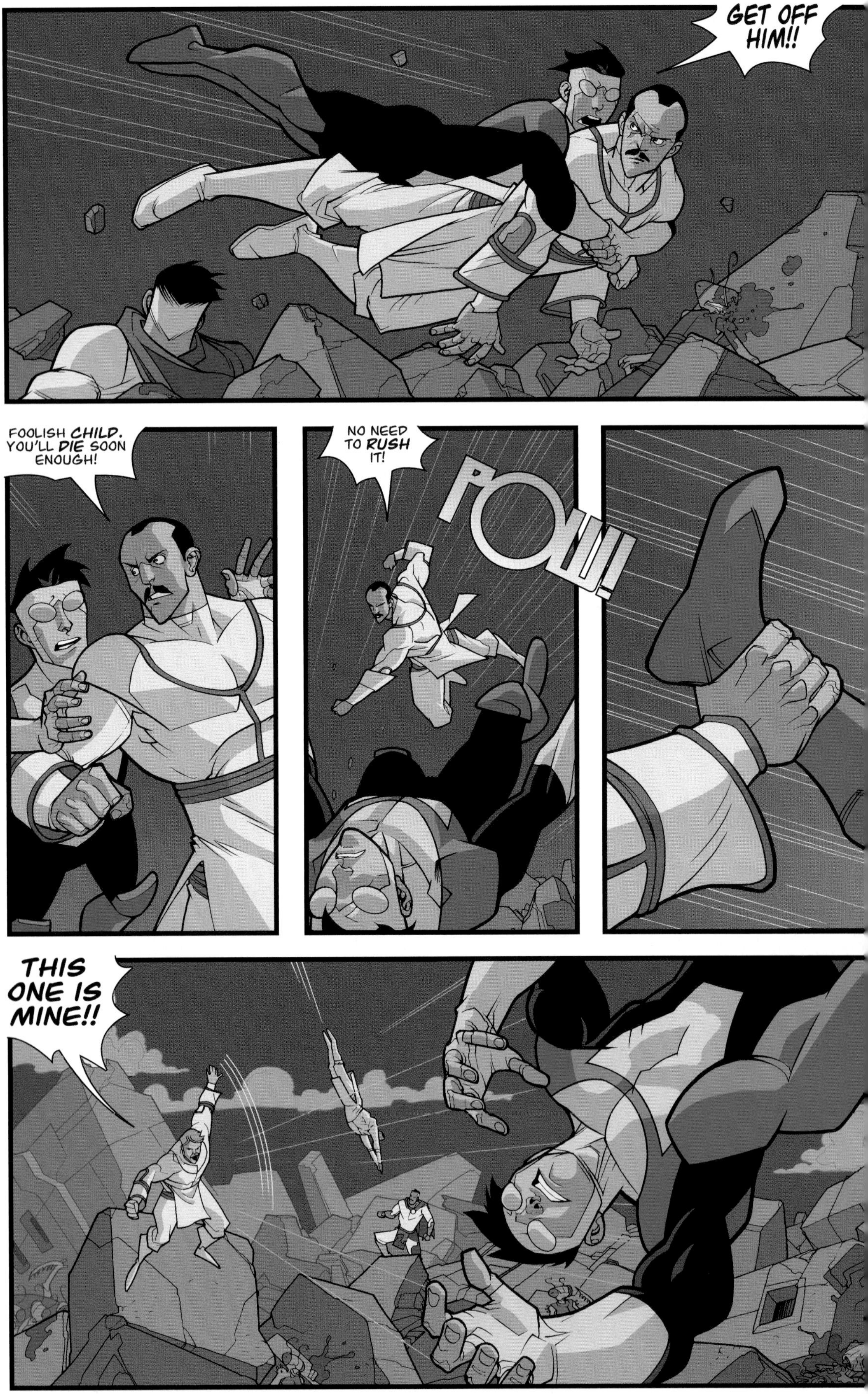
GET OFF HIM!!
FOOLISH CHILD. YOU'LL DIE SOON ENOUGH!
NO NEED TO RUSH IT!
POW!!
THIS ONE IS MINE!!

YOU KNOW-- SOME OF US VILTRIMITES ACTUALLY PREFER TO REMEMBER OUR VICTIMS. THEY THINK IT LEAVES A BETTER MESSAGE. WHEN IT GETS DOWN TO IT, I THINK THEY JUST LIKE MAKING A MESS.

ME? I PREFER TO AVOID A MESS. I LIKE TO SEE THE LOOK IN A VICTIM'S EYES THE SECOND THEY DIE-- I WANT TO EXPERIENCE THE MOMENT THEIR BODY GOES LIMP AND THEIR LIFE ENDS. YOU CAN'T DO THAT IF THEIR EYES ARE ALREADY LYING ON THE GROUND AT THEIR FEET.

I PREFER THINGS TO BE MORE PERSONAL.

WEREN'T ABLE TO TAKE A BREATH WERE YOU? YOU'RE SCARED AREN'T YOU? ADMIT IT... YOU'RE TERRIFIED OF ME. YOU'RE IN WAY OVER YOUR HEAD HERE, CHILD.

DON'T WORRY, THOUGH--IT'LL ALL BE OVER SOON.

VERY SOON.

KROK!

I COMMEND THE EFFORT, I DO, BUT IT WILL HAVE NO EFFECT. YOU ARE AS GOOD AS DEAD.

...

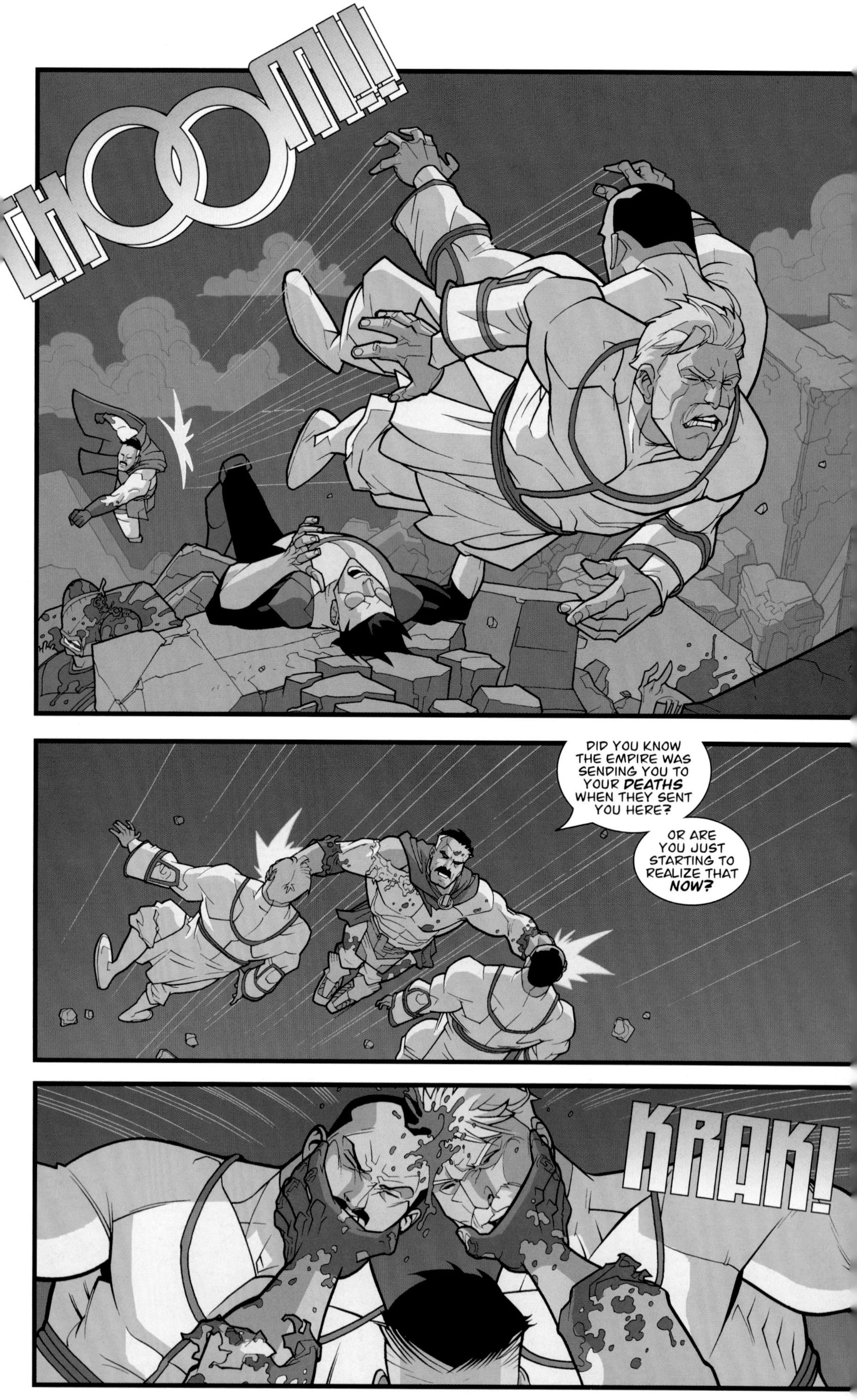
CHOOOM!!!
DID YOU KNOW THE EMPIRE WAS SENDING YOU TO YOUR DEATHS WHEN THEY SENT YOU HERE?
OR ARE YOU JUST STARTING TO REALIZE THAT NOW?
KRAK!

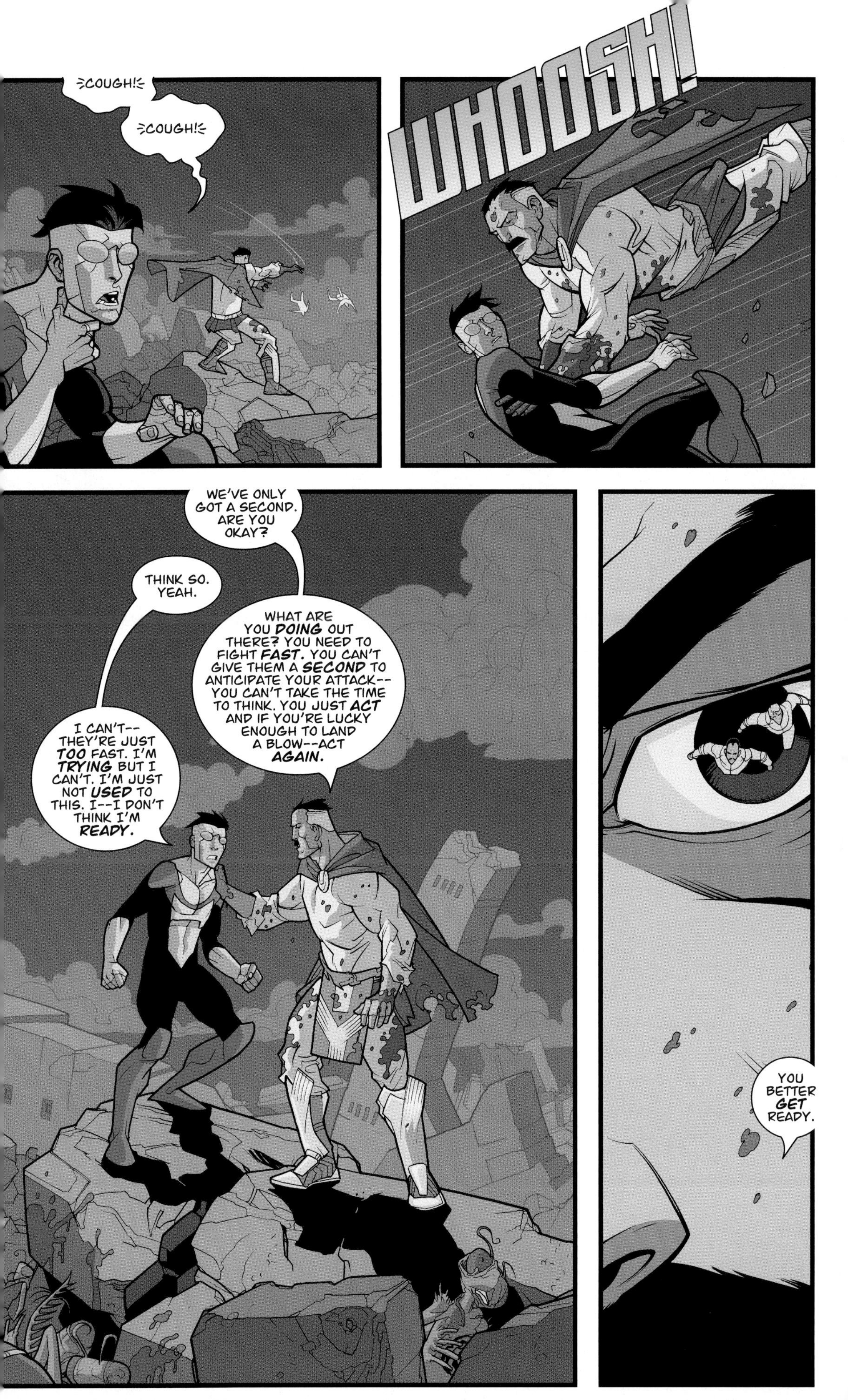
COUGH!
COUGH!
WHOOSH!
WE'VE ONLY GOT A SECOND. ARE YOU OKAY?
THINK SO. YEAH.
WHAT ARE YOU DOING OUT THERE? YOU NEED TO FIGHT FAST. YOU CAN'T GIVE THEM A SECOND TO ANTICIPATE YOUR ATTACK-- YOU CAN'T TAKE THE TIME TO THINK. YOU JUST ACT AND IF YOU'RE LUCKY ENOUGH TO LAND A BLOW--ACT AGAIN.
I CAN'T-- THEY'RE JUST TOO FAST. I'M TRYING BUT I CAN'T. I'M JUST NOT USED TO THIS. I--I DON'T THINK I'M READY.
YOU BETTER GET READY.

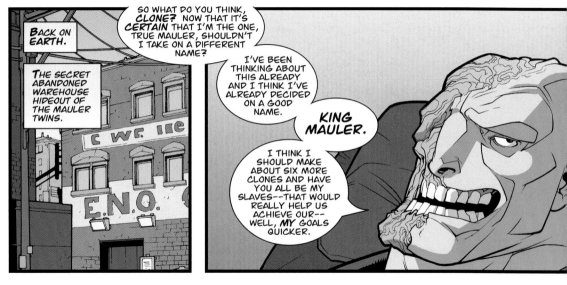

BACK ON EARTH.

THE SECRET ABANDONED WAREHOUSE HIDEOUT OF THE MAULER TWINS.

SO WHAT DO YOU THINK, CLONE? NOW THAT IT'S CERTAIN THAT I'M THE ONE, TRUE MAULER, SHOULDN'T I TAKE ON A DIFFERENT NAME?

I'VE BEEN THINKING ABOUT THIS ALREADY AND I THINK I'VE ALREADY DECIDED ON A GOOD NAME.

KING MAULER.

I THINK I SHOULD MAKE ABOUT SIX MORE CLONES AND HAVE YOU ALL BE MY SLAVES--THAT WOULD REALLY HELP US ACHIEVE OUR-- WELL, MY GOALS QUICKER.

IT'S FUNNY HOW WE NEVER THOUGHT TO HAVE MORE THAN TWO OF US BEFORE, ISN'T IT?

YES--

--FUNNY.

ARE YOU TIRED?! FINE. STOP REARRANGING THINGS AND GET ME SOME MORE LEMONADE.

CONSIDER IT A BREAK.

YES, SIR.

THANK YOU, SIR.

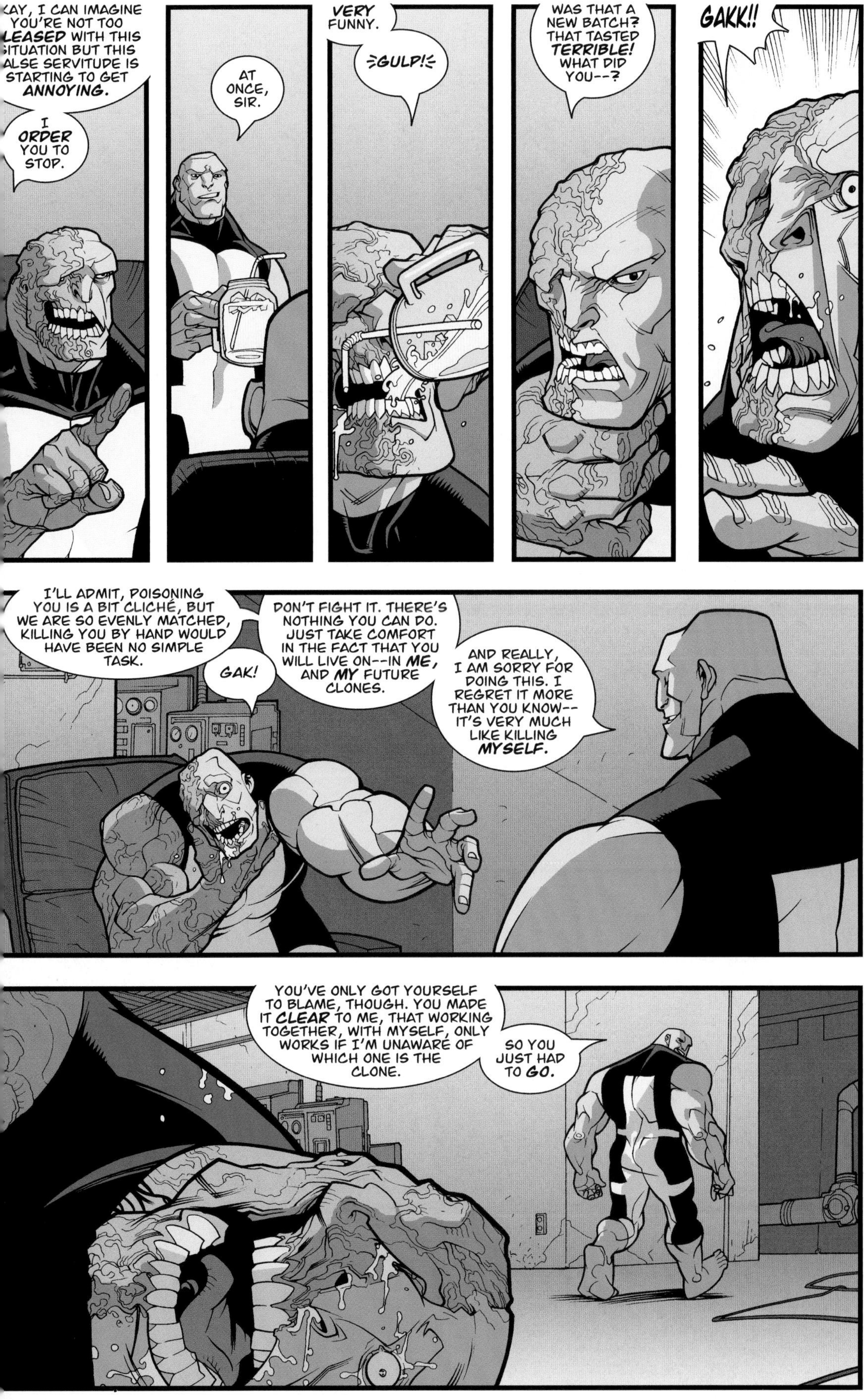
KAY, I CAN IMAGINE YOU'RE NOT TOO LEASED WITH THIS SITUATION BUT THIS ALSE SERVITUDE IS STARTING TO GET ANNOYING.
I ORDER YOU TO STOP.
AT ONCE, SIR.
VERY FUNNY.
GULP!
WAS THAT A NEW BATCH? THAT TASTED TERRIBLE! WHAT DID YOU--?
GAKK!!
I'LL ADMIT, POISONING YOU IS A BIT CLICHÉ, BUT WE ARE SO EVENLY MATCHED, KILLING YOU BY HAND WOULD HAVE BEEN NO SIMPLE TASK.
GAK!
DON'T FIGHT IT. THERE'S NOTHING YOU CAN DO. JUST TAKE COMFORT IN THE FACT THAT YOU WILL LIVE ON--IN ME, AND MY FUTURE CLONES.
AND REALLY, I AM SORRY FOR DOING THIS. I REGRET IT MORE THAN YOU KNOW-- IT'S VERY MUCH LIKE KILLING MYSELF.
YOU'VE ONLY GOT YOURSELF TO BLAME, THOUGH. YOU MADE IT CLEAR TO ME, THAT WORKING TOGETHER, WITH MYSELF, ONLY WORKS IF I'M UNAWARE OF WHICH ONE IS THE CLONE.
SO YOU JUST HAD TO GO.

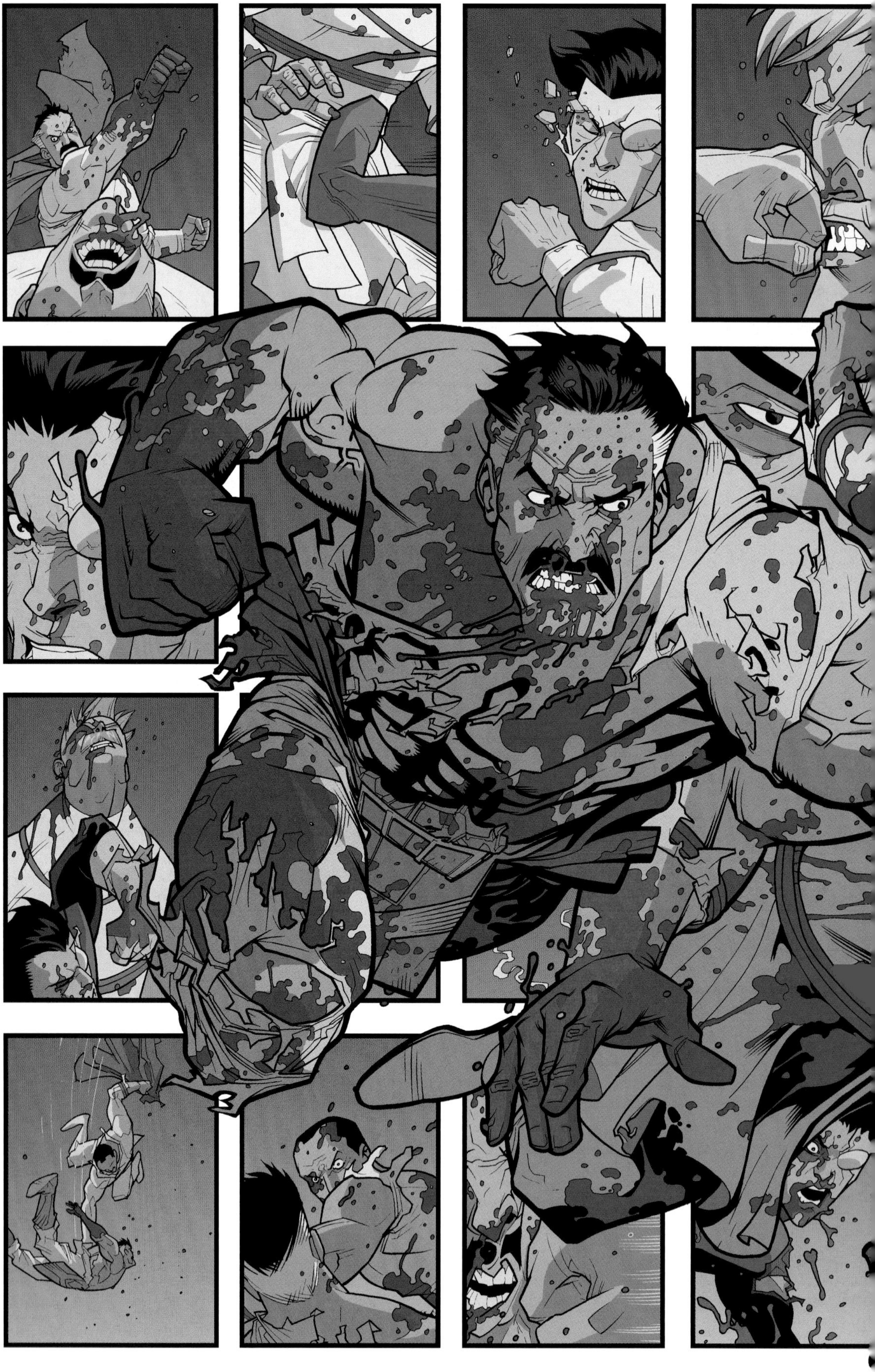

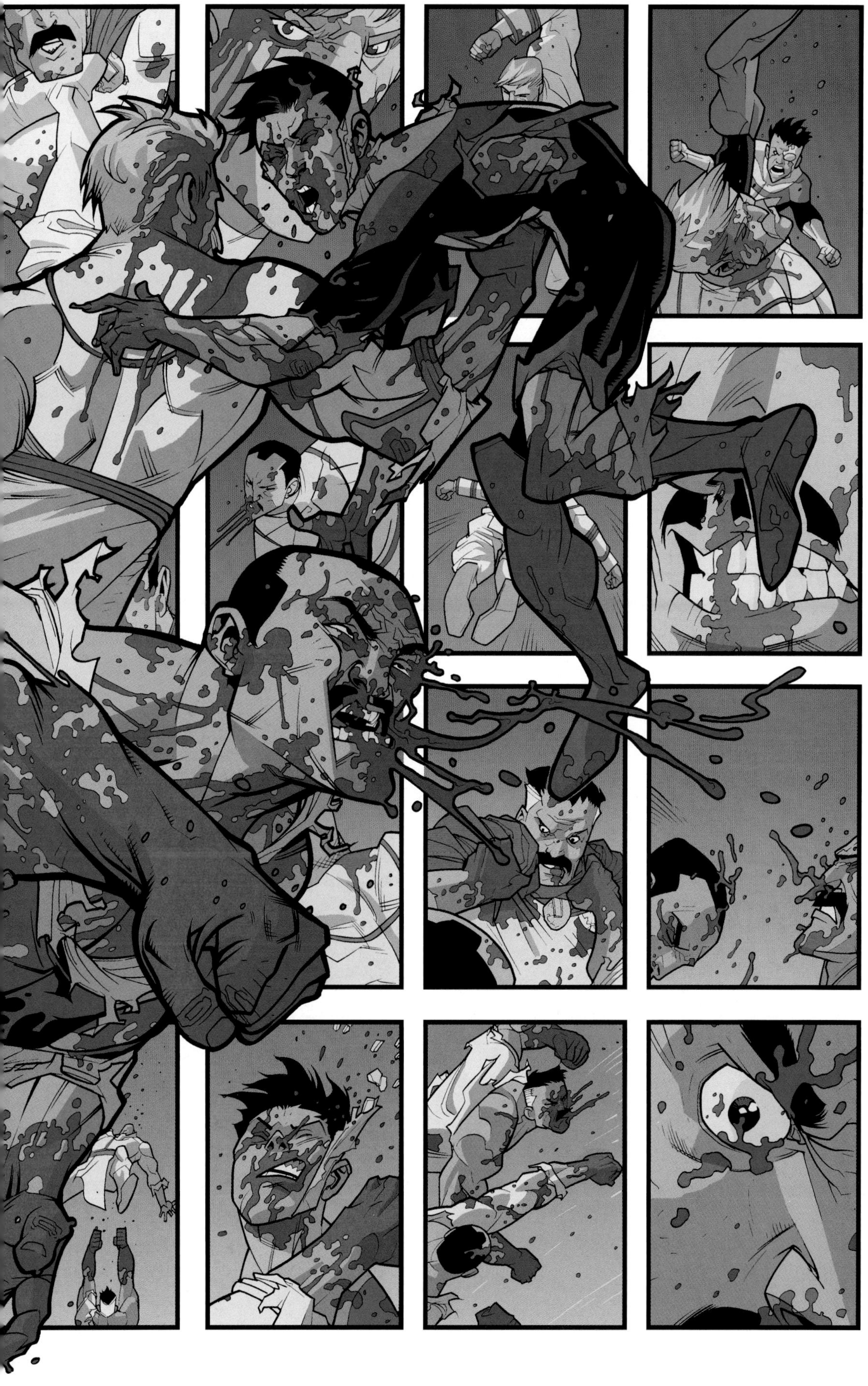

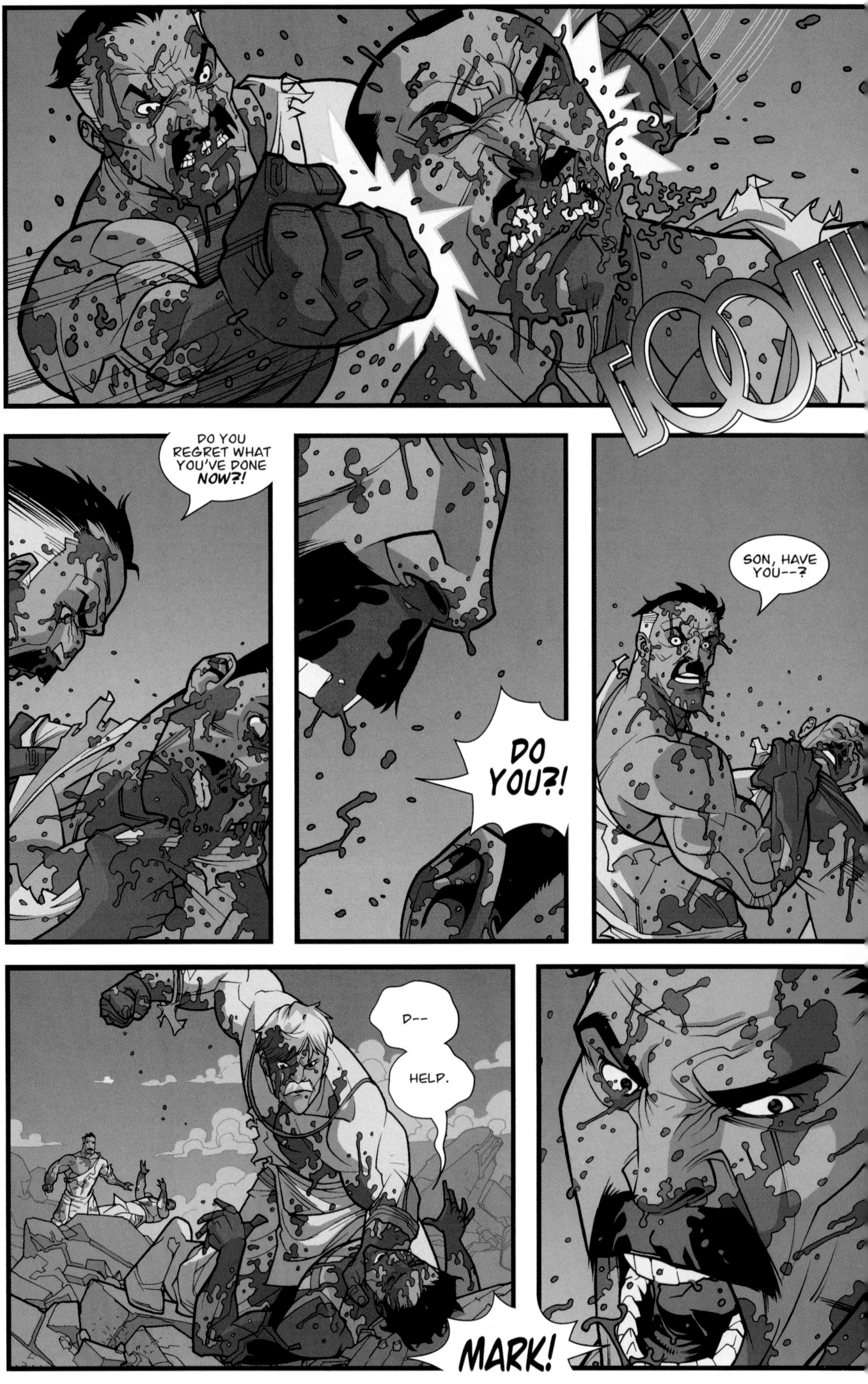
DO YOU REGRET WHAT YOU'VE DONE *NOW?!*
DO YOU?!
SON, HAVE YOU--?
D--
HELP.
MARK!

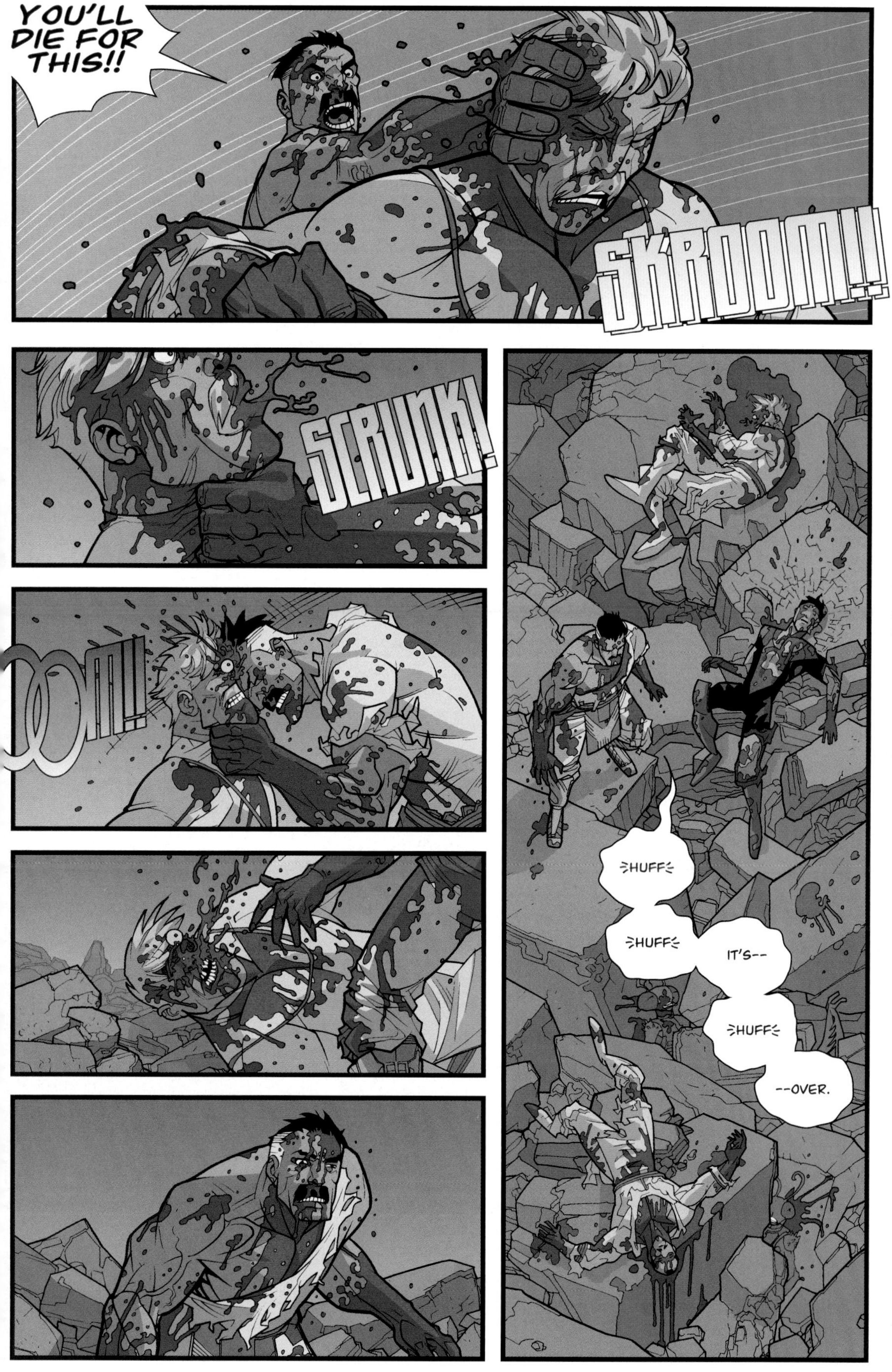
YOU'LL DIE FOR THIS!!
SKROOM!!
SCRUNK!
OOM!!
HUFF
HUFF
IT'S--
HUFF
--OVER.

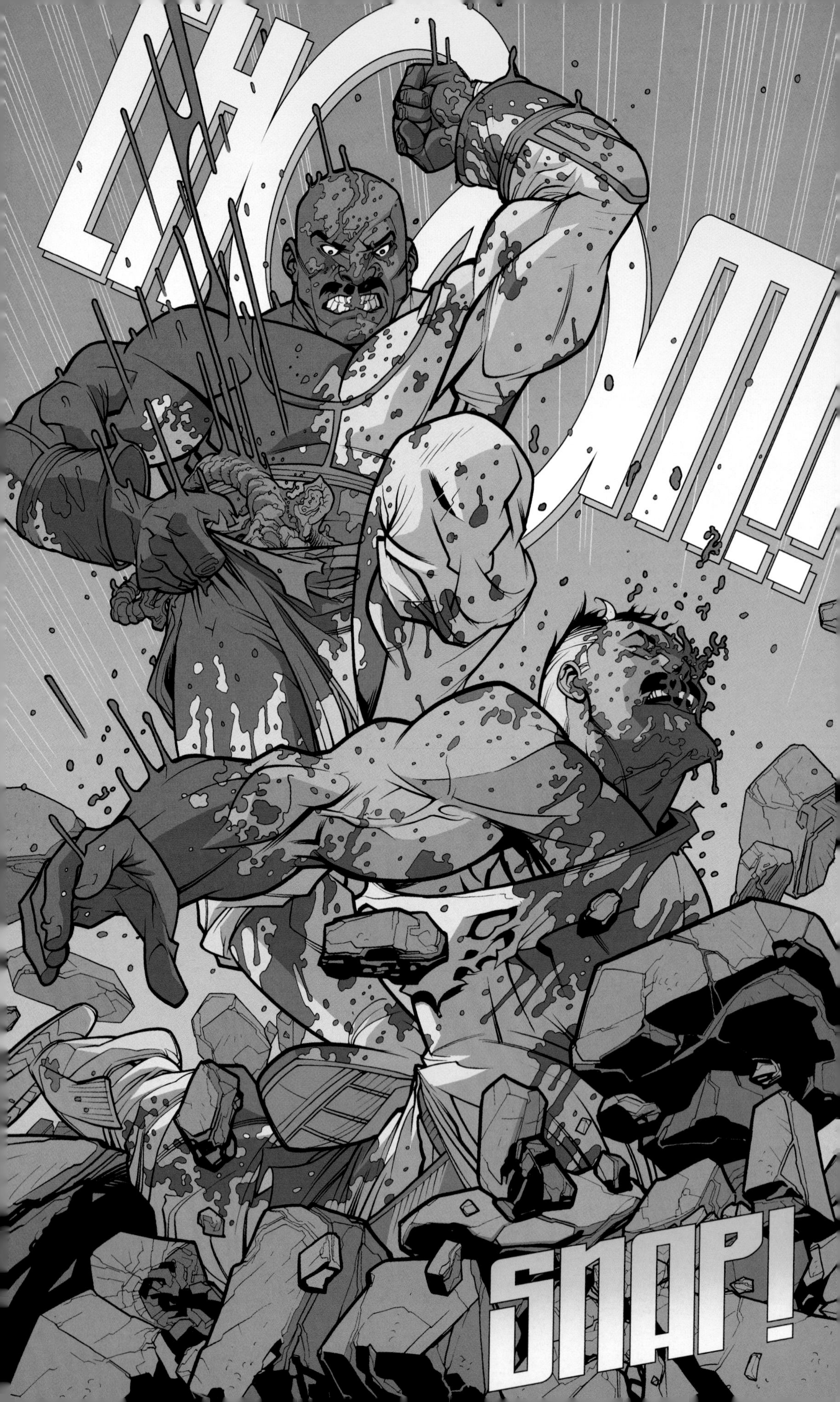
CHOM!!
SNAP!

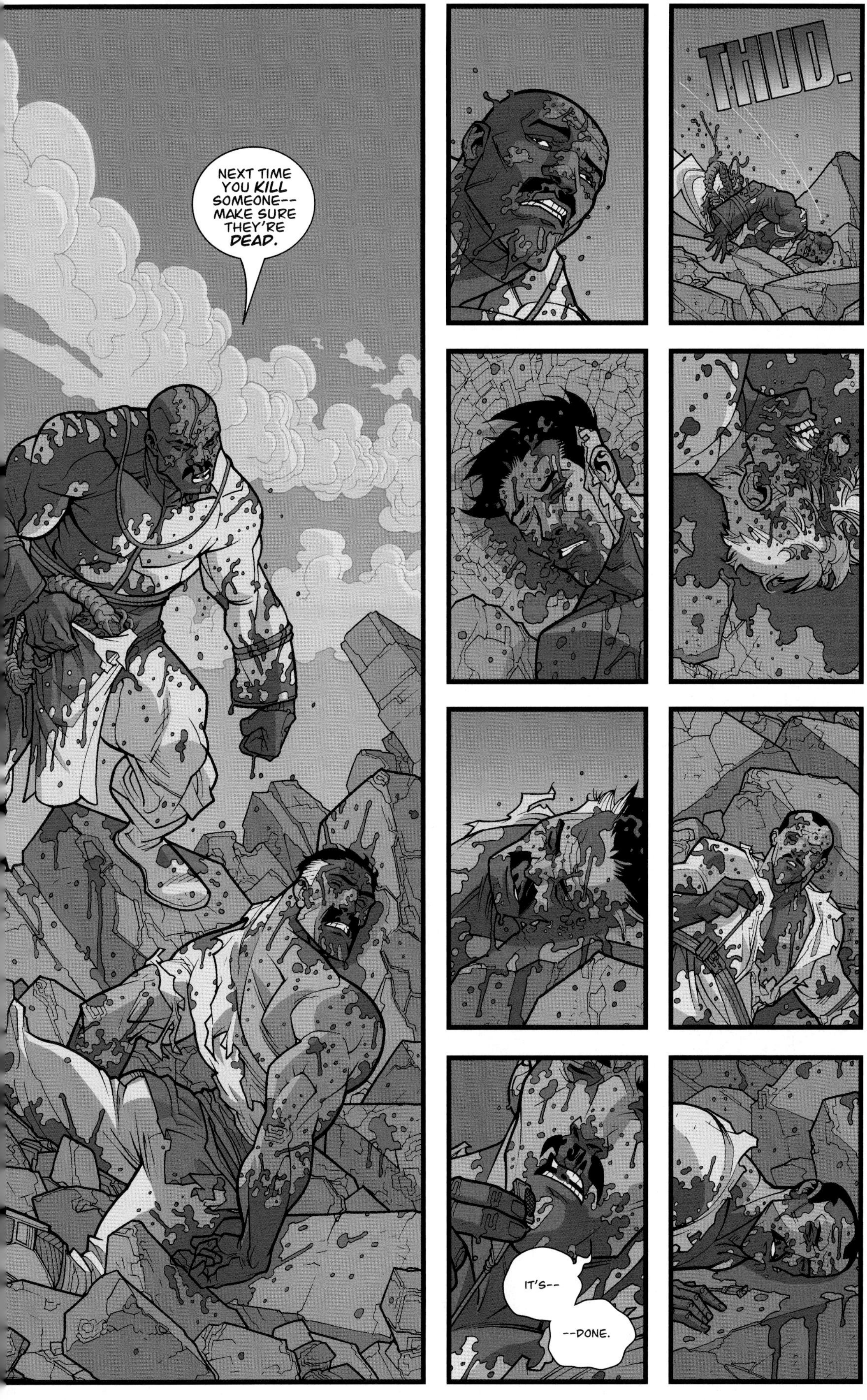

NEXT TIME YOU KILL SOMEONE-- MAKE SURE THEY'RE DEAD.
THUD.
IT'S--
--DONE.

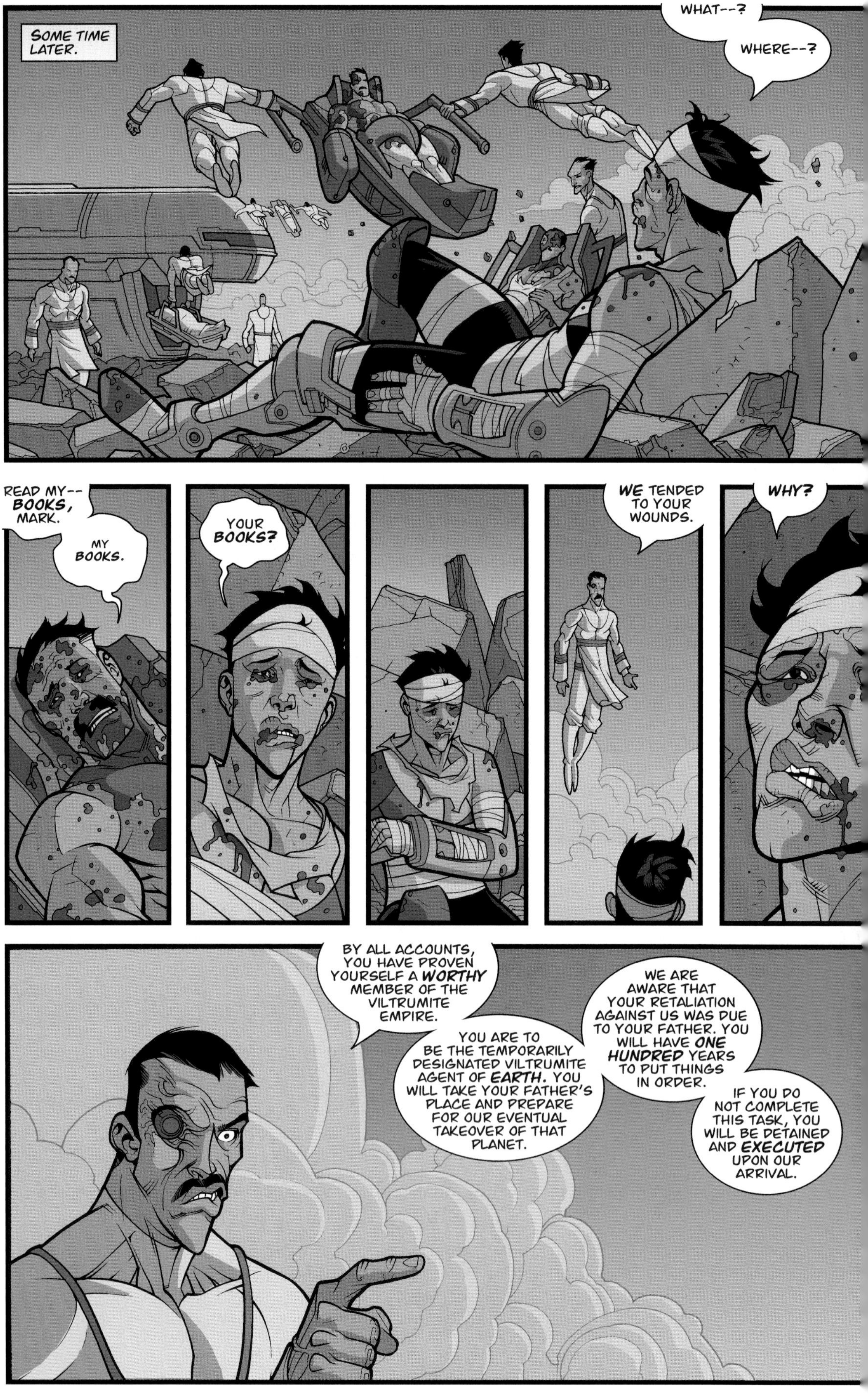
SOME TIME LATER.
WHAT--?
WHERE--?
READ MY-- BOOKS, MARK.
MY BOOKS.
YOUR BOOKS?
WE TENDED TO YOUR WOUNDS.
WHY?
BY ALL ACCOUNTS, YOU HAVE PROVEN YOURSELF A WORTHY MEMBER OF THE VILTRUMITE EMPIRE.
YOU ARE TO BE THE TEMPORARILY DESIGNATED VILTRUMITE AGENT OF EARTH. YOU WILL TAKE YOUR FATHER'S PLACE AND PREPARE FOR OUR EVENTUAL TAKEOVER OF THAT PLANET.
WE ARE AWARE THAT YOUR RETALIATION AGAINST US WAS DUE TO YOUR FATHER. YOU WILL HAVE ONE HUNDRED YEARS TO PUT THINGS IN ORDER.
IF YOU DO NOT COMPLETE THIS TASK, YOU WILL BE DETAINED AND EXECUTED UPON OUR ARRIVAL.

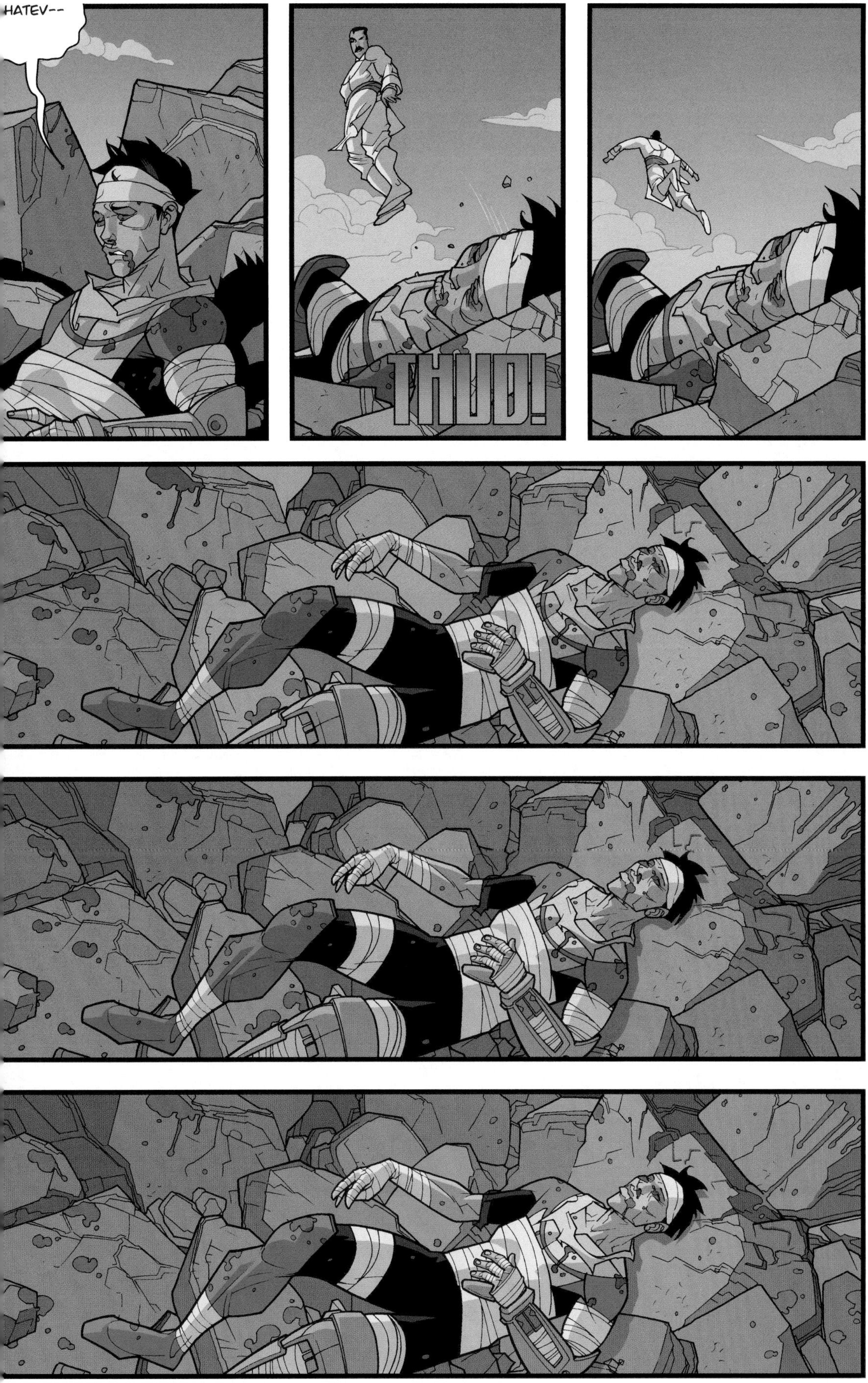
HATEV--
THUD!

THE NEXT DAY.

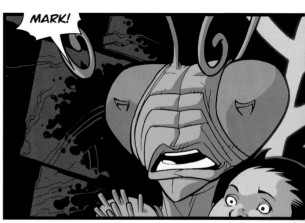

MARK!

I--

WHERE IS NOLAN-- WHERE IS MY HUSBAND?!

HE'S GONE.

THEY TOOK HIM.

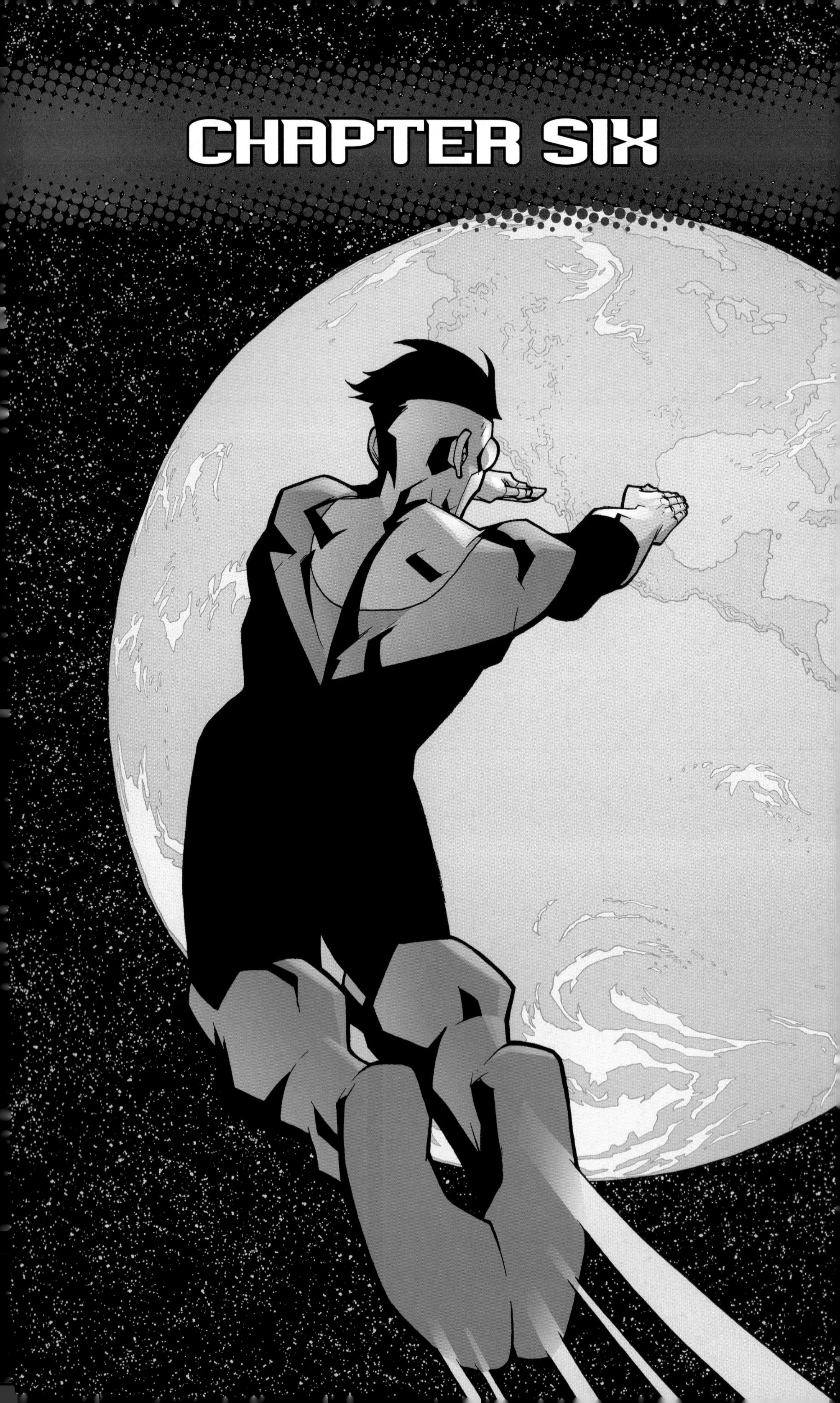
CHAPTER SIX

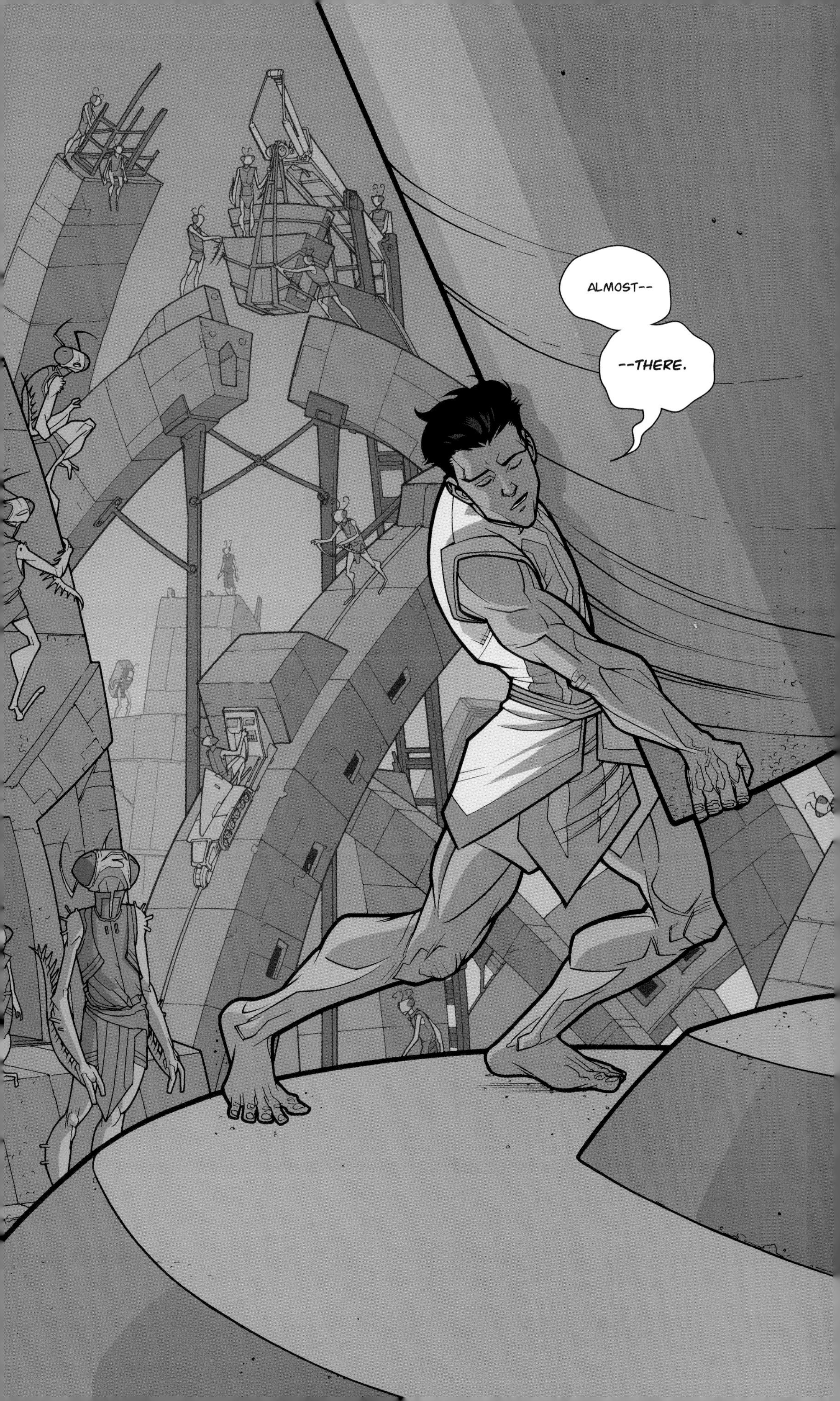
ALMOST--
--THERE.

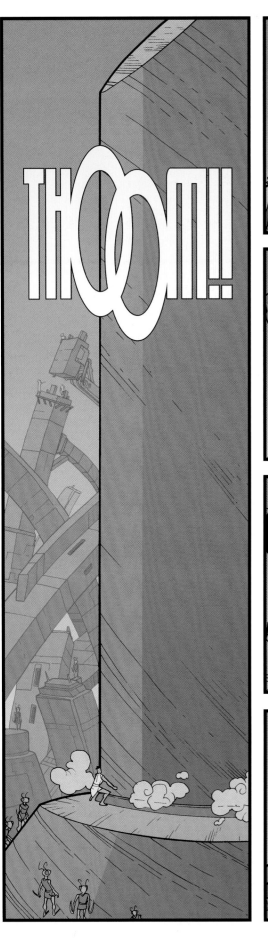

THERE-- THAT'LL DO IT.

VERY GOOD, MARK. THIS BEAM WILL BE THE SUPPORT STRUCTURE FOR A **GRAND PALACE** THAT WILL BE BUILT HERE. I CAN'T THANK YOU ENOUGH FOR ALL YOU'VE DONE.

WITHOUT YOU-- THIS CLEANUP WOULD HAVE TAKEN **GENERATIONS,** BUT WITH YOUR HELP I MAY VERY WELL SEE THE REBIRTH OF OUR GREAT CITY IN MY LIFETIME.

I'M JUST GLAD I COULD HELP--AFTER EVERYTHING YOUR PEOPLE HAVE GONE THROUGH, IT'S THE **LEAST** I COULD DO.

I'M SORRY FOR THE INTERRUPTION, QUEEN ANDRESSA--BUT YOU TOLD ME TO INFORM YOU THE MINUTE A NEW **SPACE VESSEL** WAS COMPLETED THAT COULD RETURN THE MARK GRAYSON TO HIS PLANET.

IT'S READY.

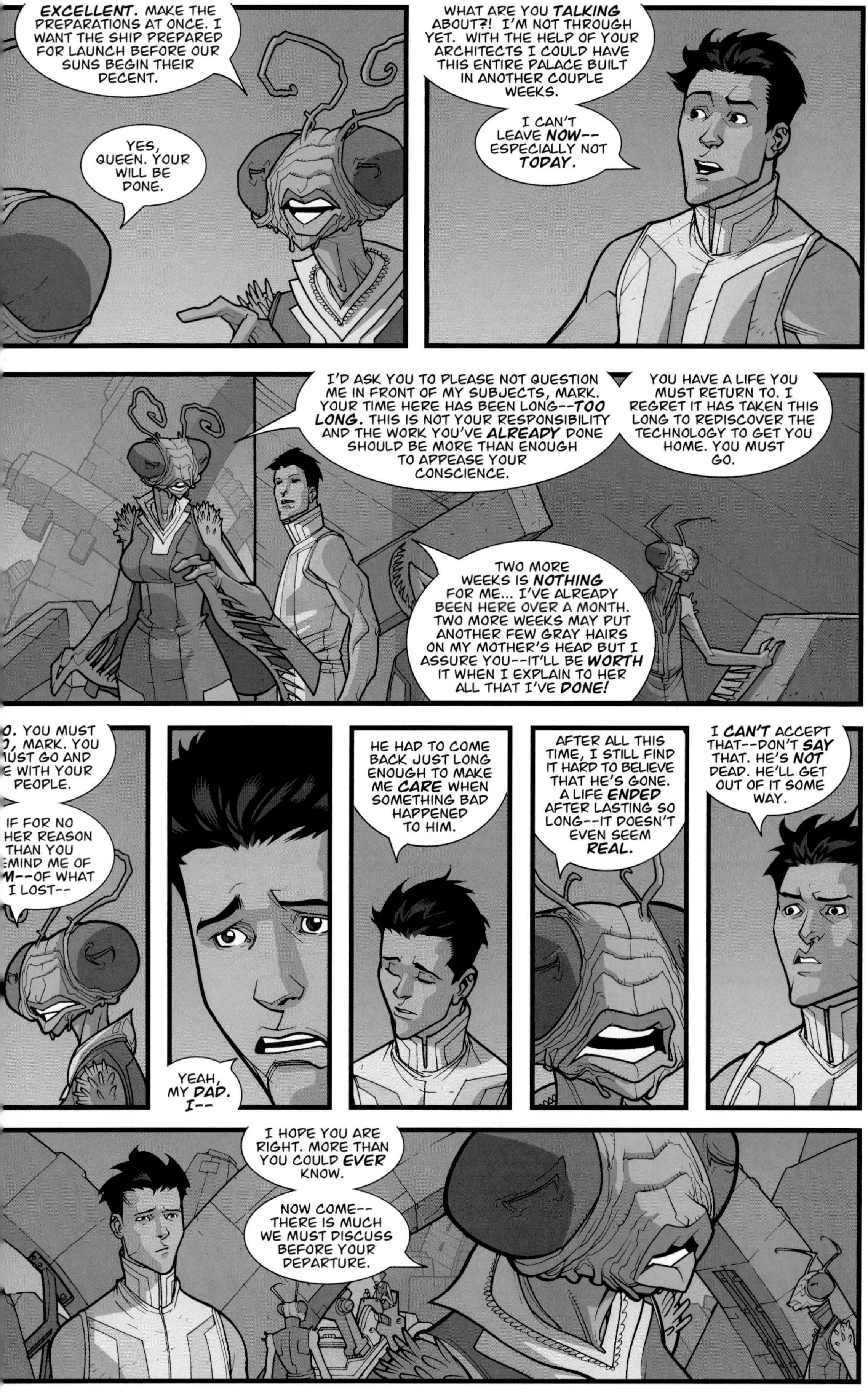
EXCELLENT. MAKE THE PREPARATIONS AT ONCE. I WANT THE SHIP PREPARED FOR LAUNCH BEFORE OUR SUNS BEGIN THEIR DECENT.
YES, QUEEN. YOUR WILL BE DONE.
WHAT ARE YOU TALKING ABOUT?! I'M NOT THROUGH YET. WITH THE HELP OF YOUR ARCHITECTS I COULD HAVE THIS ENTIRE PALACE BUILT IN ANOTHER COUPLE WEEKS.
I CAN'T LEAVE NOW-- ESPECIALLY NOT TODAY.
I'D ASK YOU TO PLEASE NOT QUESTION ME IN FRONT OF MY SUBJECTS, MARK. YOUR TIME HERE HAS BEEN LONG--TOO LONG. THIS IS NOT YOUR RESPONSIBILITY AND THE WORK YOU'VE ALREADY DONE SHOULD BE MORE THAN ENOUGH TO APPEASE YOUR CONSCIENCE.
YOU HAVE A LIFE YOU MUST RETURN TO. I REGRET IT HAS TAKEN THIS LONG TO REDISCOVER THE TECHNOLOGY TO GET YOU HOME. YOU MUST GO.
TWO MORE WEEKS IS NOTHING FOR ME... I'VE ALREADY BEEN HERE OVER A MONTH. TWO MORE WEEKS MAY PUT ANOTHER FEW GRAY HAIRS ON MY MOTHER'S HEAD BUT I ASSURE YOU--IT'LL BE WORTH IT WHEN I EXPLAIN TO HER ALL THAT I'VE DONE!
YOU MUST , MARK. YOU UST GO AND WITH YOUR PEOPLE.
IF FOR NO HER REASON THAN YOU EMIND ME OF M--OF WHAT I LOST--
YEAH, MY DAD. I--
HE HAD TO COME BACK JUST LONG ENOUGH TO MAKE ME CARE WHEN SOMETHING BAD HAPPENED TO HIM.
AFTER ALL THIS TIME, I STILL FIND IT HARD TO BELIEVE THAT HE'S GONE. A LIFE ENDED AFTER LASTING SO LONG--IT DOESN'T EVEN SEEM REAL.
I CAN'T ACCEPT THAT--DON'T SAY THAT. HE'S NOT DEAD. HE'LL GET OUT OF IT SOME WAY.
I HOPE YOU ARE RIGHT. MORE THAN YOU COULD EVER KNOW.
NOW COME-- THERE IS MUCH WE MUST DISCUSS BEFORE YOUR DEPARTURE.

WHAT IS IT YOU WANT TO TALK TO ME ABOUT?

YOUR BROTHER.

BROTHER!

HEY, LITTLE GUY. YOU BEEN PLAYING?

WHAT *ABOUT* HIM?

LOOK AT ME, MARK. WHAT DO YOU *THINK* I WANT TO TALK TO YOU ABOUT?

I'M NOT FOLLOWING YOU. YOU'RE NOT SAYING--

DON'T YOU SEE HOW *MUCH* I'VE AGED SINCE YOU GOT HERE? I UNDERSTAND THAT TO YOU NOT MUCH TIME HAS PASSED--BUT FOR ME--

MARK, BY YOUR STANDARDS I DON'T HAVE MUCH TIME LEFT TO LIVE. BY *HIS* STANDARDS I DON'T--

ANDRESSA PLEASE--H YOUR SON. Y CAN'T ASK ME TO--

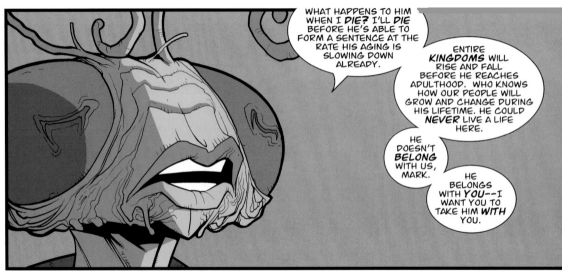

WHAT HAPPENS TO HIM WHEN I *DIE?* I'LL *DIE* BEFORE HE'S ABLE TO FORM A SENTENCE AT THE RATE HIS AGING IS SLOWING DOWN ALREADY.

ENTIRE *KINGDOMS* WILL RISE AND FALL BEFORE HE REACHES ADULTHOOD. WHO KNOWS HOW OUR PEOPLE WILL GROW AND CHANGE DURING HIS LIFETIME. HE COULD *NEVER* LIVE A LIFE HERE.

HE DOESN'T *BELONG* WITH US, MARK.

HE BELONGS WITH *YOU*--I WANT YOU TO TAKE HIM *WITH* YOU.

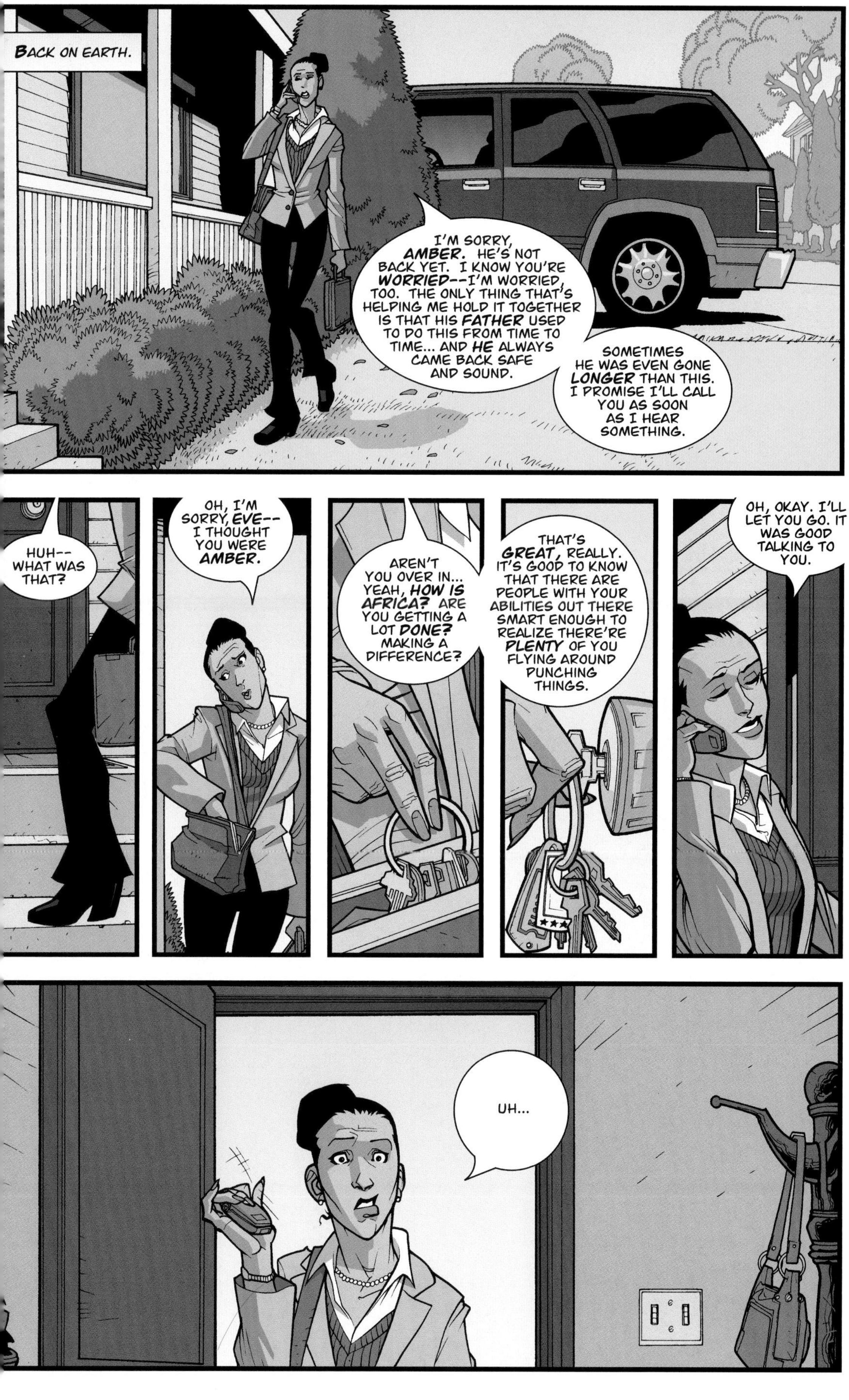
BACK ON EARTH.
I'M SORRY, AMBER. HE'S NOT BACK YET. I KNOW YOU'RE WORRIED--I'M WORRIED, TOO. THE ONLY THING THAT'S HELPING ME HOLD IT TOGETHER IS THAT HIS FATHER USED TO DO THIS FROM TIME TO TIME... AND HE ALWAYS CAME BACK SAFE AND SOUND.
SOMETIMES HE WAS EVEN GONE LONGER THAN THIS. I PROMISE I'LL CALL YOU AS SOON AS I HEAR SOMETHING.
HUH--WHAT WAS THAT?
OH, I'M SORRY, EVE--I THOUGHT YOU WERE AMBER.
AREN'T YOU OVER IN... YEAH, HOW IS AFRICA? ARE YOU GETTING A LOT DONE? MAKING A DIFFERENCE?
THAT'S GREAT, REALLY. IT'S GOOD TO KNOW THAT THERE ARE PEOPLE WITH YOUR ABILITIES OUT THERE SMART ENOUGH TO REALIZE THERE'RE PLENTY OF YOU FLYING AROUND PUNCHING THINGS.
OH, OKAY. I'LL LET YOU GO. IT WAS GOOD TALKING TO YOU.
UH...

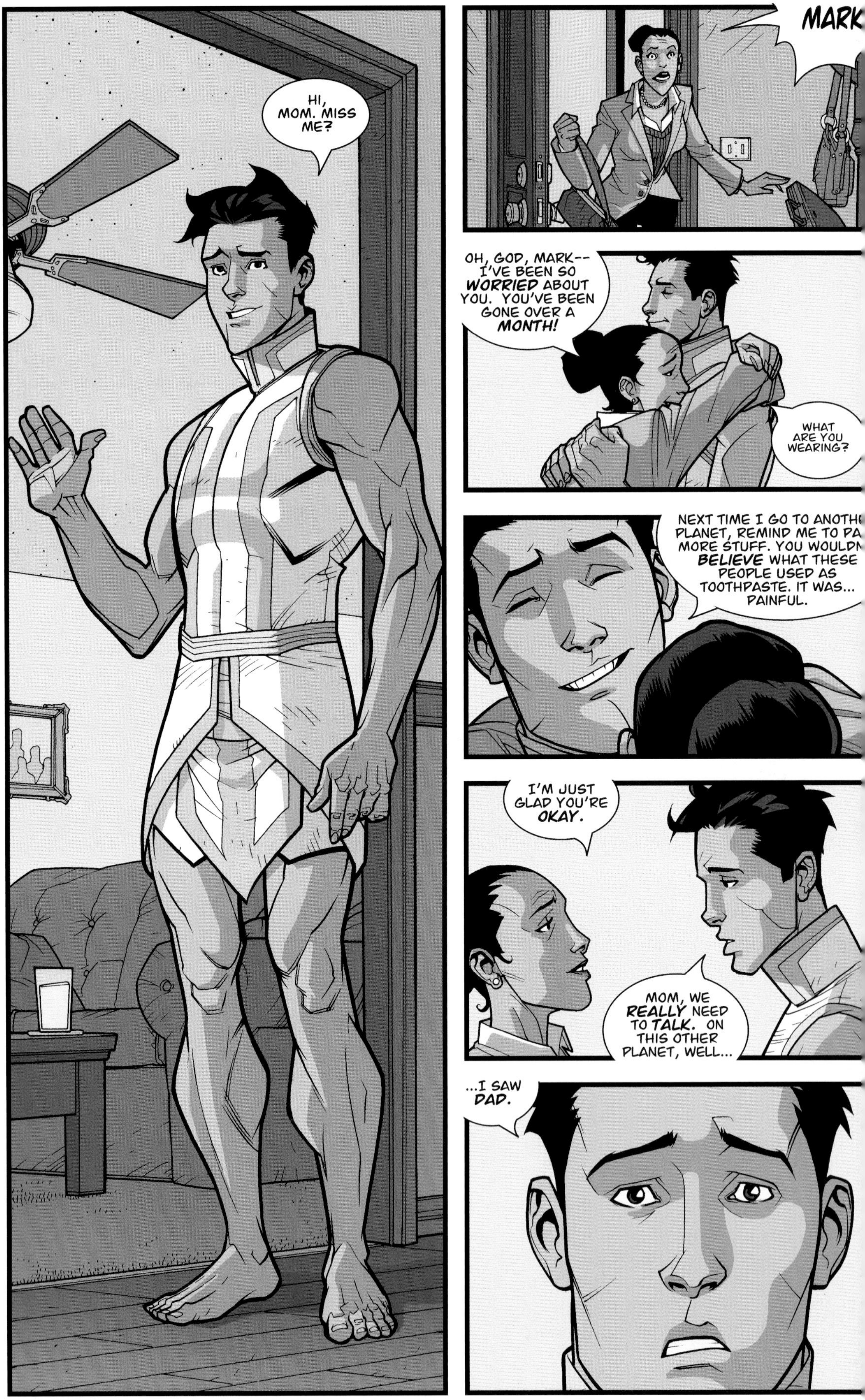

HI, MOM. MISS ME?
MARK
OH, GOD, MARK-- I'VE BEEN SO WORRIED ABOUT YOU. YOU'VE BEEN GONE OVER A MONTH!
WHAT ARE YOU WEARING?
NEXT TIME I GO TO ANOTH PLANET, REMIND ME TO PA MORE STUFF. YOU WOULDN BELIEVE WHAT THESE PEOPLE USED AS TOOTHPASTE. IT WAS... PAINFUL.
I'M JUST GLAD YOU'RE OKAY.
MOM, WE REALLY NEED TO TALK. ON THIS OTHER PLANET, WELL...
...I SAW DAD.

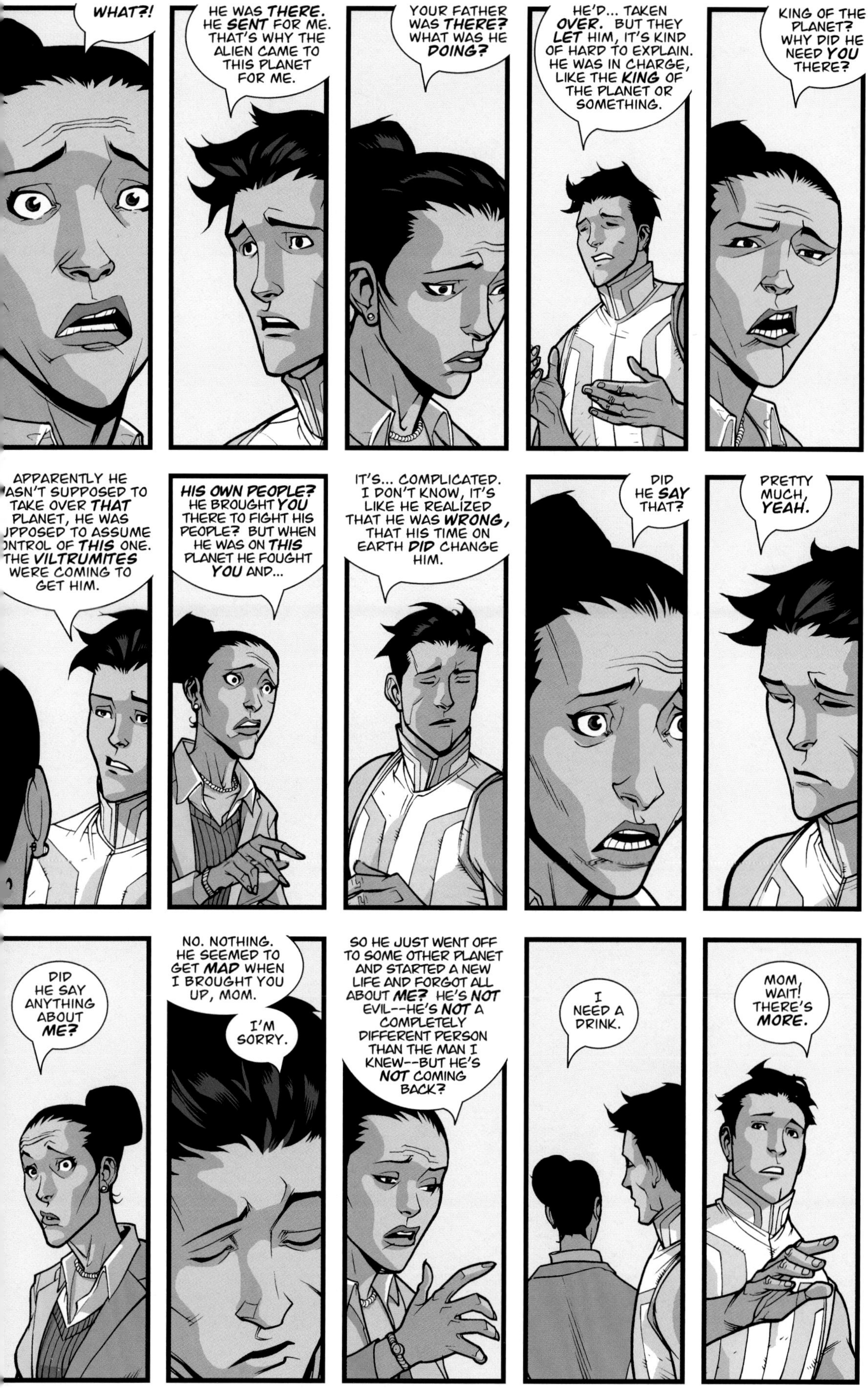
WHAT?!
HE WAS THERE. HE SENT FOR ME. THAT'S WHY THE ALIEN CAME TO THIS PLANET FOR ME.
YOUR FATHER WAS THERE? WHAT WAS HE DOING?
HE'D... TAKEN OVER. BUT THEY LET HIM, IT'S KIND OF HARD TO EXPLAIN. HE WAS IN CHARGE, LIKE THE KING OF THE PLANET OR SOMETHING.
KING OF THE PLANET? WHY DID HE NEED YOU THERE?
APPARENTLY HE ASN'T SUPPOSED TO TAKE OVER THAT PLANET, HE WAS UPPOSED TO ASSUME ONTROL OF THIS ONE. THE VILTRUMITES WERE COMING TO GET HIM.
HIS OWN PEOPLE? HE BROUGHT YOU THERE TO FIGHT HIS PEOPLE? BUT WHEN HE WAS ON THIS PLANET HE FOUGHT YOU AND...
IT'S... COMPLICATED. I DON'T KNOW, IT'S LIKE HE REALIZED THAT HE WAS WRONG, THAT HIS TIME ON EARTH DID CHANGE HIM.
DID HE SAY THAT?
PRETTY MUCH, YEAH.
DID HE SAY ANYTHING ABOUT ME?
NO. NOTHING. HE SEEMED TO GET MAD WHEN I BROUGHT YOU UP, MOM.
I'M SORRY.
SO HE JUST WENT OFF TO SOME OTHER PLANET AND STARTED A NEW LIFE AND FORGOT ALL ABOUT ME? HE'S NOT EVIL--HE'S NOT A COMPLETELY DIFFERENT PERSON THAN THE MAN I KNEW--BUT HE'S NOT COMING BACK?
I NEED A DRINK.
MOM, WAIT! THERE'S MORE.

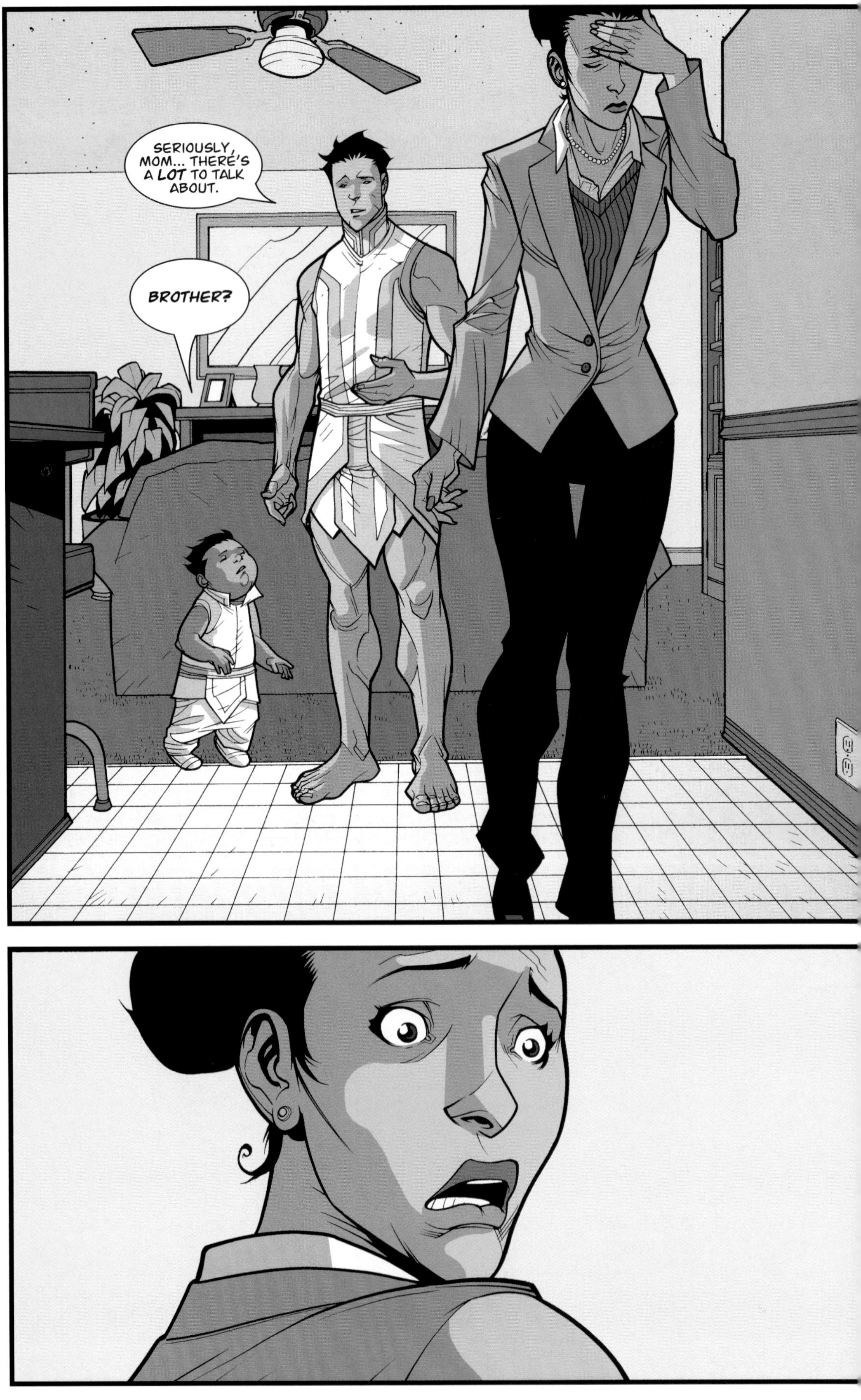
SERIOUSLY, MOM... THERE'S A LOT TO TALK ABOUT.
BROTHER?

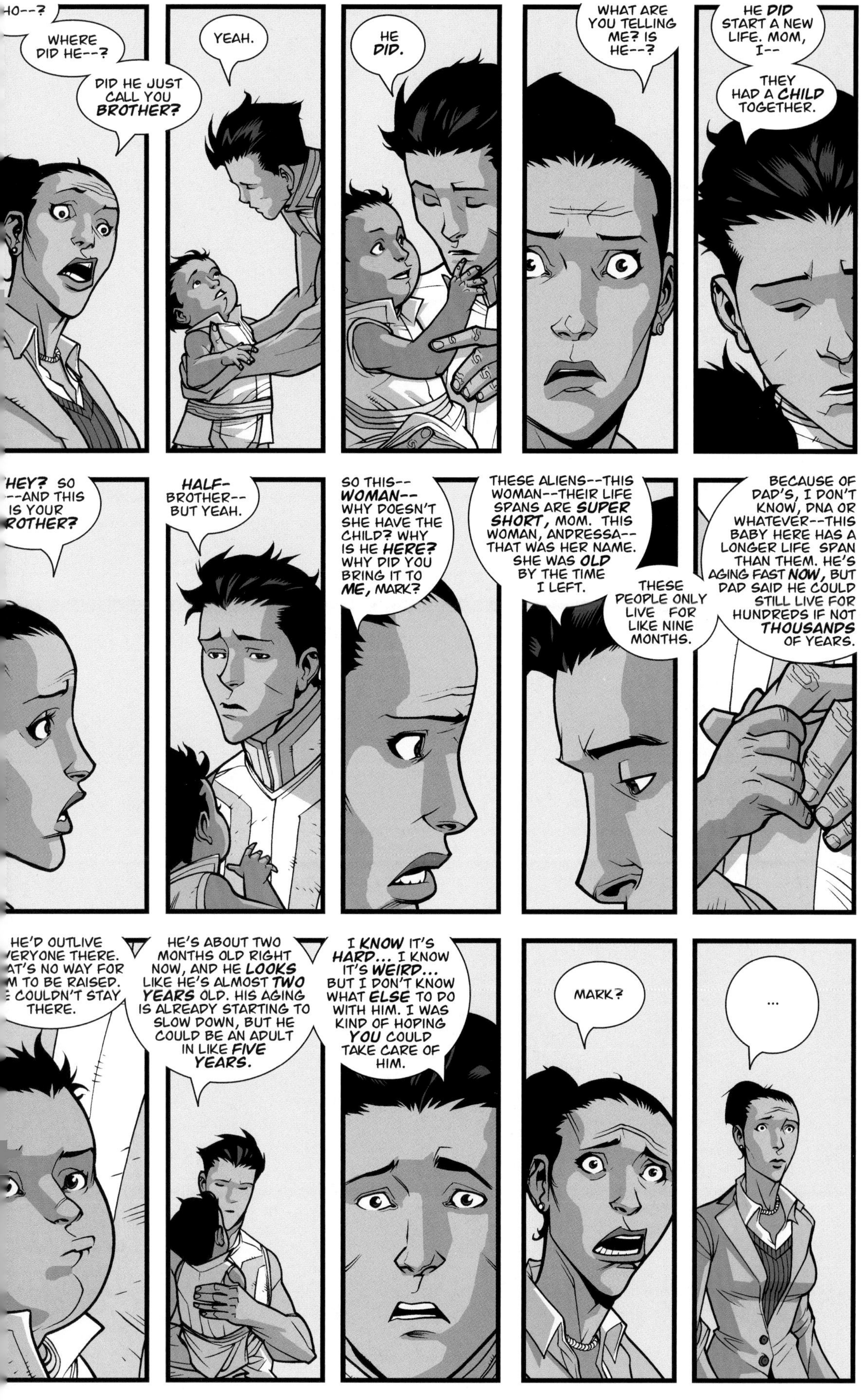
HO--?
WHERE DID HE--?
DID HE JUST CALL YOU **BROTHER?**
YEAH.
HE ***DID.***
WHAT ARE YOU TELLING ME? IS HE--?
HE ***DID*** START A NEW LIFE. MOM, I--
THEY HAD A ***CHILD*** TOGETHER.
HEY? SO --AND THIS IS YOUR ROTHER?
HALF-BROTHER-- BUT YEAH.
SO THIS-- ***WOMAN--*** WHY DOESN'T SHE HAVE THE CHILD? WHY IS HE ***HERE?*** WHY DID YOU BRING IT TO ***ME,*** MARK?
THESE ALIENS--THIS WOMAN--THEIR LIFE SPANS ARE ***SUPER SHORT,*** MOM. THIS WOMAN, ANDRESSA-- THAT WAS HER NAME. SHE WAS ***OLD*** BY THE TIME I LEFT.
THESE PEOPLE ONLY LIVE FOR LIKE NINE MONTHS.
BECAUSE OF DAD'S, I DON'T KNOW, DNA OR WHATEVER--THIS BABY HERE HAS A LONGER LIFE SPAN THAN THEM. HE'S AGING FAST ***NOW,*** BUT DAD SAID HE COULD STILL LIVE FOR HUNDREDS IF NOT ***THOUSANDS*** OF YEARS.
HE'D OUTLIVE VERYONE THERE. AT'S NO WAY FOR M TO BE RAISED. E COULDN'T STAY THERE.
HE'S ABOUT TWO MONTHS OLD RIGHT NOW, AND HE ***LOOKS*** LIKE HE'S ALMOST ***TWO YEARS*** OLD. HIS AGING IS ALREADY STARTING TO SLOW DOWN, BUT HE COULD BE AN ADULT IN LIKE ***FIVE YEARS.***
I ***KNOW*** IT'S ***HARD...*** I KNOW IT'S ***WEIRD...*** BUT I DON'T KNOW WHAT ***ELSE*** TO DO WITH HIM. I WAS KIND OF HOPING ***YOU*** COULD TAKE CARE OF HIM.
MARK?
...

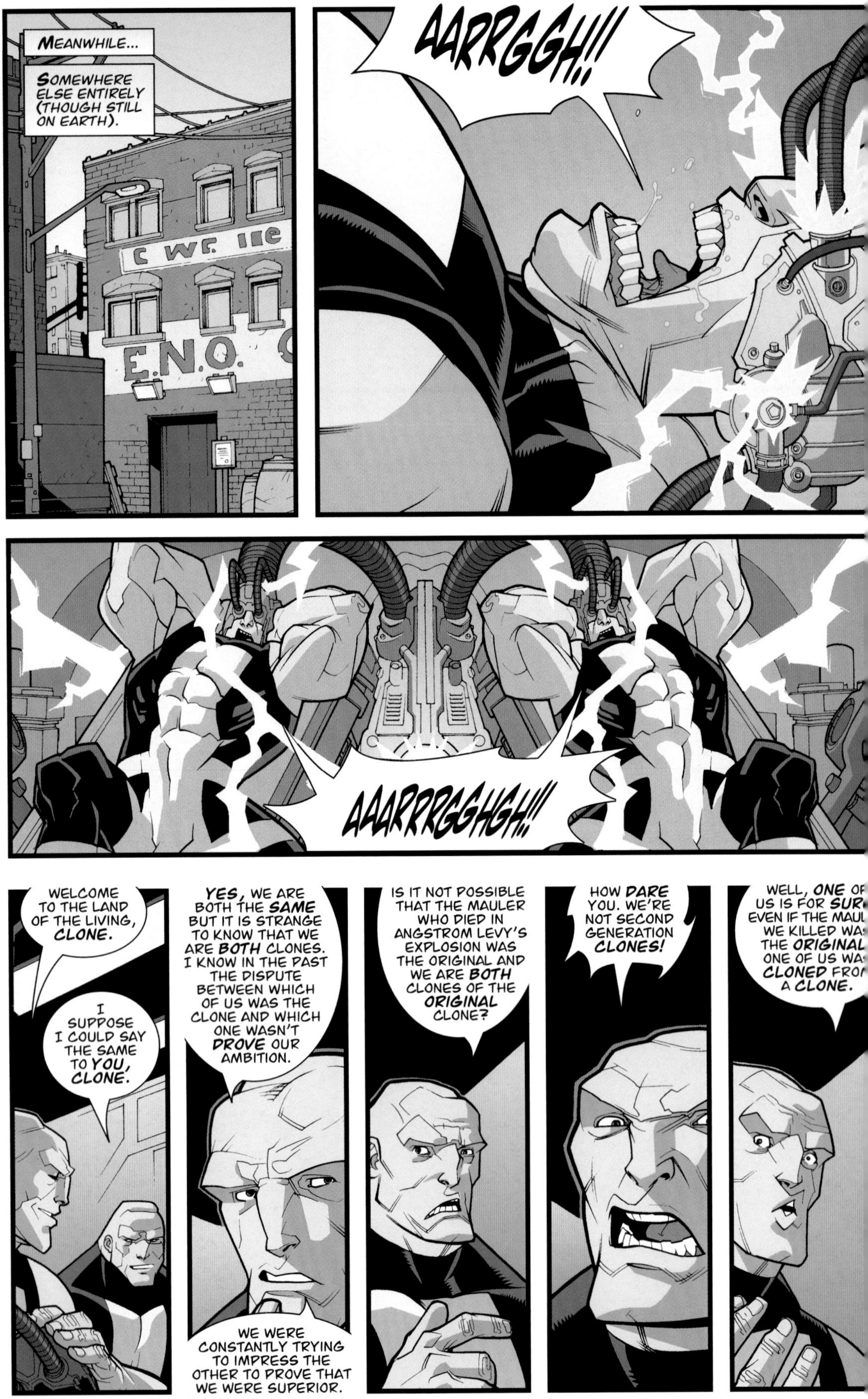
MEANWHILE...
SOMEWHERE ELSE ENTIRELY (THOUGH STILL ON EARTH).
E.N.O.
AARRGGH!!
AAARRRGGHGH!!
WELCOME TO THE LAND OF THE LIVING, CLONE.
I SUPPOSE I COULD SAY THE SAME TO YOU, CLONE.
YES, WE ARE BOTH THE SAME BUT IT IS STRANGE TO KNOW THAT WE ARE BOTH CLONES. I KNOW IN THE PAST THE DISPUTE BETWEEN WHICH OF US WAS THE CLONE AND WHICH ONE WASN'T DROVE OUR AMBITION.
WE WERE CONSTANTLY TRYING TO IMPRESS THE OTHER TO PROVE THAT WE WERE SUPERIOR.
IS IT NOT POSSIBLE THAT THE MAULER WHO DIED IN ANGSTROM LEVY'S EXPLOSION WAS THE ORIGINAL AND WE ARE BOTH CLONES OF THE ORIGINAL CLONE?
HOW DARE YOU. WE'RE NOT SECOND GENERATION CLONES!
WELL, ONE OF US IS FOR SURE EVEN IF THE MAULER WE KILLED WAS THE ORIGINAL. ONE OF US WAS CLONED FROM A CLONE.

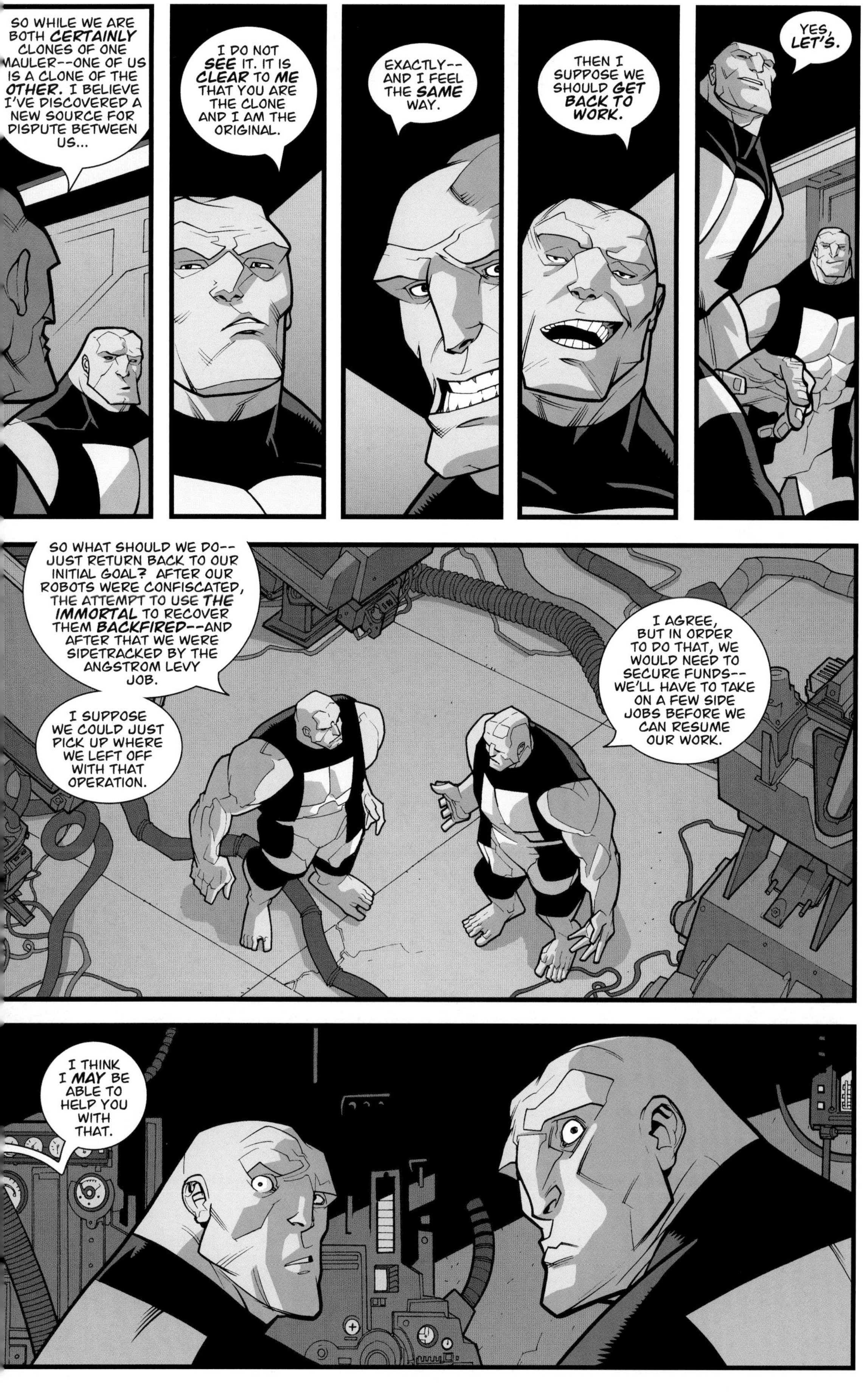

SO WHILE WE ARE BOTH CERTAINLY CLONES OF ONE MAULER--ONE OF US IS A CLONE OF THE OTHER. I BELIEVE I'VE DISCOVERED A NEW SOURCE FOR DISPUTE BETWEEN US...
I DO NOT SEE IT. IT IS CLEAR TO ME THAT YOU ARE THE CLONE AND I AM THE ORIGINAL.
EXACTLY--AND I FEEL THE SAME WAY.
THEN I SUPPOSE WE SHOULD GET BACK TO WORK.
YES, LET'S.
SO WHAT SHOULD WE DO--JUST RETURN BACK TO OUR INITIAL GOAL? AFTER OUR ROBOTS WERE CONFISCATED, THE ATTEMPT TO USE THE IMMORTAL TO RECOVER THEM BACKFIRED--AND AFTER THAT WE WERE SIDETRACKED BY THE ANGSTROM LEVY JOB.
I SUPPOSE WE COULD JUST PICK UP WHERE WE LEFT OFF WITH THAT OPERATION.
I AGREE, BUT IN ORDER TO DO THAT, WE WOULD NEED TO SECURE FUNDS--WE'LL HAVE TO TAKE ON A FEW SIDE JOBS BEFORE WE CAN RESUME OUR WORK.
I THINK I MAY BE ABLE TO HELP YOU WITH THAT.

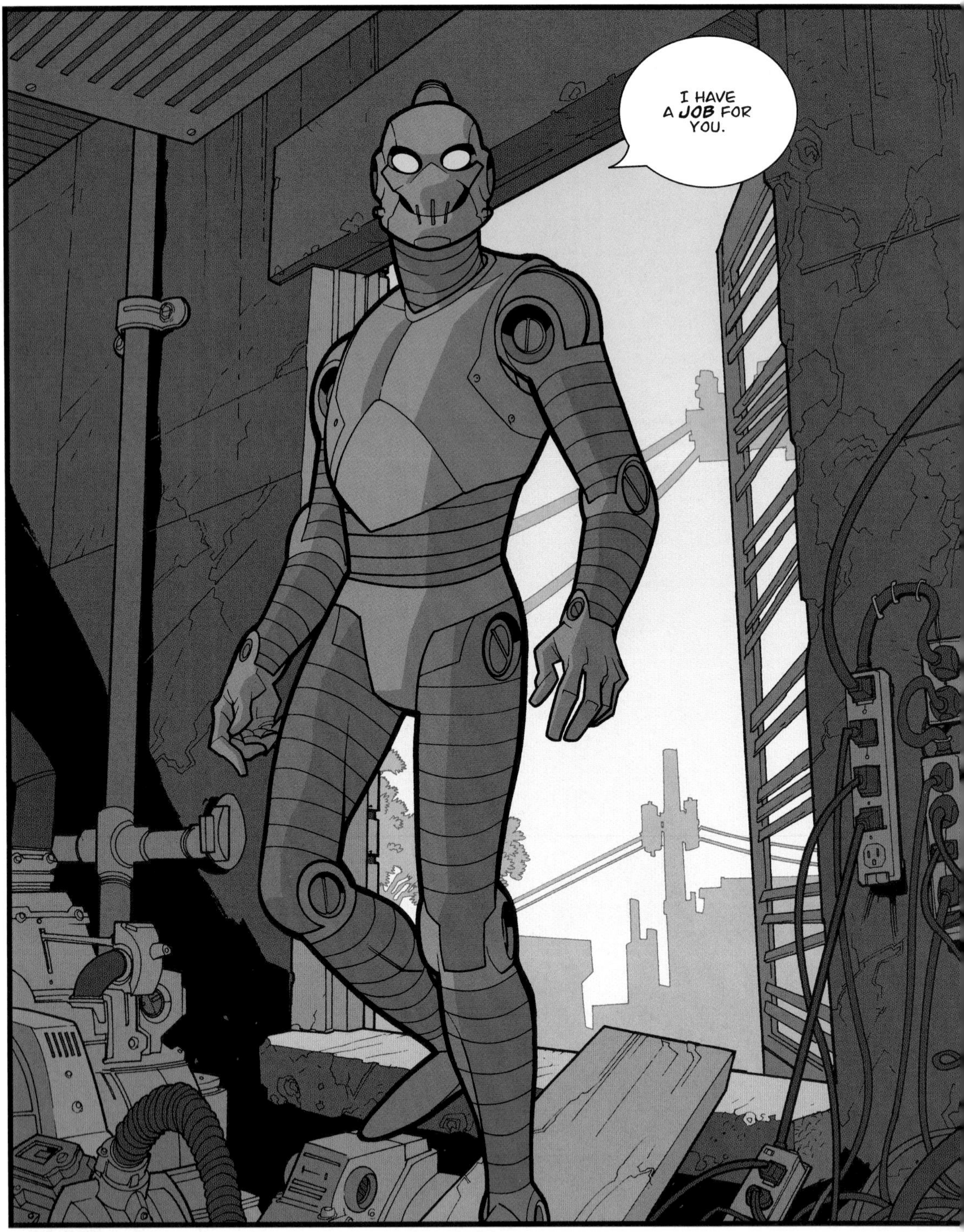
I HAVE A **JOB** FOR YOU.

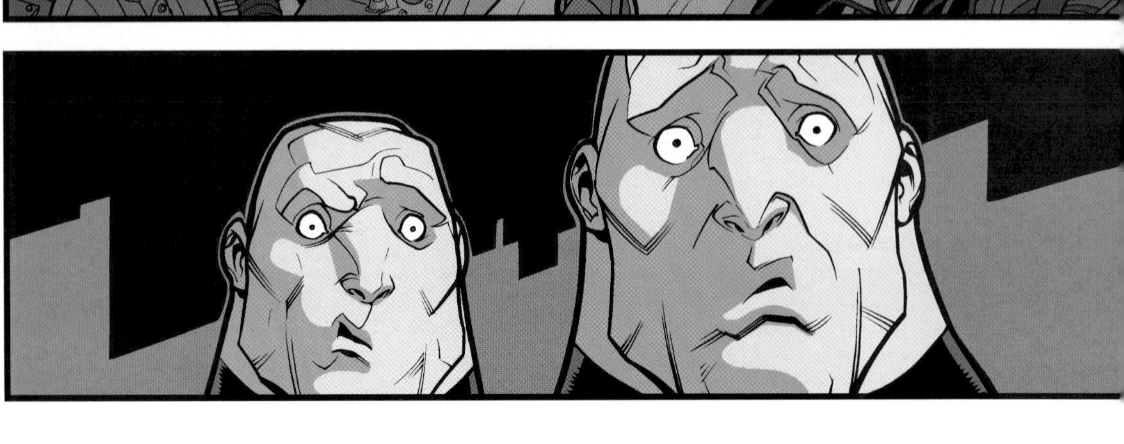

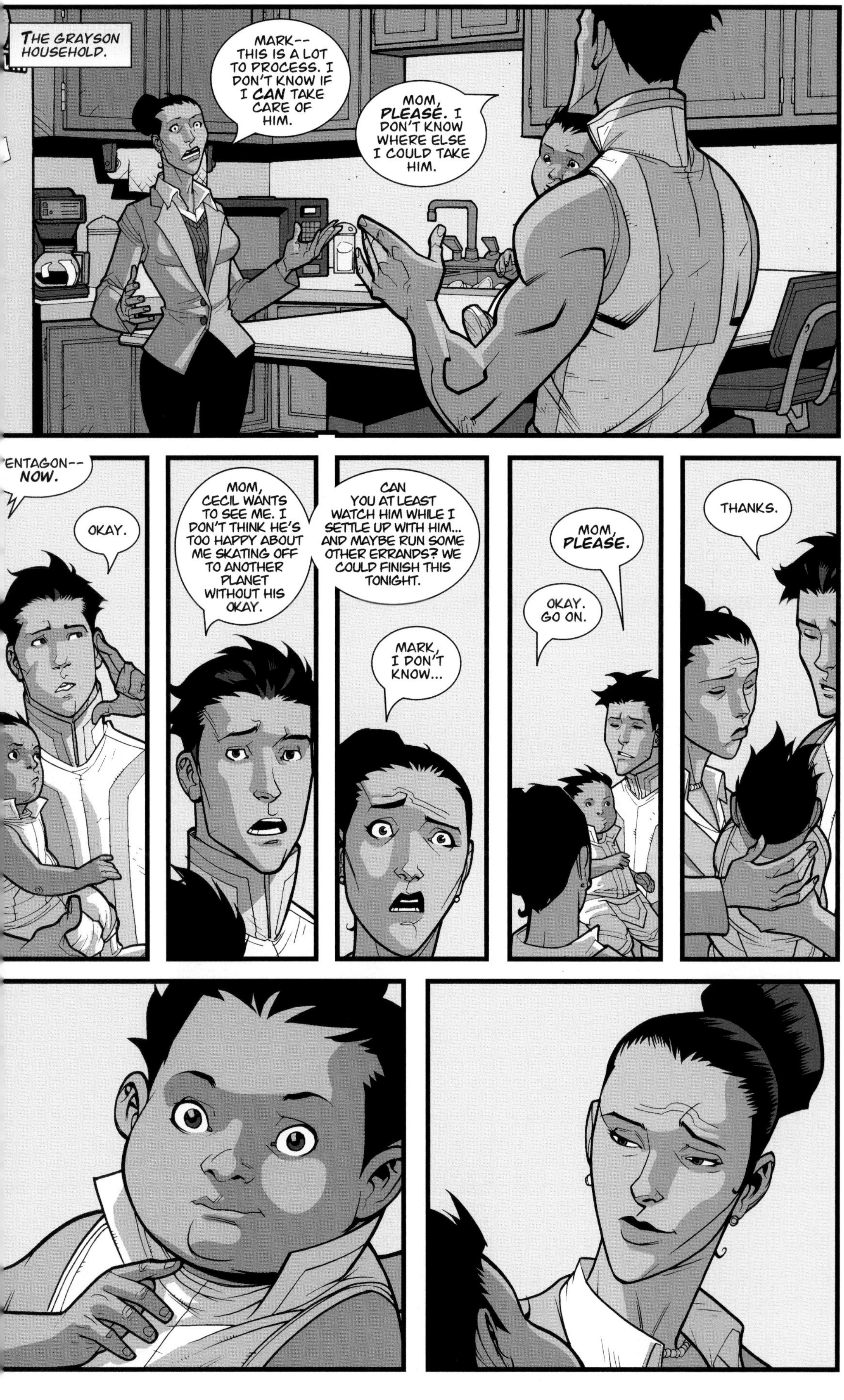
THE GRAYSON HOUSEHOLD.
MARK-- THIS IS A LOT TO PROCESS. I DON'T KNOW IF I CAN TAKE CARE OF HIM.
MOM, PLEASE. I DON'T KNOW WHERE ELSE I COULD TAKE HIM.
ENTAGON-- NOW.
OKAY.
MOM, CECIL WANTS TO SEE ME. I DON'T THINK HE'S TOO HAPPY ABOUT ME SKATING OFF TO ANOTHER PLANET WITHOUT HIS OKAY.
CAN YOU AT LEAST WATCH HIM WHILE I SETTLE UP WITH HIM... AND MAYBE RUN SOME OTHER ERRANDS? WE COULD FINISH THIS TONIGHT.
MARK, I DON'T KNOW...
MOM, PLEASE.
OKAY. GO ON.
THANKS.

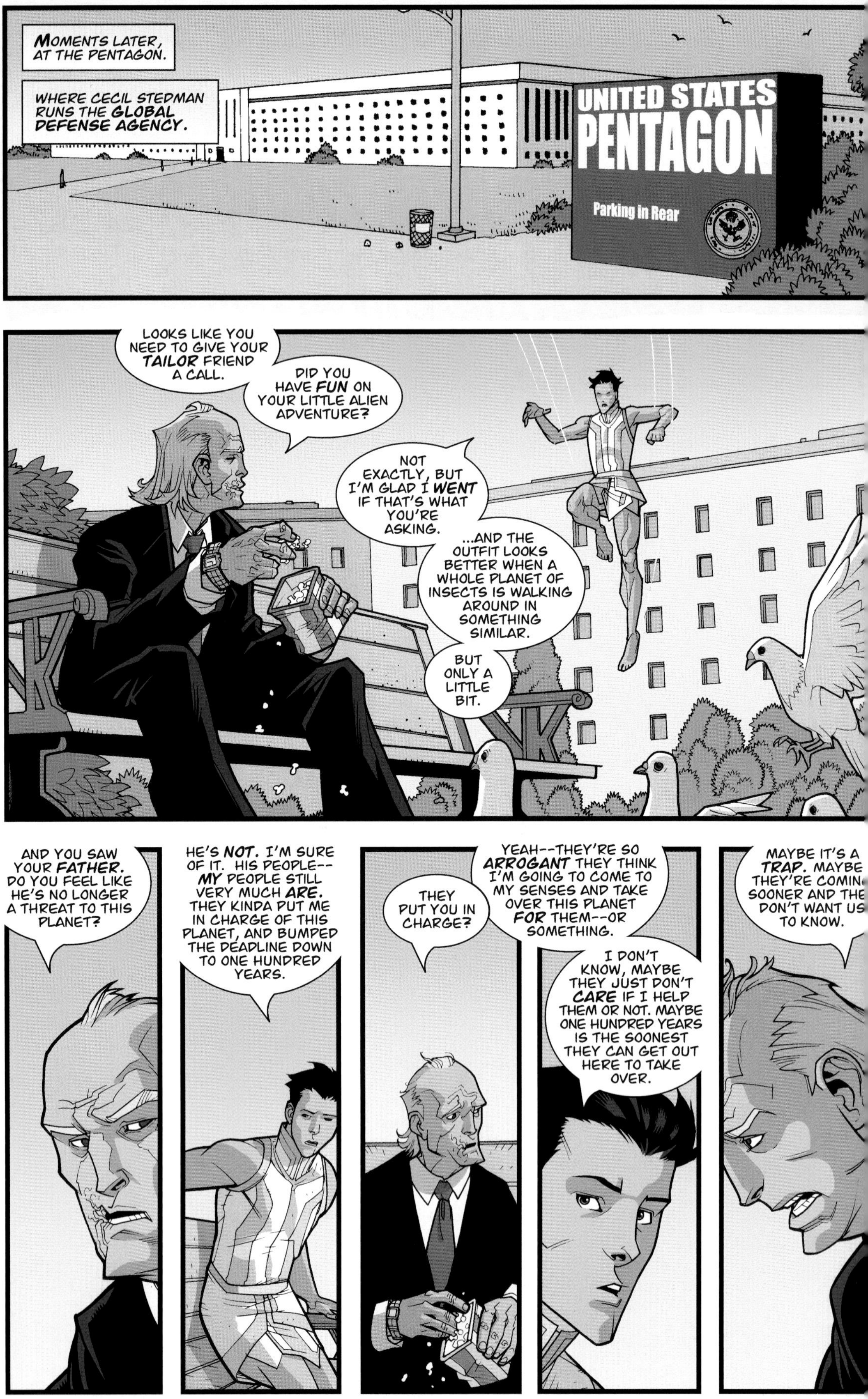
MOMENTS LATER, AT THE PENTAGON.
WHERE CECIL STEDMAN RUNS THE GLOBAL DEFENSE AGENCY.
UNITED STATES PENTAGON
Parking in Rear
LOOKS LIKE YOU NEED TO GIVE YOUR TAILOR FRIEND A CALL.
DID YOU HAVE FUN ON YOUR LITTLE ALIEN ADVENTURE?
NOT EXACTLY, BUT I'M GLAD I WENT IF THAT'S WHAT YOU'RE ASKING.
...AND THE OUTFIT LOOKS BETTER WHEN A WHOLE PLANET OF INSECTS IS WALKING AROUND IN SOMETHING SIMILAR.
BUT ONLY A LITTLE BIT.
AND YOU SAW YOUR FATHER. DO YOU FEEL LIKE HE'S NO LONGER A THREAT TO THIS PLANET?
HE'S NOT. I'M SURE OF IT. HIS PEOPLE-- MY PEOPLE STILL VERY MUCH ARE. THEY KINDA PUT ME IN CHARGE OF THIS PLANET, AND BUMPED THE DEADLINE DOWN TO ONE HUNDRED YEARS.
THEY PUT YOU IN CHARGE?
YEAH--THEY'RE SO ARROGANT THEY THINK I'M GOING TO COME TO MY SENSES AND TAKE OVER THIS PLANET FOR THEM--OR SOMETHING.
I DON'T KNOW, MAYBE THEY JUST DON'T CARE IF I HELP THEM OR NOT. MAYBE ONE HUNDRED YEARS IS THE SOONEST THEY CAN GET OUT HERE TO TAKE OVER.
MAYBE IT'S A TRAP. MAYBE THEY'RE COMIN SOONER AND THE DON'T WANT US TO KNOW.

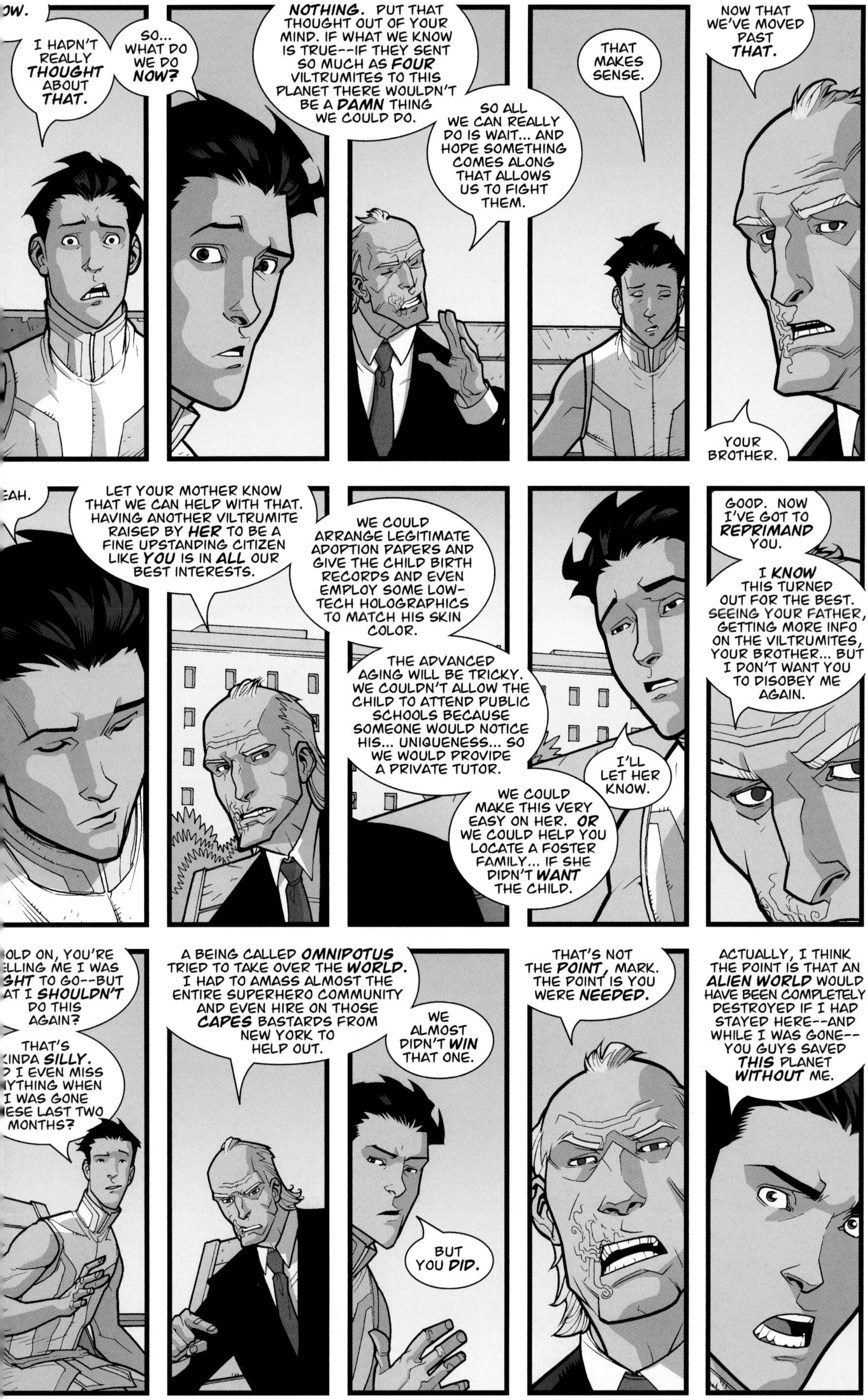

OW.
I HADN'T REALLY THOUGHT ABOUT THAT.
SO... WHAT DO WE DO NOW?
NOTHING. PUT THAT THOUGHT OUT OF YOUR MIND. IF WHAT WE KNOW IS TRUE--IF THEY SENT SO MUCH AS FOUR VILTRUMITES TO THIS PLANET THERE WOULDN'T BE A DAMN THING WE COULD DO.
SO ALL WE CAN REALLY DO IS WAIT... AND HOPE SOMETHING COMES ALONG THAT ALLOWS US TO FIGHT THEM.
THAT MAKES SENSE.
NOW THAT WE'VE MOVED PAST THAT.
YOUR BROTHER.
EAH.
LET YOUR MOTHER KNOW THAT WE CAN HELP WITH THAT. HAVING ANOTHER VILTRUMITE RAISED BY HER TO BE A FINE UPSTANDING CITIZEN LIKE YOU IS IN ALL OUR BEST INTERESTS.
WE COULD ARRANGE LEGITIMATE ADOPTION PAPERS AND GIVE THE CHILD BIRTH RECORDS AND EVEN EMPLOY SOME LOW-TECH HOLOGRAPHICS TO MATCH HIS SKIN COLOR.
THE ADVANCED AGING WILL BE TRICKY. WE COULDN'T ALLOW THE CHILD TO ATTEND PUBLIC SCHOOLS BECAUSE SOMEONE WOULD NOTICE HIS... UNIQUENESS... SO WE WOULD PROVIDE A PRIVATE TUTOR.
WE COULD MAKE THIS VERY EASY ON HER. OR WE COULD HELP YOU LOCATE A FOSTER FAMILY... IF SHE DIDN'T WANT THE CHILD.
I'LL LET HER KNOW.
GOOD. NOW I'VE GOT TO REPRIMAND YOU.
I KNOW THIS TURNED OUT FOR THE BEST. SEEING YOUR FATHER, GETTING MORE INFO ON THE VILTRUMITES, YOUR BROTHER... BUT I DON'T WANT YOU TO DISOBEY ME AGAIN.
OLD ON, YOU'RE ELLING ME I WAS GHT TO GO--BUT AT I SHOULDN'T DO THIS AGAIN?
THAT'S KINDA SILLY. D I EVEN MISS YTHING WHEN I WAS GONE ESE LAST TWO MONTHS?
A BEING CALLED OMNIPOTUS TRIED TO TAKE OVER THE WORLD. I HAD TO AMASS ALMOST THE ENTIRE SUPERHERO COMMUNITY AND EVEN HIRE ON THOSE CAPES BASTARDS FROM NEW YORK TO HELP OUT.
WE ALMOST DIDN'T WIN THAT ONE.
BUT YOU DID.
THAT'S NOT THE POINT, MARK. THE POINT IS YOU WERE NEEDED.
ACTUALLY, I THINK THE POINT IS THAT AN ALIEN WORLD WOULD HAVE BEEN COMPLETELY DESTROYED IF I HAD STAYED HERE--AND WHILE I WAS GONE--YOU GUYS SAVED THIS PLANET WITHOUT ME.

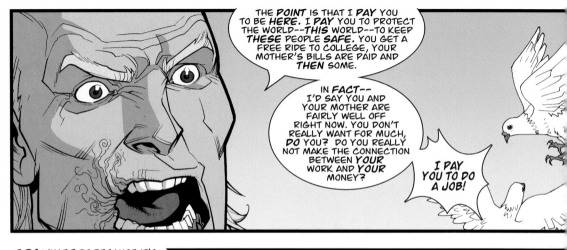

THE **POINT** IS THAT I **PAY** YOU TO BE **HERE**. I **PAY** YOU TO PROTECT THE WORLD--**THIS** WORLD--TO KEEP **THESE** PEOPLE SAFE. YOU GET A FREE RIDE TO COLLEGE, YOUR MOTHER'S BILLS ARE PAID AND **THEN** SOME.

IN **FACT**-- I'D SAY YOU AND YOUR MOTHER ARE FAIRLY WELL OFF RIGHT NOW. YOU DON'T REALLY WANT FOR MUCH, **DO** YOU? DO YOU REALLY NOT MAKE THE CONNECTION BETWEEN **YOUR** WORK AND **YOUR** MONEY?

I PAY YOU TO DO A JOB!

I **DO** WHAT I DO BECAUSE IT'S THE **RIGHT THING TO DO**. I'VE GOT THESE POWERS AND I'M TRYING MY **BEST** TO DO WHAT'S **RIGHT** WITH THEM. I DON'T DO THIS BECAUSE YOU **PAY** ME.

I **ALLOW** YOU TO **PAY** ME BECAUSE YOU PUT ME WHERE I NEED TO **BE**. YOU **HELP ME DO MY JOB**. YOU THINK I'D BE AT HOME PLAYING VIDEO GAMES IF YOU WEREN'T **PAYING** ME TO DO THIS?

IF SOMETHING COMES ALONG AND I THINK IT'S THE RIGHT THING TO **DO**--I'M GOING TO **DO IT**.

YOU'RE TREATING ME LIKE THIS AND YOU'RE NOT EVEN TELLING ME I DID SOMETHING **WRONG**. ARE YOU JUST UPSET BECAUSE I'M NOT A GOOD LITTLE SOLDIER TAKING ORDERS WITHOUT ASKING **QUESTIONS?!**

MARK. **CALM DOWN.** YOU'RE A GOOD PERSON. THAT'S WHY I WANT YOU TO WORK WITH ME.

I JUST NEED YOU TO TRUST MY JUDGMENT IN MORE CASES.

I APPRECIATE EVERYTHING YOU'VE DONE FOR MY MOTHER AND ME. REALLY, I **DO**-- BUT I'LL START TRUSTING YOUR JUDGMENT **MORE** AFTER I DO SOMETHING **WRONG**. RIGHT NOW I DON'T THINK **MY** JUDGMENT WAS IN THE WRONG HERE.

I'VE GOT A COUPLE MORE STOPS. IF YOU NEED ME, YOU KNOW WHERE TO FIND ME.

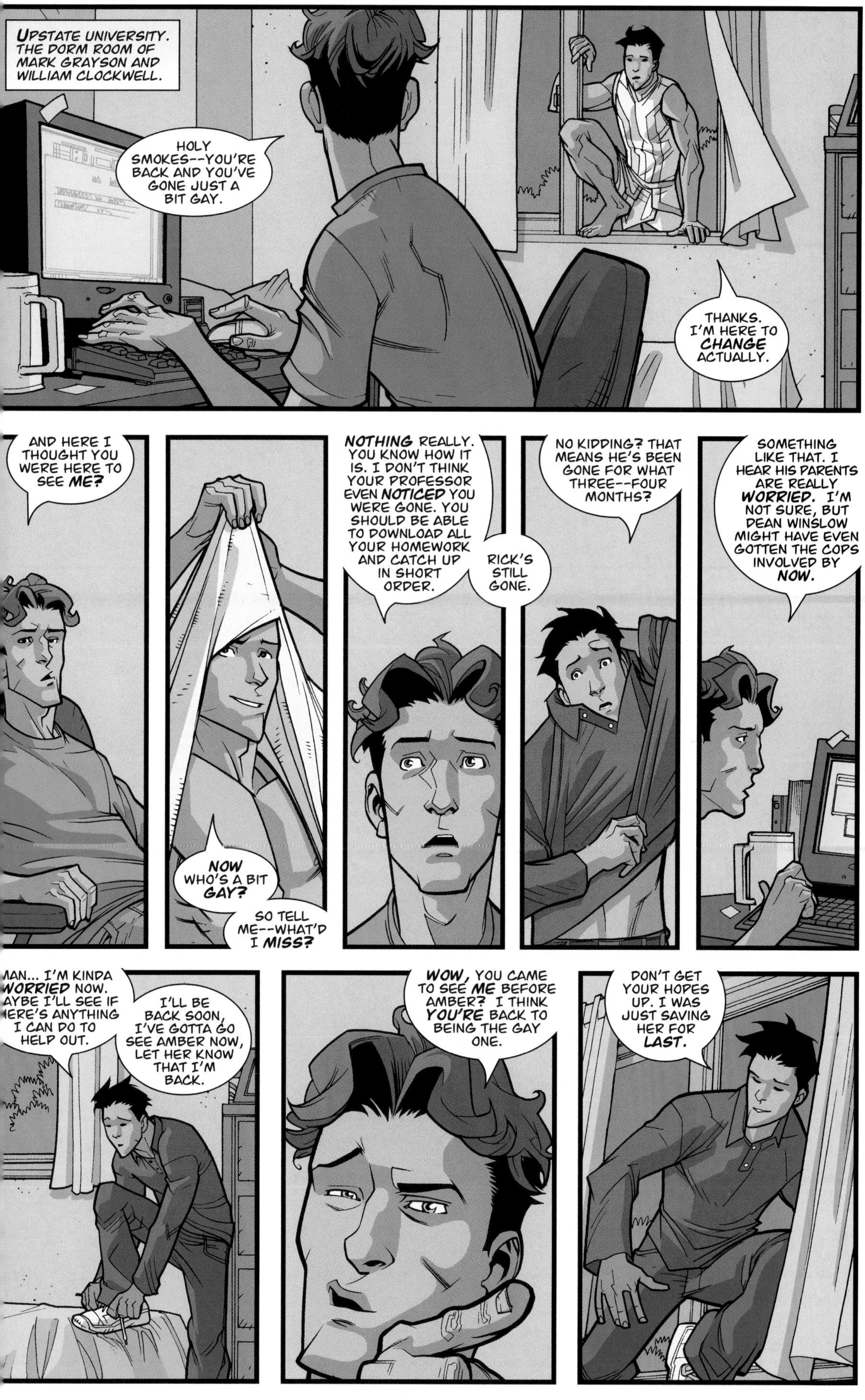
UPSTATE UNIVERSITY. THE DORM ROOM OF MARK GRAYSON AND WILLIAM CLOCKWELL.
HOLY SMOKES--YOU'RE BACK AND YOU'VE GONE JUST A BIT GAY.
THANKS. I'M HERE TO CHANGE ACTUALLY.
AND HERE I THOUGHT YOU WERE HERE TO SEE ME?
NOW WHO'S A BIT GAY?
SO TELL ME--WHAT'D I MISS?
NOTHING REALLY. YOU KNOW HOW IT IS. I DON'T THINK YOUR PROFESSOR EVEN NOTICED YOU WERE GONE. YOU SHOULD BE ABLE TO DOWNLOAD ALL YOUR HOMEWORK AND CATCH UP IN SHORT ORDER.
RICK'S STILL GONE.
NO KIDDING? THAT MEANS HE'S BEEN GONE FOR WHAT THREE--FOUR MONTHS?
SOMETHING LIKE THAT. I HEAR HIS PARENTS ARE REALLY WORRIED. I'M NOT SURE, BUT DEAN WINSLOW MIGHT HAVE EVEN GOTTEN THE COPS INVOLVED BY NOW.
MAN... I'M KINDA WORRIED NOW. AYBE I'LL SEE IF ERE'S ANYTHING I CAN DO TO HELP OUT.
I'LL BE BACK SOON, I'VE GOTTA GO SEE AMBER NOW, LET HER KNOW THAT I'M BACK.
WOW, YOU CAME TO SEE ME BEFORE AMBER? I THINK YOU'RE BACK TO BEING THE GAY ONE.
DON'T GET YOUR HOPES UP. I WAS JUST SAVING HER FOR LAST.

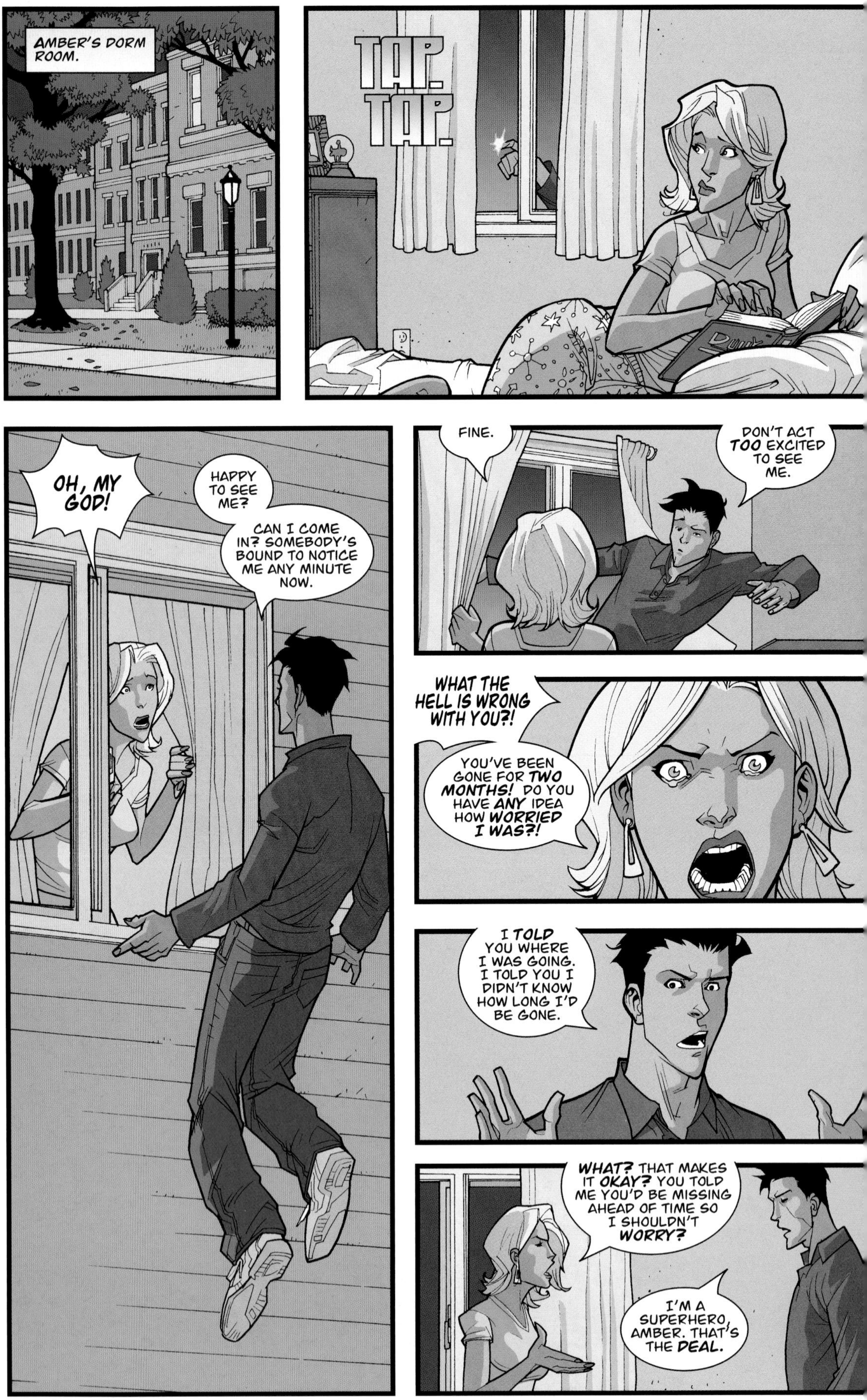
AMBER'S DORM ROOM.
TAP. TAP.
OH, MY GOD!
HAPPY TO SEE ME?
CAN I COME IN? SOMEBODY'S BOUND TO NOTICE ME ANY MINUTE NOW.
FINE.
DON'T ACT TOO EXCITED TO SEE ME.
WHAT THE HELL IS WRONG WITH YOU?!
YOU'VE BEEN GONE FOR TWO MONTHS! DO YOU HAVE ANY IDEA HOW WORRIED I WAS?!
I TOLD YOU WHERE I WAS GOING. I TOLD YOU I DIDN'T KNOW HOW LONG I'D BE GONE.
WHAT? THAT MAKES IT OKAY? YOU TOLD ME YOU'D BE MISSING AHEAD OF TIME SO I SHOULDN'T WORRY?
I'M A SUPERHERO, AMBER. THAT'S THE DEAL.

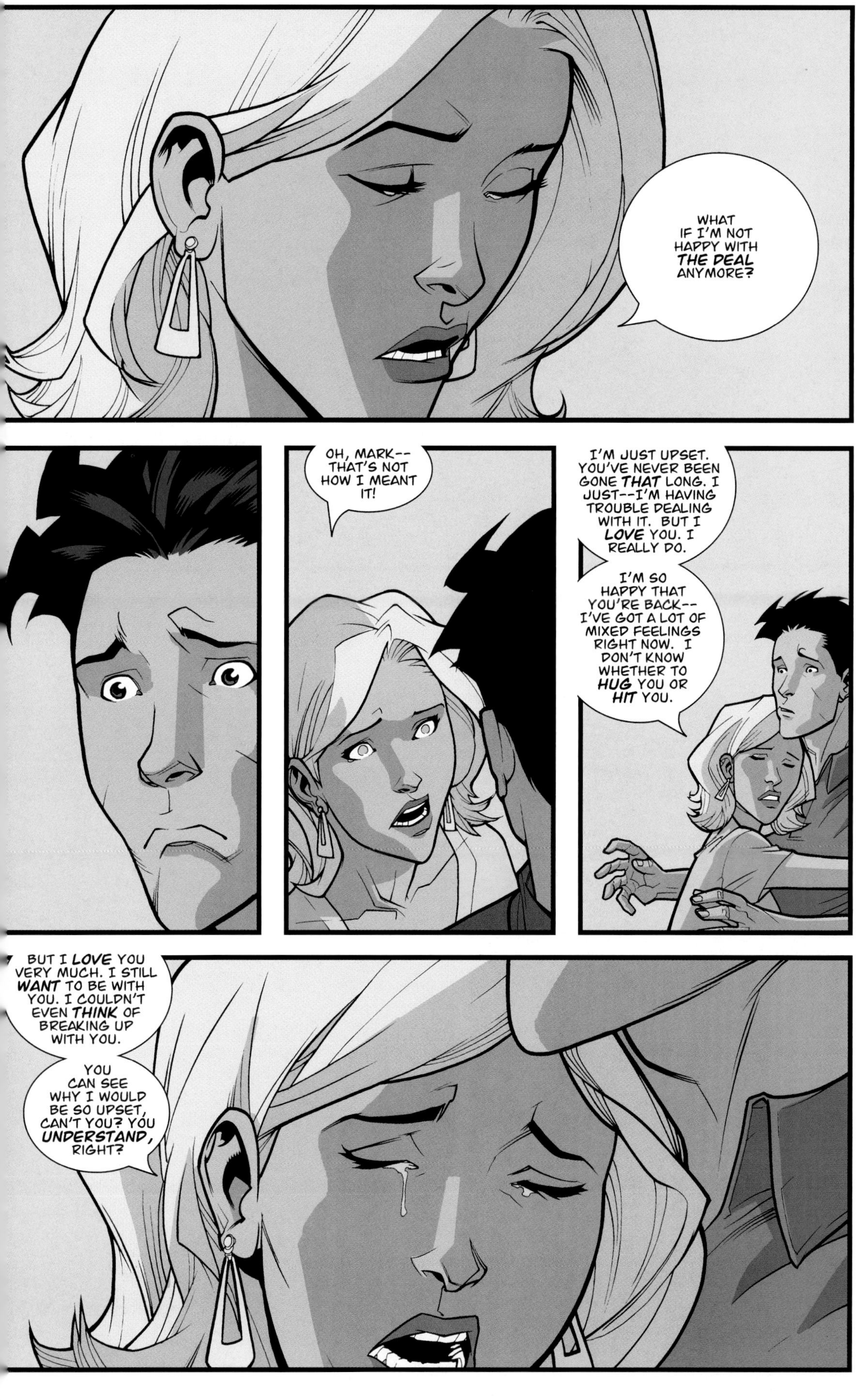
WHAT IF I'M NOT HAPPY WITH THE DEAL ANYMORE?
OH, MARK-- THAT'S NOT HOW I MEANT IT!
I'M JUST UPSET. YOU'VE NEVER BEEN GONE THAT LONG. I JUST--I'M HAVING TROUBLE DEALING WITH IT. BUT I LOVE YOU. I REALLY DO.
I'M SO HAPPY THAT YOU'RE BACK-- I'VE GOT A LOT OF MIXED FEELINGS RIGHT NOW. I DON'T KNOW WHETHER TO HUG YOU OR HIT YOU.
BUT I LOVE YOU VERY MUCH. I STILL WANT TO BE WITH YOU. I COULDN'T EVEN THINK OF BREAKING UP WITH YOU.
YOU CAN SEE WHY I WOULD BE SO UPSET, CAN'T YOU? YOU UNDERSTAND, RIGHT?

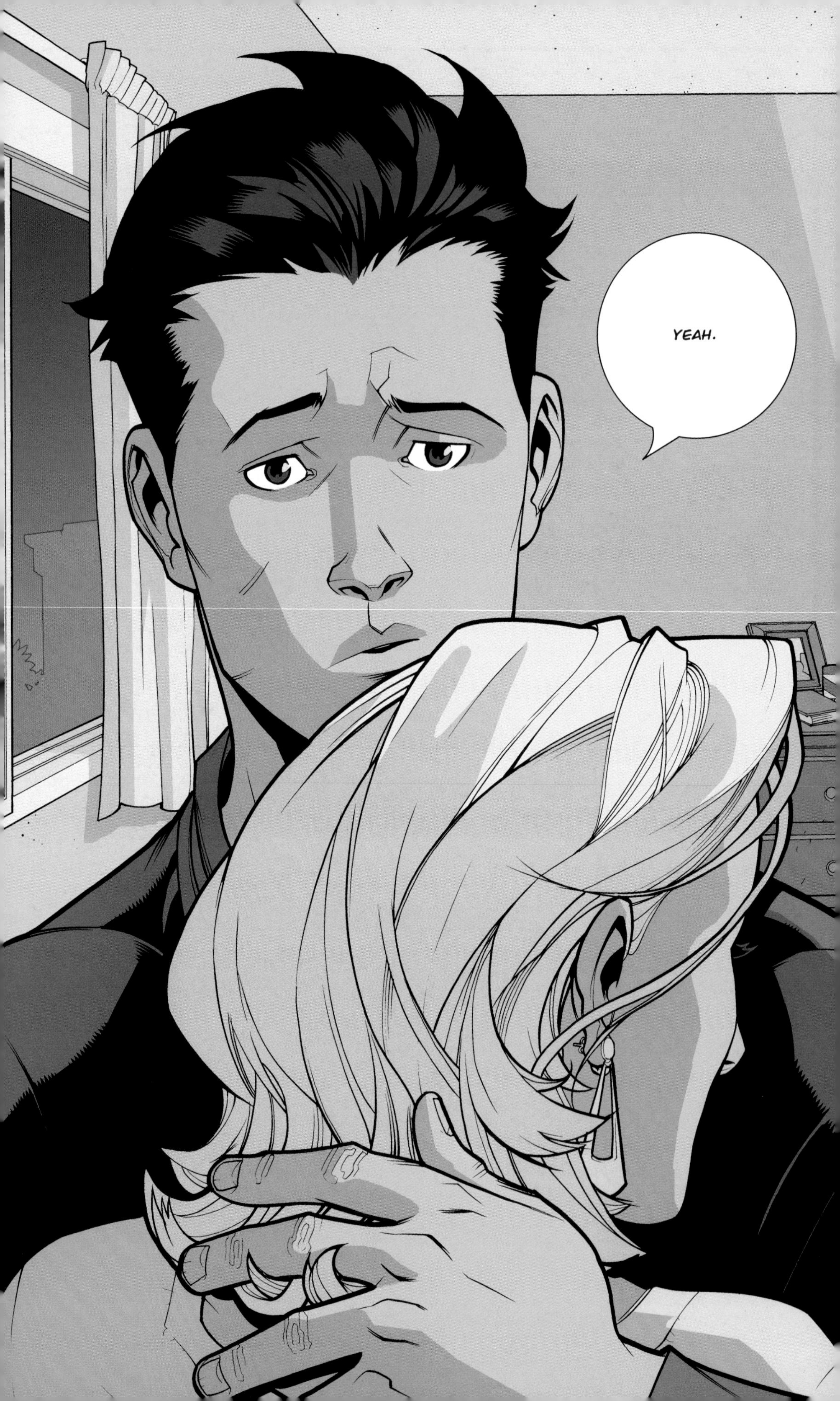
YEAH.

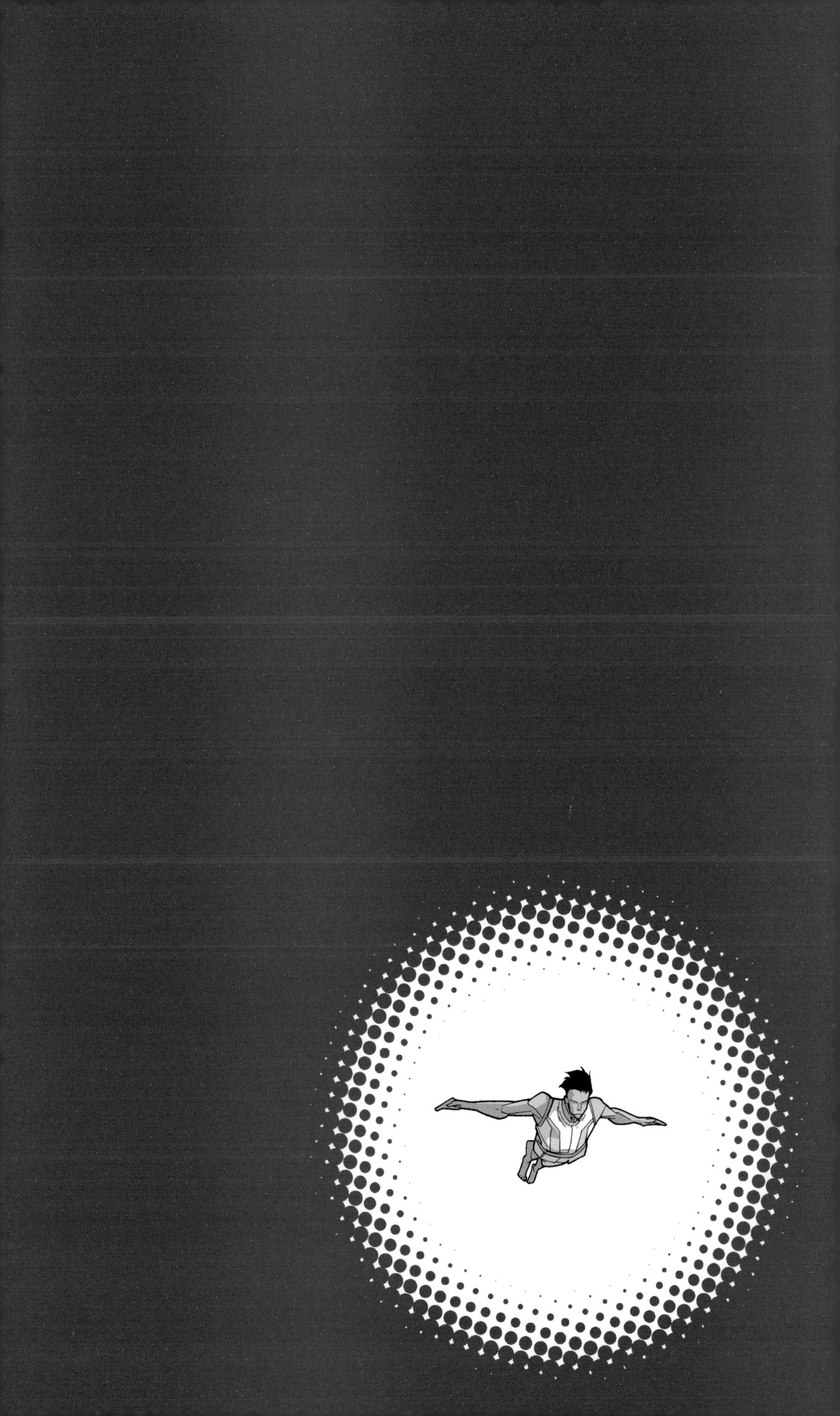

TPB 6

VILLAINITES

MANTIS

When it came time to reprint Volumes 1 and 2 of this series I had Cory Walker go back and do new covers for both. We used the original design for the first issue's cover, but with a different figure, for volume 1. (some of you may already know this.) That cover had a figure in the foreground, posing and panels behind it. I dug it. I'm also insanely anal about this stuff. When volume 4 was accidentally printed with a gloss finish on the cover instead of matte, I freaked out, then grew to like it, and then switched over to glossy covers on all the subsequent printings and new volumes of this book. I like things to match, sometimes a little too much. Case in point... these trade paperback covers.

After the cover for Volume 1 was changed I suggested Cory put panels on the volume 2 cover... and while the cover for volume 3 had been drawn, it hadn't been printed yet, so he went in and added panels to that cover too. Then, starting with volume 4, young Ryan Ottley took over, and he continued the trend. But the thing is, by the time we got to volume 6, you kinda run out of cool flying poses for Invincible... or at least, five is more than enough. Also, Bill Crabtree HATES these covers. With three or so panels on the page and a character that's blue and yellow, he has to come up with other colors to make the panels in order to pull them back from the figure and make it pop of the page... without using blue and yellow, because that's the color the figure is. Anyway, he hates it... and with good reason. But I like things to match.

When it came time to draw this cover, Ryan suggested doing something a LITTLE different. I agreed, it was time for a LITTLE bit of a change... and it still kinda matches. So I can sleep at night.

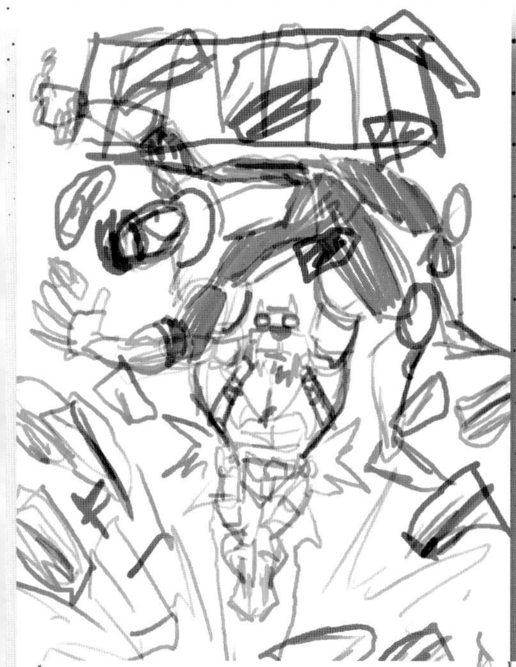

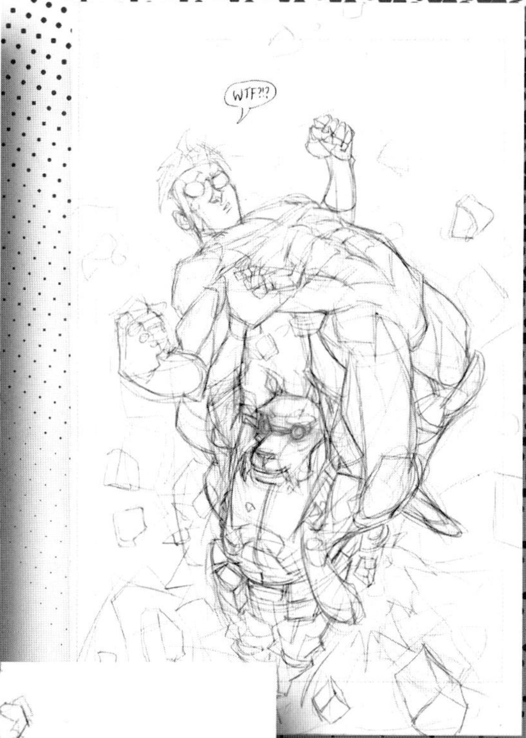
WTF?!?

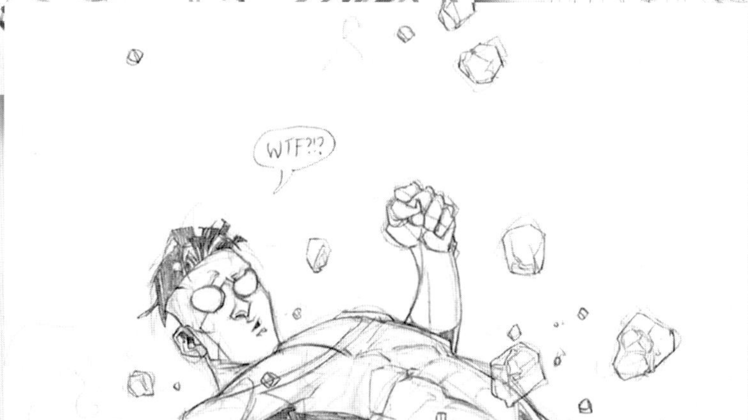
WTF?!?

On this page you'll see my crappy layout for issue 25 and Ryan's attempt at making it not suck (he succeeded). From time to time when I have an idea for a cover I'll do a little layout. It's easier than describing it in email I guess. Ryan did a great job with this cover. Notice Science Dog was originally smiling. I had Ryan change it because it made him look silly. And Science Dog should never look silly, he's the coolest comic book character EVER.

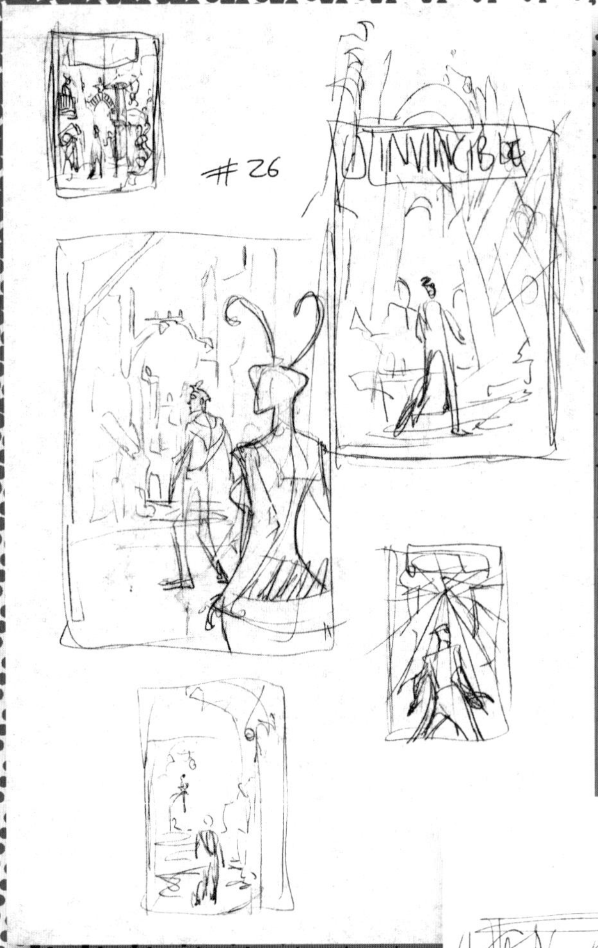

26

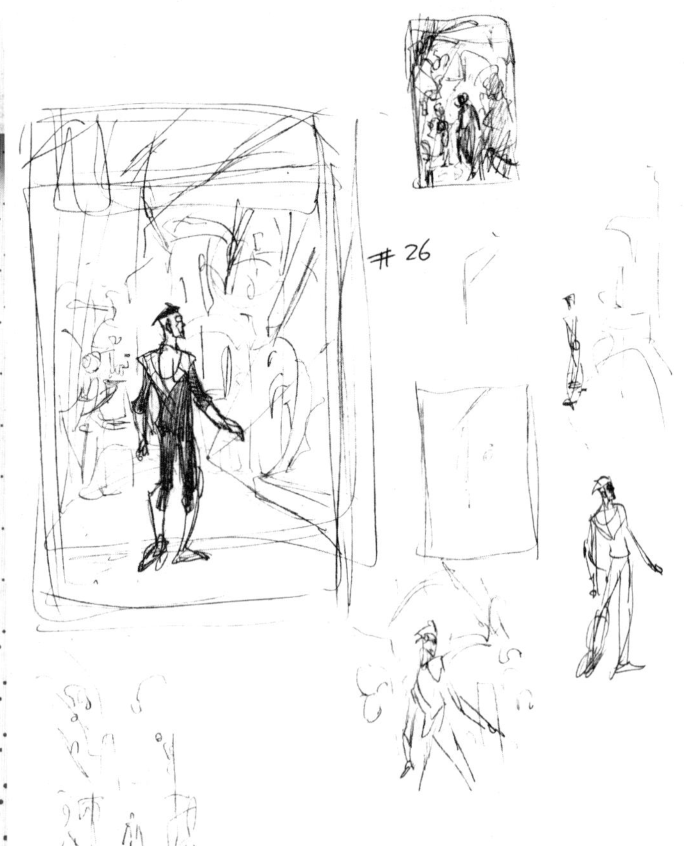

26

Here's Ryan's sketches for the cover to issue 26. I told Ryan "Have Invincible walking around the alien city, looking around." Not a lot to go on, I know... but Ryan knows what he's doing and like always, ran with the idea and did something great with it.

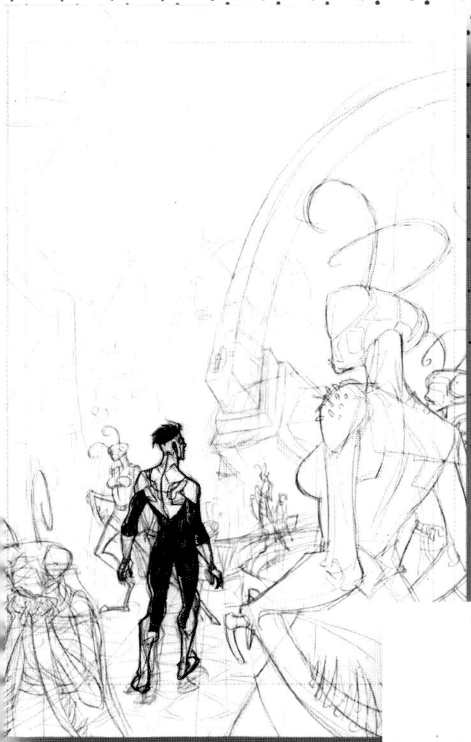

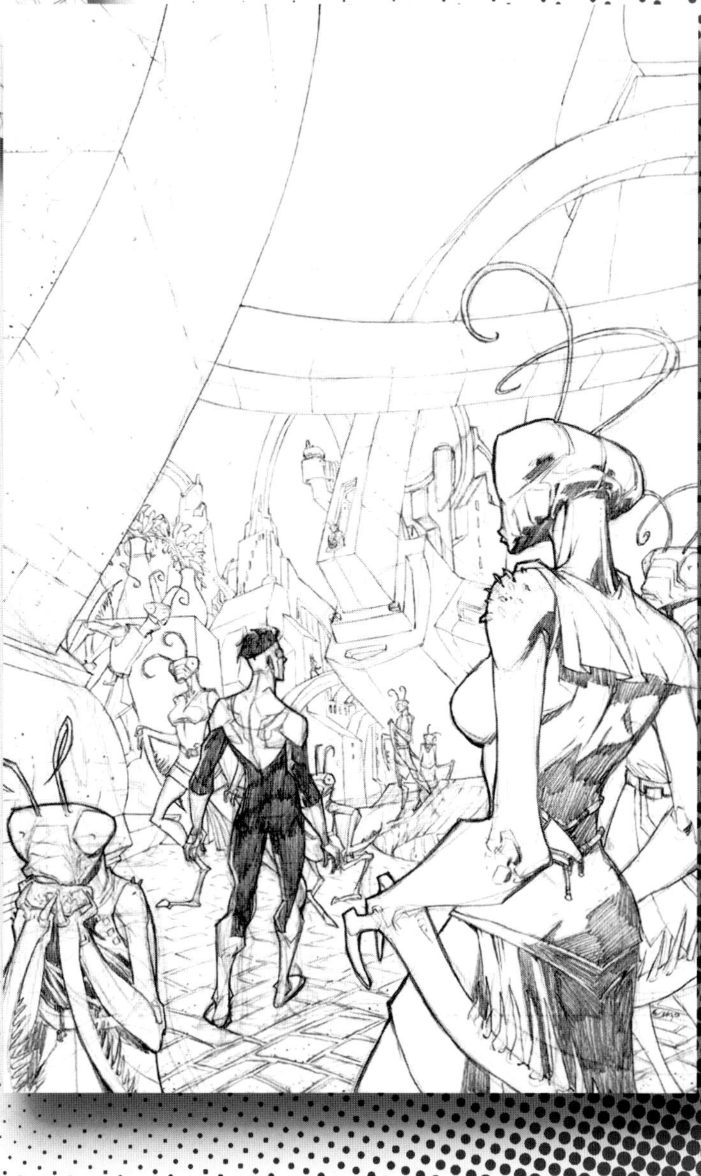

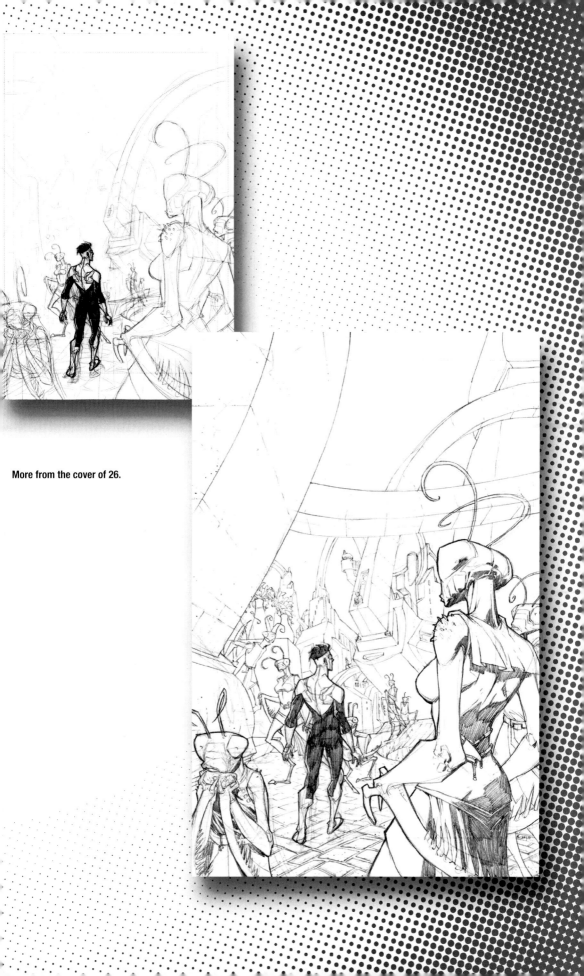

More from the cover of 26.

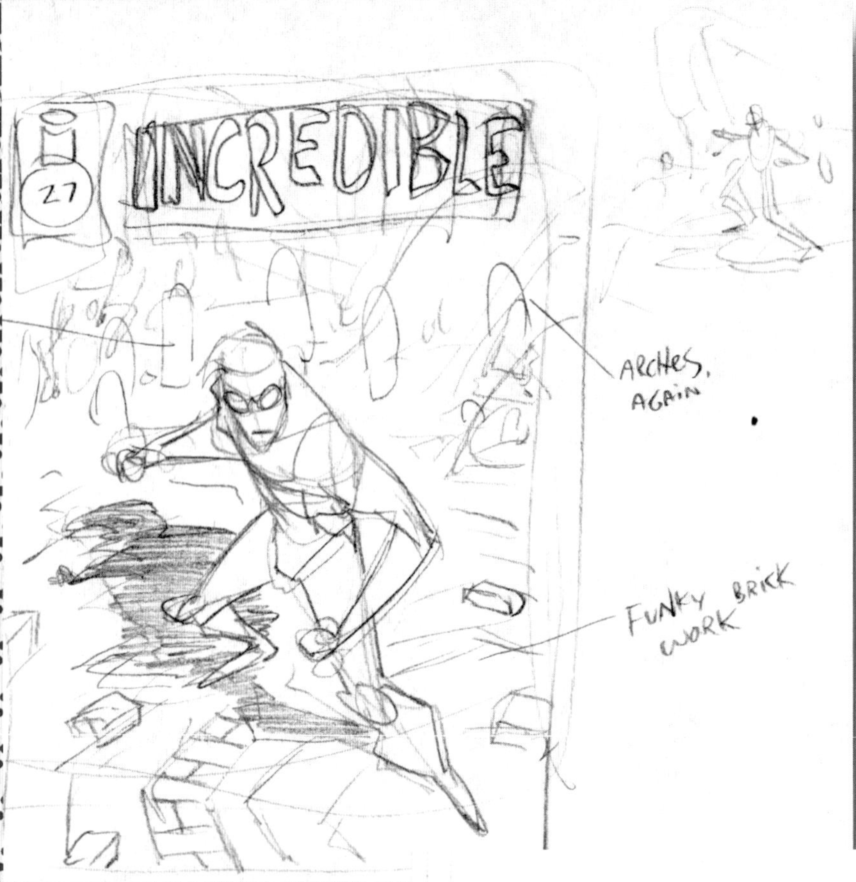
INCREDIBLE
27
ARCHES, AGAIN
FUNKY BRICK WORK

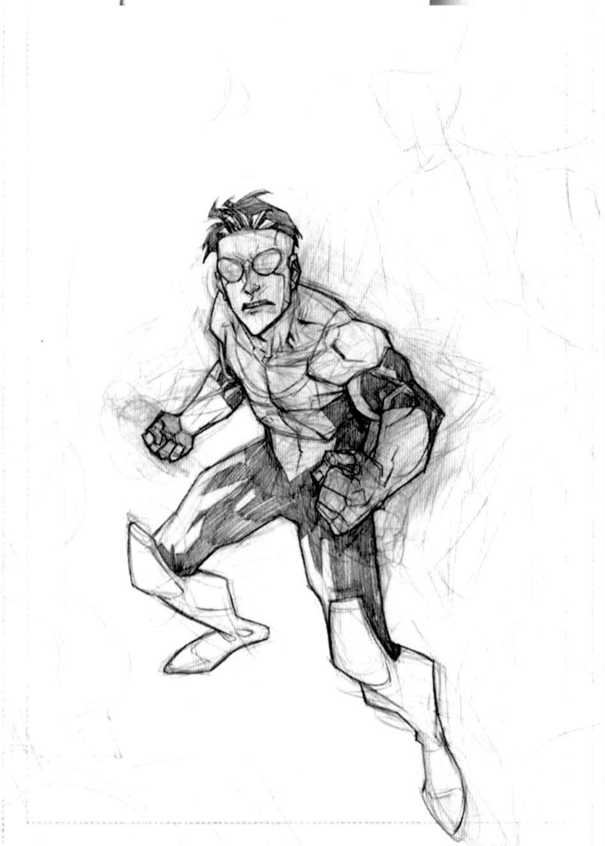

Here's Ryan's layout and the pencils for the figure of the cover to 27. Ryan got the title wrong. He always forgets what this book is called. Idiot.

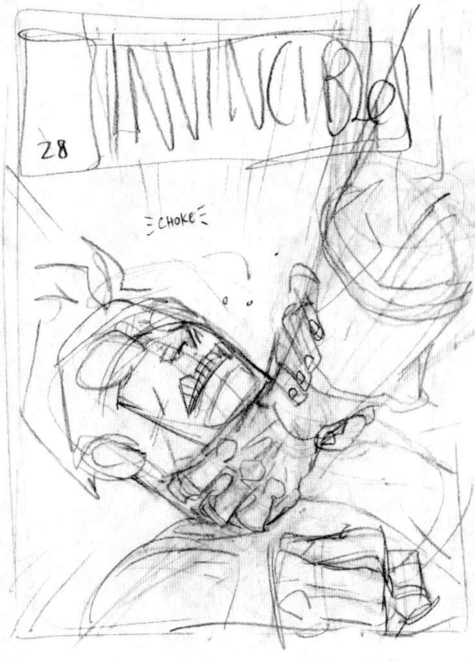
28
CHOKE

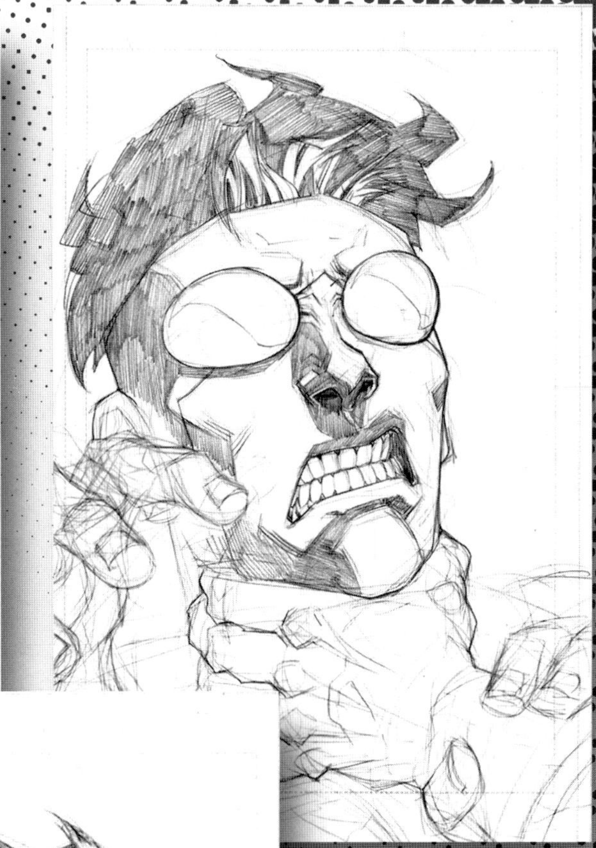

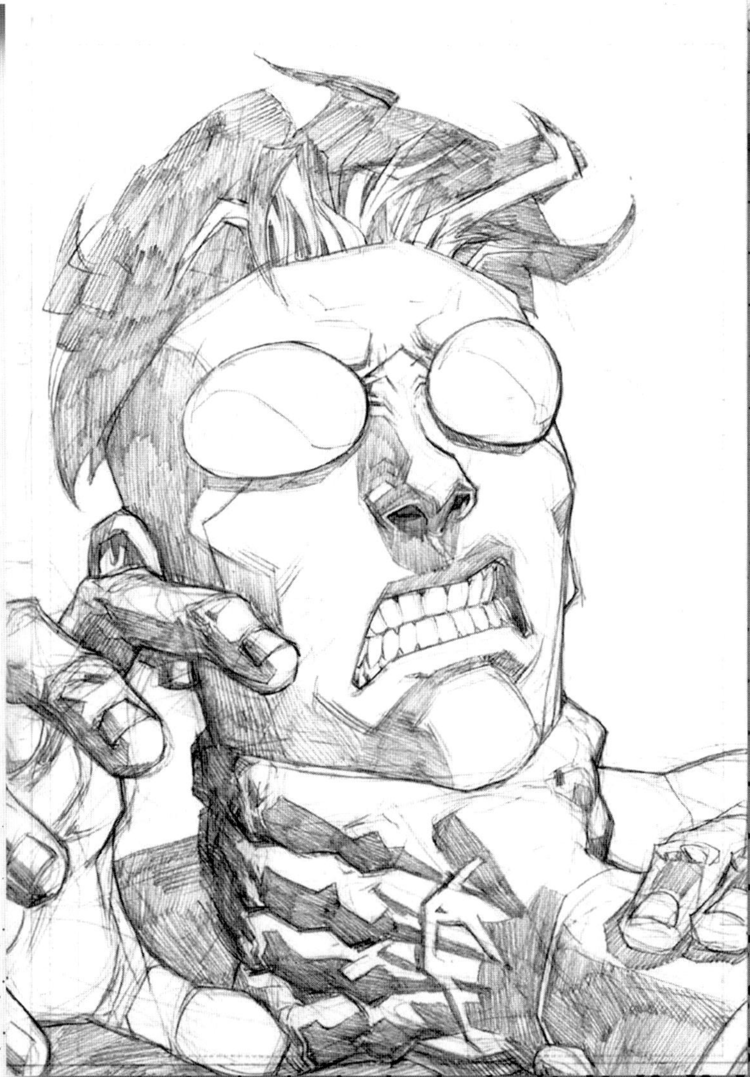

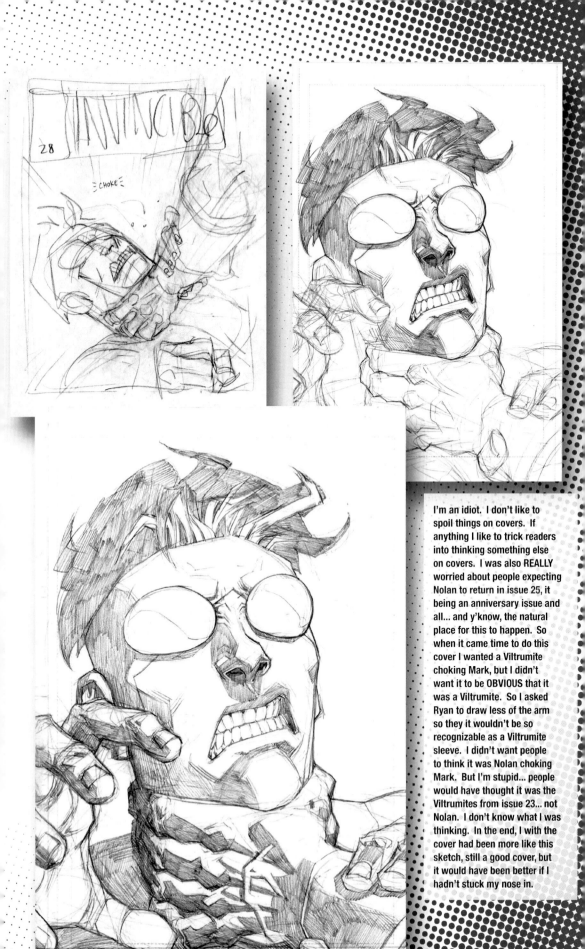

I'm an idiot. I don't like to spoil things on covers. If anything I like to trick readers into thinking something else on covers. I was also REALLY worried about people expecting Nolan to return in issue 25, it being an anniversary issue and all... and y'know, the natural place for this to happen. So when it came time to do this cover I wanted a Viltrumite choking Mark, but I didn't want it to be OBVIOUS that it was a Viltrumite. So I asked Ryan to draw less of the arm so they it wouldn't be so recognizable as a Viltrumite sleeve. I didn't want people to think it was Nolan choking Mark. But I'm stupid... people would have thought it was the Viltrumites from issue 23... not Nolan. I don't know what I was thinking. In the end, I with the cover had been more like this sketch, still a good cover, but it would have been better if I hadn't stuck my nose in.

pissed?.
SAD?.
LAUGHING
Hysterically?

SHADOW

Issue 29 cover sketches.

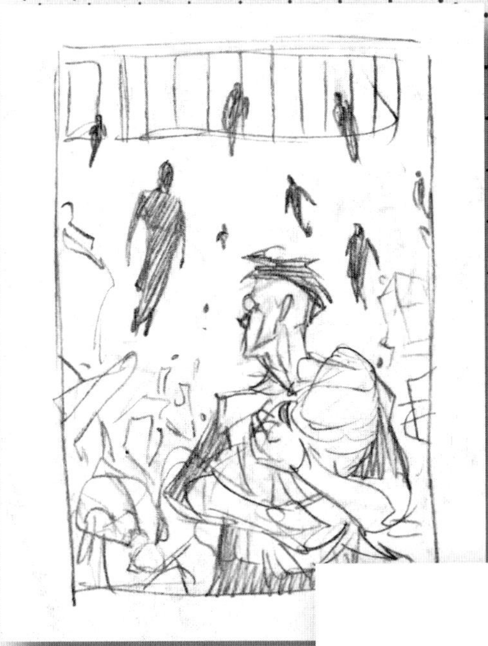

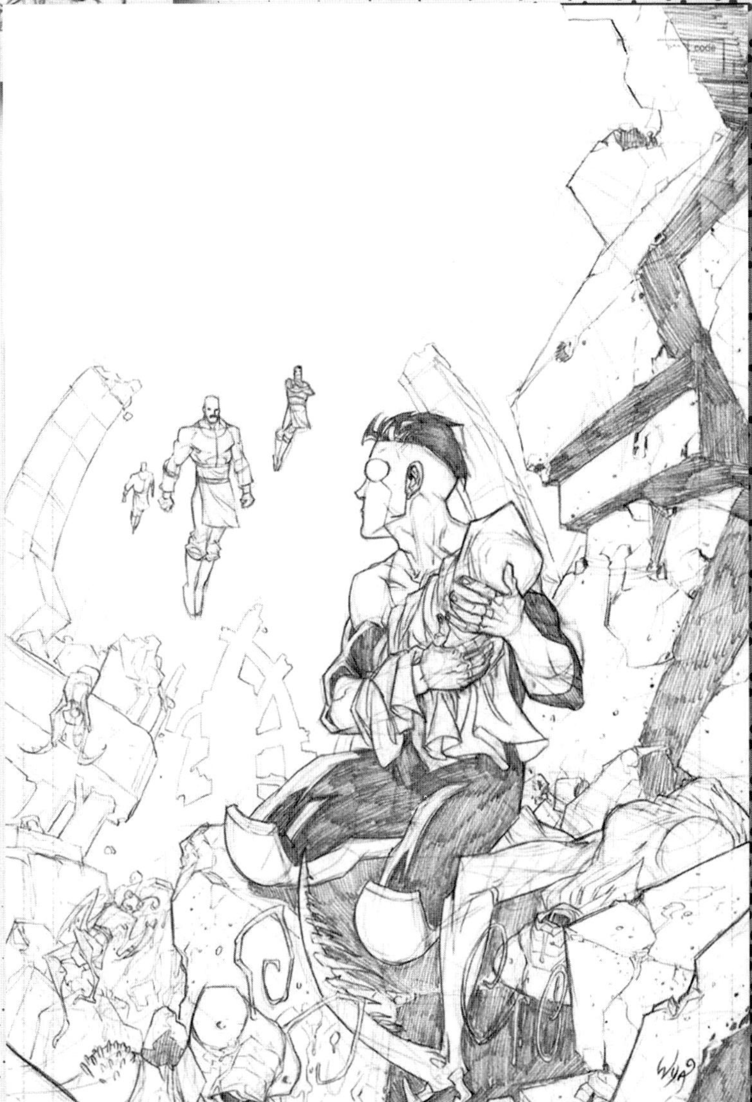

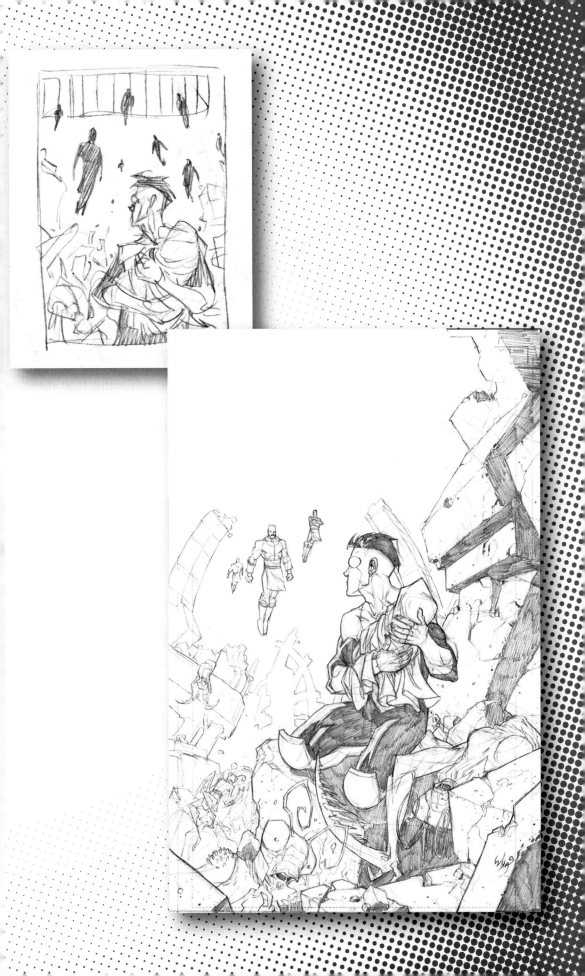

For the cover to issue 30 I wanted a shot of Mark flying home. Ryan did the first version with him cut off at the waist, seen here in sketch form and on the following page in its full glory, but I guess he didn't like it. I dug it. I thought it was fine. I may have joked about it looking weird with Mark being cut off at the waist but still, I was fine with it, really. But Ryan wanted to redo it and I was fine with that. So he did the second version. Seen here in sketch form with the most realistic drawing of the Earth I've EVER seen.

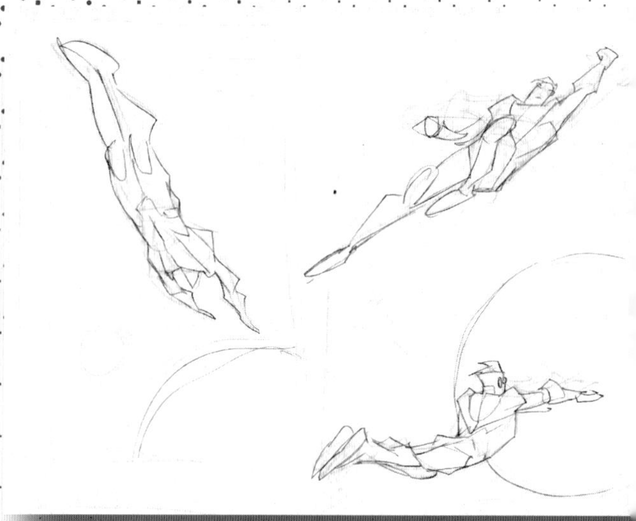

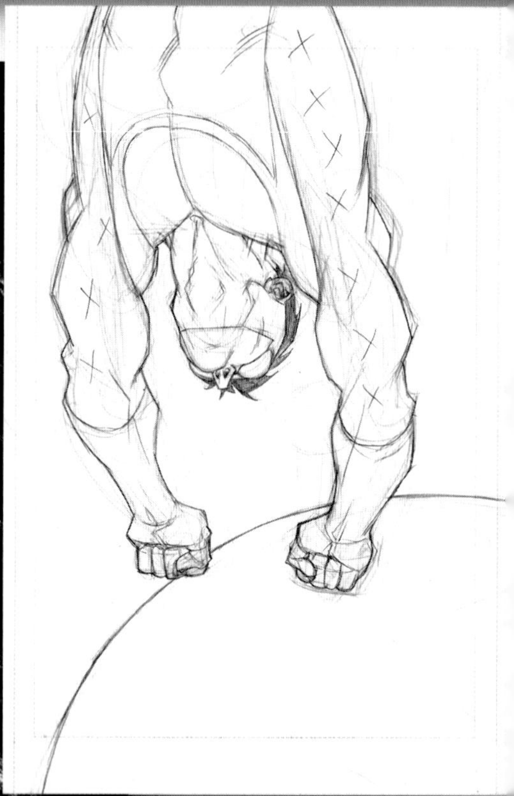

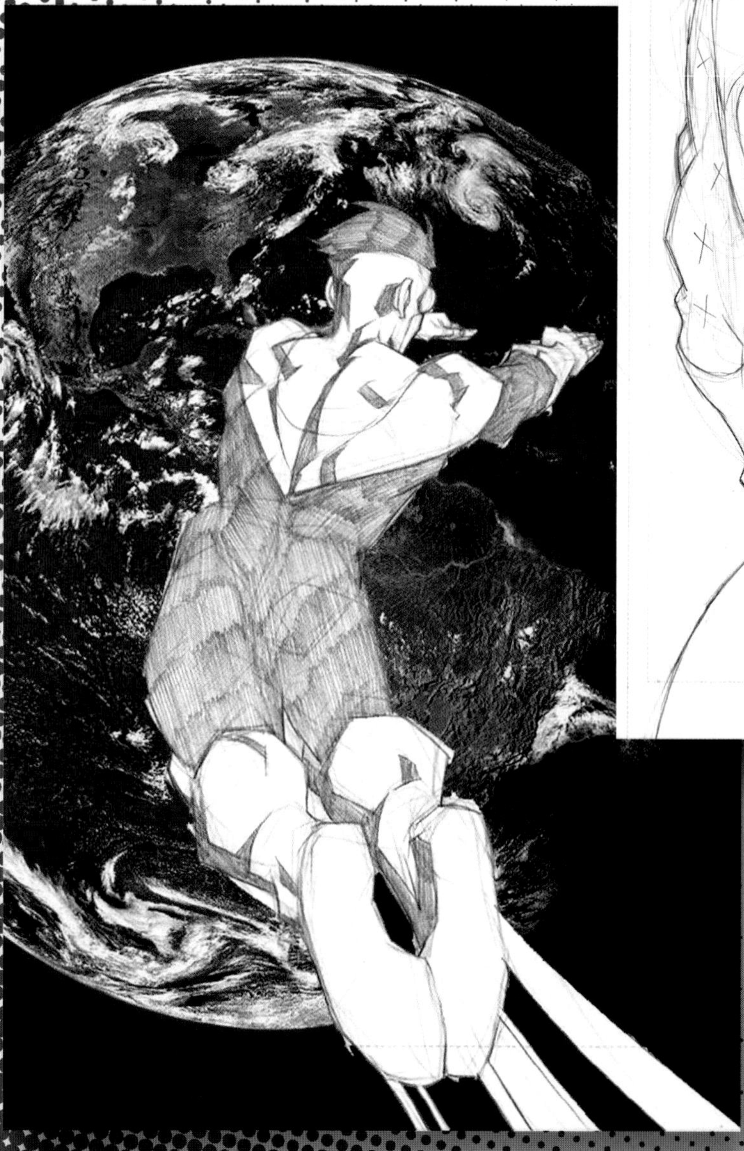

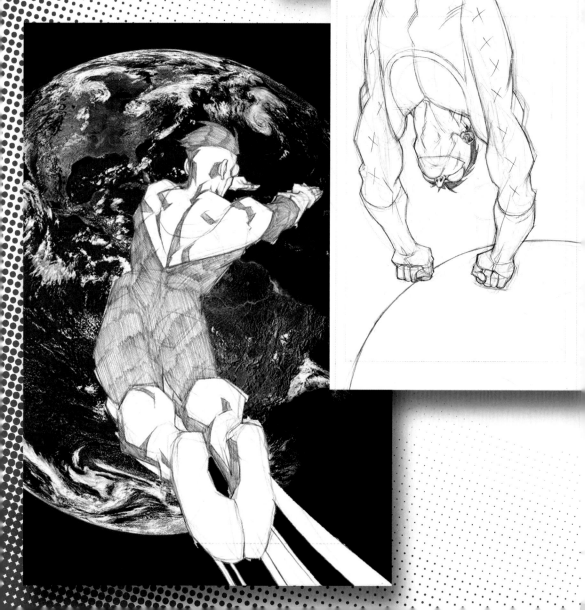

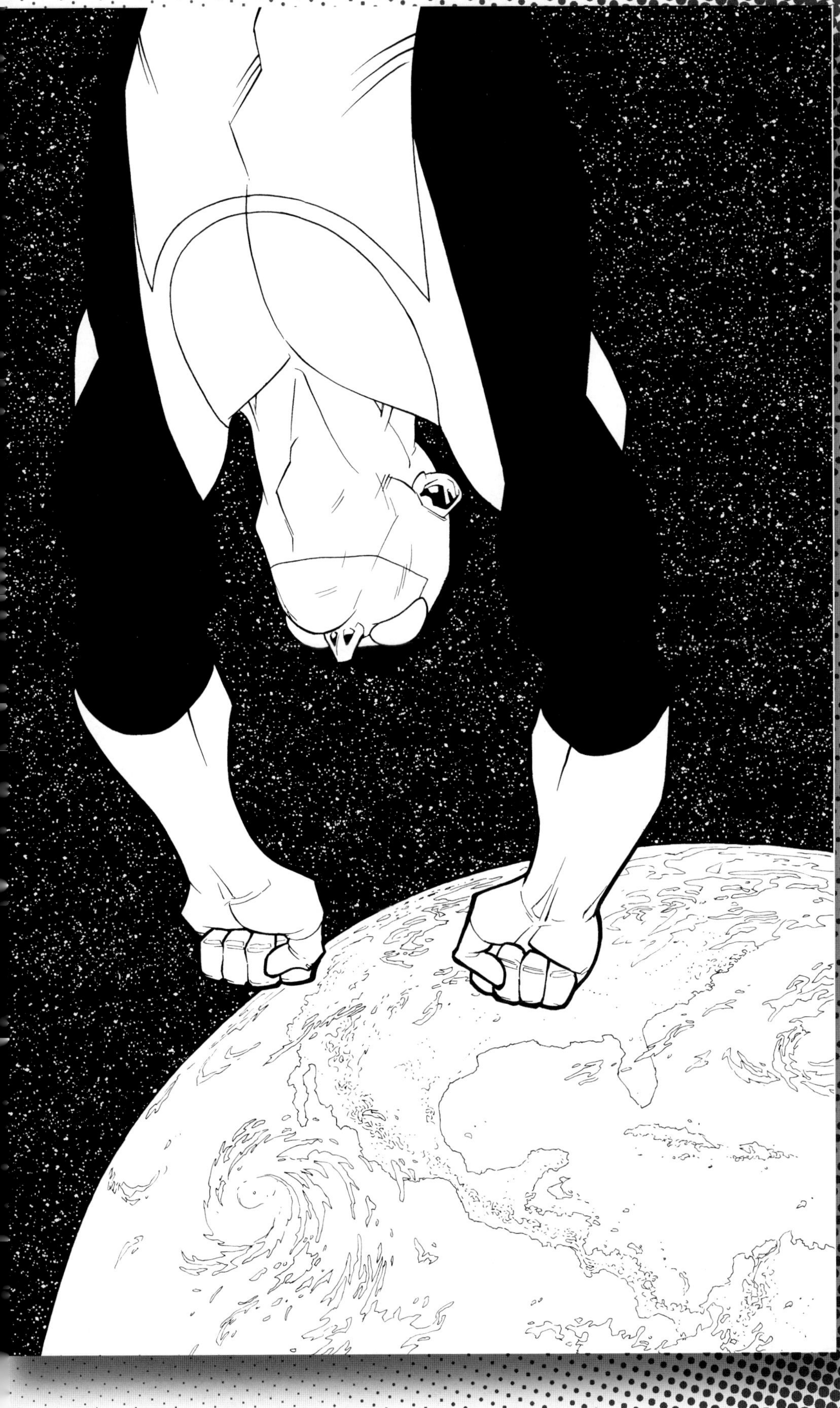

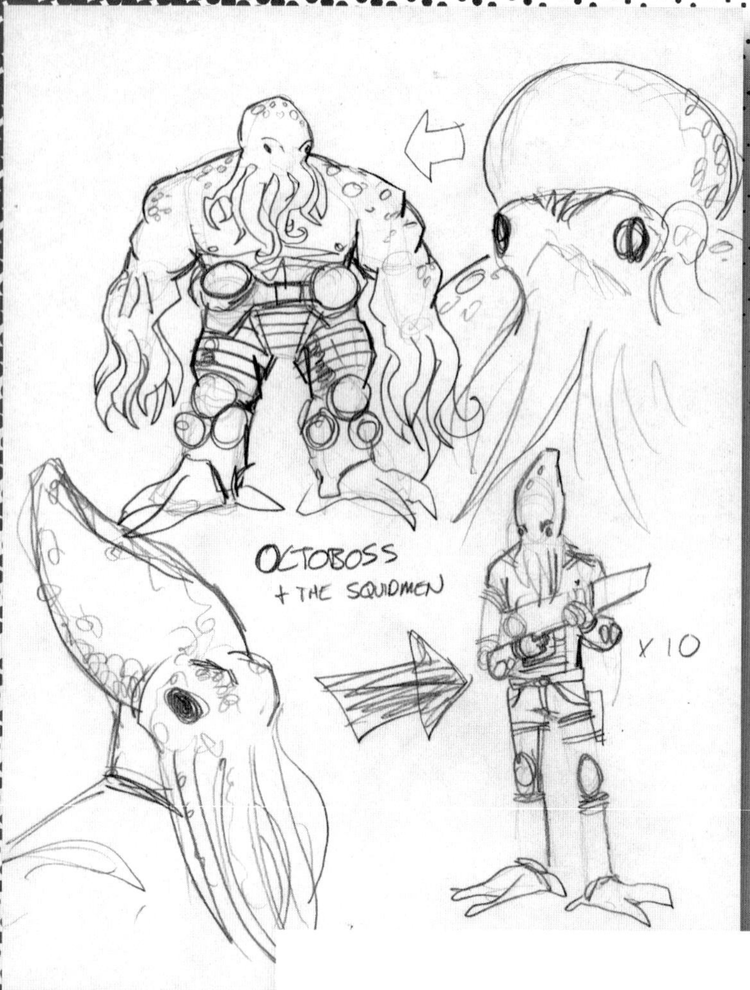
OCTOBOSS
+ THE SQUIDMEN
X 10

My design for Octoboss and then Ryan's tweaks on my designs. I DARE you to guess which one is which!

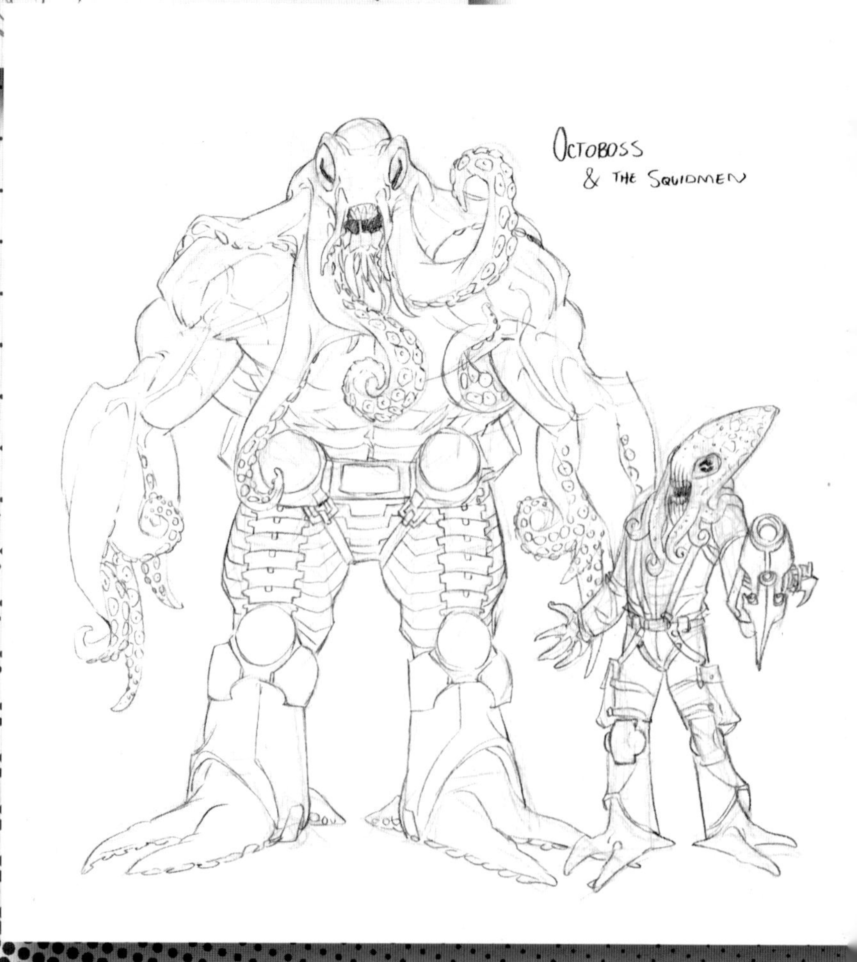
OCTOBOSS
& THE SQUIDMEN

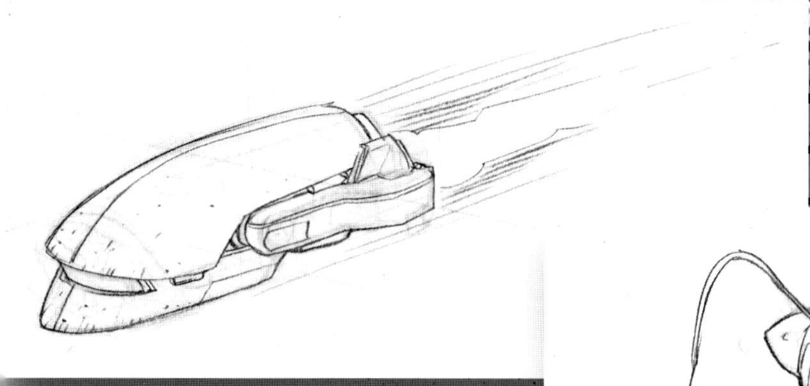

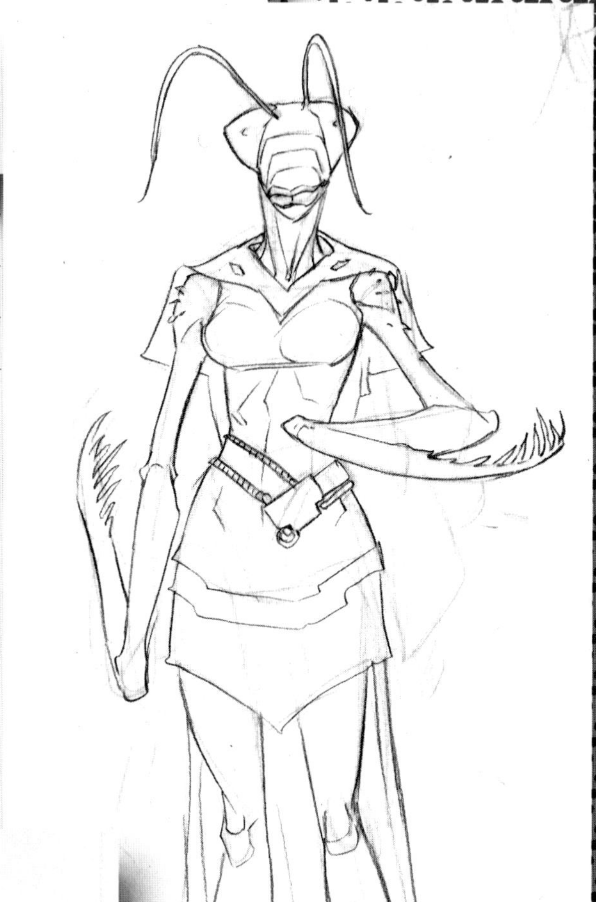

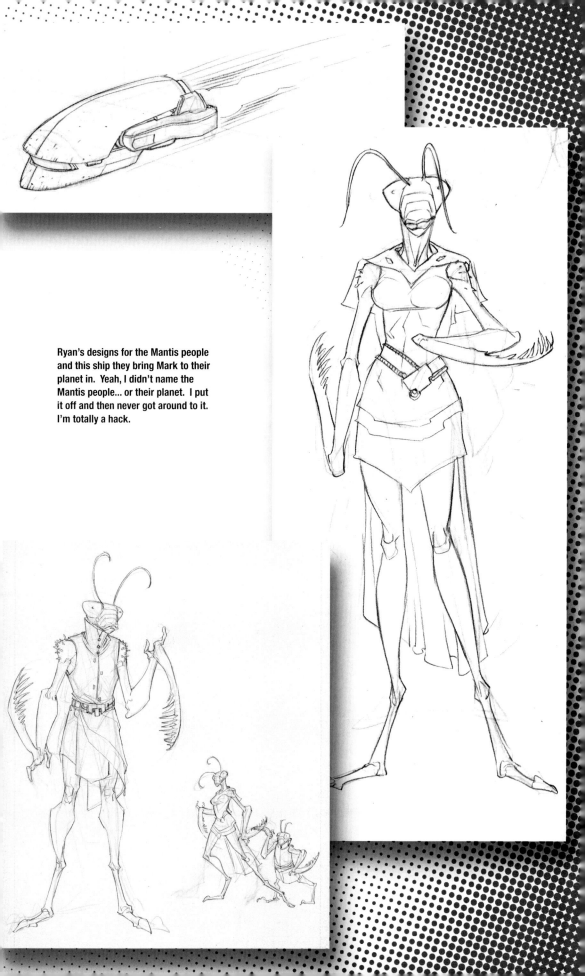

Ryan's designs for the Mantis people and this ship they bring Mark to their planet in. Yeah, I didn't name the Mantis people... or their planet. I put it off and then never got around to it. I'm totally a hack.

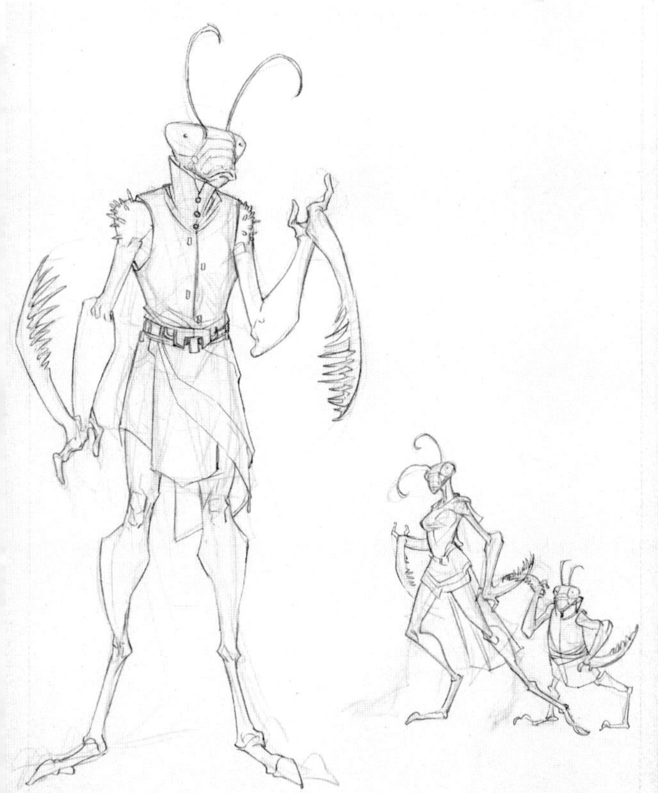

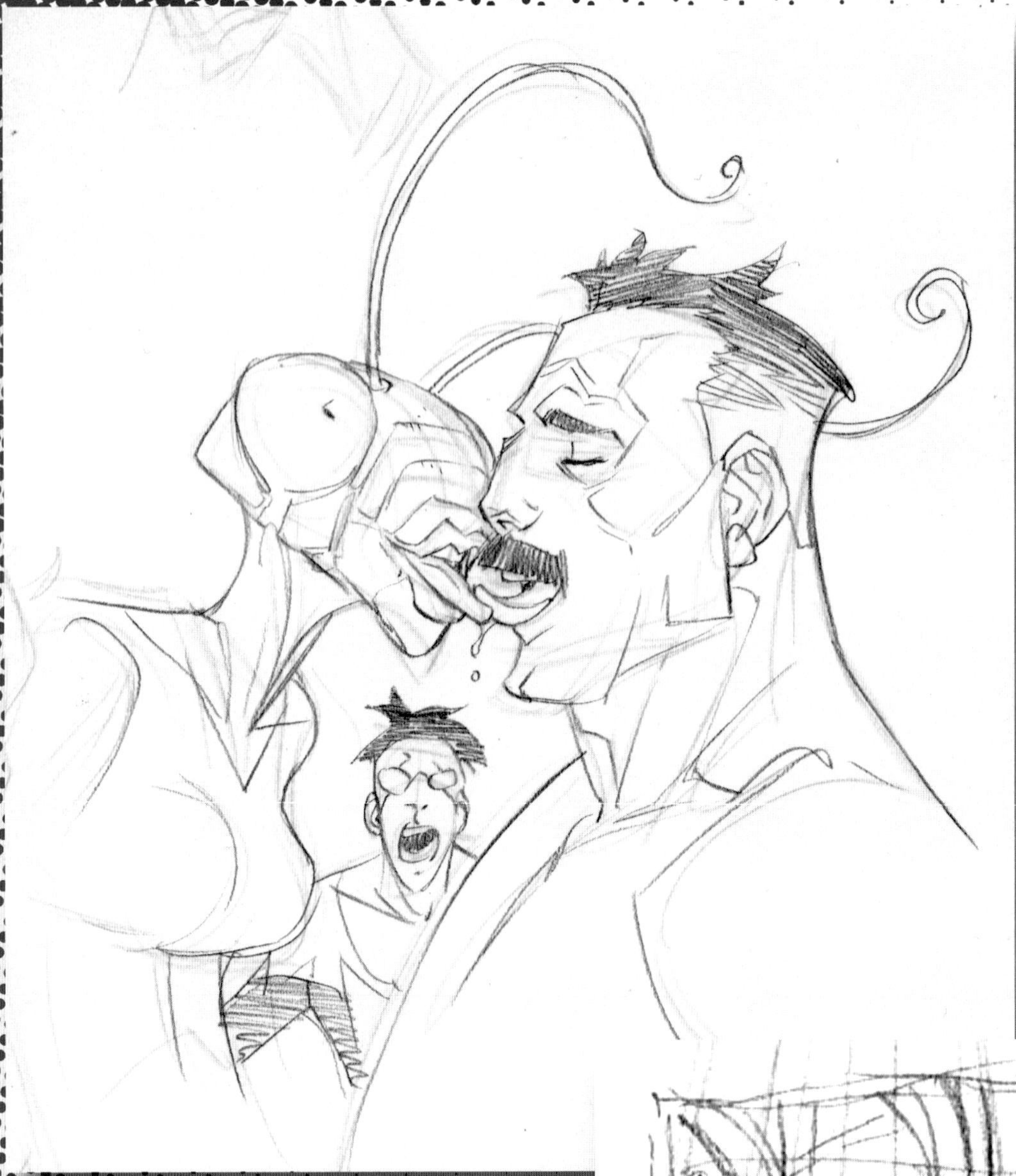

When designing the Mantis people Ryan did this kissing sketch for fun. I loved it... thought it was damn funny so I just HAD to write it into the book. Thank Ryan, for that scene. Also on this page, Ryan's sketch for the last page of issue 25.

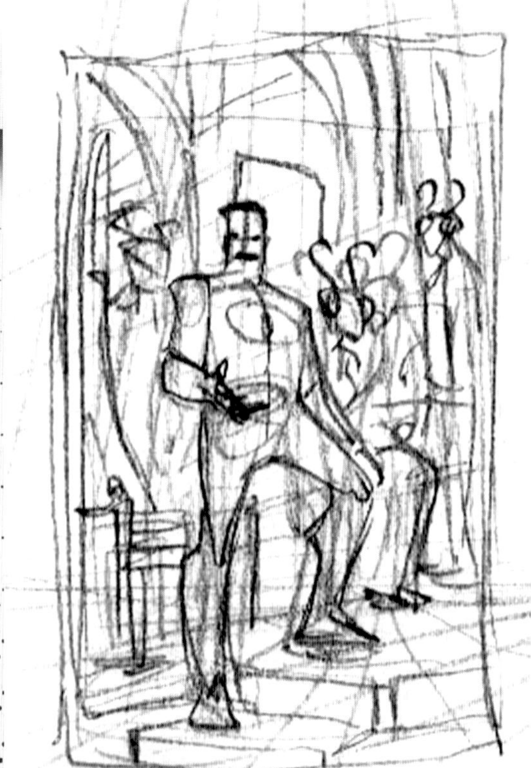

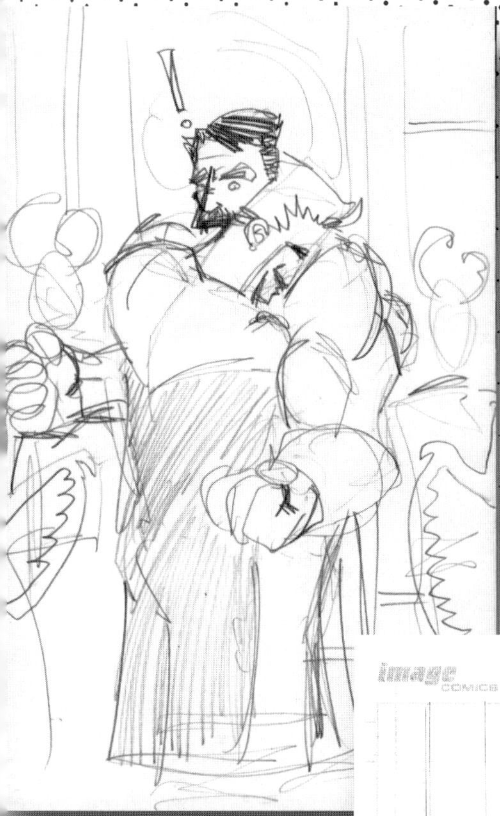

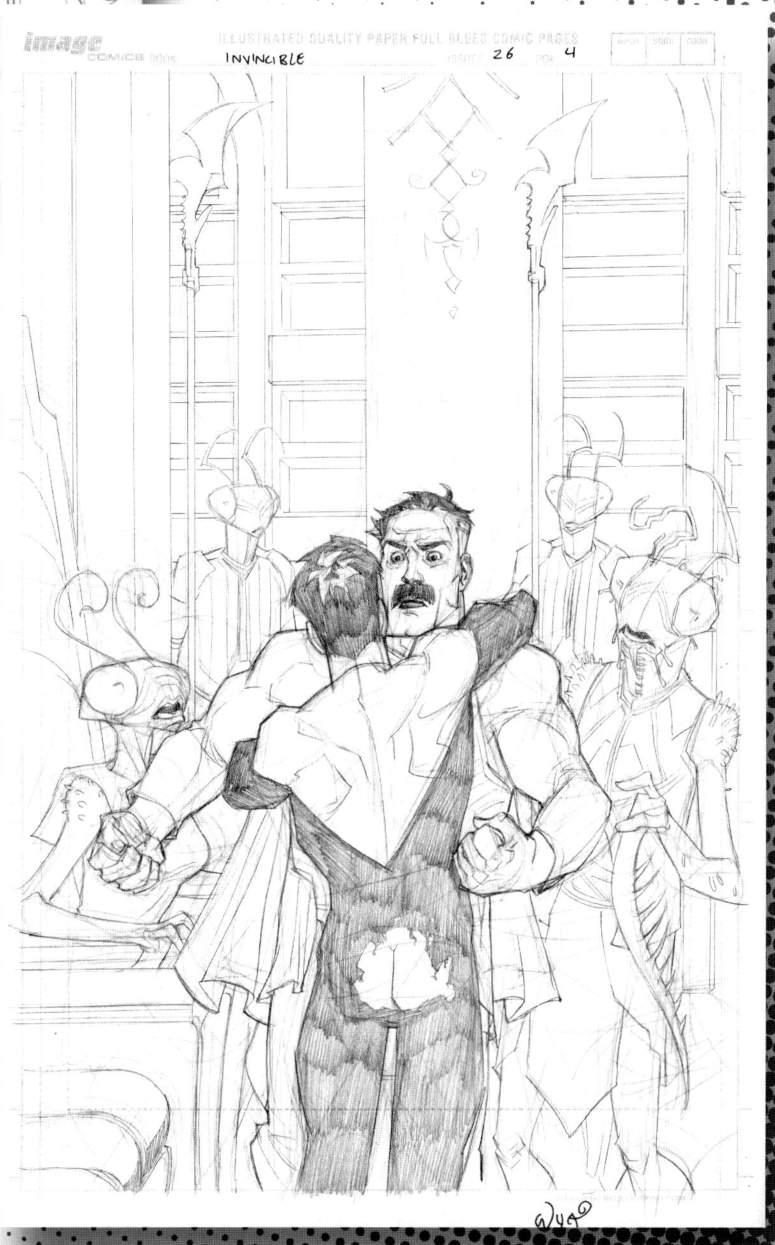
ILLUSTRATED QUALITY PAPER FULL BLEED COMIC PAGES
INVINCIBLE
26
4

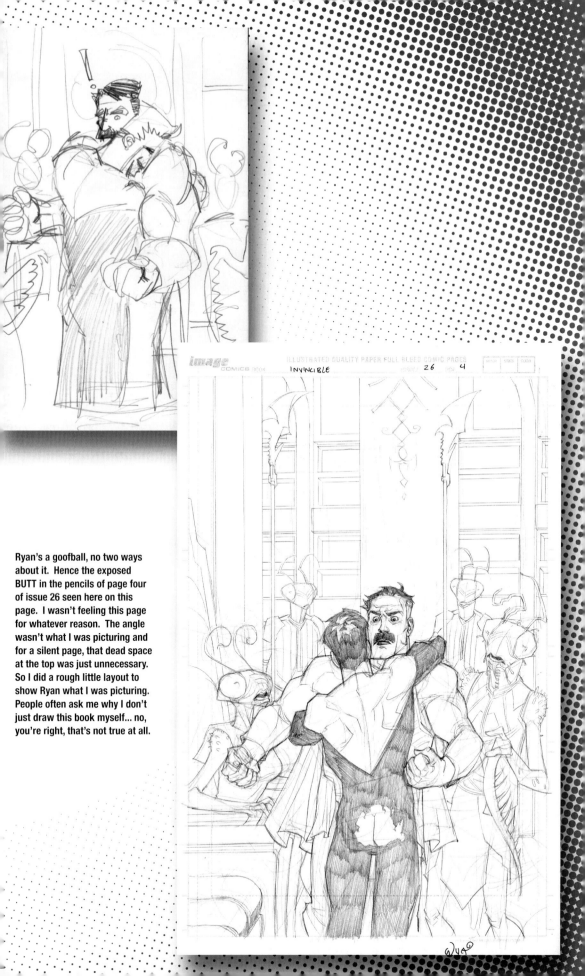

Ryan's a goofball, no two ways about it. Hence the exposed BUTT in the pencils of page four of issue 26 seen here on this page. I wasn't feeling this page for whatever reason. The angle wasn't what I was picturing and for a silent page, that dead space at the top was just unnecessary. So I did a rough little layout to show Ryan what I was picturing. People often ask me why I don't just draw this book myself... no, you're right, that's not true at all.

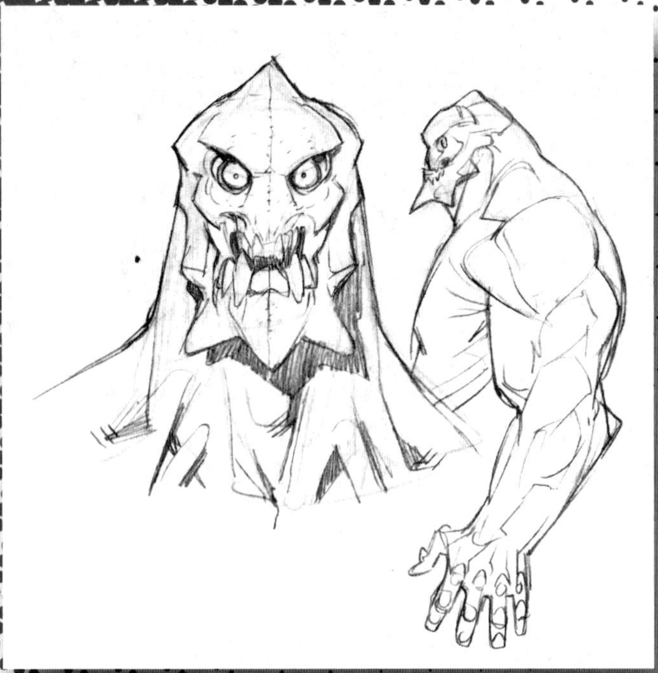

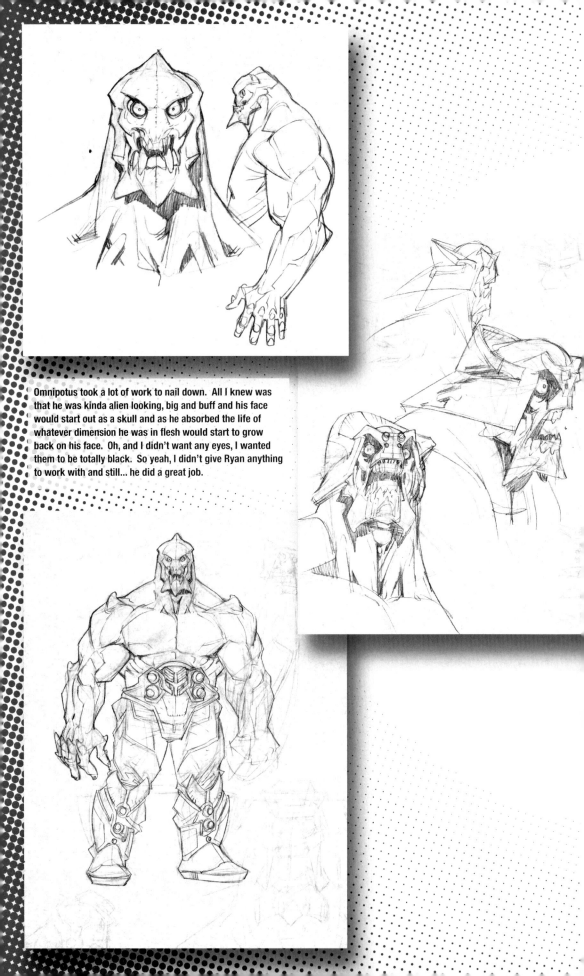

Omnipotus took a lot of work to nail down. All I knew was that he was kinda alien looking, big and buff and his face would start out as a skull and as he absorbed the life of whatever dimension he was in flesh would start to grow back on his face. Oh, and I didn't want any eyes, I wanted them to be totally black. So yeah, I didn't give Ryan anything to work with and still... he did a great job.

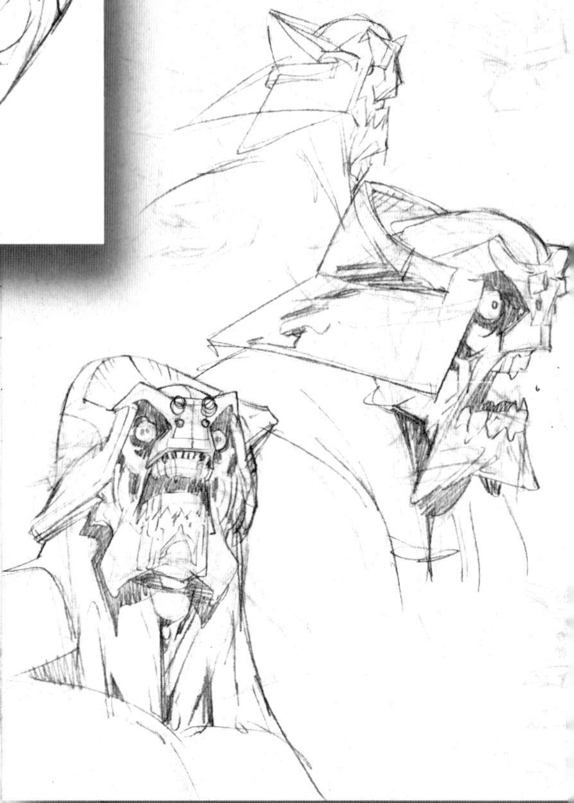

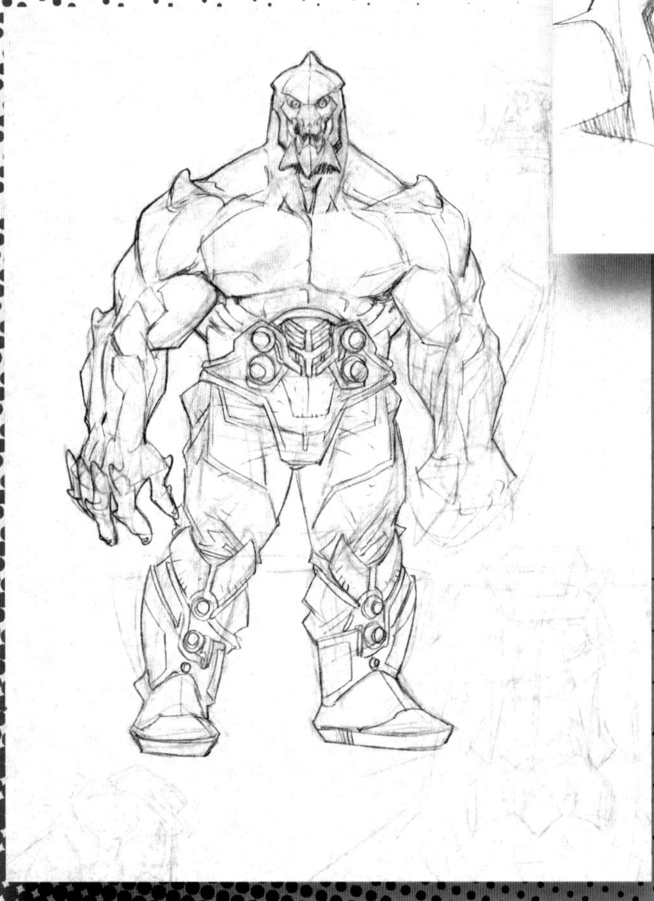

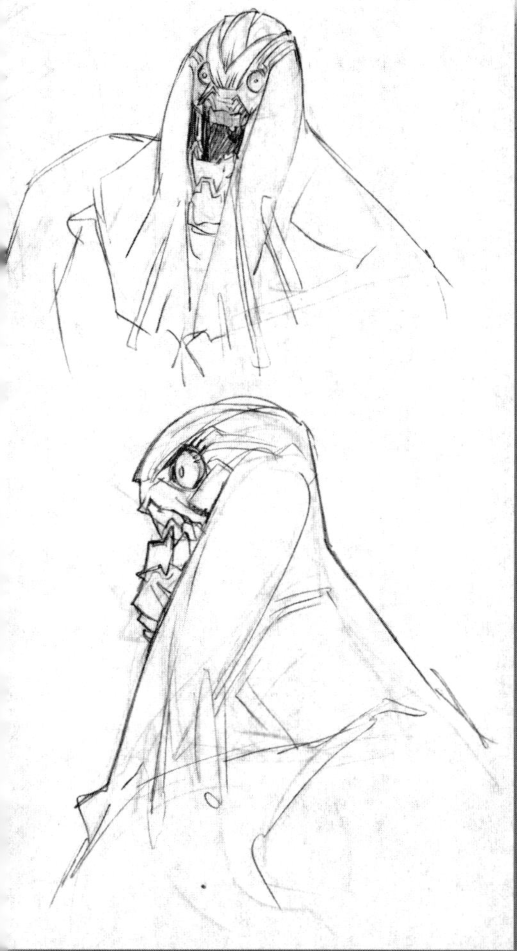

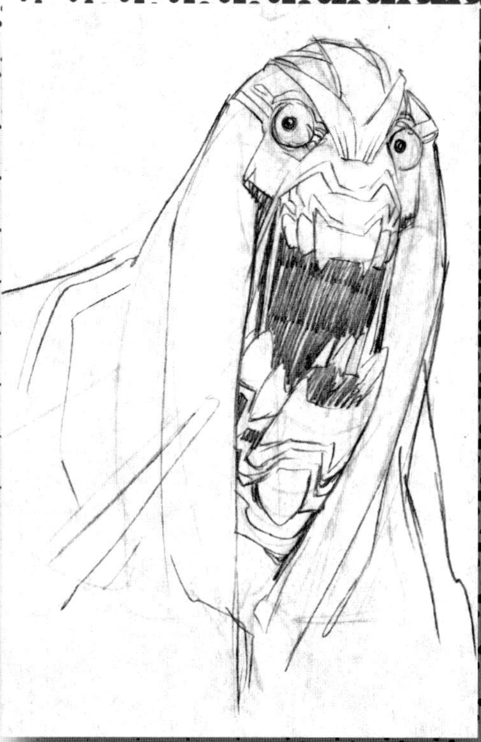

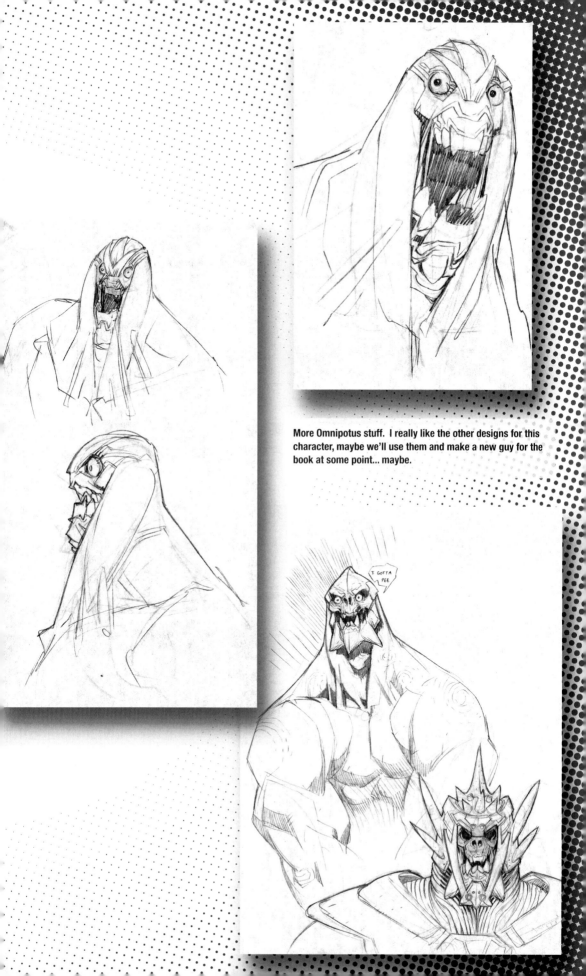

More Omnipotus stuff. I really like the other designs for this character, maybe we'll use them and make a new guy for the book at some point... maybe.

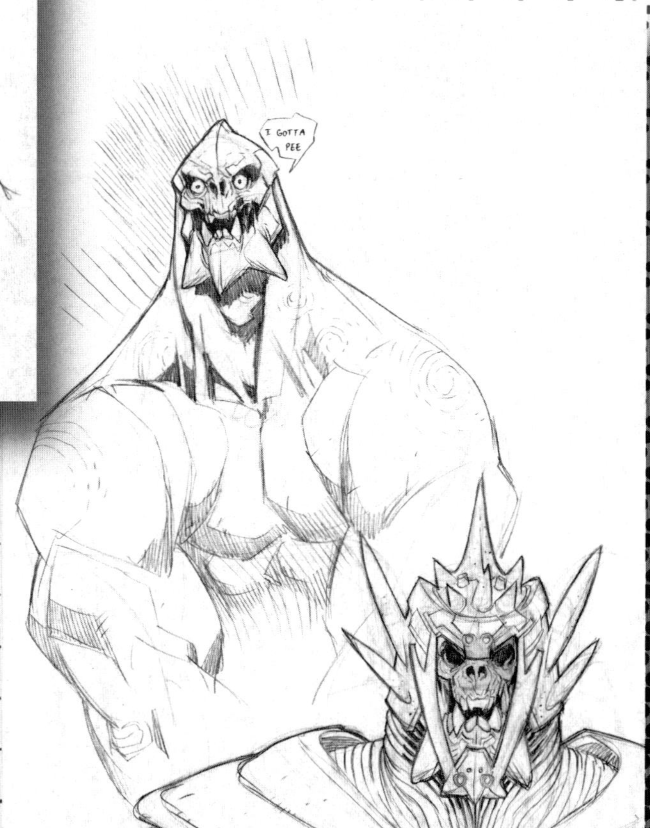
I GOTTA PEE

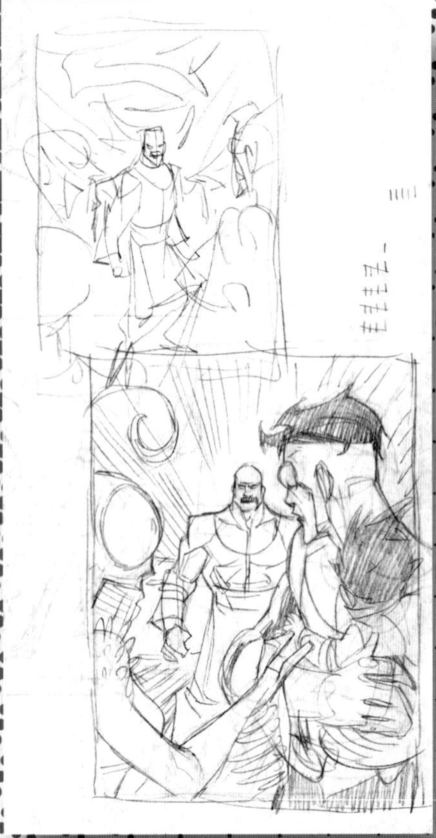

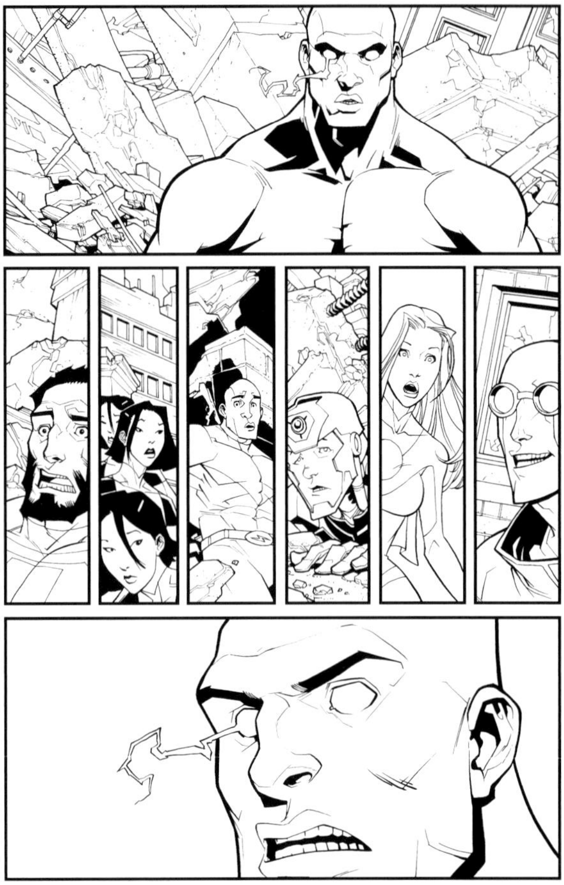

Funny story. I forgot to finish writing the last panel on page 8 of issue 27. So in the script it read "wide panel: Black Samson" and then the dialogue. But it was supposed to be Samson tackling Omnipotus. Sadly, Ryan had to redraw that panel. Also on this page some of Ryan's pencils. Cliff Rathburn pitched in to help with the book on issues 28-31 with a little inking and so Ryan wanted to show just how much work he put into his pencils.

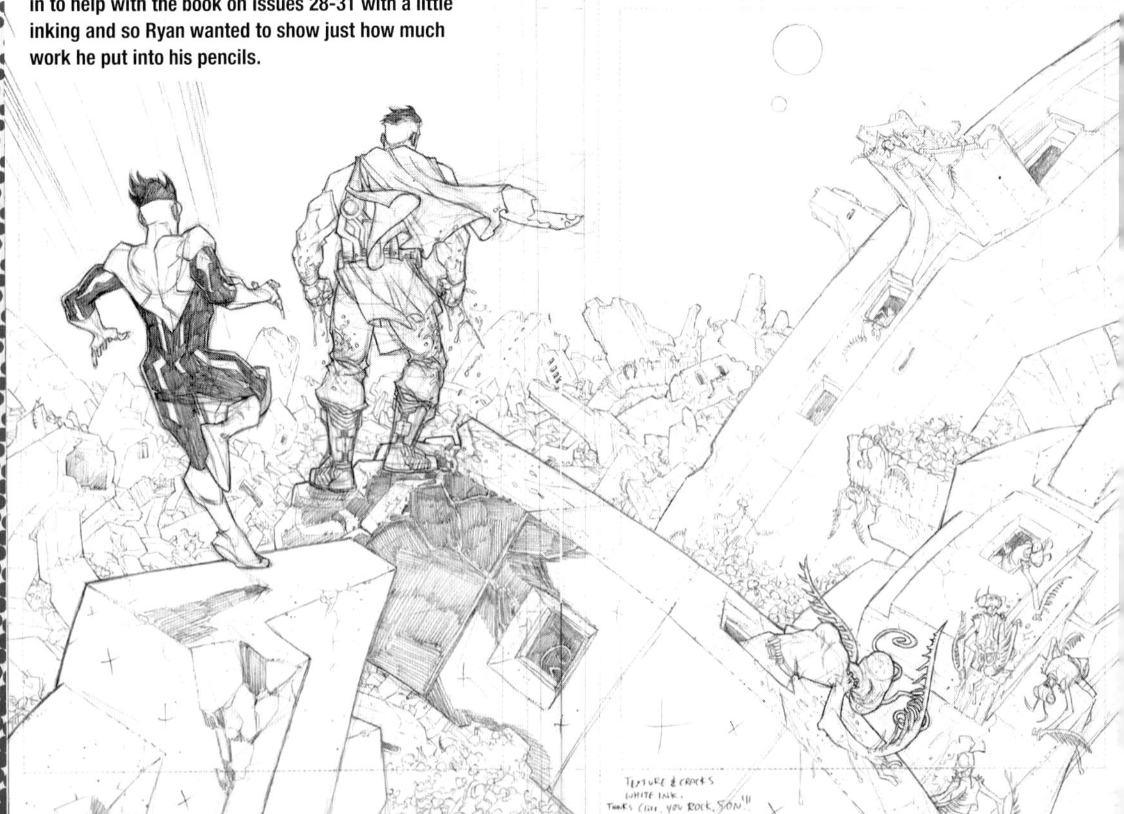
TEXTURE & CRACKS
WHITE INK.
THANKS CLIFF, YOU ROCK, SON!!

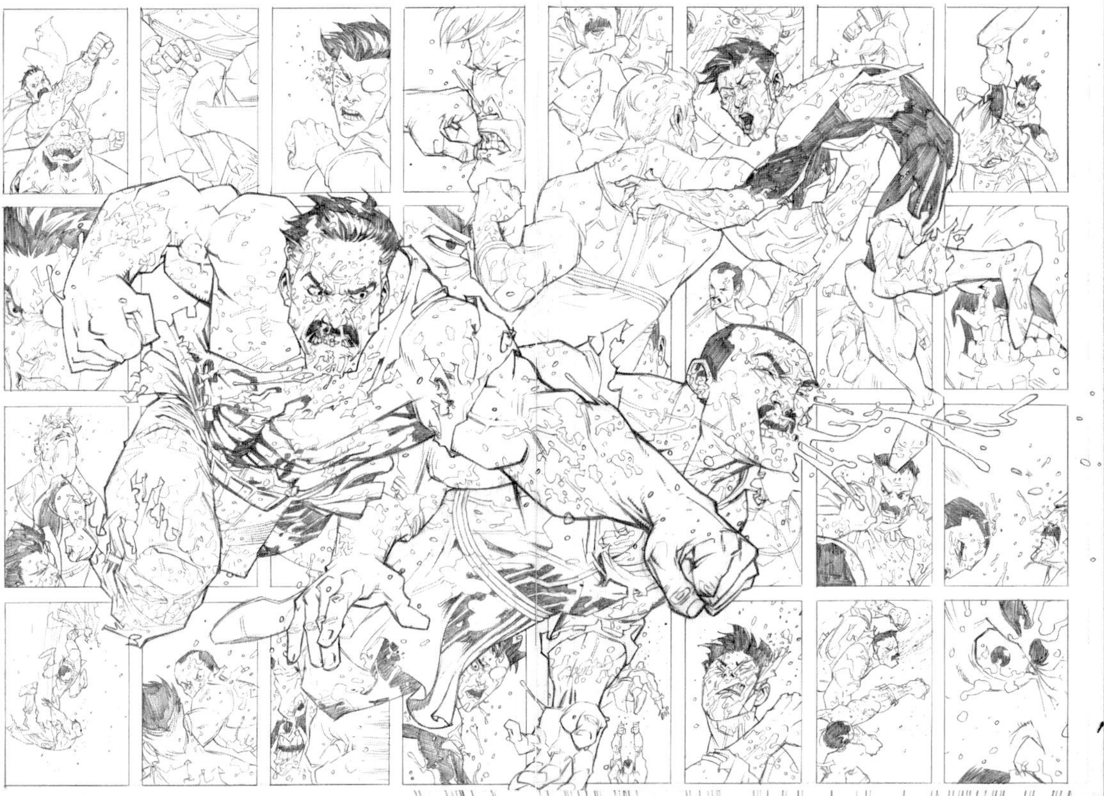

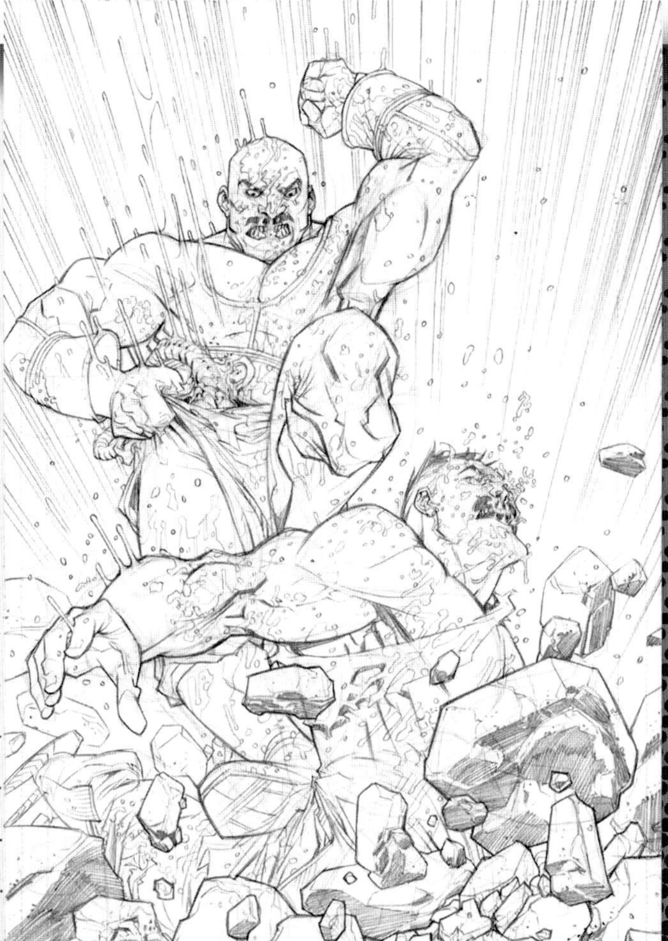

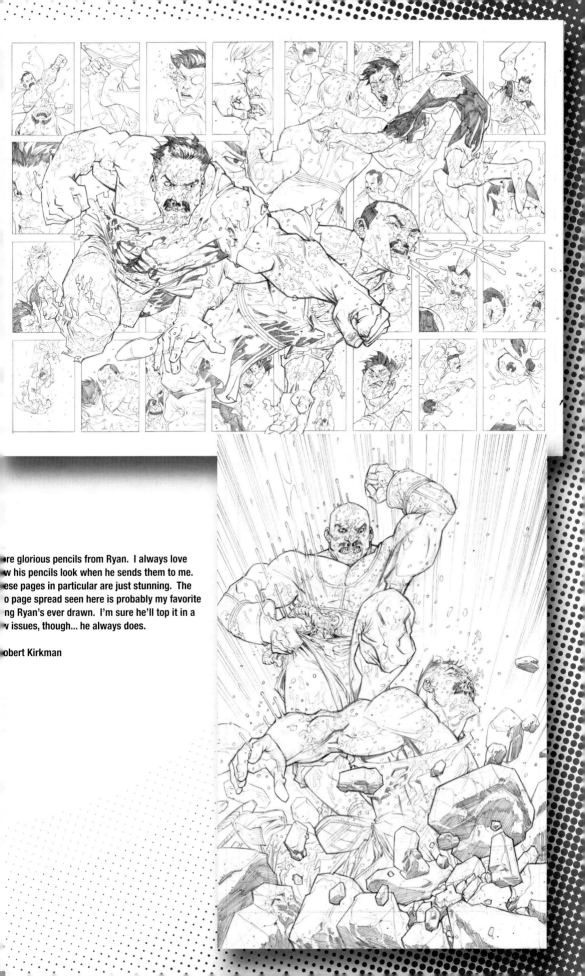

ore glorious pencils from Ryan. I always love
w his pencils look when he sends them to me.
ese pages in particular are just stunning. The
o page spread seen here is probably my favorite
ng Ryan's ever drawn. I'm sure he'll top it in a
v issues, though... he always does.

obert Kirkman

BUY MY BOOKS!

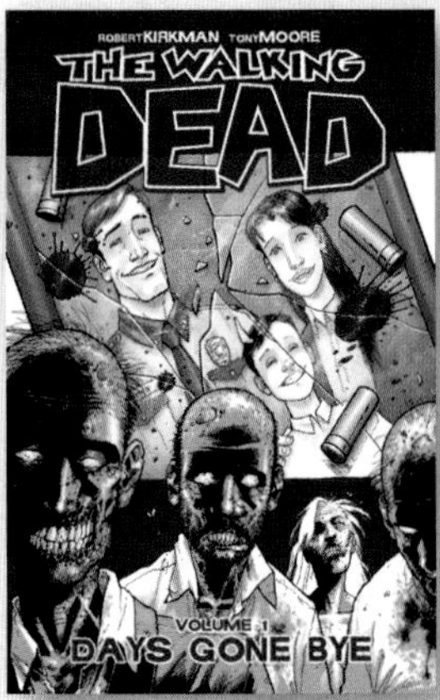
ROBERT KIRKMAN TONY MOORE
THE WALKING DEAD
VOLUME 1
DAYS GONE BYE

THE WALKING DEAD
VOL. 1: DAYS GONE BYE
$9.95 • ISBN# 1582403589

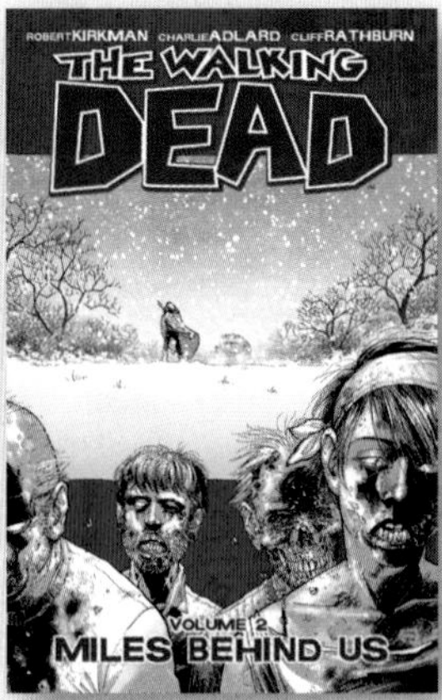
ROBERT KIRKMAN CHARLIE ADLARD CLIFF RATHBURN
THE WALKING DEAD
VOLUME 2
MILES BEHIND US

THE WALKING DEAD
VOL. 2: MILES BEHIND US
$12.95 • ISBN# 1582404135

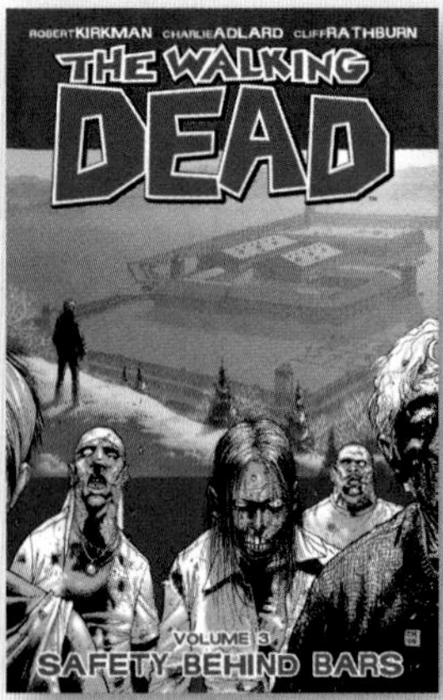
ROBERT KIRKMAN CHARLIE ADLARD CLIFF RATHBURN
THE WALKING DEAD
VOLUME 3
SAFETY BEHIND BARS

THE WALKING DEAD
VOL. 3: SAFETY BEHIND BARS
$12.95 • ISBN# 1582404879

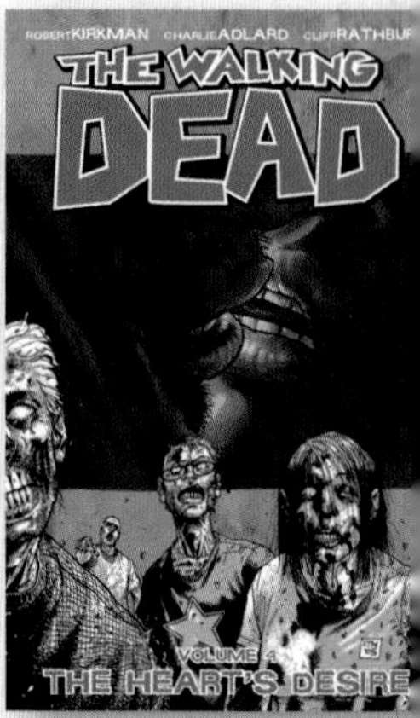
ROBERT KIRKMAN CHARLIE ADLARD CLIFF RATHBURN
THE WALKING DEAD
THE HEART'S DESIRE

THE WALKING DEAD
VOL. 4: THE HEART'S DESIRE
$12.99 • ISBN# 1582405301

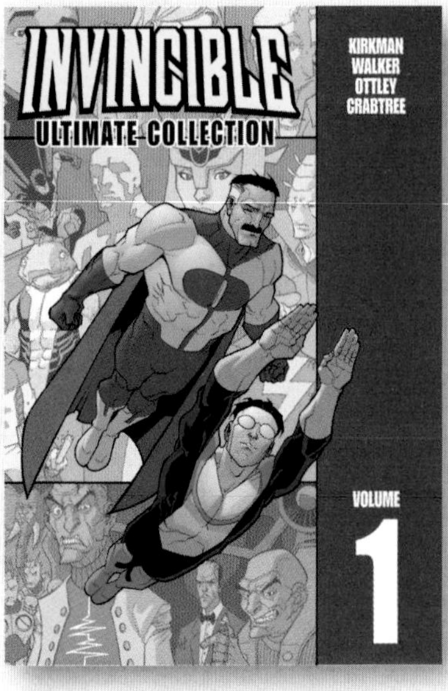
INVINCIBLE
ULTIMATE COLLECTION
KIRKMAN
WALKER
OTTLEY
CRABTREE
VOLUME
1

INVINCIBLE
ULTIMATE COLLECTION, VOL. 1

COLLECTING ISSUES #1-13 IN ONE OVERSIZED HARDCOVER!

$34.95 • ISBN# 158240500X

ASK FOR THESE AND OTHER GREAT BOOKS FROM ROBERT KIRKMAN & IMAGE COMICS FROM YOUR LOCAL COMIC BOOK RETAILER.

TO FIND YOUR NEAREST COMIC BOOK STORE, CALL:

1-888-COMIC-BOOK

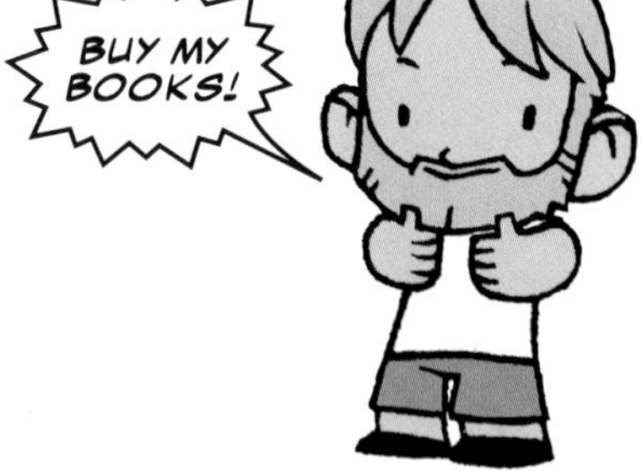
BUY MY BOOKS!

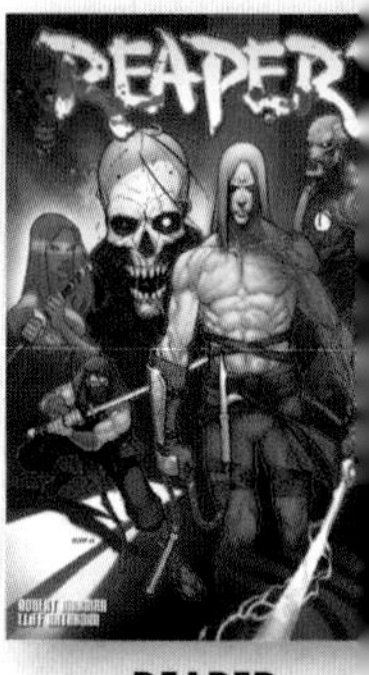
REAPER

REAPER
$6.95 • ISBN# 1582403546

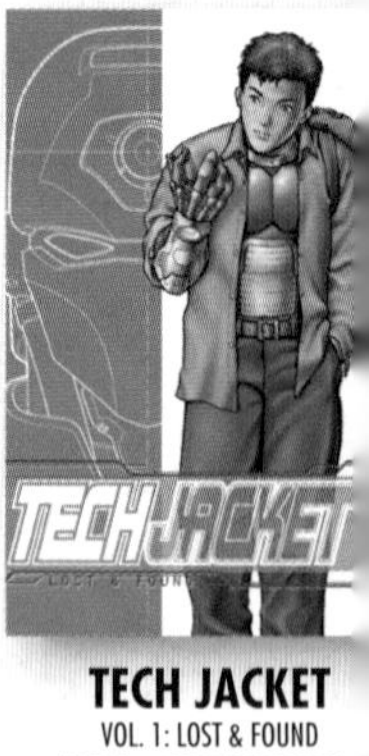
TECH JACKET

TECH JACKET
VOL. 1: LOST & FOUND
$12.95 • ISBN# 15824038

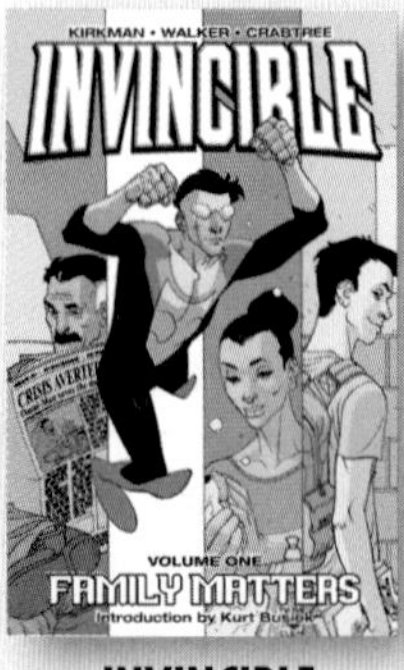
KIRKMAN • WALKER • CRABTREE
INVINCIBLE
VOLUME ONE
FAMILY MATTERS

INVINCIBLE
VOL. 1: FAMILY MATTERS
$12.95 • ISBN# 1582403201

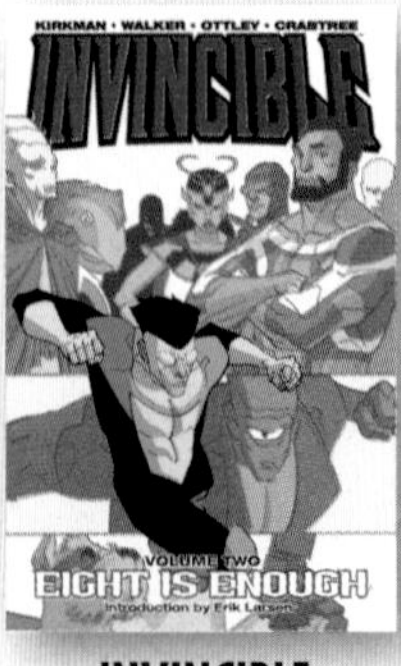
KIRKMAN • WALKER • OTTLEY • CRABTREE
INVINCIBLE
VOLUME TWO
EIGHT IS ENOUGH

INVINCIBLE
VOL. 2: EIGHT IS ENOUGH
$12.95 • ISBN# 1582403473

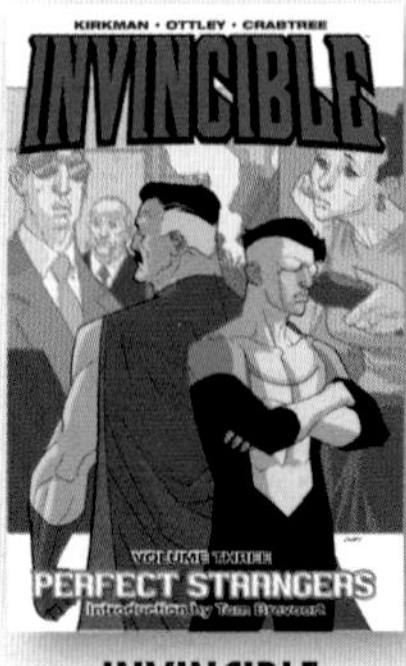
KIRKMAN • OTTLEY • CRABTREE
INVINCIBLE
VOLUME THREE
PERFECT STRANGERS

INVINCIBLE
VOL. 3: PERFECT STRANGERS
$12.95 • ISBN# 1582403910

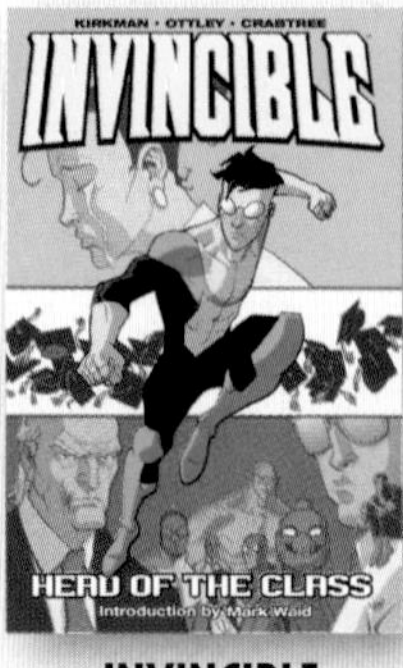
KIRKMAN • OTTLEY • CRABTREE
INVINCIBLE
HEAD OF THE CLASS
Introduction by Mark Waid

INVINCIBLE
VOL. 4: HEAD OF THE CLASS
$14.95 • ISBN# 1582404402

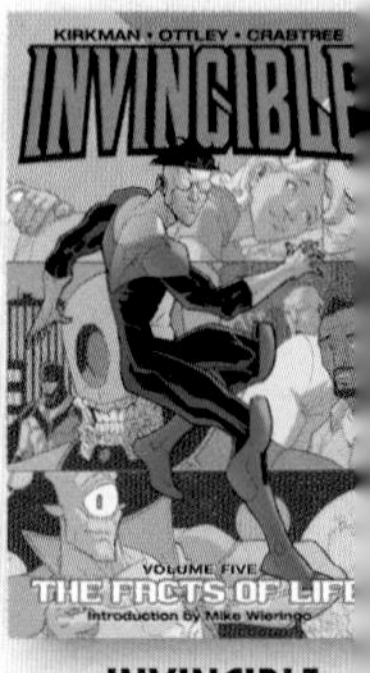
KIRKMAN • OTTLEY • CRABTREE
INVINCIBLE
VOLUME FIVE
Introduction by Mike Wieringo

INVINCIBLE
VOL. 5: THE FACTS OF LIFE
$14.99 • ISBN# 158240554